Praise for the Space Opera of John C. Wright

"This is much more than a space opera, and fills your mind with intriguing, startling possibilities. John Wright's novel is bursting with ideas, blending mythology, machine and human evolution, mathematics, space travel, and much more." —Brian Herbert on *Count to a Trillion*

"Science fiction in the grand tradition." —*Booklist* on *The Judge of Ages*

"The author's talent for imagining the future on a large scale places him in a category with David Brin and Iain M. Banks." —*RT Book Reviews* on *The Hermetic Millennia*

"It's a pity the word 'awesome' has been misused to the point of meaninglessness: it would once have been an ideal description of *Count to a Trillion*. Instead, I'll say that the novel came perilously close to overloading my capacity for wonder, burning out all my 'gosh' circuits—and I've been reading science fiction assiduously since 1954." —Spider Robinson on *Count to a Trillion*

"Spectacularly clever . . . in weaving together cutting-edge speculation along the outer fringes of science. Highly impressive." —*Kirkus Reviews* on *Count to a Trillion*

"Wright moves breathlessly from one exciting idea to the next, using science fiction to examine the biggest ideas he can." —*The A.V. Club* on *Count to a Trillion*

"R. A. Lafferty meets A. E. van Vogt in a cakewalk through a future full of antimatter, alien artifacts, transhumans, an Iron Ghost, a Texas gunfighter, and a Space Princess. Well worth the price of admission." —Michael Flynn on *Count to a Trillion*

"Wright is at his best." —*Publishers Weekly* on *Count to a Trillion*

TOR BOOKS BY JOHN C. WRIGHT

THE JUDGE OF
AGES

———————

JOHN C. WRIGHT

TOR®

A TOM DOHERTY ASSOCIATES BOOK

NEW YORK

THE JUDGE OF AGES

Copyright © 2014 by John C. Wright

All rights reserved.

A Tor Book
Published by Tom Doherty Associates, LLC
175 Fifth Avenue
New York, NY 10010

www.tor-forge.com

Tor® is a registered trademark of Tom Doherty Associates, LLC.

The Library of Congress has cataloged the hardcover edition as follows:

Wright, John C. (John Charles), 1961–
    The Judge of ages / John C. Wright.—1st ed.
        p. cm.
    "A Tom Doherty Associates book."
    ISBN 978-0-7653-2929-5 (hardcover)
    ISBN 978-1-4299-4712-1 (e-book)
    1. Human-alien encounters—Fiction.   2. Interstellar travel—Fiction.
    3. Cryopreservation of organs, tissues, etc.—Fiction.   I. Title.
    PS3623.R54J83 2014
    813'.6—dc23

                                                    2013025457

ISBN 978-0-7653-7580-3 (trade paperback)

Tor books may be purchased for educational, business, or promotional use. For information on bulk purchases, please contact the Macmillan Corporate and Premium Sales Department at 1-800-221-7945, extension 5442, or write to specialmarkets@macmillan.com.

First Edition: February 2014
First Trade Paperback Edition: January 2015

Printed in the United States of America

0 9 8 7 6 5 4 3 2 1

CONTENTS

Far along the worldwide whisper of the southwind rushing warm,
With the standards of the peoples plunging thro' the thunder-storm;
Till the war-drum throbb'd no longer, and the battle-flags were furl'd
In the Parliament of man, the Federation of the world.
There the common sense of most shall hold a fretful realm in awe,
And the kindly earth shall slumber, lapped in universal law.

—Alfred, Lord Tennyson

PART FIVE

The World Beneath
the World

1

The Instrumentality of the Hyades

A.D. 10515

1. In the Tombs

"O Rania, I was better off dead," muttered Menelaus Montrose, in English, a language which, he reflected, was also long dead. "Unearthed and outmaneuvered, how in pestilent perdition am I going to outsmart getting myself killed entirely? How am I ever going to see you again?"

Above, the sky was gray with snow clouds, and leaden. A storm was gathering along the southern horizon, above the glaciers now shrouding the Blue Ridge Mountains, the source of some immense, unnatural disturbance.

Downhill, the pines and frozen rocks were bare of life. The prison tents were empty, the deadly wire was motionless, and the odd seashell-shaped buildings beyond the wire were silent.

Directly underfoot, down a dizzying drop of catwalks and scaffolds, lay the darkness of the archeological dig. No coffins moved or fired. They were deactivated, returned meekly to their recharging plugs, and were no longer attempting to defend their precious, slumbering contents.

Instead, wild packs of the dog thing soldiers were dancing, whooping, and barking with elation among the ruins, whirling swords and pikes, flourishing muskets, in the triangle of light that spilled from the broken doors across the silent firing range. Montrose saw none of the dwarfish little bald Blue Men in their jewel-adorned coats.

He wondered how many hours he had before the persons of ordinary intelligence figured out that Corporal Anubis, allegedly a Beta-rank Chimera of the Sixth Millennium A.D., was instead Menelaus Illation Montrose, experiment in intelligence augmentation gone awry, of the Third Millennium A.D., the so-called Judge of Ages and Guardian of the Cryonic Tombs of the Slumbering Dead—or how many minutes before Del Azarchel figured it out.

(That man was surely still alive! Fate was not kind enough to have killed off mankind's other experiment in human intelligence augmentation, mechanical rather than biological, during the thousands of years while Montrose slept in suspended animation. The two of them were still in mid-duel, a deadly fight momentarily put on hold during the immensities of human evolutionary history.)

Maybe they would not find the coffeepot, or his notebooks, or his gun collection, or his clothing closet. Of course, there was still the giant Texas flag he had pinned up, or the portrait of Rania, or his collection of history books, Witch idols, magazines and old coins with his image on them . . . sweet Jesus up a tree! There were a lot of clues lying around.

Montrose watched in helpless anger as Rada Lwa was taken from him. He had carried the unconscious albino Scholar over his shoulder from the torture cell of the Blue Men. Rada Lwa was placed by the dogs into a sling and lowered from platform to platform into the Tombs.

Back in A.D. 3090 (over seven thousand four hundred years ago by the calendar, but just shy eight years ago by his oft-interrupted inner biological clock) Rada Lwa had attempted to assassinate Montrose. It was unforgivable. And yet the man, by entering the Tombs of the Judge of Ages, was under Montrose's protection. He was a client. To have Blue Men excavate Rada Lwa, thaw him, torture him, in Montrose's book, merited execution. But not ten minutes ago, he had discovered to his shock that the Blue Men were Thaws as well; in theory, his clients also under his protection. He blamed himself for not seeing it earlier. In hindsight, it was obvious.

While the dog things were busy lowering Rada Lwa, Montrose spoke to them in Intertextual: *"You know your masters ain't really and truly archeologists, don't you, you sons of bitches?"*

The Blue Men, all but whoever was behind them, thought they were looking for the mythical founder of the Tomb system, the demigod called the Judge of Ages: so called because he condemned to death any age of history which dared forget the reason for the Tombs, the point of accumulating slumbering knights and scientists.

The mythical founder was no myth, but stood among their prisoners, unrecognized, helpless as a child, and angrier than hell.

Montrose was answered by snarls and a prod in his back with the muzzles of muskets. The captain of the dogs, a stately Great Dane of heroic build, pointed with his cutlass, motioning Montrose to descend.

Montrose, with a smirk and a shrug, politely raised his hands in surrender, and walked and climbed down the last length of scaffolding into the cleft.

He tried once again, this time only addressing the Great Dane by name: *"Rirk Refka Kak-Et, you do know your masters are Thaws who just so happened to wake up earlier than their fellow clients, and looted our coffins and thawed us against our will?"*

Looking down, he saw that the armor was gone, peeled away by some immense force, along with the bedrock and the first three levels of the Tomb. Avalanches and snowfall had toppled this first level onto the second, and the second had been cut or blasted open to reveal the third, leaving only a set of protruding decks to the east and west like bookshelves.

As he descended, he saw above a squad of dogs lowering an oversized coffin using a block and tackle. As it passed him, swaying in the wind, he was close enough to read its alert lights: The Giant inside was awake, only mildly sedated, fully thawed and healed. The coffin was being used as a claustrophobic prison, not a hibernation unit.

Creaking, the lines lowered the Giant's coffin faster than Montrose (with dogs above him and dogs below) could negotiate the rungs of the synthetic tubing which formed the ladder. Montrose ached with the desire to speak with the Giant. His brain, due to its size, could match the feats Montrose's, due to its composition, could perform. A short conversation with him, and the many mysteries plaguing Montrose might be answered.

The wind grew soft as the sky shrank to merely a narrow blue ribbon above, and the sunlight grew dim. It was cold between the narrow canyon walls of stone, and colder still between the metal walls of the Tomb.

"Your masters, they do not know any more than I do who or what—if anything—is alive out there in the snowy wilderness of the Ice Age. Some human civilization is still on the surface, perhaps extremely advanced, and they will surely notice this activity here."

The armored floor here was all but gone, and at the lip of this huge hole, the scaffolding the dog things had erected led down to the third level. Roofless, the floorplan of the third level was exposed.

To one side, the southern half was a labyrinth of cells and corridors wormridden with smaller passages designed for coffins to slide easily through, where men must duck walk or crawl, and murder-holes and ambush vents led from the smaller passages to the maze of main corridors. The northern half of the floorplan was an empty space of metal like a firing range, overlooked by a massive door. This door was thirty feet tall, with gunblisters and energy emitters thick as grapes on a trellis on its massively armored doorposts and lintel. The beetling cliff above the door to the fourth level was intact, so that the door was like a metal plug at the back of a throat of stone.

And the door was open. Gold light poured up from shining stairs.

"You know that, right? You savvy? Thaws are clients of the ultra-long-term hibernation tombs—sleep in the ground, under the armor, for centuries, millennia, waiting for the End of Days when the star monsters come from the Hyades."

Montrose did not mention that he, personally, was waiting for an event predicted to happen long, long after that. Driving off the Hyades invasion was meant merely to preserve the Earth in her Earthly state until Princess Rania returned.

He looked down at a noise. He saw Oenoe, garbed in her green mantilla, walking serenely between two lines of cavorting and howling dog things. The strange angle of the light from the open door cast the shadows of the dog things like angular phantoms across the walls, whose jerking dance was a thing from boyhood nightmares.

With her was Soorm the Hormagaunt, unconscious, or dead, being hauled limply in the metal clamps of a lumbering automaton. Preceptor Naar, looking bored, rode atop the walking machine.

"Did your little Blue bosses warn you about the star monsters? They will be here in a century. A dark mass, equal to a small gas giant, has been approaching us from Oculus Borealis for the last eight millennia."

Down the final ladder, there was steel floor underfoot. Menelaus and his dog escort stood in a narrow corridor which connected both halves of the level. The connecting corridor was supposed to be the most dangerous spot here. To the east were powerhouses and storage vats for the dangerous nanomaterial used in biosuspension, as well as the main and secondary refrigerant systems. To the west were staff living quarters and utility rooms and guard stations with periscopes leading to the surface. This corridor was open both to the massive guns of the door, and to the sniper fire from the secretive coffins.

"When the Hyades arrive, the Master of the World, a posthuman named Del Azarchel—even you have heard of him, I see—and the externalized Machine Intelligence of Del Azarchel, Exarchel, wise beyond all the genius of the Blue Men, will sell mankind into slavery, and the Blue Men will be to the Domination of the Hyades as dogs are to men—no matter how smart, still just pets."

The artificially anthropomogrified creature did not speak, but from the flex of its spine and the prick of its ears, Montrose saw that his words had struck home. Now the dog captain was listening carefully.

"Is that what you want for your masters? For Mentor Ull and Invigilator Illiance? Lives of servitude? Or worse?"

The dog thing said nothing, but looked at Montrose with eyes as hard as stones, ears laid flat against its skull.

"Do you know Ull and Illiance and all the Blues here are serving the Machine? Well? Did you know that?"

The Great Dane's answer was to cuff him backhand across the mouth.

2. The Connecting Corridor

By the time Montrose had reached the level in the gloomy corridor where the other prisoners were being kept, the Giant's coffin was out of sight. There was a splash of light on the wall opposite, a reflection of the golden light pouring out from the opened door, which was blurred and darkened for a moment with shadows as the bulky coffin of the Giant was maneuvered into the stairwell. A moment later the shadows passed, and the reflections gleamed again undisturbed.

At the northern mouth of the connecting corridor, the Blue Men had piled their sandbags, raised square shields of refractory reflex metal, pulled up floor plates, and dug in their gunnery nests. A second line of defense had been erected at the other end of the long corridor, to fend off still-active coffins that attempted from time to time to sally and dislodge them. Beyond this line of sandbags, the wreckage of such sallies clogged the labyrinth of corridors to the south.

Menelaus, his robes of metallic tent material clashing as he stepped, walked down the connecting corridor.

Larz the Fixer, one of the prisoners, relaxed, chuckling to himself. Larz was lying on his back atop an impromptu cot of toppled sandbags with an enormously smug look on his face and his hands tucked behind his head. Next to him was a bowl and several small bottles of rice wine, some empty and some not.

This was the man, this worthless little man, a low-caste Kine from the time of the Chimerae, who had boasted to the Blue Men that he could force open the Tomb door.

Larz was not dressed in his prison overalls, but was in an extravagant civilian costume from the late 5900s: The half cloak of the overalls of the Kine, instead of bearing his name and assignment, was covered with gauds and bezants, with coils of braid at the shoulders and colored scarves hanging from the armpits. He wore the bright pink boots of a professional kick-fighter. The switchblades in the boot toes clicked open and shut like little blunt-nosed creatures flicking out their tongues as Larz idly drummed his heels against the deck.

The serpentine stolen from Yuen the Alpha Chimera was lying near his hand, and it was extended to its full length: it lay like a thread of silver water across the empty expanse of steel floor, winding here and there to avoid buried mines and pressure plates, reaching from the sandbags to the door controls, where it had found a compatible plug.

"Impossible," Montrose muttered in English, his eyes narrowed. Larz could not have hacked his locks and wards. Either Soorm had opened the Tomb doors from the inside, or something equally unlikely. Could Larz be a Hospitalier in disguise?

He tried to stop and speak to Larz, but Larz, thinking him a Beta Chimera from his era, cowered back, whimpering and calling on the dogs to protect him, and the dogs in turn hustled Menelaus down the corridor past Larz.

Midway between the northern and southern defensive positions were bales of ammo and other supplies, as well as angry digging automata in need of minor repair.

Nearly a score of figures could be seen there, separated by armed automata and watched by their assigned guard dogs, who were looking with envy at their dancing brothers not far away, yapping and yammering, tails wagging.

The prisoners were all dressed in their period costumes. Menelaus wondered why the prisoners, now, had their garments returned to them. The Blue Men were very naïve and stupid in some ways, but sharply intelligent in others, close enough to posthuman in their thinking patterns that they could control lateral thought-techniques to see gestalt patterns in events. A man with his clothing and possessions on him altered his "tells," his body language and subconscious reactions. All the Blues need do, if they were as smart as Menelaus thought they were, was observe the prisoner's behavior in the Tombs, and compare this to the reactions of any undamaged information systems in the Tombs to the prisoners. Any wrong reactions would pinpoint the imposter. Had Montrose been visible to the Tomb systems, this tactic would have no doubt already revealed him.

Coming down the corridor, passing within perhaps three feet of Menelaus, was Invigilator Illiance in his jeweled coat. He gave Menelaus a polite nod, but did not pause to exchange any words.

In his hands was the coffeepot from Menelaus' workroom.

Illiance glided down the corridor toward the silent firing range chamber.

He was too small to block the light from the door when he went downstairs, or at least, not enough to alter the reflection of the light bouncing from a distant floor to the nearby wall, but Menelaus could hear the soft, light footsteps passing without hurry down and down.

Menelaus observed his fellow prisoners.

There were seventeen Thaws here: First was the waif perhaps named Alalloel from the Eleventh Millennium. Only four hundred years displaced from her native time. He attempted to contact her with his implants, but the signal did not generate any return. Perhaps she was ignoring him, or perhaps the Blue Men were wise enough to dampen her instruments.

Second and third were the two gray twins, a male and a female, from the Ninth Millennium. They were very similar to the Blue Men, but seemed to be a later development from them.

Next were two Hormagaunts, two Clade-dwellers, and three Donors from the Iatrocracy period in the Eighth Millennium.

After that were four Chimerae and three Kine from the Sixth Millennium.

The Thaws were not standing together, but rather were grouped by aeon, so that Alalloel had a group of cringing dogs around her, away down the corridor, out of sight; the gray twins were next, and armed dogs separated them from Alalloel on the one side and the Iatrocrats on the other.

There were more guards blocking the way between the Iatrocrats and the Chimerae, the group to which Menelaus was brought. He saw no Nymphs, nor anyone of earlier eras. He wondered if they had been taken below.

The Chimerae were closest to the line of sandbags facing the firing range; Alalloel was farthest. All prisoners were huddled against the eastern wall, since the wind was less there.

Now he was among the Chimerae. Here were three underfed and over-worked Kine, muscular dark-haired men with dark and stoical expressions. There were subtle asymmetries and incongruities in their features, odd shapes to their teeth or ears, which hinted at experiments done on generations of their forefathers. Their names were Franz, Ardzl, and Happy.

Their native garb was not that different from the overalls the Blue Men provided, except that each sported a short half cape, where emblems showing their names and assignments were displayed. Menelaus was pleased to see, from certain irregularities in the way their overalls hung, that they had sharpened tent pegs into knives and had them hidden under their clothes.

Near them were two Beta maidens. Above knee-length skirts they wore tight, dark pinch-waisted jackets that buttoned up the side like fencing jackets, tight at the neck, with decorations on the exaggerated shoulder pads. Menelaus was reminded of doormen's costumes at old hotels. Their world had been warmer than that of the gray twins: instead of boots, they wore sandals with laces that ran up their thighs.

The warrior maidens had carved serviceable bows out of the branches of yew trees and strung them with strands of their gene-modified, nigh-unbreakable hair. Each maiden had fletched a dozen arrows, feathered from slain owls, but knapping flint to make a workable arrowhead was beyond what their auxiliary corps girls' schools had taught them. The arrowheads were shards of glass taken from shattered bottles from the infirmary tent, lashed to the arrow shafts with adhesive medical gauze. From the way their tunics hung, he guessed that wider strips of medical gauze had been used to bind their breasts flat: impromptu plastrons. More medical tape wrapped their left arms from palm to elbow, as protection against the bowstring, and their left sleeves were folded up and buttoned short.

Here also was a Gamma. His skin was peeling and pockmarked, a mixture of dark and white patches, and his lower jaw protruded like a Neanderthal's. He had clipped a lock from his long brown hair and woven the strands into a functional Goliath-killing-type sling.

The sleeve of his uniform bulged, showing he kept the water-smoothed stones that formed his store of ammunition in his rolled-in shirtcuffs. His name was Buck Gamma Joet Goez Phyle of Bull Run, Lineage Discontinued.

The male uniform was severe and unadorned, except for a cloak of livid scarlet; shoulder boards extended a hand's length beyond his shoulder, giving his costume something of the look of an ancient samurai's. On these shoulder boards were small electric pins displaying his line, rank, and regiment. His only other adornment was a cloak pin of brass shaped like an upside-down letter L. On his head was a cap of leather and horn.

Alpha Lady Ivinia, splendid in the metal breastplate and tiara of her dress gear, a jet-black tunic decorated with silver skull ornaments, and a long black leather skirt hemmed with iron bosses, still carried her spear. Her red cloak was pinned with a letter shaped like a fish.

3. Reporting for Duty

In his role as Beta Sterling Anubis, he crossed over to her, and knelt, head bowed and hand out in a straight-armed salute. "Milady. Uh, reporting for duty, Ma'am."

She bent and touched him on the shoulder, which surprised him; and drew him to his feet and kissed him on the cheek, which surprised and alarmed him. (She was a tall woman, but even she had to stand on her tiptoes to do this.)

Lady Ivinia said, "This is not I who gives you this kiss, Loyal and Proven Beta, but, rather, the motherhood of all the race, including your own mother, who is not present to give it."

Menelaus touched his cheek, strangely moved. He knew what a horrid and bloodthirsty race the Chimerae were, and yet still they were human beings. Almost.

Lady Ivinia spoke in a hushed voice, with great dignity, "That is the farewell kiss of the race that bore you, for it may well be that we die this day, and reach the longed-for oblivion which will quench the memories of all our crimes and shortcomings in beautiful, unending nothingness. They have taken away Alpha Daae and greatly I fear for his safety. I charge you that should the chance come, his life must be saved, even at the expense both of your life and honor, and of his honor. No glorious death is to be his: Should he so command, and with the strongest oaths bind you, I charge you by the womb of the mother that bore you, and the paps that nursed, to betray that command, and break those oaths. If the name of Anubis must be sunk forever in shame and cursed, let it be so, but he must survive." She did not even mention the name of Alpha Yuen.

Menelaus then realized that the Alpha Lady meant to marry, no doubt to begin the Chimera race again, and that her only choices for the next Adam were between gray-haired Daae and young Yuen. And she had selected Daae.

He felt both awed and saddened by the ambition of her daydream, and its unlikelihood. It was nearly as unlikely as his own dream of finding his own true love again.

Menelaus said, "Ma'am, I will do what I might to save him. The sacrifice of the name Anubis to shame I do not regret, nor will I hesitate." (It was not, after all, his name.)

She inclined her head regally, but then turned her nose aside, to look at him sidelong, a strangely coy and demure look on the face of a woman whose normal expression was one of cold and direct ferocity. "You speak as one almost not fully a Chimera. There is more to you than seems at first inspection. And yet Yuen says you bested him . . ."

"By a trick, Proven and Loyal Ma'am. He is Alpha; I am Beta."

". . . but I am convinced you are loyal to the race. You do not apprehend how near the race teeters to being utterly expunged, nor your own role in these events."

"My role? Beggin' your pardon, my Lady?"

Her eyes grew vivid as she stared at his face. "Alpha Daae realized that the Blue civilian named Illiance interrupted our briefing, and took you from us, merely to have you away from the field of action, while the camp was broken down and withdrawn with all personnel to the belowground here. You were meant not to be present when Kine Larz forced the great door to the lower levels. They did not return your uniform to you. This was not to shame you: they understand you are significant."

Menelaus did not mention that he had not been buried with a uniform, Chimerical or otherwise.

He looked again at the Beta girls with their bows, Phyle with his sling; not to mention the belt capsules of the gray twins, or the poisonous oil in the hair barbs of Zouave Zhigansk.

Menelaus wondered at the nonchalance of the Blue Men. Perhaps the Blues wanted the Thaws to be armed, to have an excuse to slaughter them that would ease their consciences.

It took him a moment to realize that something more was involved in returning the native period garb to the prisoners. They had been allowed to retain their makeshift weapons in order to provoke a disturbance in the behavior patterns of the prisoners.

With hope of violence in the air, their actions would be tested under stress, and once again anomalies in behavior would be more obvious. It was a dangerous tactic meant to flush out the imposter among the prisoners, and it bespoke desperation on the part of the Blue Men.

Something was terrifying them into rash action.

4. Hairdressing

The Chimerae also sensed the terror in the air, and it gladdened their hearts. The Chimerae were relaxed, which was an odd sight, like seeing a pack of wolves suddenly learn how to smile. A certain degree of informality seemed to have overcome them: they did not address each other by rank.

Lady Ivinia whistled and doffed her tiara, pushed back Menelaus' hood, and gestured for him to sit on the cold metal floor beside her. Then the Chimerae took out oils and combs and began dressing each other's hair. Gamma Joet Phyle stood behind Lady Ivinia, who maintained a stoical expression as her hair was yanked by the apologetic Phyle. Vulpina and Suspinia stood behind Menelaus and began combing his hair, marveling at how short he wore it. The three Kine, Happy, Ardzl, and Franz, backed away on their knees, bowing, as far as the dog things would permit, frightened to see their master race wax merry.

Lady Ivinia said, "Brothers and sisters! For you are all ennobled to my blood this day: The oblivion we crave is upon us now! Let us each, in our hearts, curse the nonexistent God for his indifference, and dare him to destroy us! The more lingering the death inflicted, the longer the time to display the stoicism and bravery by which our descendants and lineages shall be judged by future Eugenics Boards . . ."

Her voice trailed off. Her words had no doubt been something she had been wont to say, a habit, and spoken before she could catch herself. A pall of silence hung in the air after this; no one of the Chimerae was willing to say that there would be no more Eugenics Boards, and no lineages, forever.

Menelaus stirred and said, "Well, don't give up hope yet; it's possible we can talk our way out of this. We all might make it out alive, if we only keep our heads . . ."

They looked shocked for a moment, and then, suddenly, the Chimerae opened their mouths and laughed peals of laughter, Gamma Phyle in bass, Lady Ivinia in a contralto, the two Beta maidens in sopranos.

Phyle, the scabrous-skinned Gamma, spoke up, "Good one, Sterling! Had me going!"

Vulpina, behind him, giggled and shrieked and said, "Oh, Anubis, you are too *funny*!"

Suspinia, the other Beta adolescent, said doubtfully, "He wasn't really, I mean, not for real, wanting to live, right? It was just a rec hall prat, right?"

Lady Ivinia said, "Of course, my sister. Merely a comical word to unknot the tension! All Chimerae know that life is pain. Life is grief. The only joy of life is to inflict death on those who want so desperately to live. The only peace in life is to yearn for death, so that those who inflict death on you are cheated of this same joy. That is the Chimera way. In our blood, and in our genes, we are half beasts, and we despise the nature of pure men, who love good things." But she said this not in a stern tone, but lightheartedly, as if she were speaking sentiments known to all; reminding, not instructing.

Menelaus jumped when Beta Vulpina spoke in his ear. He had not forgotten that the hands rubbing oil into his hair belonged to the maiden pressing against his back, but now her lips were dangerously near his ear, and he felt the intimate tingle of her breath on his cheek. She said softly, "Listen to the Alpha Lady! We must learn to love pain, and to love to inflict it!"

"Lovely," muttered Menelaus in deadpan sarcasm. "How old are you, what, sixteen? Fourteen?"

"I am as old as I will ever be! This hour you and I will die together! Won't that be *fun*? If we time it right, we can have the entrails of our corpses mingled together in a huge pool of blood. I ask this as my dying request. *Do you really think me lovely?*" And she kissed him on the ear.

He brushed her lips away from his neck like a man brushing a fly. "I am still married until death us do part, sister. I appreciate the offer—who does not like a romantic double murder-suicide in battle?—but let's keep our guts inside us to digest food, and spill *theirs* on the floor."

She pouted. "You un-face me! If I were not about to commit suicide in battle, I'd commit suicide just to spite you!"

Lady Ivinia was done with her coiffure, and now she had Vulpina sit down before her, and began combing out the girl's hair with practiced, businesslike strokes. "Sister Vulpina! Self-demotion is a sacred rite among us! And too good for you!"

All the Chimera laughed again, and Vulpina turned beet-red, but she also laughed, and did not draw her suicide dirk and plunge it into her own throat.

Lady Ivinia said, "The duty of virgins is to survive combat and be raped by their conquerors, so that they may bear male children, teaching them to slay their fathers and avenge us. Remember this! I am the mother of seven I can name with pride and others I do not name. My duty to the race is fulfilled, and painful death in melee is an honor I can claim."

Suspinia said in a saucy voice, "Well, you're too *old* to get raped anyway!"

Instead of drawing a weapon and killing her on the spot, Ivinia threw back her head and emitted a peal of laughter, and Gamma Phyle slapped the ground, guffawing, and said, "Aye! But them blue Kine ain't got no wagglies bigger'n my pinky nohow, so who could they plumb?"

Menelaus said, "Since we are all about to die, let me just be frank and say, Chimerae are a sick, sick race. The only thing that is really good about Chimerae is that we are not as disgusting as Nymphs."

Suspinia sniffed and snapped her fingers under his nose. "Well, that's not fair! Chimerae have good points! We love fighting, for one thing. And we are tidy. Have you seen how squared away our tents and grounds in the prison camp are, compared to those sloppy Witches'?"

More laughter. Vulpina chimed in, "She is right! The Witches don't even walk in step when they walk. They are like toddlers who haven't learned how to march. At dawn they are still in their sleeping rolls when the dogs blow reveille—except unless they stayed up all night!"

Phyle said, "Anubis! You're not saying aright, Brother Beta! Chimmers are the best o' the best. 'Specially our womenfolk. I figures there be but two kinds of frails, those what like getting beaten a bit before bunk-up time, and those what stab their men in the kidneys with a stiletto whiles we're asleep. Meek and feisty. Both have their good points, mind you! But both kinds likes them to kill strays and ferals like whats facing us here in this place, so I'll bet you that these two girls and the lady will kill more of the foe than all the others in the room combined! If I win the bet, I cut off your left nut; and if you win the bet, you cut off mine! What'ya say?"

Stray and *feral* meant any one not bred according to the sound principles of eugenics.

Menelaus clapped him on the shoulder and said, "Joet, you're a man after my own heart! And I do appreciate you wanting to stick up for the womenfolk— that's right gentlemanlike of you. Unfortunately, I just found out early today that wagering is an undue complexity of life. On another topic, let me explain what these archaic words in the long-dead language called English mean: *engaging-in-copulation, guano-of-bats, not-sane*. Now, each separately means nothing, but, taken together as a phrase, the stalwart men of Texas in elder times used this expression (abbreviated *FBC*) to refer to anyone like yourself, who was (well, if I can be frank one more time) simply Fu—"

Lady Ivinia interrupted, "Do not be frank, Sterling! It erodes discipline, and in any case our cause will prevail, despite any losses. The Judge of Ages is real—Alpha Daae has convinced me of it—and will hand us victory."

Menelaus wished he were equally confident.

5. Separated

The widow Aanwen, Preceptor Naar (along with four of his automata that had been outfitted with steam-powered machine guns), and a squad of excited and yammering dog things rose out of the stairwell, and crossed the metal floor of the firing range. Larz favored them with an airy salute of his wine-bowl.

They entered the connecting corridor. Naar uttered a command in his sing-song language. The dog things lowered the bayonets and began urging the cold-faced and defiant Chimerae toward the big door. The Blue Woman, Aanwen, gestured toward Menelaus. *Not him.*

Like wolves separating a stray from the herd, a trio of dog things thrust their way, snarling, between Menelaus and Lady Ivinia. She brandished her spear. The Kine fell to the deck, hands over their heads, whimpering. The two Beta teenagers, blithely ignoring the ferocious dogs and their threatening bayonets, stopped and strung their bows. The Gamma soldier, Phyle, shrugged, and as if by magic, dropped his sling out of his sleeve, stone already in the pocket, and set his shoulders as if ready to sling a stone at the nearest Blue Man.

Menelaus saw that resistance was suicide. The metal walls of the narrow corridor would scatter ricochets and shrapnel in every direction, and any intact panels of reflex armor would ignite grenades and petards in counter-fire, chopping everything in the corridor to bits neatly as a steel thresher on overdrive. The gray twins might have nerve weapons that would stun or benumb Naar or Aanwen, or the Hormagaunts release spores that would sicken or slay the dog things, but neither one could affect the automata, nor prevent all the dogs from opening fire; nor could the sling, arrows, spear, and knives of the Chimerae damage the machines.

Menelaus estimated that a trained fighting-Chimera could kill ten or twelve armed dog things barehanded; but Gamma Phyle had been recently released from the infirmary tent, and was not in top shape, and Lady Ivinia and the teenaged girls could not match even his performance.

Menelaus called out in two languages not to attack, and the dogs, annoyed by the noise, struck at his face and chest with their musket butts, knocking him from his feet. He had hardened the substance of his cloak before the blows landed, and he stayed on the ground, hood over his face, unwilling to show himself lest Aanwen and Naar realize that Menelaus could not be harmed by the weapons present.

He heard the noise and commotion of footsteps receding as the other Chimerae were herded away. To his surprise, he heard no noises of struggle, smelled no blood.

Dimly, he was amazed that they had been persuaded by him, and then he realized to his chagrin that they had not been persuaded. He was the ranking male present, and by Chimera law, women were noncombatants and must obey—including armed women who were ready to fight in combat. And, of course, Beta outranked Gamma, and freemen outranked Kine.

The dog things pulled him to his feet, and pushed him to stand with the gray twins. Alalloel was not far away, and stood to one side, and the Hormagaunts and their Clades and Donors stood to the other.

6. The Gray Twins

The Grays were blue-haired: the male wore his short, and the woman's reached past her shoulder blades. The male had no trace of facial hair. The pair were also slightly taller than the Blue Men or the onyx-skinned Locust men, and the gestures more fluid and graceful.

The woman wore a fur-trimmed black parka of a smartmetal substance not unlike the tent material, trimmed and lined with seal fur and webbed with heating elements. From her belt hung a fur muff, as well as gold capsules Menelaus' implants told him contained energy sources. Her boots had soles of smartmetal as well, and could probably be programmed to various degrees of friction or traction, or to form snowshoes, cleats, or skates, depending on the substance underfoot. Her twin was likewise wearing a parka of black metal of the same design; heavy fur gloves were tucked in his belt. Gold capsules hanging from his belt likewise gave off a faint radio signature. Both wore snow-blindness goggles with thin slits over their eyes, giving them a sharply alien look.

Menelaus studied the energy contour coming from the golden capsules clamped to their belts, and realized it was consonant with certain types of non-lethal, short-range electroshock weapons, or radiant neural agents. The gray twins were armed.

Menelaus was burning to speak with them, because of Alpha Daae's cryptic unfinished sentence: "It is far more important that we get underground as soon as possible. You see, we found something dreadful. The gray twins discovered it . . ."

What had they said to Daae?

Said? Rather, since they shared no language in common, what had they *shown* him?

Menelaus turned to the man and the woman, and said in Intertextual, *"Do you happen to understand this language?"*

Seen closely, the gray skin was many-hued and subtle, like the color of a pigeon's wing, or silvery silk. Highlights and subtle shadings of pearl and platinum differentiated the eyelids, cheekbones, and jawline, lending the faces a peculiar exaggeration and vivacity. This close, Menelaus could see through the slits of their goggles that the pupils of their eyes were as silvery-white as polished foil. The blue and cerulean hair formed a handsome contrast. Their faces were like works of art, and their features were stamped with the signs of refined and energetic personalities.

The man said, *"All Locusts are programmed with the applicable prenatal speech templates."*

Menelaus, with some surprise, said, *"You are Locusts?"*

A smile answered him: *"Yes, if isolated individuals without tendrils, and with no connection to any outside mental environments, can be called Locusts. I am Linder Keir and this is my daughter Linder Keirthlin. We call ourselves 'Linderlings' or Reestablishmentarians, since we still hope to restore the disintegrated Noösphere to working coherence. We adhere to protocols devised by a man named Elton Linder, and became Inquiline. As nonessentials, we entered hibernation at the time of the Reductions, in order to escape the coming of the ice."*

Menelaus looked back and forth. Daughter? She looked like a twin sister. Cloning? Gene manipulation? It implied a longevity technique that not merely slowed aging, but halted it altogether. That implied a sophisticated genetic correction system, which, in turn, implied Xypotechnology.

Eager as he was to learn what they had shown to Daae, he thought it best to follow up this other thread first.

Menelaus said, *"An inquiline is a bug that lives in an ants' nest or termite mound without being one of them."*

Keir said, *"Such is the relation of our order to the planetary neurocybernetic mental hierarchy. Inquiline are in the Noösphere but not connected to it."*

Keirthlin spoke up for the first time. "Do you also speak English?" She had a flawless Oxonian accent.

Menelaus looked even more surprised. "I'll be hornswoggled. How could y'all possibly know English?"

Keirthlin said, "Earlier, we were placed in close confinement with the Savant called Ctesibius. He has a fully functioning emulation broadcast path woven into his brain from cortex to brainstem, with pinpoint emitters that were only switched off, not removed. I was able to pick up a signal through a short-range resonance, and induce signal flow from his cache. The traces were enough to use a holographic memory technique—you understand this technique works both for endogamic and exogamic memories?—to build up a perception of his language structure."

"He only spoke Pre-Anglatino."

"But the earlier language forms can be deduced from traces, residuum, and atavisms. I used a negative information intuition procedure to fill in the patterns. It took the better part of a day. Language patterning is not my strong suit."

Keir patted her hand with fatherly affection. "There, there. Under less adverse conditions, results would have differed; and we judge by intention and effort, which you can control, rather than by any result influenced by factors no one can control." He lowered his slitted goggles onto his nose, and, peering over the top of them, transfixed Menelaus with his bright, silvery eyes. It seemed an oddly avuncular or professorial gesture. "Can you understand us at a conversational level?"

"Uh, sure. It was an ancient language in my day, but I reckon I can speak it well enough."

Keirthlin fixed him with a particularly penetrating gaze, her head tilted to one side, as if toying with a thought. "You *reckon* so, do you? It is your native language. I cannot determine whom you want to fool. I assume it is the Witches. Anyone from a time later than the Chimerae would see your deviations from their behavior standards. As for contemporaries, well, Mr. Slewfoot Larz the Pinkerton—that is the correct term in English?—the Pinkerton knew immediately you were not a Chimera when you failed to punish him for remaining seated while you stood . . ."

Menelaus said, "Wait, wait. You *saw* my interview with Larz?" Thunderstruck, he realized these two had some implanted system to pick up what the Blue Men were recording or sending to each other with the gems on their coats. They had been spying on the camp. They knew the Blue Men's plans. "What are the Blue Men planning?"

Keir said placidly, "Our ability to intrude is hindered by those rather complex codes of behavior that the Blue Men have decided no longer to follow. Some of their information is proprietary, and since the Blue Men have violently trespassed on our integrity, we can audit certain streams of it, in certain ways, but our retaliation has to fulfill specific requirements before we can act more directly. Take my daughter's hand."

Menelaus shook her hand. It was small and slender in his fist. Keir looked at his daughter, and said, "Well?"

She puffed out her cheeks in a sigh. "I can detect that he has a short-range electromagnetic aura of the first complexity. It should allow him to neurointerface with certain simple circuits and switches, but he lacks the direct thought-to-thought inputs of a Locust. He is not legally an Inquiline because he has some active wiring, but he is not ethically or aesthetically one of us, because we can never reciprocate his mental information. But I think we have to trust him in certain areas, more than what would be expected by the intersection of our limited altruism precept against zone-of-privacy considerations."

"Do you guys run through this kind of rigmarole every time you decide to answer a question?" Menelaus asked sardonically. "My rock-bottom respect for the Blue Men has lifted a half centimeter from the floor of hell. *You* are the people they are trying to live more simply than?"

Keir said sternly, "The complexity you mock is the byproduct of a successful attempt to sculpt laws and customs to a sufficient level of detail as to allow for both world peace and personal liberty, considering both the complication of every possible scenario of human interaction and considering the innate depravity of the human race. The difficulty of all previous cultural systems was that they were insufficiently tailored to reality: all laws had to be broad stereotypes to be simple enough to rational men to anticipate what conduct was permitted, but Divarication ensured laws soon would become corrupt. In contrast, Xypotechnological modeling and emulation of major possible behavior patterns is more efficient than having legislators make laws, or allowing blind chance to establish arbitrary or historically specific customs and cultural habits. The Noösphere makes this level of detail possible."

Menelaus said sharply, "Your Noösphere was based on Xypotechnology?"

Keir said, "We are reconciled to a certain degree of cooperation with the Exarchel Machine, and allow it to influence our legislative modeling process."

Menelaus said, "The Machine means to exterminate the human race. Ctesibius thinks it has already done so, and that now all that need doing is to clean up the biological life left—us relics from the past, in other words."

Keir said, "If the humans are guided slowly and gently to underpopulation, and then extinction, where is the harm? If the process is voluntary on all sides, no specific rights are being violated."

Menelaus said, "It's still wrong."

Keir said, "The thought-process of biological life will continue in the nonbiological matrix, if needed. The Noösphere is not simply the Exarchel Machine. It is the conceptual unity of all thinking systems, both human and posthuman, machine emulation and neural emulation. Our brainpaths are not like yours. We have a solid mass of three-dimensional logic tissue rather than ordinary gray matter. Within this matrix we can construct or emulate any number of minds of human levels of complexity, to suit our needs and interests. The system is completely fluid: basically, in my head, I could make a virtual version of any sort of nervous system or brainpath and emulate it, play it out. That is what Illiance did when the Naturalist Oenoe forced him to accept emotional communion to her story, when she was being interviewed; you translated for them. You recall the event?"

"Sure. That's when he turned off his weirdness chip, and I started liking him."

Keir said, "There is no physical computer chip in his brain. It is a complex of logic crystal energies tainting his nervous system in a delicate balance of path preferences. You are speaking metaphorically, I assume?"

"Very metaphorically," agreed Montrose. "Unduly so."

Keirthlin said, "Oenoe the Naturalist did not know what she was asking. It is a classic example of symmetrical misunderstanding across two mutually incomprehensible mental texts."

At that moment, once again, a squad of dog things accompanied by four clanking automata came up out of the fourth door, passed where Kine Larz lay, and herded the Hormagaunts back down into the depths, along with their Clades and Donors.

7. Last of the Iatrocracy

Montrose watched as the Iatrocrats were marched past him down the cold, dim, and roofless corridor.

Two looming Hormagaunts glowered at the guard dogs, eager to slay and careless of being slain. One was a man who looked like a leopard walking upright, thin and wiry, with elongated legs, walking on his toes, with an impressive array of barbs, spines, and knife-points growing from his spine. His neck was like that of a boneless giraffe or monster snake; his head like that of a saber-toothed tiger. This was Crile scion Wept.

The other had no head at all, merely a lump of bone between his shoulders, and he had placed his eyes in his chest, his shark-toothed mouth like a zippered band across his stomach. His body was apelike but hairless, squat and low to the ground, and his back was a tortoise shell. His tail was an armored limb of muscle tipped with an orb of bone. His genitalia and buttocks cheeks were bright red, like those of a baboon. This was Gload scion Ghollipog.

Scurrying after them were three nondescript and cringing men, dull-eyed and sullen, covered with the scars of old surgeries. These were the slaves "Anubis" allegedly had freed when he bargained with Soorm to form an alliance between the Hormagaunts and the other prisoners to cooperate in an escape attempt. With a pang, Menelaus realized that he had done nothing of the sort, having had no time to train the Donors out of the grip of their mental habit of servitude, or even to explain the new situation to them.

Prissy of Clade Pskov was from the same period as Crile and Gload. With her was a male of her subspecies, a Clade-dweller who looked more human than the Hormagaunt caste. Both Clade-dwellers had hawklike, high-cheeked features, and masses of bushy hair set with spines and quills trailing down their necks. The two stood as far apart from each other as the laxity of the dog guards would permit. The male was Zouave of Clade Zhigansk.

Prissy Pskov wore a blue fur coat embellished along the shoulders and upper back with amber and bezants of golden ivory. A wide scarf of woven zigzag pattern gathered the fur coat hem beneath her breasts, exposing them, but a diaphanous veil of antiseptic fiber modestly covered her nose and mouth. Her apron and skirts were embellished near the hem with clattering scrimshaws of horn and tusk. Her buckles and bracelets and the bells that fringed her shawl were all made of wood or pearl or enamel or horn: her metal-poor era made little use of gold or iron. She had tied a fan of colored feathers and beads in her hair, which would stand like a peacock's tail when she spread her quills.

By contrast, the garb of Zouave Zhigansk was simple and severe: a bear pelt pelisse worn over a dark tunic, with split skirts below. His only ornaments were the bear claws that adorned the toes of his fur boots. He had the mouth-cup of a filtermask made of black ivory hanging by a strap around his neck, but he did not have it over his mouth and nose at the moment, because he was menacing the dog things with his retractable fangs. The porcupine quills that rose from his hair were glistering as if with oil: he had combed additional poisons into their tips, to make them more sweetly scented, and deadlier.

Seeing his eyes on her as she was hustled past, Prissy Pskov said aloud, "Anubis! These *culls* here-now understand not my speech. My kit has been returned, and primary formulations are mine to command. I can release a spore that will induce seizures in the dogs and leave the humans nauseous but mostly alive."

Blackie del Azarchel was obviously expecting a fight between the Thaws and the Blue Men. But why? On general principle, it was better not to let him get his way.

"Do nothing! Nothing!" he shouted back to Prissy Pskov. "Await my signal." But this shouting attracted the anger of the dog things, who brandished their muskets and cutlasses in his face and barked furiously. Menelaus raised his empty hands, backing away.

His voice roused the Hormagaunts, who roared and reared, and at their barking, more dog things rushed up to subdue the Hormagaunts.

So large a number of dogs escorted the Hormagaunts down the stairs that only a dozen were left to guard Menelaus, Keir and Keirthlin, and Alalloel.

8. The Principle of Absolute Trust

Events were coming to a head. Menelaus turned back to the two strange and strangely elfin gray-skinned people. "You have to help me. For starters, tell me what you told Alpha Daae."

Keirthlin took off her slitted goggles, revealing a pair of lovely yet eerie silvery-white eyes, fringed with long, dark lashes. She said, "Wear this. Look within."

Menelaus did not don the goggles. "An image? Live or locally stored?"

Keirthlin looked uncomfortable, but did not answer.

Menelaus said, "You showed Daae a picture, right? But he could not ask you what data system you were using for transmitting the picture. If you have access to the Blue Man logic crystal system, you may be able to deactivate their weapons and energy sources, and trace their lines of information back to their real boss. How broad is your format? Can you make contact with the Tomb brains? And give me control of the major weapons systems?"

In the eyeslits of his goggles, Keir's eyes of silver glinted with a stern light. "Your purposes are warlike, violent, and that behavior is unendurable to us. Even our right to retaliate in self-defense is severely curtailed by an overarching principle of long-term utilitarian altruism. We can only make local and limited exceptions under closely defined circumstances, which do not here and now obtain. We must respect the ethical claim of the Simplifiers."

Menelaus said sharply, "*Ethical* claim? You mean you could meddle with the automata and muskets, maybe even deactivate them—and you choose not to? So you are the ones in charge of the camp, but you are sitting on your gray little butts, doing nothing while they run rampant?!"

Keir said loftily, "Our choice was defined when our order vowed devotion to world and racial reunification across all the disparities, mutations, and violent recriminations which the shattering of the Noösphere brought forth. That is the great evil we are oathbound to undo. The Linderlings are devoted to rapprochement even with Inquilines who reject mental unification, and so we are enjoined to nonreprisal, nonaggression, and noninterference."

"Why do the tomb-robbers have a greater claim to your moral protection than the innocent clients here?" Montrose shouted.

Keir drew back fastidiously. "How innocent are any here? In any case, the Blues are a cousin species to the Grays, and we must reestablish our broken communion with them. We were designed for this cause by our creator-parents' cells."

Menelaus gritted his teeth. "The cause you serve is long dead. These Blue Men are killers. Your indifference aids and abets their crimes. They killed the three Locusts who tried to help me when I first woke up. I promised to save them, and I failed to do it. The least I can do is make sure blood is paid out for blood spilled."

"Their names were Crucxit, Axcit, and Litcec of Seven-Twenty-One North Station. They were from a century when the Inquiline and nonjurors were not recognized as independent entities with any right to exist. They overstepped the ethical claim I respect, attempted to suborn the mental environment of the Blue Men, and were murdered in retaliation. Shall you indeed retaliate for that retaliation? If so, be deliberate and cautious: perspectives of differing ages disclose differing aspects of the complex edifice of proper conduct."

Menelaus said, "The Blue Men are trespassing on the Tombs."

Keir said, "If the Tomb system were functioning, it would not have brought us forth by accident in a time when the human world is dead. The failure of the Judge of Ages to carry out his obligations must be taken into account. There is no current civilization. Hence the Blue Men must trespass on the Tombs for supplies. They are compelled by necessity, which is your excuse for the deceptions you practice."

Menelaus spat, "Nothing here has been an accident. There *is* a current civilization; and your damned Machine you love so much, Exarchel, that ran your age, is still active and no doubt running this one. He just has not shown his hand yet."

"You speak in ignorance. Exarchel was merely one participant in a complex social and mental organization, treated warily, hemmed in by certain checks and balances and . . ."

". . . And actually running things because he is smarter than you."

Keirthlin interrupted. "Father, I submit that we are operating on partial information, and should assume the negative information space of the missing data matches the contour in the fashion most favorable to the case leading to the minimal-maximal solution to the conflict of ethical-legal claims here."

Keir said to her, "You are urging we both act on the principle of absolute trust? But I cannot deduce his motives."

Keirthlin said, "That is because our minds are complex, whereas his motive is simple. He is, in his own person, what the Blue Men artificially attempt to be: a man with no affectations or ulterior motives. The moral category distortions are caused by circumstances, not by him. The Blue Men are, after all, tomb-looters! That is the crucial trespass that defines and limits the possible legal resolutions."

Keir said, "Violence is unthinkable!"

She flashed him a pert glance of her odd, metallic-white eyes. "Then don't think about it."

He said, "My internal emulation of you is not reaching the same conclusions you are. What additional thing does the real you know that my projection of you does not?"

Menelaus looked back and forth, his face almost blank with wonder, as if too many conflicting emotions, wonder and impatience among them, had canceled each other out on his features.

Keirthlin said, "I know his energy aura contains keys compatible with the coffin mechanisms." She pointed a finger at Menelaus dramatically, accusingly. "The speculation of Aanwen must be correct. *This* is one of the Tomb Guardians. That means he is under a moral obligation to protect the revenants, including us, and including the Simplifiers; which means in turn we are under a moral obligation, even at our own expense, to assist him. Did we not take advantage of the Tombs to escape an era of glaciers? Is there no reciprocity for that?"

Father and daughter stared at each other. His eyes were troubled; hers were bright.

Menelaus said mildly, "Is this how your whole society worked? It is amazing anyone ever did anything. How did you decide when to take a coffee break, or when it was OK to filch a cigarette from the pack your brother kept hidden under his bed? Just curious."

Keirthlin turned toward Menelaus, her eyes flashing. "Will you trust me, completely and absolutely, if only for a short time?"

Menelaus looked taken aback, but spoke in the voice of a man who comes to a quick decision. "If you are servants of the Machine, you would not know how Exarchel has been manipulating your memories or perceptions. But I will trust you now. I am desperate. It's not like things can get much worse."

"Then tell me your identity and motives."

He put out his hand. "Okay, maybe they can get worse. I'll make you a deal. You trust me first. Your personal infosphere is carried in capsules on your belts. Hand me one, attune it to me, and establish a link to any working Tomb channels. Once I am armed and dangerous, I can tell you who I am and what I mean to do."

She unclipped one of the little cylinders at her belt and put it in his hand. Immediately he felt an ache in his back teeth as the two semi-incompatible systems worked out mutual formats and eventually—almost four seconds later—shook hands.

He clicked open the little golden tube with his thumb. It was a line of gems, just like the ones the Blues wore on their coats, held together one atop the next, like a finger wearing so many rings it could not bend: sardonyx, carnelian, chrysolite, beryl, topaz, chrysoprase, jacinth.

From his implants, he received two sets of signals. The main and secondary power on the level where he was had been locked out. There was no response except for a simple denial signal. However, from the next level down, he could log on to the secondary and nonlethal weapons. Something or someone was blocking him from reaching the main batteries of the heavier weaponry. He gritted his buzzing teeth in frustration. Something in the Tomb brain was broken, or corrupted, or someone else was active in the system. He knew not which it was.

If he could get the dogs to carry him belowground, he would be within range to give commands to at least some nonlethals and automatics. It was something.

Like a whisper, he then picked up a third signal, a blank carrier wave. He moved his eyes without turning his head. It was coming from Alalloel. His implants, by themselves, had not been able to reach the strange-eyed woman. Whether she had been ignoring him or the Blue Men had been jamming him was still not clear, but these Gray instruments had opened a channel of communication.

He spoke in a low tone. "Your guess falls short. I am no servant. I am Montrose, the Judge of Ages. My men are buried here, and are starting to thaw. As soon as they wake, I will enact a bloody vengeance on those who trespassed in my Tombs. The horror of my retribution must be so great that it will echo through history for thousands of years, that generations yet unborn will fear to trespass again."

Keir said in a voice hollow with horror, "You are the one who condemned the Noösphere to destruction. You introduced Cliometric variables into the scope of history to preordain its disintegration!"

Menelaus said roughly, "You should be grateful. That world was one big termite hive. It was one creature with infinite bodies and only one head. Well, brother, that one-headed world creature had only one neck, to make it easy for Exarchel to snap a collar on it, and then hand the leash to the Hyades. Whatever ain't an individual ain't rightly human."

The gray twins stared at him with wide and silvery eyes. He could not tell if they were afraid because they thought him mad or speaking lies, or thought him sober and speaking truth.

He said, "Machinophiles or not, I will spare you. I will protect you and all innocent clients of the Fancy Gap Hibernation Facility, without reservation to the best of my ability, and yes, if there is a way to spare them, I will try to save the guilty clients too—but only if they surrender, and restore each thing they have looted or touched, and only if the persons directly responsible for the deaths of the three black Locusts are executed. Can you deduce my motives now?"

Keirthlin looked at her father.

Keir was scowling darkly. "All you have said is inconsequential. There is no need for vengeance. There will not be any future generations."

An icicle of dread formed in the pit of Menelaus' stomach. "What did you see?"

"The First Sweep. Look within. This is a true image."

9. Raleigh

He seemed to be in midair, and snowy hills, green with pine, were flowing by underfoot. Menelaus said, "This image is coming from the missing wind-craft that Mickey launched."

Keirthlin's voice was at his ear. "The serpentine that your friend cycled into its more primitive and self-aware phase of behavior gave out its normal call and response to find other mechanisms loyal to the Machine. Those process codes, being in the public domain of our Noösphere, were part of our Confraternal heritage."

Kier added, "We violate no precepts by availing ourselves of the information content."

Menelaus said, "You are telling me that even back in the Witch days, Exarchel had all the ratiotechs bugged?"

She said, "From even earlier. The Gigantic precautions limiting Sylph ratiotechnology to isolated handheld systems were not an overreaction. I will now show you an earlier image."

The wind-craft hung like a kite over the scene.

Blocks of glacier, hundreds of feet high, reared above a ruined city. Even softened by shapes of snow, the soaring towers and lofty domes of glass gave the metropolis an air of classical beauty. The traces left by boulevards showed a clean gridwork of streets, and four public squares surrounded by a central square. He could see statues hooded with ice and the broken feet of triumphal arches mounded high with snow. He looked closer, and realized that those towers were merely stumps of what must have been superscrapers, and the domes were no more than surface vents for deeply dug geothermal power taps. From the arrangement, he guessed that these were an example of the very pyrohydroponic gardens whose quests to reach ever deeper levels long ago forced Pellucid to sink into ever more cautious secrecy.

Then he realized that the high, square shapes of white looming like titans above the scene were not glacier cliffs, but arcologies: massive, windowless buildings not meant for human life, containing nothing but mostly buried cubic miles of logic crystal. These were the Granoliths Pellucid had mentioned in his final report. These vast rectilinear monasteries represented land-based biological man's last desperate attempt to understand and control the multiple-minds of the Melusine, semiartificial seagoing creatures apparently constructed from men, sea mammals, and Xypotechs.

The image seemed melancholy, but nothing to put a fright into so stolid a soul as Alpha Captain Daae.

Then he wondered if he was looking at the wrong part of the image. It was not until he turned his head that he realized this image was from a 360-degree camera, a global lens. Turning the goggles brought other parts of the recorded image into view.

Away to the south, past the barren white hills beyond, Menelaus saw what seemed to be giant dark thunderclouds gathered.

Menelaus realized there was something odd about the cloud. There was a band of blue sky (slightly brighter in hue than the sky to the left and right) issuing from the top of the thunderhead. It looked like a blue road, or perhaps a crack, as if the sky were pure blue glass that had developed two perfectly parallel, perfectly vertical fissures several miles apart, reaching directly upward.

Menelaus craned back his head, tilting the view from the goggles upward. The road of lighter blue sky receded in the upper distance. The far ends seemed to converge, the way the parallel rails of a track seem to meet at the horizon. Only here, there was no horizon. Directly overhead, the dome of the sky was cloudless, and the highest midpoint of the dome, the very zenith, was the point to which the lighter blue stripes converged. So the whole atmospheric disturbance or optical illusion or whatever it was looked like a very narrow and very tall triangle, perhaps a few miles wide at its storm cloud base, and hundreds of miles high as it reached to the top of the sky. Because of the fact that, to the human eye, the sky does seem to be a dome, the triangular stripe of lighter blue color seemed to bend like a hook or a claw, as if a Titan with his shoulder at the horizon were reaching a curved arm up and overhead, to place a menacing finger at the zenith.

It was certainly ominous looking, as if an immeasurably immense tower shaped like a half circle were about to topple on the scene.

Keirthlin, who could see him tilting back his head, gave a noise smaller than a sigh, as if anticipating what Menelaus was about to see. That small noise came just as his eyes adjusted, or perhaps his brain, and he realized what he was seeing. Perhaps he consciously noted now how disturbed the thundercloud was, or how large it was, or how far away. Perhaps he glimpsed, where the black clouds parted, the vast and round metallic surface of the lower part of the structure.

It was not blue, not really, any more than mountains seen on the horizon are blue. Mountains seem blue at a distance because of the hue of the mass of the intervening air. When they are closer than the horizon, of course, there is less air, and therefore the color is not as dark.

What he was seeing was a solid object. It was a cylinder, too large and far away for any surface details to be distinguished, reaching from the cloud level, perhaps five hundred feet off the ground, up and up through the atmosphere and stratosphere and perhaps beyond. The clouds parted as it advanced, and the air masses being displaced were condensing into a large hurricane and thunderstorm at the bottom of its foot.

The bottom was a circular plain of metal dotted with irregularities, surrounding the vast emptiness of a portal or mouth opening into the immeasurable cylindrical interior of the structure. Threadlike arms or instruments hung down, looking like the trailing tails of jellyfish.

Minutes passed, and more could be seen. The armored body of the cylinder itself was punctuated here and there with cross-shaped altitude jets, or black dots of weapon ports or antennae or instruments of some sort, about one every five or ten square miles. To be visible at this distance, the rocket cones must have been larger than skyscrapers.

Some segments of the vast curving surface were flat and dark like the oceans of the moon; others were stubbled with a pattern of irregularities, almost invisible at this distance, which may have been buildings, encampments, fortresses, or aerodromes larger than any major metropolis, their towers horizontal rather than vertical. There were some craters large enough to be visible on the sections higher in the atmosphere, or perhaps these were scars from strikes by old nuclear missiles.

With the effortless power and grace of a god, serene as a ship in full sail, the unimaginably titanic artifact moved across the face of the Earth, and the disturbed clouds formed eddies and swirls, larger than provinces, behind it as it came.

A little nimbus of glittering glints fluttered before the mouth of the cylinder, and tiny specks as if something was traveling up through the air into it.

The wind-craft that had recorded the image swooped closer to the city. Menelaus could see something being lifted up from the ground and into the opening of the cylinder.

Once the wind-craft was close enough, Menelaus could use a cortical interpretation technique to resolve the vision into meaningful shapes.

Machines, swarms of machines, on the ends of long lines like spiders on threads, descended from and ascended to the mouth of the cylinder. They were carrying buildings. Even the arcologies were but toy blocks compared to the size of the cylinder. Menelaus saw vehicles like trains, pulled out of the ice that had preserved them, drawn like links of sausage up and upward. Or they may have been lines of cable or pipe.

He saw oak trees and sculptures being lifted up. A geodesic dome, and many, many lesser buildings. Houses. Mansions. Gardens. Museums. Edifices he did not recognize.

The wind-craft moved closer to the great Bell, passing beneath the mouth. The cameras could see that inside the mouth of the Bell, the various components of the city were being put back together again, like a children's puzzle, on a series of shelves that ringed the inner hollow space.

Keirthlin said in English, "It was Raleigh, one of the cities of the Carolinas."

Menelaus snatched the goggles off. "The base of the machine was above fourteen thousand feet. The upper reaches must be above the atmosphere . . ."

Keirthlin said, "I estimate it to be 116 million feet high, or 19,100 nautical miles. To hold its own coherence under its own weight, descending from orbit to the surface, the material must exceed 200 gigapascals of tensile strength and elastic properties of over 1 terapascal. The degree of tapering between the geosynchronous altitude and the Earth's surface depends on the material: for steel, it is tens of thousands to one, whereas for diamond, twenty to one. In this case, there was no visible tapering, which indicates a strength of material above what is possible for molecular bonds: the strength is akin to the strong nuclear force. By any normal understanding of Earthly science, what we saw was impossible."

"Plague and pestilence! Who on *Earth* could build such a thing? The space elevator Rania took off with was just a frail spider-thread compared to that. How far out into space does it go? Is it anchored to a geosynchronous asteroid? And if it is—sucking abdominal wound of Jesus Christ!—how can they maneuver it?"

Keir said, "Have you not studied the Monument? The great east-southeast cartouche element of the Pi hieroglyph segment displays image-algorithms, pictoglyphs, and other representations describing the tools the Hyades Dominion uses for its deracination, as well as other schematics of traditional mechanisms and systems. This Bell is identical to one of the instrumentalities so pictured. It is a device for absorbing into confinement a planetary population along with various tools and physical artifacts of their culture, and sufficient layers of the ecosphere to sustain them, and for placing the populations as payload in Clarke orbit pending solar sail launch outsystem. Different mechanisms than this are preferred by the Hyades for deracinating superterrestrial and subjovial worlds. This contrivance seems to be a Hyades war-object that arrived far in advance of the promised World Armada."

"Impossible," said Menelaus.

Keir said, "How can we know what is impossible for them? We are as ants."

"The laws of nature are the same for ants as for bigger things. No one can exceed the speed of light; no one can create energy from nowhere."

Keirthlin said, "Someone sent out an extremely low frequency signal to attract the Bell, and it answered in Monument hieroglyphs, describing its rendezvous with this location. The Bell should be here shortly. If you note the cloud cover gathering, and the drop in temperature, and the howling of the wind, you will deduce that the near rim of the mouth of the Bell is already visible above the local horizon. Would you care to see a view from the logic crystals in the camp?"

Numbly, Menelaus handed back the goggles. He had seen enough.

Keirthlin said, "Why did you call them here? What did you intend? What do these events mean?"

Menelaus said, "I am the smartest man on the planet, and I have no damnified and pustulating idea what is going on. The Currents, whoever they are, if they had the technology to create such a thing, would surely have left some sign, some energy signal, that the Locusts would have detected, or my radio. Are they hiding?"

Keirthlin said, "While I am not a Simplifier, I do admire the directness of their approach. In this case, the simple approach is best. If you are curious about the motives of the current generation, why not ask?"

Menelaus goggled at her. "*You* are the Currents?"

Keir made a curt, negative gesture with his hand. "We are not. She is." And he nodded toward Alalloel. "Everyone else here is from our past. Only her energy signals contain fine emission nuances we cannot penetrate. Observe the small motions of her eyes and hands. She is a posthuman."

10. Girl from the Eighteenth Configuration

Menelaus still felt an astonishment, great as anger, burning in his belly. He spun and glared across the space separating them at Alalloel.

He looked at the ornamental clasps adorning her shoulders, wrists, and waist. They looked like seashells. The tiny patterns of striations showed they had been grown using the same method as the shell-like buildings outside.

"*You!* You are a Current, aren't you? World hasn't changed that much in four hundred years, has it? You are a Melusine! You are in contact with them! You know what's going on! Where is the world? Where did the human race go? What is that—that *thing* outside?"

The gold, silver, and blue antennae on her head stirred, and the second pair of ears below her human ears opened like little pink parasols, and tilted toward Menelaus as if tracking the source of the noise. But she said nothing, and there was a mocking look in her blind-seeming eyes.

He probed the clasps on her uniform with a signal from his implants; this time he used the Gray logic gems to heterodyne his signal onto the carrier wave he had detected earlier. From the energy echo, he realized she had the range and the power to reach not only the Bell, but whoever was in charge of this period of history, including whatever libraries and infosphere contained the answers to his questions. Questions she was not answering.

Menelaus adjusted the nodes the Grays had given him, and sent a signal strong enough that Alalloel winced. Aloud, he said the same words: "Who are you?"

She raised an eyebrow. She opened her tongueless mouth. From her throat issued a voice.

"Alalloel u lal rir Lree, u lal rir Enlil-Urthlolendthril."

"Nope. If the Linderlings can pick up this language at their speed, you can at yours."

The throat-voice changed, and now spoke with the same modulation, accent, and rhythm as Keir, but at a slightly higher pitch. The perfection of the impersonation was eerie. "Alalloel of the Lree of the Eighteenth World Mind Configuration."

"You hid that you can grasp our talk? Why?"

"It would lack symmetry were you, given your actions, to criticize the pretense of ignorance to lure others to speak unguardedly."

"You started to speak to me in the mess tent."

"I started to offer you my name; you offered me in return a lie. Absent reciprocity, conversation halts."

Menelaus said angrily to Alalloel, "Lady, you better tell me where is the human race."

"Measured in terms of the majority of intellectual activity, the human race is no longer significant. The Eighteenth Configuration is no longer significant. The Earth itself is self-aware."

He didn't know if that referred to Pellucid filling the core, or the self-aware Del Azarchel snow-coating the outside of the planet. He said, "Go on."

"The mentality involved has not yet achieved coherence. Rather, the conflicting polities have thought-structures issuing from two epicenters, creating mutual interference. Nobilissimus Del Azarchel and the historical and mental events he sets in motion occupy one epicenter; you and yours occupy the other. But who are you? The archives refuse to confirm that you are the Judge of Ages, Menelaus Montrose, despite your claim. There is an information lapse or blind spot when the inquiry is made. Something nulls the reply. Who are you?"

Menelaus realized she must be at least partly contaminated by Exarchel, or her archives were. He said, "What happened to the people? Where is everyone?"

She looked at him with her strange, blind-seeming eyes. "You are not forthcoming? I reciprocate. Do not resist when the Simplifiers emerge to hale you below. They make an identity error."

"What?"

"I speak now for the Final Stipulation of Noösphere Protocols, which supersedes even the Eighteenth Configuration: the Finality imposes an imperative to permit resolution of the various deceptions and aggressions involved that minimizes collateral damage to persons or historically valuable objects, information, or arrangements."

"What the poxy hell you talking about, lady?"

"The Finality requires that you go below. All events are arranged; all contingencies foreseen. Do no damage to our Tombs."

"*Your* Tombs! Pestilential hellish *pox*!"

But there was no more time. The dogs raised their muskets as Illiance, glittering in his blue coat, glided smoothly up and out from the gold shining stairs leading below. He pointed and whistled and the dog things eagerly leaped to obey. Paws grabbed Menelaus by the arms and half dragged, half frogwalked him across the wide steel floor to the shadow of the great doors.

Illiance regarded him with mild curiosity, and said in a quiet voice, "Beta Sterling Anubis."

Menelaus counted the gems on the Blue Man's long coat. "Hello, Preceptor. Got your rank back, did you? Congrats."

"Thank you, Corporal. My peers happen to admire the elegance with which an armed insurrection in the camp was averted, thanks to my forethought, and to my correct assessment of your maneuvers. You were preparing an act of insurrection, were you not? You would have killed the Followers we sent to guide you. The crime is an abomination."

"Yeah. Almost as bad as tomb-looting, theft, trespass, kidnapping, maiming, assault, torture, and murder."

Illiance said, "Now, please come this way. Your talent for translating dead languages is needed. We have found the Judge of Ages."

"Oh, this I *got* to see."

2

The Tomb of Ages

1. Payment

Mentor Ull was standing near the line of sandbags that separated the connecting corridor from the firing range, where the huge doors leading underground loomed.

Ull said to Menelaus, "Beta Sterling Anubis, please tell Kine Larz of the Gutter that, as we agreed, he may keep the ratiotechnology-based hand weapon of the Extet clan as payment for his services, but please warn him that there is no fiscal or financial structure in the current world able to exchange such a valuable antiquity for other goods and services more to his liking."

Naar and Ull returned through the door. Menelaus watched with a look of blank anger on his face as the little men glided without harm past the countless spray-nozzles, mines, gun-muzzles, and energy emission antennae lining the massive metal doorposts.

Menelaus said in Chimerical to Larz, "Now that you have betrayed us to the Blue Men, they are trying to see to it that you get killed. The one in the coat without many glitters is named Ull, and he is the Alpha here. He says you may keep the ancestral weapon of the Extet clan for your use, but he warns you that there are no pawn shops or museums to sell it to. I will warn you that if an Alpha sees a Kine holding a weapon from one of the original experiment families, he will not even bother to utter a ritual challenge."

The rice wine had given Larz artificial courage. His speech was only slightly slurred when he spoke. "A Beta would not issue a bother to a brother a pother either, a real Beta. Who in oblivion are you?"

But at this point the dog things grew restless, and began gesturing angrily with their muskets.

The gray twins and Alalloel were at the rear of the line of marching dogs. Menelaus and Larz were in the front.

Menelaus watched the great door carefully. Certain of the gunblisters were still active, and the barrels did track Larz and the dogs as they walked under the massive lintel, and other weapons followed, but nothing fired, and nothing pointed at Menelaus. Menelaus put his hand to his mouth and coughed, and started to say something aloud, but the dog next to him (no doubt fearful that a loud noise might provoke one of the many unknown weapons in the door) struck Menelaus sharply on the side of his unhooded head with a musket butt, and half dragged, half carried him across the threshold. Menelaus was eventually able to get his feet under him.

He also now had the powder horn and the wallet of musketballs which had been dangling alluringly from the dog's sabretache under his cloak. Along with his rock, the splicing knife, and the Gray capsule of logic crystals, it was not much by way of weaponry, but it was something.

The stairs were gold, and creaked ever so slightly underfoot, as each stair was a pressure plate. Menelaus looked left and right, noting that the heavy voltage conduits meant to electrify the stairs (gold was, after all, a splendid conductor) had been jacked into their safety positions.

The dogs led them down one magnificent flight after another. Down and down they went, through solid bedrock and past layers of armor like the geologic strata of a metal world, from the third to the fourth level.

The stairs were more slippery than they seemed, or Menelaus had been hit in the head more often or harder than he thought, for he fell once or twice. Larz (who was staggering a bit himself) stepped next to him, and put a hand under his arm to help him walk.

As they walked, Larz took the trouble to hide the serpentine. He unbuttoned his shoulders, wrapped the stolen smart whip four or five times around his naked waist, and pulled the top of his coveralls over it.

Menelaus said, "That won't help. Alpha Yuen already saw you touching it."

2. The Man Named Loser

"Tell me who you are, or I will tell everyone who you are not," said Larz in Chimerical. "You are not a Beta. Not no-how."

"And you are not Larz of the Gutter."

The man's eyes grew round. "They still read cheaplies in the far future? They still read Gibson? You're kidding me!"

"You should have picked a name no one would recognize, like Tarzan or Sherlock."

"So says a man named Anubis—you trying to get caught? No Chimera was ever called such. He is the ancient Egyptian death-god with the head of a jackal."

"I was hoping anyone who recognized the name would betray himself. Where did you hear it? It is not like the Chimerae let their slaves study mythology."

"Mythology? What's that? No, I know Anubis 'cause Larz of the Gutter faced the Phantom Pharaoh of the Haunted Pyramid of Mars in *Strange Tales of the Street* numbers 100 to 104, a four-part episode called *Beneath the Moons of Fear and Terror*. I consider it a five-parter, on account of 104 was a double-sized issue."

"Y'know, I read slop like that when I was younger, too. So what is your real name?"

"Loser! My Da wanted me to get into a lot of fights. But I actually, really am a merc law. I did crack-knuckle work, and some shoot-and-scoot."

"Wait, do you mean your name is *Loser*, or were you calling me a . . ."

"I mean I am as slick as the real Gutter Larz, and that is my name from now on. I got the damn door to crack, Jack! That's prudential departmental credential, a smart fix with no tricks!"

"Oh, seeping scabs of syphilis! Please, by all that is clean and sterile, don't start your stupid sales pitch again. Your coffin said *Larz*."

"And yours said Beta Stalling something-or-other Devious Anne-Ibis. So what? I figured whatever name I picked when I slumbered, that would be my name in the new world when I thawed. So stop stalling, Stalling, or I'm calling and you'll be crawling."

Menelaus said, "Anything to squelch your damned yammering! I'll talk! Do you believe in the Hermetic Order?"

"Spooks and kooks who live in the great black yonder in a starship older than history? Dark Magicians who serve the Machine? Simon the Black and his secret of eternal life? C'mon, mate, don't pork a porker. No such beastie."

"Simon the Black is myth. Ximen del Azarchel is real."

"Simon the Magician. Simon of the Moon. I know the name."

"How do you know it?"

Larz said, "The same way I know about the Pharaohs of Egypt. Larz of the Gutter had to fight mummies and mesmerists and swamp zombies, not just gangsters and assassins. It's just made-up stuff, R and R reads, not real."

"Real enough to kill us all in the next hour."

"No! It is a fairy tale for kids in boot camp. The world was burnt an aeon ago, and only Simon the Magician escaped; an aeon before that, the world was drowned to death, and only Noah the Navigator escaped."

"Old Noah with his houseboat full of zoo animals?" said Montrose, astonished. "I used to have a toy when I was a whelp—how in the world is that story still around, by your day?"

"Aha! So you might ask! There is something behind those tales. Now, you might think the latest news is the least painted-up and liar-tilted. But no sirree! My take on it is"—and here Larz seemed to puff out his chest a bit, and assumed a philosophical expression—"in general the older tales can be more trusted, on account of the brass has had less time to hack them, right? Older tales had more time to spread around the world and lodge in nooks and cracks where the truth police cannot unnook nor uncrack them, not all of them, right? Of course right. And the truest tales come from the very beginning of the world."

"Very beginning of the world?"

"You heard the one about the man named Man and the woman named Wife, and they lived in a garden called Peace? It seems a geneticist named Old Snake fed the wife a poison apple, so that her children would look like people on the outside, but be just like snakes on the inside, 'cause that is the only way the sterile Old Snake could reproduce. You know that one, right? Old stories never die, and not even the Chimerae can wipe them out."

"That is a very old story," said Menelaus. "My Ma used to tell it to me. Not sure if I believe it."

"It explains why the world is just a damned snake pit, though, don't it?"

"I allow that it might do that," nodded Menelaus.

"*You* believe Simon the Black is real. Are you going to scoff at Old Snake and his everlasting poison?"

Menelaus sighed. "I can see that kiddie yarns are more educational than I thought. Well, some of those stories are real or near enough. I think Reyes y Pastor has been adding historical vectors to keep Bible stories afloat, the way I tried to do for yarns about Englishmen raised by apes. And the stories about the great ship *Hermetic* are true, or based on truth. The Hermeticists have been diddling with your history, and all the history periods before and after, and they are hunting for me."

"What'd you do?"

"I defied them. It's not just me. They are gunning for everyone who protects the Tombs, because we are the only thing keeping the past alive, and stopping them from running history any damn which way they please. So I had to hide my ID."

"Why us? Why try to pass your sassafras ass as a big, bad Beta?"

"Simple. No one frats with a Chimera. I picked an era, the Social Wars, when the records were burnt or erased by electromagnetic pulse."

"How come the brass didn't glam your scam?"

Presumably Larz meant Daae and Yuen. "I trounced them," answered Montrose, "and their Alpha pride could not admit a Kine can trounce a Chimera."

"Ho! They is slow. I could tell you weren't no Chimera at half a glance even without you dropping your pants."

"For the love of God, I will pay you gold from the treasuries of the Judge of Ages if you will stop talking in rhymes. It makes me seasick. Yellow gold that shines like the sun. I swear by the circumcised and risen penis of Christ."

Larz was so surprised that his voice dropped to a whisper. "You know about the White Christ?"

3. Depthtrain Station

At that point, the passage was blocked by a rock slide. The procession turned aside and entered a wide arch, and here were ramps meant for coffins to slide, not people to walk, and there was no conversation as the dogs and their prisoners clambered and stooped to pass through.

They entered a short, bright corridor leading to a broad platform. It was a depthtrain station.

A vast well, covered with one transparent airlock after another, dropped into infinite distance underfoot. Poised like a ship in dry dock, or a topsy-turvy rocket ship in an upside-down launch silo, was one of the ancient depthtrains: a bullet shape coated with as many magnetic spines as a metal porcupine. The vehicle was huge, a tower leaning nose-downward, and in the racks and rails overhead, other bullet-shaped carriages and train cars rested, titanic, shining, filling a vast space like the ammunition rack of cyclopean beings. In two great half circles surrounding the lip of the vacuum well, metallic parentheses, crouched the silent bulk of a magnetic-atomic linear accelerator. There was no thunderstorm smell of ozone, no throb of dynamos; the only hint of the vast power locked in those accelerators were little alert lights like fireflies burning steadily, as they had for millennia, on the steel faces of the main leads.

The next chamber, equally vast, was a warehouse with rectilinear crates and containers and lifts and power-trucks and trolleys idle to either side, positioned to maneuver the supplies through an upper loading dock to the waiting depthtrain cars. The train yard control booth was overhead, looking down through slanted glass windows, and its ceiling was a transparent globe, finely spiderwebbed with countless brachistochrone curves of the gravity-drops.

Menelaus looked left and right, noting which crates had been broken open, and memorizing the tracking numbers, and with each number, he gritted his teeth more grimly.

Beyond that, a second storehouse just of spare parts, braces, hulls, magnetic engines, coupling, and cables. Row upon row of fully robotic workshops loomed to the right. Vault upon vault of storage for dangerous radioactive or precious metals frowned from the left.

Larz continued the conversation. "No more rhyming, Simon, I swear it on my carrot. But you gotta tell me who or what you are. Why are the superhuman magicians from the night sky looking for you? They are pookas from children's stories."

"I experimented on myself to raise my intelligence, and I fell in love with the girl they had created like a Moreau. And they think I stole her from them."

Larz said, "What are you? A little Giant?"

"Something like that."

"I thought they had two noses."

"I make do with one, just extra large, and it doubles as a can opener. Speaking of can openers, how the hell did you get the door open? The lock has so many levels of quantum encryption on it, not even the Machine can unpuzzle it."

"Puzzle, wuzzle! I was *given* the passwords and challenge responses. When I was in the hospital."

"You met Sir Guy? He wanted you to bring the Blue Men in?"

"I didn't know his name. I don't know what he wanted. He was a painted man, illuminated like an old book, all his face and skin covered over with inks. This man, whoever he was, the Blue Men chopped off all four of his limbs to put him in a talking frame of mind, and he didn't talk no-how, so they coffined him up to regrow his limbs, and I guess they were going to try again. He wasn't doing not a wringing thing for them, that's a sure deal. He would not break. He was holy."

"Holy?"

"Because of how he acted. He talked to invisible people on his knees (when he had knees) and he clasped his hands to ask the invisible people for help (when he had hands) and he was very kind and *very* not afraid. You could see it in his eyes."

"But there were no holy men in your era. Or unholy. The Chimerae outlawed churches and Witches both."

"They outlawed buildings and books. Who can outlaw holy men? All you can do is kill them, which makes them more holy. What's so funny?"

"I was just thinking about a man I knew. His idea of a perfect society was one where everyone was in uniform and no one was in church, and men slept with each other's wives like weasels in heat, and human beings were bred like dogs."

Kine Larz looked solemn. "You are talking about us."

Montrose gave him a sharp look. "You think I should talk more kindly about the works of the Chimerae? Now that the oblivion of time has swallowed all, you are a loyal fan?"

"All the higher-ups think our society is perfect, or soon will be. They dreamed great things!"

"Well, Larz old buddy, the icy waste you saw outside these Tombs is where all those dreams ended up. Their future never arrived. It is pie bye-and-bye and pie in the sky, but nothing but toil and lies now and here. This guy I mean, he would have been so very disappointed to find Christians in the catacombs in his perfect little world; I am just sorry I beefed him before he found out. I would have liked to see the dumbfounded look on his face. Well, he looked surprised enough when I shot him. That'll have to do."

"You shot one of the Alpha caste?"

"Higher rank than that," said Montrose.

Larz nodded solemnly. "The prototype."

"Who?" Montrose had not heard this term before.

"Narcís D'Aragó, our founder. He is the posthuman, the prototype toward which all Chimerical evolution is directed. The creator of all the lineages, Epsilon to Alpha."

"He told everyone y'all were supposed to evolve up to be like *him*? Man's ego was even more elephant-sized than I thought."

"Mister, why did you shoot him? I mean, I know what the story says. That he killed your Thucydides Montrose by mistake, the Roman Holy Man who made the Giants."

"That was sure one reason. The other is harder to explain."

"Tell me. I have known your tales my whole life. Tell me the truth!" The eyes of Larz gleamed with strange hunger.

"This is the truth. Narcís D'Aragó was the opposite of a holy man, the kind of man who ushers in hell on earth. It is our duty to kill such men."

"Whose duty?"

"All of us. Everyone with a trigger finger and half a pint of manhood. Ain't that the moral of all those old stories you love?"

Larz nodded solemnly. "Your Sir Guy—if that was his name—was a man from an old story, and not the kind of stories Chimerae tell, which are all about honor and shame, rapes and polygamy, and war, murder, and suicide, and mass murder, and mass suicide. Not the lies their stories are. No, he was like one from a real story. An old tale. He was a knight and a Crusader and a Hospitalier, a warlord of the light, and it was like he had stepped down from a better world to be in this one, to help us fight our wars. Just like the Crusades!"

"You know about the Crusades? No, don't tell me . . ."

"Of course. *Strange Tales of the Street* number 86 was *Curse of the Treasure of the Templars,* and one of the undead Professor Necromant raised from the Tombs of the Ages was a Crusader—a Red Cross Knight, in service to Richard the Lionheart during the King's Crusade."

"Huhn. You really can learn useful stuff from kiddie yarns. Maybe learn everything you need."

"Professor Necromant also raised a zombie triceratops, an amphibious mervampire samurai cyberassassin from Atlantis named Glaucon, and a dog-eating Witch named Melech Chemosh Shemyaza the Nagual. Hey! Do you think *this* is the very tomb the Professor used?"

"Uh, yeah. Forget what I said about kiddie yarns being useful. Tell me more about Sir Guy."

"He was every inch the perfect knight. He tried to console the black dwarfs when they were sad, even though they did not speak the same tongue. The little men with gold antennae. They knew they were going to die. He sprinkled them with water, just plain water, and for some reason that seemed to drive back their sadness. The next day, Ull had Naar's automata dig a deep pit next to the airstrip, and the trio were driven into it, and the dogs climbed in, tore the little black men to bits, and climbed out, and Naar's machines shoveled the cold dirt on top of them. They did not even put up a marker or nothing."

"Who was with him?"

"Ull? He acted alone. Just the machines were with him."

"Is he still alive?"

"The knight? He was alive when I saw him: they were moving his coffin down here with the rest of us."

"Did he tell you anything or leave any message?"

"How would I know? He didn't talk. Not a language I understood."

"Then how—?"

"We used slumber marks."

"Slumber marks? What's that?"

"In my day everyone—every Chimera or Kine—before he went into suspension was taught a set of signs to allow people from different time periods to communicate. In case you were thawed out to do work for the Judge of Ages with someone else from a different period. Or in case you wanted to join the Knights. It is not always the same knight, you know! They are allowed to quit and reenter the un-thawed world, and the Judge of Ages has to fill out his missing roster, and he recruits new men. They did not have slumber marks in your day? Little signs you put on the coffins to tell the knights when to wake you up?"

"The coffins were better designed in my day. Who else was in the hospital?"

"A Giant—but I see you believe in Giants."

"They are real, too. I glimpsed him in the pit when I first was thawed, and later, I saw his oversized coffin being lowered down when I came down from the surface just now."

Larz squinted and looked at him sidelong. "You say you do not know the slumber marks, and yet they date from the time of the Witches. Yet you are not a Sylph, nor a Giant, nor a Savant. What period are you from?"

Menelaus shrugged. Everyone was about to find out anyway, one way or the other. "I come from the days before the Giants. I am the oldest man in the world. And the damned tiredest. You see, I am really—"

"The Judge of Ages—wow!"

"Yes, yes—eh? How did you kn—"

"There he is! It's him!" Larz was looking ahead, pointing with excitement. "He must be inside! He must!"

For the dogs had brought them suddenly through a pair of huge double doors into a chamber much larger than any ordinary coffin cell, a golden chamber. "—it's the Judge of Ages! His tomb! His sanctum sanctorum! The great armored battle-crypt! Just like in the old stories!"

This was the mausoleum more splendid than that of a king. It was a sight to awe the eyes.

4. The Tomb of the Judge of Ages

The ceiling was painted in frescoes of gold and deep blue, a pattern of stars and constellations. Stalactites of yellow gold hung from the ceiling, an architectural oddity like baseless capitals of columns: these held clustered dozens of pinpoint sources for light, and from the points depended pineapple-shaped ornaments. The floor was tessellated with alternating squares of yellow gold and white marble and green malachite.

The chamber was like the nave of a cathedral, long and narrow. One wall, the south, was occupied by a doorframe and massive leaves large enough, when opened, to admit five chariots abreast. Through this door Menelaus and Larz came, escorted by a troop of dog things.

Thirty-foot-tall gold statues gilded and painted of white-bearded Father Time and the hooded Grim Reaper stood on either side of the great doors, looking inward toward the hall, and their scythes met and touched over the tops of the open doors. Opposite them at the far end of the hall and facing also inward loomed a statue of Michael the Archangel, balance scales in one hand, boar-spear impaling the jaws of a red dragon in the other, and a gigantic statue of Hades wrestling a fainting Proserpine was beside him. The white arms of the goddess were outstretched as if imploring old Chronos the Titan to come to her aid. Michael the Archangel stared with youthful defiance into the hood of the Grim Reaper, as if promising him, once victory over the old serpent won, he would be the last enemy felled.

The eastern walls, between the vast images of death and the archangel, were set with wardrobes of crystal holding the silks and costumes and suits of armor of many ages, stuffed heads of animals, pelts and skulls and other trophies.

The western wall, between the images of death and his bride and his father, was lined with crystal cases holding hunting and dueling pistols of several ages, and swords and spears and battleaxes, all polished and gleaming as if newly made. Both walls were lined with alternating pillars of white and red marble.

Above these twin rows of pillars ran two parallel balconies. Menelaus saw a shower stall, a kitchenette, a recycler, several oxy-nitrogen tanks, and other basic necessities hidden behind half-closed wooden screens along the recessed balconies. There were four staircases curving upward to the balconies, one behind each of the massive statues in the corners.

Midmost was a silver-basined fountain, sitting foursquare. A plume of water hung in the middle, burbling merrily, blocking the view of the north end of the chamber. From the plashing of the water, it seemed a very deep basin, a well or a cistern.

Level with this fountain were two alcoves or lesser wings interrupting the eastern and western walls. To the eastern side squatted a private supply of bio-suspension material; to the western, an atomic pile plated in gold and designed to last forever.

Looking back toward the doors from the fountain, as large as the doors and occupying all the wall behind and above, was hung a larger-than-life portrait of a blond young woman. She had a sharp look to her eyes and a winning smile, and the artist had perfectly captured a sense of softness and hidden strength. She wore a crown and a sash of royal office, but incongruously; beneath that she wore a close-fitting suit of dark satin with a ring-collar. This was the officer's uniform of the star vessel, the captain's uniform. Behind her, like a half wheel, part of the Milky Way galaxy held up its curving arms. Above her head was a small puff of stars lost in intergalactic darkness, a globular cluster orbiting the Milky Way. A slender silver line connected the globular cluster with one point near the edge of the Milky Way.

Eternal clocks and calendars were built into the walls to either side of the portrait, and a small jewel was held on the frame in a position only a very little of the way up the silver line toward the globular cluster above the crown of the princess.

Menelaus stood staring, with such a look of loss and longing on his features, that he seemed a different man, and younger.

5. *The Azure Coffin*

Before the fountain, not abutting, but close enough to be wetted by its spray, was a coffin of lapis lazuli, blue as the sky, and of very ancient design.

The coffin was placed on the floor in a spot of no particular significance, and reminded Menelaus oddly of a photo he had seen in his youth of the last automobile left in the last parking lot after the Age of Oil had passed away.

Menelaus slowed and stopped, staring at the coffin. The dog things with him stopped also, perhaps unsure as to which part of the chamber to take him to.

Larz spoke up, "So this is the coffin of the Judge of Ages! Do not touch it. This whole chamber is probably full of hidden weapons!"

Menelaus stirred himself. Larz was regarding the blue coffin. "See?" Montrose said. "Reading cheaplies is educational. This place damn well better be full of hidden weapons." Montrose stepped over and looked at the readout.

"I said to don't touch it! It will probably explode, and then drop you into a pit full of acid-spitting cybercobras."

"I'll risk it," he grunted, and put his fingers on the coffin surface. The coffin lid turned transparent. The interior was blue-white, and the coffin was layered with some sort of gel or ice, on both its sides and bottom. Inside it was a young woman, naked. She was thin-faced, no older than seventeen, and her hair was treated with a purple hue that glowed in the dark, her closed eyelids darkened with mascara or kohl. In the center of her forehead, a purple gem was planted, a teardrop seemingly fused to her skin.

"A naked woman!" exclaimed Larz. "What year is she from? I bet she's a cavegirl!"

"No staring at the nipples!" Montrose said dourly.

"You're looking!"

"I am a doctor." But Menelaus shaded his own eyes with his hand, partly blocking the view. From beneath his fingers, he could still see the readout. "She's perfectly healthy. This is a voluntary hibernation: the code indicates she's waiting for someone, linked to another coffin calendar. The name line says 'Changed Frequently.' So unless her family name is *Frequently* and her Christian name is *Changed*, my guess is that she changed her name too often for the records system. She was interred A.D. 2537, she is too short to be a Giant, so she is a Sylph."

Larz looked down with particular interest. "A Sylph! I have never seen one before. I bet she needs to be rescued!"

"Maybe we all do."

"What pert breasts she has!"

Menelaus slapped the coffin lid again, and it turned opaque. "Down, boy. I think she is underage."

"How so? She is at least a zillion years old!"

Coming suddenly around the edge of the fountain came Mentor Ull and Preceptors Illiance and Yndech. The sounds of the falling water hid the sounds of their light footfalls.

Ull said crossly in Iatric, "What is this tardiness, Beta Anubis? Why do you pause to consider this coffin? It is of no consequence. You are needed to facilitate conversation."

Menelaus said, "Your pardon, Mentor. I thought perhaps this coffin, being alone in the midst of the floor, was significant."

Illiance said, "An understandable misapprehension, for we were also puzzled by this coffin. But it holds no particular concern for us at this time. The

Judge of Ages awaits us at the end of the chamber. He is not in this coffin. He is risen."

And at that moment came a loud chime of noise from the blue coffin, like the reverberation of a crystal gong.

Larz screamed an astoundingly loud, high-pitched scream, and threw himself to the golden floor, covering his head with both arms.

The dog things nearby, startled, barked and raised their muskets, some aiming at Larz, some at the coffin, some at Menelaus, who raised his empty hands, saying, "Good boy. Good doggy."

Ull stepped forward, his half-lidded eyes brimming with even more contempt and weariness than was his wont. "Eschew these antics. Events converge! Depart to the dais fronting this chamber, Relict Beta Sterling Anubis."

Illiance raised a slender hand. "Your indulgence is craved but a moment, Mentor, for my curiosity is piqued. What do these things mean, Corporal Anubis?"

Menelaus said, "Something you said was picked up by the coffin brain, and it triggered the thaw cycle. Should be a matter of minutes, rather than days, because she is unwounded and prepped for a quick thaw, like a Hospitalier."

"Interesting. And why did Relict Kine Larz of the Gutter impel himself prone, and utter an energetic vocal commotion? Please ask him."

Menelaus translated the question. Larz, looking up with panic-wide eyes at the gun muzzles of the snarling dogs, raised his trembling hands. "Tell the blue Alphas I meant no harm by it! Besides, I don't have any kin in this age to be torn up before my eyes, so there is no use giving me punishment detail!"

Menelaus said, "The Blues aren't as barbaric as, well, us." He put his hand down and helped Larz to his feet.

Larz muttered. "Why do you say 'us'? I know you are no Beta."

"Don't make me civilized, neither. I'm from Texas."

Larz suddenly was full of vim and pluck again, and so he waved his hands in the air, crowing loudly, "Well, tell them this ain't no way to plunder a dungeon! Don't they know anything? First, you check for traps! Always send in the native guide before you, because he is usually secretly a-working for the cult that worships the Mummy, so it won't matter if he trips the tripwire. Second, always leave the gold on the ground, because the Judge of Ages circuits it into the electrocution system. And third, the beautiful captive always knows something important, so talk to her right away, and if she is gagged, take out the gag before you untie her feet, because that way she can warn you if the Beast of the Crypt is sneaking up from behind.

"And check for secret passageways behind the wall," cried Larz, warming to his topic. "And follow the money; because the guy who makes out like a bandit is usually the bandit. Oh, and the adjutant or the mess-hall staff, or someone in the background who just helps out, like the interpreter following the Sultan of the Space Chimerae around, he is always the key to the whole thing. Folks what reads *Bloody Half-breed Murderer at Large Picture Weekly* or (what's that good one?) *Gladiator, the Son of Gladiator,* we all know how it's done! Not to mention *Doctor Vengeance Versus the Decapitator.* You've read *Doctor Vengeance,* right? 'The Cure for Crime Is Bitter Medicine!' or when he laughs his laugh and whispers, 'Time to Amputate!' Remember? You must've read 'em."

"I read something like that when I was way young," admitted Menelaus. "But it was about space pirates and moon maidens and suchlike."

"How come none of these smart guys know what to do in situations like this? Wake the girl, check for secret panels, check for traps, and keep an eye on the adjutant! Common sense!"

"First, they're too smart to read the cheaplies, and second, why are you trying to help them? These are our abductors, and the Judge of Ages is going to blast them, so don't give anything away." Menelaus turned his head, and said to the Blue Men in Iatric, "Kine Larz reports that the sudden noise startled him, and he hit the deck to avoid shrapnel. The coffin is armed, after all."

Illiance nodded sagely. "The precaution was no doubt wise. He may return to his prone situation on the ground if he wishes, or put himself where he deems best. You must come farther."

Larz decided to stand far away from Menelaus, and the dogs allowed him to step away. He avoided the vat of biosuspension material, which he recognized as nanotechnology and a source of danger; so he ducked into the opposite alcove. Maybe he did not recognize the large golden sphere as the containment dome for a small atomic pile.

6. Dais, Sarcophagus, Throne

Passing to the other side of the fountain, they could now see that the western wall was ivory panels carved with a bas-relief of two stallions rampant, facing each other, framing the rest of the scene with their uplifted hoofs, fiery manes tangled with the ceiling.

Between them on the wall was a stark black field, cut with silvery-white lines of nonhuman mathematical hieroglyphs forming a triangle within a circle, and at the corners of this triangle were symbols written in ovals of various eccentricities and triangles isosceles, equilateral, and right, written in turn into dodecagons and parabolic curves, radiating out in two great arms to nested fields of eye-defeating sine waves on the right like a restless ocean and rigid rectilinear shapes on the left like an army entrenched and encamped.

Written in the stone on the wall above the horses and the dark fresco were the words *NE OUBLIE.*

Before this wall was a three-tiered dais, and each tier was over ten feet broad.

Atop the lowest tier, to the far left stood a suit of powered armor for a knight, looking like an ape made of shining steel. As far to the right was what looked like barding for a horse, with breathing gear built into the champron or skull armor, instrument housings built into the crinet and crupper, strength-amplifying modules in the flanchard, and emission weapons dotting the peytral along the steed's chest. Both suits of armor were emblazoned and caparisoned with the Maltese Cross. Oddly enough, it was powered armor for a horse.

Atop the middle tier midmost rested a huge, gold-plated sarcophagus with the relief figure of a sleeping warrior carved into its lid. This lid was slid half-open. The sarcophagus rested at a slight angle, the footboard lower than the head, so that the slumberer upon thaw would find the larger-than-life portrait of the woman the first thing before his eyes, along with the calendar and star-map of her location.

On closer inspection, the figure carved into the half-open sarcophagus lid was not quite a warrior. Sculptured folds of long and magisterial robes, such as warlords in battle would be unlikely to wear, lapped the figure in rising runnels like a frozen cascade. The image of a balance scales rested in one hand, and a flat-pointed, two-edged sword in the other. His hair was long ringlets that reached to his shoulders, and on his head was a tasseled square, almost a hood, such as judges in a forgotten land in days long gone were wont to wear when issuing death sentences. Below the carved boots of the reclining figure were skulls and broken swords.

Atop the highest tier, beneath a canopy upheld by four tall and pallid wands, was a black iron throne.

The dark throne was covered with the bright, silver-dappled scarlet leathers of extinct or re-extinct dinosaurs. The backrest was a pattern of argent and gules lozenges. The armrests, oddly, were carved in the shapes of friars in kirtles, so that the fingertips of one seated there would rest on the down-bent hoods, who bore the armrests on their heads like monkish versions of caryatides. The carved images of the kirtle friars carried long swords in their hands, points upright, blades mirror-bright. Above the throne, the canopy was adorned with images of scallops and roses. Below, the footstool was a tortoise made of iron.

The sarcophagus stood empty. The throne was occupied.

Here sat a stern-eyed man, almost the image of the image on the coffin lid.

He dressed in a costume of brilliant scarlet robes trimmed with white at the cuffs, with ermine at his throat and across his shoulders. He sported a black scarf and girdle, and down his back hung a scarlet casting-hood. A wig of long white curls framed his severe face.

Across the man's knees he held a straight and naked sword, with an unadorned crosspiece of steel. The blade was square and short at the tip, as if the point had been sheered off. The blade was black synthetic that looked like glass, and shined with a violet light. It was logic crystal.

Menelaus stared in bafflement, wondering who the fellow was.

7. The Dark Judgment Seat

Menelaus saw before him where Preceptor Illiance and the knot of other Blue Men, two squads of dog things, and a trio of automata stood contemplating the figure on the throne. Mentor Ull glided up and was standing with the older Blues named Saaev and Orovoy, all three looking as wrinkled and decrepit as mummies.

Ull had folded his arms like a Mandarin, tucking each hand into the opposite sleeve. Menelaus with great interest perceived from the way the folds of the garment fell that Ull was wearing some metal device at his elbow, like a large bracelet pushed as far up the forearm as it could go.

Menelaus patted Illiance on his bald, blue, waist-high head, which made all the dog things snarl.

"You found him sitting here?" said Menelaus, baffled by the scene, and the stern man.

Illiance, serene and unperturbed, said, "Not at all. He happened to be in his sarcophagus."

Menelaus stood below the dais, with the open sarcophagus between him and the throned figure, and stared up. The man's face was long and bony, lantern-jawed, and a scattering of freckles touched his cheeks. He had deep-set eyes that seemed never to blink. His mouth was a nearly lipless gash that never flexed far from the horizontal. In the shadow of his long and curling white wig, his eyebrows were a dark orange.

Illiance said, "We are puzzled that he lacks the dark skin and slanted eyes that Kine Larz and Scholar Rada Lwa reported. We have not yet determined his hair color or the size and fineness of his hands. Perhaps he undertook a minor biological adjustment when thawed in the time of the Chimerae, to appear more as they? We will address him: many ambiguities will be resolved." Illiance stepped up onto the first tier of the dais.

Menelaus only then saw that the ornamented sarcophagus was an active one. Its alert lights were gleaming softly, and to either side of the prow, snub muzzles were poking from gun blisters to the left and right like the eyes of a chameleon.

Menelaus waved Illiance back, but the little man ignored (or, more likely, did not understand) the gesture, and kept walking forward. The Blue Man glided up the dais, and around the coffin to approach the throne. The sarcophagus weapons twitched but did not open fire.

Illiance, with no sense of private space or standing on dignity, sat down cross-legged at the stern man's feet, his nose almost touching the man's knees.

The man raised a hand and beckoned Menelaus. With a wary eye on the sarcophagus, Menelaus walked around it and stepped forward, his metallic robes slithering and jingling. He halted again and gave a stiff-armed open-palm Chimerical salute.

A twinkle of amusement appeared in the man's eye, and he also held out his hand in the same form of salute. *"Seig Heil,"* he said sardonically.

3

The Court of Ages

1. Justice High and Low

Menelaus stared in confusion at the bewigged man, who, sternness gone, was observing him with a raised eyebrow, a look of relaxed good humor on his features.

"*Sprechen Sie Deutsch?*" asked Menelaus.

"*Nein. Sprechen Sie Spanisch?*"

"*Sí, hablo español muy bien,*" said Menelaus.

The man laughed shortly, and replied, "*No tan muy bien. Usted tiene un acento del gringo. ¿Usted habla Inglés?*"

Menelaus looked astonished, and answered, "I reckon I do." He spoke with a thick Texan accent.

The man had a milder version of the same accent: a Dallas accent rather than the accent of a rural county. He spoke in a voice of quiet dignity and power, saying, "My wife—is she yet returned? The time—is the aeon for which I await yet come?"

Menelaus took a step back, his face blank and expressionless. "Who are you, sir?"

"I am the architect, founder of the biosuspension hibernation Tombs here and throughout the world," said the other, his face once more set in stern, hard lines. "I am the sole owner and director of the Endymion Syndicate. Those who have dared to trespass on my place of rest shall endure retaliation, I assure you. My name is Menelaus Illation Montrose."

Even if they did not understand the rest of the sentence, the Blue Men understood the last three words. The chamber rustled with echoing murmurs of surprise, in which a note of victory could be heard.

Menelaus looked back at Mentor Ull. The weary old eyes, for once, did not seem dead, but were lit up and glistering with something like hunger. Menelaus, through his implants and nodes, detected a power surge in the large bracelet Ull wore above his elbow. It was an instrument, not an ornament. But whatever it was, it was not active yet: it was warming up.

"Now that you know of me, tell me of you. Who is the Interactor?" the throned man said sharply, as if annoyed that Menelaus had turned his back. Menelaus turned quickly to face him again, and saw the man nod his bewigged head down at Illiance.

Interesting. The word *interactor* was from the Twenty-sixth Century. It referred to someone with cybernetic neural implants, that is, someone able to interact directly with an infosphere.

"One of our captors," said Menelaus. "His name is Illiance. Your Tombs have been broken open and looted, and the people and systems set to guard them are compromised, captured, or dead. We who are your clients are their prisoners, and as soon as they get what they want of us, we are to be killed—but you do not seem worried."

"I am in the stronghold of my power, and have allies both seen and unseen. Tell them I command to know of them what they want."

Menelaus said, "I can answer for them. They seek the Judge of Ages."

"And who is that?"

Menelaus kept a straight face, and said, "They all say the Judge of Ages is the man named Menelaus Montrose, the posthuman. Yourself, in other words."

"And you say something else, I take it?"

"I am not saying much of anything at the moment, but you can interpret my silence as a sort of skeptical silence."

"Silence is wise. In that case, they may address me as the Judge of Ages. That title will serve, for now. As for you—what name do you go by?"

"High-Beta Sterling Xenius Anubis of Mount Erebus, from A.D. 5292."

The Judge of Ages did not laugh, but his eyes twinkled. "Captain Sterling?"

"My rank is Corporal."

"Of course it is. Clear ether and hot jets, Captain Sterling! Any sign of the Atom Monster from Mercury? Tell me. In A.D. 5292, was everyone named after a character from a boy's adventure series from the Second Dark Age? Or just you?"

"Well, I could been named *Montrose*, after a starfarer from the Second Space Age, but that name was already taken. I understand it gets used a lot."

"I am glad we respect each other's privacy. But I do not doubt you are Captain Sterling, because your companions come from similar futurist cartoons. I see you brought along the Masterminds of the Moon, a group of Musketeer wolfmen, some Insectobots."

"The bald blue dwarfs wearing logic crystals on their coats are our captors, and the Moreau dogs are the prison guards. The automata are digging machines looted from your facility at Saint Nevis Island, brought here to dig up coffins. Anyone else you see later will be a prisoner. I hope to bring them all into this chamber."

"Which one of the masterminds is most master?"

"The leader is named Ull. The one whose eyes look like they were pried out of the skull of a dead snake, that's him."

The Judge of Ages said, "And how much English do they understand? Not much, I take it?"

Menelaus said, "Let's assume the conversation is being recorded and will be analyzed later."

The Judge of Ages nodded, and said, "I saw them come alert when I said the name *Montrose*. Have I put the lives of the Thaws in danger?"

"Basically, yes."

"Since there are clients of the Hibernation Syndicate who have been unlawfully meddled with, the danger must be put to rest before I go to my rest once more."

"If you can think of an excuse to get me next to the sarcophagus, I can aid your effort, Your Honor," said Menelaus very softly.

In a rustle of his scarlet sleeve, the Judge of Ages now held aloft his dark sword.

"Oyez! Tell all who have need to approach, and I will administer justice swift and terrible to those in need of justice, both high and low of birth, both thawed of old and current of year. Tell this Ull, and his people, that he and his are jointly and severally liable to whatever penalty this hearing shall determine. Repeat to them my words, and ask of him first why he dares disturb my slumber."

The throned figure pointed with his dark glassy sword toward the sarcophagus. "Captain Sterling, I appoint you my bailiff. Administer the oath. There is a Bible in the footlocker of my sarcophagus, just in case any of them are civilized men, but I will accept their affirmation if they are not."

2. The Motive

Menelaus turned and translated these comments to the Blue Men, most of whom were still on the far side of the fountain, looking on with what seemed expressions of aloof academic interest. Their instinctive sense of position was simply odd: people in his day would have crowded forward to hear more clearly. He wondered if the technology in their gems, which could put information directly into curious eyes and ears, had long ago habituated these members of a cybernetic culture to stand any which where, since they could point a sensor and get a clearer view than walking and peering would give.

It was an odd thought. Perhaps their desire for simplicity was not just a game or an affectation. Maybe their culture had lost something precious, not just a natural instinct for where and how to stand, but a thousand little, almost unnoticed, habits, patterns, and civilities.

Menelaus stepped away from the throne and toward the sarcophagus, but Mentor Ull called out, "Halt! Deception is suspected! The sarcophagus contains live weapons. Do not approach it!"

Menelaus said, "Mentor, I am merely retrieving the book of"—(there was no word for *sacred* in the Iatric language, or *heavenly*)—"the very significant things of the sky, in order that you may promise to tell the truth."

Ull looked skeptical. "The act would be without meaning. We hold aloof from all ceremony, both secular and *spiritual*." He used the word in the Witch language, *iki-hebereke-ren*, indicating a public coven ceremony performed while intoxicated.

Menelaus was surprised by the venom in his voice. "What is your objection to sky things? Do not sky things protect men from devils and hungry shadows of the dead?" There was no word for heavenly matters, but there were words in Iatric for supernatural malice and for restless souls that haunted graveyards. The Iatrocrats were still human, after all.

"Many lapses of logic are found within the lore of the *seirei*," said Ull condescendingly. This was another Witch-word, that meant both *spirit* or *ghost*, but also *order* and *regulation*, which were all one and the same concept in Virginian. "*Seirei* hence is fit only for relics, underlings, and primitives. Simpler to eschew such paradox and nonsense."

"If you have no *seirei*, then what will you swear by?" said Menelaus. "Your honor? As if you had any. Do you believe in anything?"

"We Blue Men hold that all matter-energy contains nuances of eternal and conceptual meaning, which only becomes self-aware according to embedded particulate hierarchies, ultimately embedded as pure potential in the primal pinpoint of the Big Bang. In effect, all rational life is merely a sense organ or a limb of the universe by whose means the universe decides to become aware of itself."

"Gee, no paradoxes there," muttered Menelaus sarcastically. Louder, he said, "But you are on trial, Mentor Ull. Your whole race is on trial. You have to take an oath to tell the truth, and nothing but the truth. The Good Book here is part of the ceremony."

Ull said, "Insignificance! We revere no ceremonies." And he whistled, and sent five dog things forward, three standing between Menelaus and the sarcophagus and two crouching atop it, muskets at port arms or dirks clenched between sharp, white teeth.

Menelaus backed away. "Then your words cannot be trusted."

Ull did not stir, but merely gestured with a jerk of his chin toward Illiance. "The Preceptor has predominance in this area. It is better that he should speak."

"Ah! In that case, with your permission, Mentor Ull, I will recover the book from the sarcophagus to present it to Preceptor Illiance . . ."

"Approach not the sarcophagus, neither to recover books nor other objects, neither for this nor for any purpose!" snapped Ull.

Illiance explained apologetically to Menelaus, "Any oath would be redundant: it is innate to the Way of Simplicity that the words of those of my order conform to our thoughts, and that our thoughts conform to reality."

Menelaus turned and said in English to the Judge of Ages, "Your Honor, the defendant refuses to swear. He also wishes benefit of counsel. The little blue man sitting at your feet like a dog will do the talking. If that is acceptable to the court?"

The throned man showed no reaction on his face. He said merely: "Do the defendants understand the gravity of the charge they face?"

"I don't think so, Your Honor."

"Have the years forgotten my statutes and commandments? I am not to be wakened before the appointed time, no, nor none of those under my charge. Explain to the defendants that the penalty is mortal if no circumstances demanding leniency arise, and that both they, and all the civilization they represent, its records and accomplishments, stand in the dock! Repeat to them precisely my words!"

Illiance listened gravely while Menelaus translated.

Illiance said, "Reassure the Judge of Ages that our attention to his ceremonial is sincere, and we find this ritual quite interesting. Nonetheless, can he confirm his identity? There are some incongruities between his appearance and the description we were given."

"He says he is the Judge of Ages. His exact words were these: *My bride, is she yet here? My aeon, is it yet come?*"

And because those words stuck in the throat of Menelaus, they came out hoarse and harsh, and with an echo of majestic anger, as if some dark, great power of the ancient world had spoken.

There was a visible stir of uneasiness among the Blue Men. Calm and reticent as they were, the recital of the phrase was like an unseen breath of silent winter moving among them, words that brought chill.

"Hear him!" Menelaus roared into the silence. "He demands to know why you dared rouse him from his long slumber. He demands to know why you seek and woke him."

His voice echoed from the far wall. . . . *why you seek and woke him . . .*

Illiance seemed to need a moment to gather his nonchalance. "This we did for the simplest and most honorable reason imaginable: we wish him to judge our age and vindicate it."

Menelaus stared at Illiance for so long that even the Blue Man, abnormally patient as he might be, grew restless under the hot gaze. Illiance said, "Am I unclear? The Judge of Ages must judge us. We wish to be preserved by him and not destroyed by him."

Menelaus spoke in a soft, dangerous voice through clenched teeth. "You mean you want him to use the Tombs, and what is stored in them, for your benefit? If so, you have done exactly the *opposite* of what you need to do to win his favor. You have trespassed on his sanctuary, used his healing equipment to torture the weak, and killed the clients he vowed to protect. In order to deter generations yet unborn, to make them fear even to think about committing similar crimes, he must visit upon you a vengeance so huge that the echo and rumor of its terror must last fifty thousand years!"

Illiance nodded. "We find that regarding other men as means to an end, such as when the innocent are punished to deter the guilty, results in linguistic and conceptual complexities so convoluted as to become paradoxical. Hence considerations of the sort of which you speak are nonoperative with us."

"You cannot get someone's help by doing the things that make him your enemy! Are you totally insane?"

"Not insane. We think differently than relicts like yourself, but more directly."

Menelaus said scornfully, "Direct is right! You directly mean to kill him."

Illiance said, "A character from remote prehistory? Unlikely. What would be the motive? We are simple men, an order of ascetics. Abstract or symbolic motivations form no part of the principle to which our mental environment coheres." Illiance gestured toward the chamber around him. "Behold, we have Followers and to spare, not to mention energy pistols and remote weapons; and yet here sits the Judge of Ages, unharmed, unmussed. If murder were our object, why would we have gone to such eccentric efforts to detect and thaw him? We could have consumed his sarcophagus with explosives, tampered with the feed, hoisted it aloft to dash it down the cliffs outside, or (more simply) stepped aside to observe the coming of the Bell." Illiance shook his head dismissively, a gesture identical to that of a Dawn-Age man. It made him look more human than his normal expression. "Kill him? You have misconstrued our purposes."

Mentor Ull spoke up, his voice high-pitched and querulous, "And you delay rather than aid the conversation, Beta Sterling Anubis, in which you have no part and which does not concern you! Please repeat the words given you to the Judge of Ages, promptly and accurately. It is not the endorsement of a middle-rank Chimera of limited mental accomplishment we seek, but the judgment of a being superior to human beings."

Then Ull added, ". . . If this indeed be he!"

3. Priority

Mentor Ull stepped toward the throne, and spoke, "Relict Beta Anubis, ask the throned man to confirm that he is undeniably Menelaus Illation Montrose, and the Judge of Ages. The question of his identity is best settled definitively before further events proceed."

At that same moment, the Judge of Ages stood up, and pointed the sword toward Ull. His voice rang, and his deep-set eyes had a cold stare. "Enough! Interruptions will be punished as contempt of court! Captain Sterling, do these blue dwarf men understand the firepower I have buried under my mountain?" This comment was in English.

Menelaus said, "Your Honor, this is not the facility under Cheyenne Mountain."

"So, then . . . tell me where the hell I am."

Menelaus was standing close enough that he could see the hollow look of shock in the man's eyes, but the tone of voice was so even and calm that it carried no hint of the disorienting bewilderment which was behind the question.

"Fancy Gap in Carroll County, Virginia, inside a cave formation called Devil's Den."

"Fine. Tell the blue dwarf men I have a, uh, a den full of deadly weapons."

Ull was staring at the sword, and did not wait for a translation. "What is he saying? Does this gesture indicate threat? Or is it a symbol of dominance? Please inform him of the circumstances of his environs. The coercive power at my call is sufficient to render such symbols incongruous." He drew his pistol. The dog things brought their muskets to their shoulders with a metallic clatter of noise. The gun muzzles were pointed at the Judge of Ages. The dog muzzles were wrinkled in snarls.

Menelaus lunged up the dais, stepped before the throne, and spread his arms, so that his metal cloak hung like a drape, blocking Ull's line of fire. "Mentor Ull, the sword is symbol of the dominion of justice, which must be orderly. Invigilator Illiance, you'd better say something to calm everyone down."

Illiance said, "You know my task has been elevated to that of Preceptor."

"I know, but you'll get a demotion for sure if your dumb doggies here shoot the Judge full of explosive pellets."

Illiance turned to Ull, and said, "Mentor, the time has finally come to present our case to the Judge of Ages. This is the reason for all this great effort, these distasteful and immoral acts, the coercion of people and conversion of property?" For the first time, a look of doubt, almost of fear, flickered across the face of Illiance, and one eyelid twitched and narrowed. "It *is* the reason justifying our otherwise unconscionable acts, is it not?"

Ull scowled and holstered his pistol. "Of a certainty. I merely prefer his identity be confirmed."

The Judge of Ages said, "Captain Sterling, tell me what they said."

Menelaus said, "An argument over pecking order, near as I can make out. The creepy-looking old bald dwarf was in charge a moment ago, but the nice young bald dwarf with puppy-eyes who looks like he's high on tranquilizers is in charge now. He says he is not hunting for Montrose to kill him. We might as well believe him."

"And what about the creepy-looking old bald dwarf?"

"Him? You and I will be lucky if we both make it out of here alive," said Menelaus, not turning his head. "He thinks you are not Menelaus Montrose."

The Judge of Ages stood, put his left hand on the shoulder of Menelaus, and gave it a squeeze. "Then let us act, for now, as allies and comrades, and let us do nothing to shame the name of Montrose, which must endure. All the future, no matter how remote, is just one slumber away."

Menelaus turned and looked into the other man's eyes, but he was not sure what expression to read there. He stepped aside.

4. Who Is Montrose?

The red-robed and white-wigged man, seated once more, again raised his blunted sword. "Sterling, tell them the Judge of Ages speaks: Let none here question my name nor my right to pass judgment. Hear me! I will tell you who is Menelaus Montrose."

He spoke in a voice as if he were reciting a poem or play recalled from his youth: "Montrose is a man, a mortal man who has set himself the task of out-waiting eternity. His greatness is in the greatness of the obstacle he undertakes. That is who he is!

"What is his time? It shall be A.D. 70000 before the earliest possible date of the return of the Swan Princess Rania. She will spend the lion's share of that eternity at near-lightspeed, such that no words of love or hope pass between her and the cold universe encircling, since one beat of her precious heart is as a year to us; or thousands of our years, to her, the space of a sigh."

The man seated on the throne then did sigh, and silence filled the chamber around him.

"Men of the current and temporal world! Each hour, no, each moment of delay parting me from that sweet reunion and vindication is as torment! Who trifles with the Tombs of the Cryonarchy of Man? I myself am the First Cryonarch: all the slumbering dead below the Earth are mine. Do you think whatever few and soon-forgotten years the current kings or empires savor their suzerainty matter to me? Whatever greatness you pretend to possess is already dust to me. When you approach the Judge of Ages, remind yourselves that you, to him, are already things of the long-dead past. His heart lives at the date of her return, sixty thousand years from now; the rest of him, without his heart, endures here.

"Do not trifle with the Judge of Ages, for he is not a man of this time, nor of any time. He is a creature of eternity. Ask of him what you will, but ask at your peril, for he will answer from an eternal coign of vantage.

"Let those with petitions to set before me approach."

Menelaus translated the words, and for some reason, his voice held a majesty and passion not present in the calm tones of the Judge of Ages.

There was no motion in the chamber, and no voice spoke.

5. Prayer

The Blue Men exchanged twitters in Intertextual. The discussion was technical. Montrose listened with curiosity. Illiance summed up their conclusions: *"These words fit the established psychological pattern our negative information calculus has deduced as a normal axis for the person sought. If this is not he, then he composed those words, and this man here is merely reciting them, but this is dismissed as an unlikely eventuality."*

Illiance turned back toward the throne, and spoke again in Iatric. "Most of the surface of the Earth is glaciated, Your Honor. Where the glaciers have receded, only the most primitive biology has reestablished itself: lichen and moss, mushrooms and ferns, but no trees; insects and worms, but no mammals. In the areas surrounding old ruins, or the openings of Tombs, very small oases of older forms of life survive: tundra and taiga, grasses and pine, owls and foxes, and a plethora of simpler creatures."

Montrose translated. The Judge of Ages asked, "Are you survivors of a war? Or, perhaps, a plague?"

"Consider us the survivors of a plague of Locusts," said Illiance with a small, sad smile. "The genetic mechanism that ensures strict monogamy among us is counterproductive in situations where rapid repopulation is called for. We seek a biological corrective for this which your faculties could provide. Further, our inquisition has already established that reindeer, walruses, caribou, and other biotic forms which could prevail under current conditions are preserved somewhere in the Tomb system, here and at other sites."

The Judge of Ages lifted his hand, looking stern. "Do you know the reason why the Giants from the time of the Great Consensus besieged my mountain?"

Illiance said, "Ah . . . not in every particular. The details are lost to history."

"They held I was in violation of current laws against preserving biocontaminants. Many of the sick and ill my Tombs preserved were infected with vectors of diseases that Giants had both wiped out, and had lost the technological ability to detect and resist. Before you ask me to repeople your dying world, or restore some dead animal species to stock, I must be certain to introduce no malignancy to your ecology, except perhaps such things as the current generations of flora and fauna can combat. Each vector of the growth and predation and decay rate-changes between all participants in the food chain clusters must be extrapolated, especially of microscopic biota. The calculus involved is immense and immensely multivariable. Put me in contact with whatever self-aware computer system holds sovereign sway over the globe."

Illiance said, "I express surprise and chagrin. Your Honor, there is none such."

"Then put me in contact with the Xypotech sovereigns of other spheres. There are surely worlds and moons in space colonized by human intellectual machinery?"

"Your Honor, not to my knowing."

Menelaus was confident that the Blue Men did not have the upbringing, and might not have had the right-hemisphere neural structures, necessary to interpret facial expressions correctly. They seemed to have as much trouble reading the nonverbal cues of unmodified men as anyone not a zookeeper might have reading the facial and social signals of a monkey. But Preceptor Illiance was slightly sharper, perhaps because of whatever brain modification he had done on himself at the plea of Oenoe the Nymph. Menelaus asked himself whether Illiance saw the Judge of Ages turn pale with shock, or saw his pupils dilate with fear, and whether he would interpret those signs correctly.

The man was breathing slowly through his nose, making a credible job of keeping his face as masked and closed as the face of a poker player. Preceptor Illiance seemed blithely unaware.

For the first time, the Judge of Ages seemed ill at ease. Menelaus was standing closely enough to see the man's eye movement: his glance darted to the various musket-bearing dogs, pistol-bearing dwarfs, and armed automata positioned about the chamber; glanced at the only exit; looked at the coffin fire-control board and ammo register. But the reaction was still somewhat subtle, and he regained control of himself in a shorter period than might have been expected.

The Judge of Ages said, "What is the date?"

Menelaus answered without translating the comment. "It is A.D. 10515, sir. October thirty-first—Happy Halloween."

The Judge of Ages said, "The World Armada of the Domination of the Hyades is expected to arrive in this solar system by A.D. 10917—which is in roughly four hundred years. Does the current generation have some method for increasing the rate at which a self-reproducing machine, such as a Von Neumann system, can break down the total mass of a planet and convert it to cognitive matter, into submolecular rod-logic diamonds, and so on? The estimates with which I am familiar were based—or so I thought—on theoretical maximums. We cannot possibly star-lift, mine, and convert a sufficient mass-energy of Sol to form a Dyson Sphere of self-aware logic diamond around the solar system within this time frame, not if the gas giants have not yet been converted to cognitive matter. Ask the Blue Men: was there some other plan developed by the current dominant subspecies of mankind to oppose the Hyades?"

Menelaus had to explain many unknown terms to Illiance. The Iatric language did not have words for megascale engineering, star-mining, inanimate thinking-substances, shells that englobed entire star systems, submolecular engineering, or any word for the idea of self-replicating machines. The combination of ideas—using nanotechnology to convert the gas giants into thinking machines, which would in turn skim hydrogen-helium plasma out of the sun and use the compressed and frozen metallic hydrogen to make a spherical thinking machine larger in diameter than the asteroid belt, and controlling all the electromagnetic forces generated by Sol and the Inner System—this required considerable explanation.

Before the full explanation was done, Preceptor Illiance held up a slender blue hand to interrupt. "Beta Sterling Anubis, please inform His Honor that there has been a misapprehension. We are Inquilines, not members of the Noösphere, which all evidence suggests has been annulled, perhaps destroyed. The Order of Simplified Vulnerary Aetiology hails from A.D. 8500 and later. I am one of the last members of my order, and I entered hibernation in the early Eighty-ninth Century. Of events of the intervening two millennia we have no knowledge and little indirect evidence.

"To our knowledge, there are no plans and never have been any to resist the Hyades by force of arms, not in any era of mankind except the very earliest. An examination of the Monument describes tactics and strategies beyond human power to resist. As has indeed proven to be the case.

"And, be that as it may, the discussion is moot. We have flown extensive search patterns around every energy-use our instruments could detect. Only Tombs as unguarded as the one in which we woke were discovered. We have found no surface life, aside from the forms mentioned. Evidence suggests that the Bell of the Hyades has been here operating since A.D. 10484, and has already swept the globe clean of developed life."

Illiance blinked owlishly. "As best we can tell, there are no Currents. The world is empty of Man in any form. The Bell has swept it all away. We Simple Men shall inherit and repopulate the Earth once the Bell departs again into heaven."

6. Darwinian Competition

Menelaus had trouble translating this, merely because he kept pausing to swear and grind his teeth.

At the end of it, the bewigged Judge of Ages wore an odd expression: that of a man trying to look blank-faced because he was pondering, and hiding the blankness of his face because he was confused and clueless. He nodded sagely, obviously unable to imagine what these things meant.

Menelaus said to the Judge of Ages in English, "Say something, sir. Ah, something judicial. Use some legal phrases."

"Writ of Certiorari. Cloture. Acclamation. Ways and Means. Breach of Privilege. Division. Dissolution. Gentleman Usher of the Black Rod. Ah . . . Bicameralism? Oh, here is a good one: antidisestablishmentarianism." The Judge of Ages raised an eyebrow. "You said they were going to record and review the conversation. Are events going to move too swiftly for that?"

Menelaus said to him in English, "If the Montrose luck holds out, sir."

Menelaus turned and said to Illiance in Iatric, "The Judge of Ages notices what he calls signs of haste surrounding your whole setup here, and wants to know what the hurry is. Why were you in such a rush to find him?"

Illiance widened his eyes in surprise, and looked at the dog things and automata in the chamber with him. "He was able to determine this by one glance at our equipment?"

Menelaus said without cracking a smile, "I am only reporting what he asked, Preceptor. If his brain is a posthuman neural array, it may be capable of unique structures of thought or intuitive logic. Don't let's keep him waiting—with someone at his brain speed, each moment might seem like an hour's worth of boredom."

Illiance said, "In that case, I am surprised the answer is one he could not deduce without error. Tell him that it was necessary to find the Judge of Ages, and within a very short period of time, because we need his permission and blessing to replenish and colonize the surface of the Earth with biological forms from our own time, which we have reason to believe exist within his archives and mausoleums. We also would be advantaged by his aid in finding all members of our order entombed anywhere in the world."

Menelaus said to the Judge of Ages, "Keep it going."

The Judge of Ages said, "Quorum. Filibuster. *Sine Die.*"

Menelaus spoke in Iatric, "The Judge of Ages wishes to know by what justification you hindered the liberty and converted the property of his clients, the other Thaws here?"

"Naturally, because we prefer our race to inherit the Earth rather than older and more primitive forms, we were not at liberty to allow previous generations we unearthed their freedom, lest we fail in the Darwinian competition against more fertile races. We are particularly loath that the Locusts be released into the ecosphere or whatever infosphere may soon take shape."

Menelaus said in English, "One more time."

The Judge of Ages said, "I am running out of law Latin. *Corpus Juris. In vi et armis.*"

Menelaus turned to Illiance. "He demands if this is the reason why you killed the Locusts Crucxit, Axcit, and Litcec?"

"It was a contributory cause, of course. The more direct cause was that they attempted to induce a hypnogogic state in our docents, which we interpret as an act of rapine."

Menelaus said in English, "Once more."

"You really have to, ah, *Lex Parliamenti,* tell me your scheme, if you want me to continue the, ah, playing-along-ness. *Ejusdem generis.*"

Menelaus answered, "Just trying to get both of us out of here alive, sir."

The bewigged man nodded regally. "Make it snappy. I am not sure how long I can keep up my public speech face in a live event like this. Usually my soul helps me."

Menelaus turned and called out in Iatric, "The Judge of Ages demands to know whether you have anything further to say in your defense, to mitigate the atrocious crimes you have committed, trespassing in his stronghold which is the sanctuary for all who are ill or exiled of time, murdering his guests and clients, robbing and despoiling their goods, assaulting their persons, imprisoning and kidnapping them, extracting slave labor from them. The crimes are doubly inexcusable because you yourself are his clients, under his protection, and therefore know full well how solemn is the sanctuary of this power, and took full advantage, while it was offered to you, of the asylum and refuge from the passing years these Tombs offer—a right of sanctuary you have violated in your neighboring and fellow slumbering dead."

The Blue Men began to murmur frantically among themselves in their own language of hissing and twitters until the Judge of Ages brought his black glass sword blade down with a ringing clash on metal floor panels. "Order!"

Preceptor Illiance, still seated at his feet, raised a hand. "Tell His Honor that our actions, under ordinary circumstances, would have no excuse, and that his anger, under ordinary circumstances, would need none.

"But we have reason to believe that the Tomb site here will be destroyed in less than a full day, and therefore we offer as our defense this mitigation: that by acting as we did, we found the Judge of Ages as quickly as we could, enabling him, with such help as we can provide, to preserve the remaining coffins and buried materials, as well as to take himself from the area and therefore to preserve his life. Had we been respectful of your property and privacy, and left you and these other to slumber, you and they would have perished without waking."

Menelaus said to the Judge of Ages in English, "Say something longer. Any unusual grammatical constructions might be, uh, not unhelpful."

"Anything to make translating less easy, eh?

> *But see where the* Hermetic *vessel flies, loftier than pride itself, whose wings of light, fraught with sorrows, wheel and mount the air more lucid than the crystal sea before the Judgment Seat feigned of old to crown the high empyrean, wherein the blessed quench the tears of life. Is there no drop of those heavenly waters to slake the sorrow burning as hot as those aeronautical fires that mount the upper night? Man breaks the dour chain of mundane gravity and time, and, lo, the zenith is appalled at that supreme ascendance. Rally, spirits, and gather to the shining banners of my pride! I am not less in dream than such stature as the brave* Hermetic *soars; by my sacred name and the blood within my veins, I swear the future times shall be more golden and majestic than times of old. Tomorrows of glory, Hail! Receive the salute of one who vows your forefather to be, shades of heroes unborn, heroic years uncounted!*

And if they can puzzle out what that means, many years be added to them, because my classics tutor could never untangle that argle-bargle argot to me as he beat it into me."

Menelaus knew these were words penned as a monologue in a historical play honoring him by a poet named Peerworthy at the patronage of the Cryonarchs claiming descent from the Montrose line. Menelaus thought it somehow unfair to have words put in his mouth by historians while he slumbered, especially such high-sounding words as he'd never use.

During this gush of poetical excess, Menelaus put a look of fear upon his face, and bowed very low to the bewigged man, and turning to Illiance, he said, "The Judge of Ages is inclined to be most severe, and to locate and annihilate each member of your race and every cell in any genetic base that might be used to reconstruct them, sparing only a few of you, or only one, to survive and carry the tale to other generations."

Preceptor Illiance seemed surprised. "Then, that we acted so as to preserve him and also all this Tomb site accounts for no mitigation?"

Menelaus said, "I don't pretend to understand his posthuman reasoning process, but you must realize that you could have found a way to find him without robbing and enslaving his clients!"

Illiance said, "Not a way that economized our effort. Naturally we acted also to advantage ourselves: if there is no mutual benefit to mutual action, congruence or cooperation of mingled actions is impossible. Does he seek to impose a verdict that will discourage future contemplation of such mutuality?"

There was a murmur of agreement from the other Blue Men in the room. Their voices held a note of surprise, even indignation.

"We also do not understand this insistence on privacy of property: that all property should be held in common is a moral absolute," Illiance continued. "We treated the relicts, his clientele, with as much civility as was possible given the needs of the task before us. Examining the historical record, we knew that they all came from cultures where conscription to public use of levies of laborers was allowed or even encouraged, with the exception of the Nymphs, whom we therefore did not force to labor. All these rest are slave-keepers, and hence have consented, in principle, to the institution. Likewise, in the case of the Locusts, after their attempt, we merely applied to them the laws and customs of their own native era, which would have likewise penalized interruption of interdicted thoughtspace as a capital crime.

"This line of questioning disorients. Are you certain you translate correctly? I am not sure in what respect we did wrong, or what prohibition we offended. He hid his resting place, and we sought among our fellow revenants to see if any had knowledge thereof. We did not allow them their liberty because they are dangerous creatures from barbarous aeons. I emphasize again that we had no other practical means to preserve the Tombs from annihilation!

"Tell the Judge of Ages, if he is unaware, that an instrumentality of the Hyades is at large, sweeping over the surface of the globe, and drawing into its hollow interior any ruins, artifacts, or forms of higher life it finds. It was in operation before we woke. We assume all of the current-day races of mankind have already been taken into the interior."

7. Summoning Other Witnesses

Illiance continued: "The leading edge of the Bell will be over the Tomb site in an hour. There is no reason to believe it will not act here as it has acted heretofore, and draw up the persons and materials found here.

"Moreover, tell the Judge of Ages that we have been cautious enough to bring his other clients underground with us. We have located his depthtrain launching platform, but have been unable to restore it to function. We propose that he unlock the depthtrain, and carry us and his other clients to some remote distance beneath the surface of the Earth, where the Hyades instrument cannot reach.

"Finally, tell the Judge of Ages that he must mitigate his severity toward us, on the grounds that our acts performed in the attempt to locate and thaw him were committed to save him, and his clients, and us, from annihilation or capture. Had it not been for our acts, the Bell would have descended upon him unawares, unforeseen.

"For our benevolent act of waking him and warning him of the impending danger from the Hyades, we anticipate that, in return, once the Hyades instrument departs and returns to deep space, our order and our ecosphere will be released from his Tomb sites here and elsewhere, and be biologically adjusted to become the sole inheritors of the Earth."

Montrose translated all this to the figure on the throne.

The Judge of Ages made a steeple of his fingers, and seemed to be brooding. He said softly to Menelaus, "I cannot fix the depthtrain system. It stopped working in the first half of the 2400s. About a zillion years ago. I don't know how to find whatever other slumbering blue people there are, and I cannot restore the ecology, and I cannot fight the Hyades. Do you have any suggestions? I am completely out of ideas." He said this very calmly and very softly.

Menelaus said, "Not to worry, sonny. I am never out of ideas. They get me in trouble, sometimes, but I'm never out."

"Never out of ideas or never out of trouble?" asked the throned man wryly.

"Both." Menelaus turned and proclaimed in High Iatric, "Men of the Order of Simplified Vulnerary Aetiology! The Judge of Ages has heard your plea! He decrees that it is unlawful and unwise to wake him from his slumbers, but that you, his petitioners, claim to have done so seeking his justice, wishing your era and aeon, species and ecosystem, to be vindicated and restored. However, there can be no hearing, and no justice done, while the Blue Men rob others of the right they themselves seek to exercise. Men of other ages and eras have been thawed, and are being held in confinement against their will.

"He commands you to gather all here into this, his presence chamber, that he may examine them before determining your fate, and theirs!"

8. An Eye for Detail

There was a murmuring from several Blue Men when they heard the command.

Preceptor Ydmoy stepped closer, saying, "There are security considerations involved. The minds of the before-men are strange and undomesticated: odd and eccentric behavior is to be expected. The suggestion of gathering all here is less than wise."

Menelaus turned to Illiance, saying, "Preceptor, if I translate that last stupid comment to the Judge, he might destroy everyone in this chamber."

Illiance said, "On what grounds do you conclude he has such an ability?"

Menelaus said, "On the grounds of the terrible weapon he commands. Do you not see that sword in his hand?"

Ull spoke up, saying, "The sword is ceremonial, and not of much danger should he use it."

"The danger is should he *not* use it. That sword represents his justice. He is called the Judge of Ages because all he need do to condemn an age to oblivion is to fail to act to preserve it. Time will pass, and you will be extinct. His power so simple in its operation even you Simple Men must be impressed with the elegance: to kill you and kill your dreams, all he need do is nothing at all."

He paused to let that sink in.

Then he said, "Gentlemen, you are here asking him for help, remember? Begging? If he refuses to hear your case, all your effort is for nothing." Menelaus looked down at Illiance.

Illiance was staring at Ull with a look of suspicion on his normally serene features, perhaps a hint of anger. Illiance said, "We have followed your leadership without doubt, Mentor Ull, and it has led us to this situation. Instead of finding an architect of the Tomb System willing and eager to aid us, we face recriminations and possible extinction for our acts. Our only reasonable course is to make amends and cooperate unreservedly. Yet now your words and actions cannot be reconciled with your expressed and apparent purposes."

Ull scowled, and put his hand under his coat. It was an ominous gesture, as if he were reaching for his weapon. But Ull said only, "As a Simplifier, it is beneath me to practice deception. Words conform to thoughts, which conform to reality. That is our code."

Illiance said, "Then let the other relicts be brought in."

Menelaus spoke up, saying, "His wording was specific: every prisoner must be brought here, including those imprisoned, despite their full health, in your field hospital." (There was a slight stir of wonder among the Blue Men at this, not being able to fathom how the Judge of Ages knew their secret deeds). "The Judge of Ages must be assured that his clients are safe before any hearing can proceed."

Illiance said fretfully, "But what fashion of hearing? We are simple men, not accustomed to formality and ritual."

Menelaus said, "He will investigate, and decide among all the races of man, and all the aeons of history, and render judgment which age is most worthy to inherit the barren and deracinated Earth. Your conduct now before him will weigh heavily on that judgment."

9. Scipio

Illiance, Ull, and the blue triplets departed the chamber to oversee gathering the Thaws. Naar and Aarthroy and Aanwen and the other Blue Men were near the door.

The Judge of Ages said softly to Menelaus, "Is the young Mastermind of the Moon telling the truth about the Hyades, Captain Sterling? They are not due yet for four centuries. I don't care how advanced they are: no one can jinx Einstein."

"My name is Beta Corporal Sterling, not Captain. His name is Illiance. I think the Bell is an artifact of the current civilization. Man-made. I don't think Illiance is lying; but I think there are two layers of deception involved here. The Hermetic Order has an agent or agents somewhere on the scene, and they are looking for the Judge of Ages—the real one. The Currents are hiding. The world is coated with logic crystal nanomachines in the shape of ice glaciers. Has it made radio contract with you?"

"No. The, ah, ice coating the world hasn't talked to me. I hope you are not a crazy person, because I am relying on you to have a plan. The blue dwarfs took over the Tomb because they woke first?"

Menelaus nodded slightly.

"Who woke them?"

"I don't know. I think it was the Hermeticists."

"So where are the Knights of Malta? The armed men who are supposed to be in charge of this icebox? Our jailers?"

The man was a penal hibernation case, then. Menelaus said, "The Tombs are damaged, and the thaw systems are not being triggered correctly. You are a Savant, aren't you? A Machinist? You mentioned your soul helping you. That is your Ghost. You were expecting it to be alive to greet you when you woke. You expected to be put in contact with the infosphere, because you assumed the version of you recorded there might still be alive? Hate to disappoint you, but all the Ghosts died in A.D. 2525. That was a long, long time ago."

The Judge of Ages raised his hand as if to stroke his chin in thought, and his hand covered the expression of his mouth. "I am a Savant. What gave me away?"

"You recognized Captain Sterling from *Asymptote*. The only other person I met recently who did that was Ctesibius. You recognize the name?"

"Sure. *Asymptote* became famous when it was found that Mad Montrose the Fallen Hermeticist read it as a kid, and one of the characters was Cyrano Widget the Living Brain, and he became a mascot for the Order of Transhumanitarian Emulation Advocates. Aside from that, I read the dumb thing in First Ancestor class in school. As a comic, it was juvenile trash."

Menelaus was taken aback for a moment. "Trash? It was about the dreams of the future."

"Dreams of adolescent idolatry of science, you mean. Just everything gets better and better, and the women get fast and the cars get faster and the sky-scrapers get scrapier, until one day we all download into machines that live forever and ever? Ri-iii-ight. I downloaded myself into a machine, and what did I get for my pains, my biofeedback training, and my radical brain surgery? My soul is dead, and I don't look like I am going to waltz out of here whistling. Here I am buried alive in a Tomb with a bunch of poxy gene-tweaked freaks, and overhead is an empty world and a talking glacier. As far as happy predictions go, the comic missed the bull's-eye."

"I wasn't talking about the comic. You recognize the name Ctesibius? You Savants were not in charge of the world for all that long, and there were not that many of you."

"Fifty years is pretty long! How long do most Advocacies last? Yeah, I knew him. He was a Copt. He was one of the main planners for the Day of Gold. That is what pushed me over the edge."

"Is that why you are a 'sort of' Savant?"

"That is why. You can call me a traitor, if you like. No sooner was I done betraying the Clan to the Machine, when I betrayed the Machine to the Giants. I turned myself in to the Giants to warn them about the Day of Gold. I let them make yet another copy of my thought patterns, a soul to serve them, so there could be no doubt of me. Maybe I thought if I had souls on both sides, I would survive no matter what happened. Then I realized that the Giants were crazy. They were planning to burn the whole Earth. They called it the Ecpyrosis. They gave me, and any other Savant they caught, a choice between burning up or long-term slumber: fire or ice. They did not want to kill us, just our Ghosts."

"When were you interred? Before 2525? You didn't live long enough to see it, but they did their job. The Giants burned all the power plants and cable nodes and torched the cities, towns, and villages; any outhouse large enough to house a mainframe."

"Why are any people still alive?"

"It's sort of a Noah's Ark deal, except there were flotillas of arks, and they floated like Zeppelins."

"You're poxy kidding me."

"Zeppelins with tentacles. That were atomic powered. And supersonic. And could turn into submarines. And strip all the proteins and complex molecules out of any life-form they passed over. With simple decentralized ratiotech brains. Which adored their masters and sang them songs."

"Atomic-powered supersonic amphibious Zeppelin airships with tentacles . . . ?"

"Right."

". . . that sing?"

"Um. If you saw the construction details, it is not as strange as it sounds."

"Who built these again?"

"The Giants built them for the Sylphs, so that they could airlift the entire earth, all the populations of billions of survivors, to become nomads in these air-skiffs, while the world underneath them smoked like the crater floor of hell."

"And who were they?"

"The Sylphs?" said Menelaus. "Call them Noah's family. Or his zoo. Sylphs were gene-engineered for lightweightness, with birdlike direction sense in their heads, and some were grown with an inbuilt moder-voder so to interface with their Mälzels and shipboard gimcracks more easily."

"Jesus pissing in Palestine!" said the Savant. "Slumber for a few centuries, and you miss all the cool, weird scat."

"Millennia. And there is a twenty-mule-team wagontrainload of weird scat left. All your Ghosts are long dead. Why are you pretending to be Montrose?"

"Just a misunderstanding," the man said. "I was talking to the blue dwarfs through their little boxes, but those don't do such a good job of translating. They got all a-twitter when I said my name. They took a blood sample and checked it against gene traces they found on a coffeepot. They offered me a cup of coffee. It twitter-pated them even more when I drank it." He shrugged. "It seemed best to go along with their misapprehension."

"What is with the fancy room?"

"Like it? It's family only, direct lineage from the main bloodline. Even though I am incarcerated here, the local Prior for Knights of Malta, Sir Romegas, let me slumber here with my cousins. Once I made a hefty donation to their cause, of course. Even the damned Papists and bead-mumblers were not so bold as to deny me, keeping me locked up in my own stronghold. They were pretty decent about everything, considering. In any case, the whole chamber used to be packed full twice and thrice deep. Weird to see it empty. I assume my cousins got their Thaws as soon as the we took over the world again. I mean, if you run the Tombs, you run the Currents, right?"

"Why do you assume there are any Currents?" asked Montrose.

"You just said so. Besides, the Montrose family will live forever, so that means the human race will."

"I hear Montrose did not get along with his descendents. Yanked the rulership of the Earth out from under them and gave it to the Uniate Catholic Orthodox Church."

"That did not last, did it?"

"Not forever."

"But the Cryonarchy is back in charge by now, isn't it?"

"Nope."

"Ah, give it a few more years! People need the Tombs. We form the bridge between past and future. Without us, what happens to tradition? It is not like the Europeans have the population levels to sustain a Current-to-Thaw ratio, what with their aging rates, that can . . ."

"Europe is gone."

"W—What?"

"That land mass is called *Baltica* now. The Cryonarchy is not coming back. The Dawn-Age men, that is us, we are not coming back either."

The other man was silent a while, appalled by the crushing weight of aeons that had gathered on his coffin while he slept. Menelaus waited patiently. He was so familiar with the sensation that he had dubbed it with a name of its own: chronovertigo.

Eventually Menelaus said, "I'm curious. Why did you call this *your* stronghold?"

"Sorry, but I was kind of famous in my day, so I guess I am used to people recognizing me on sight."

"I know the feeling. But sometimes you just don't recognize the people you know, even if you look right at 'em. Funny, ain't it?"

"Well, I call this our stronghold because it belongs to us. The whole chamber here—it was designed by Gascoigneux himself, you know—used to be at Cheyenne Mountain. That statue there is the *Abduction of Proserpine* by Phidias. The ceiling is by Jourbert and programmed by Lockheed-Smith-Wesson. That Rania Clock is an original by the Pitcarne Studio, foremost radioactivists in France . . ."

"Yeah. Swell room. Who is 'us'?"

"The World Advocacy. The government. The Clan."

Menelaus was staring at him in puzzlement. "Mister, what is your name, anyway?"

"Montrose."

"Uh?"

"No, really. Advocate-General Scipio Cognition Montrose of the World Concordat, Regent at Large, Lord Protector of the Dead, Director of the Endymion Hibernation Syndicate, and so on. After the First Ancestor blew the Cryonarchy to smithereens and stole our antimatter, leaving us shamed and penniless, I thought I would try working for the other team."

"*Your* antimatter?"

"Simon-pure straight it was ours! If I ever get my mitts on that thieving crowbait of a First Ancestor, I'll knock him galley west till he screams like a whore on nickel night," said Scipio.

"Mm. He likely deserves it."

"Amen, and you're not stringing windy, brother! Anyway, my other name is Glorified Scipio Montrose, Endorcist of One and a Half Donations, but I don't cotton to that name so much no more, as I am not really a Savant. Sure, I got holes drilled in my head, and for a while I had a supergenius copy of myself I could talk to on the phone, who could solve all my problems for me. Gave me personal advice, too, which I did not much appreciate. He seemed to think I was screwing up my life and the lives of the people he cared about, our friends and family. He was trying to keep me married to that shrew. I think she called him behind my back, the trollop! After a while, he got spooky."

"Spooky how?"

"I think the Machine got him. Ate him. Ate my soul." Scipio shuddered. "The Machine had all my memories and personality and habits, so he could talk like me when I called on the phone, and what he said was possibly things I might have thought if I were smarter than myself, but I had this hunch I just could not shake. Creeped the plague out of me. I kept thinking of this . . . copy . . . of the Nobilissimus going over my memories of my wedding night. I guess I don't much care for being a Savant. I am actually a Cryonarch, one of the Lords of the Slumber. I am in exile, until we get our rightful power back."

"Sure. Good luck with that. What is with the getup?" Montrose nodded toward Scipio's costume.

Scipio looked slightly miffed. "It is my right. This is Cryonarch court wear of the first form." Then with an eyebrow he made something resembling a microscopic shrug. "At least, it was in the sixties."

"The sixties of what century?"

"Sorry; The Twenty-fifth Century. Just before the Fifth Global Civil War, in 2461 the Gallic Directorship granted the Northern Advocacy judicial dignities, and we started dressing this way. In Northern Europe."

"You don't have any glow-in-the-dark tattoos. No diamond showing your donation."

"You mean like kids wear? What do you take me for? A plague-carrying newborn-greenhorn *Current*? I am a Second Ancestor. I hail from A.D. 2409, the Nevada branch of the Clan, and I made my first hibernation when Del Azarchel fled to Prussia, with orders to wake me for the next war, which I knew was coming. I thawed again in 2413, in 2439, 2450, 2467, every time Ximen the Black struck. I was there to fight him. The Montroses are a fighting breed!" Scipio laughed softly at himself, shaking his head. "Listen to me go on. Like anyone cares how often I slumbered, or what my seniority is. The First Ancestor robbed us of all our power and threw us into the cesspit. We used to run this place, these Tombs, the whole world. We were the men immune from time, the changeless ones. I guess that is all changed now. It is no fun being Rip van Winkle, though. Every time I thawed, things got weirder. It was like waking up on Mars."

"And what about the wig? Cryonarchs don't wear wigs."

"Savants do. The wig is to cover and protect the ugly in-jacks they had to drill in my skull for my donation. And to show we are as good as Scholars. Nobilissimus del Azarchel gave the Scholars the right to wear such wigs, when the sumptuary laws denied it to everyone else."

"And where are your loyalties now? With the First Ancestor, or with the Master of the World?"

"What the hell year did you say it was? The fight between them must be long over."

"Nope. In about five minutes, we are going to see the next round of it, and if I have calculated a-rightly, Blackie his own damned self will show up, guns blazing. So pick a side, Cryonarch."

"Which side are you on?"

"I am a good guy. Mostly."

"Okay, I'll trust you, Mister Good Guy. You did not give me away. And you seem to know what's what."

"I know a Scholar and a Savant contemporary with your era are about to enter the chamber. Ctesibius the Savant will recognize you. There is a Scholar named Rada Lwa who will at least know you are not Menelaus Montrose. I have a theory that he will not recognize me even if he looks me straight in the face, due to contamination."

"I recognize his name. Rada Lwa Chwal is from the Argent-Montrose branch of the Clan. It was a junior branch that got involved in some scandal; I forget the details. Him, eh? So the plan is, you sent the dwarfs to gather those two guys here, so that they can shout out I am a fake. Thanks a lot, Captain Sterling! Sorry I trusted you."

"Shout out in a language no one speaks but me."

"And then what happens? The real Judge of Ages pops out of a hidden coffin and saves us from this Bell? What is it going to do, anyway, ding-dong at us?"

"It's shaped like an Oriental bell, a cylinder; not an Occidental bell, a cone. It is an orbital skyhook, a massive one, big enough to hale a major city aloft easy as a chickenhawk snatching up a peep, and it's made of some impossibly strong material. What is going to happen is very simple: I am going to jam the door shut, and trap them in here with me."

"Lock yourself in the room with the musketeer dogs and the pistol-packing blue goons. Good plan. What happens when they scald your ass with laser-guns set to *deep fat fry*, Space Captain Sterling?"

"Their weapons will be not much use. I'll destroy whoever opens fire first."

"Destroy how?"

"The coffin is armed with twin infinite repeaters and rocket-propelled grape-shot. The vents can flood the room with phosgene gas. The floor is wired for electrocution. Those pineapple-looking ornaments all over the ceiling are self-aiming heavy-caliber guns. There are secret panels in the upper walls behind which are other automatics and emitters. The fountain in the middle of the room can be switched to spray the chamber with lethal fluid. The doorposts are armed with chemical shot, linear accelerators, jellied gasoline, sonic weap-ons, and particle-beam projectors. The globular structure to the left of the fountain is a working atomic pile, and to flood the room with radioactives, all I'd need do is release the magnetic containment. I won't tell you what I can do with the nanomedical fluids in the structure to the right: give you bad dreams. And you've got a sword in your hand. And I have a rock."

"That is why you wanted to get over to the sarcophagus: to reach the general security channel from the local channel. Let's say those dogs let you by. And what exactly makes you think you can operate all these weapons? Or that they are still loaded? For that matter, how do you know they are there?"

"Because I know the architect who built the place, and I know any changes to any chambers made by the Hospitaliers would follow his designs. I do not think there is an object in this room that does not have a weapon built into it, except maybe the portrait. For her sake, I'll try to spare as many as I can. I pacify them, disarm them, and then we sit and wait for my men to thaw out. I hope Soorm set the process in motion. I have been having a lot of trouble with my systems, which have been partly compromised. I've been getting better responses from the lower levels, however, so . . ."

"*Your* men? *Your* systems?"

Menelaus drew back his hood and stared at the man, giving him a good look at his face.

"Jesus poxing Christ up a tree," breathed Scipio.

"Don't poxing swear," said Menelaus. "And congratulations. You passed the test. I thought you might have the Machine in your head. You're just un-observant."

4

Witnesses

1. Entrance

The Blue Men were gathering everyone into the chamber in order by age: Alalloel first, her walk stately, the gray twins next, followed by the Hormagaunts and their Donors and Clade-dwellers. Soorm was on his feet, and appeared unharmed, but his shoulders drooped, and his fluked scorpion tail lashed.

The Nymphs danced in, graceful as willow branches in the breeze. They wore green tunics, and the women had long green scarves in their hair, shedding petals. They had been given their lutes and fiddles and flutes and panpipes, and they filled the chamber with a wild, elfin air like the sound of the robin, the thrush, the lark, and the loon. A quartet of effete, sloe-eyed males were they, and the quartet of slim-ankled hetaerae flinging their dark hair in twirling ecstasy. The smell of wine and the scent of roses came with them. The green silks of the girls' curving girdles or corsets were tied tightly about their slender waists, to emphasize the exaggerated roundness of their hips, the overfullness of their breasts. Male and female both had oiled their luxurious midnight-black hair so that it shined like fresh ink. As she whirled past, Oenoe tossed a petal toward Menelaus—it was a myrtle blossom, which meant *I am ready*.

Next came the Chimerae marching through the doors, bows strung and spears ready.

Menelaus caught the gaze of Daae and Lady Ivinia, and saw that they were ready, too. Alpha Yuen had his bone truncheon in his hand, not hidden, but he was staring at the floor, his one eye sullen, his posture tense with anger.

Mickey the Witch strode ponderously through the door as if to grand and inaudible music. The crones next came stalking in, grave and solemn in black, leaning on their charming wands, and the more mundane menfolk in their various heraldic robes came after, and fierce Demonstrators in their coats of human-skin leather. Mickey, less solemn than the rest, gave Menelaus a cheery smile, and an eye-decoration on his ridiculous pointed hat winked. He mouthed the words *what's going on?* The other Witches were behind his broad back, and did not see his facial contortions.

Menelaus could think of no way to answer the question.

2. Scipio in Storybook Land

Scipio, seated on the throne of the Judge of Ages, raised his hand to cover his mouth, and said softly, "Okay, First Ancestor, I take back what I said about your cartoon. Looks like it came true. This menagerie doesn't have a single un-modified nonfreak in the lot. Who the pox are the half-naked dancing girls in flowers, and the dead-eyed SS troopers in samurai drag whose girls are dressed like Minerva and the Drum Majorettes? And the gross hags looking like they were stretched on racks? And that thing with no head? Are those space aliens?"

"Lemme sum up," sighed Montrose. "The sequence of extinctions goes like this: That girl with antennae and weird eyes is a Melusine, and her kind wiped out the two gray dwarfs in the parkas toward the front, called Linderlings. The gray dwarfs and the blue dwarfs are part of a race of black dwarfs called Locusts, who are radio-telepaths that formed a mass mind and are color-coded for your convenience. The Locusts exterminated the Hormagaunts, who are the biotech monstrosities there. The Hormagaunts are Nymphs gone mad, who are the Geisha girls and the sissy-looking boys. The Nymphs drugged the Chimerae, who are the Spartan Nazis there. The Chimerae wiped out the Witches, who are the tall ugly women there, and that whole group from Halloweenland. The Witches wiped out the Giants, whom you know all about and I can hear one coming now. We also have coming a Savant and a Scholar from your times, and, if God is in a good mood and decides to stop cat-playing with my life, my knight will be here too. He's from the poxy Middle Ages."

"You have got to be poxy kidding me. Chimerae and Witches and Nymphs and knights? Plagues of Locusts and the Seven Dwarfs? What is this, the Land of Storybooks? Those cannot be their real names."

"It is not what they call themselves, but, by the prickly cap of bleeding Christ, that is what they really are. The way to remember who is who is that the Witches want to sacrifice babies, the Chimera want to breed them like dogs, the Hormagaunts want to eat them, and the Locusts want to absorb their brains. What the Melusine want, I have no idea, and that worries me."

"None of 'em sound like nice people," said Scipio.

Menelaus gave him a sickly grin. "They are damned sick, believe you me. But no worse than the folk from our day, mister."

"Our day was civilized!"

"Meaning we threw rockets instead of rocks. Civilization makes it easier to earn ourselves the mark of Cain, which is the goddam star-spangled banner of the human race. Remember how many World Wars the Cryonarchy fought? Four? Five? How many cities of innocent civilians were wiped out by atomic or antimatter space-bombardment? Man has not progressed a whisker's length in all this time: Like a mad dog on a chain tearing up a circle centered on his stake, all we've done is change and change. Ain't moved. Ain't bettered us none. Ah, is that him—?"

Montrose was staring in naked eagerness.

3. A Familiar Face

The old knight entered. Menelaus increased the visual cortex activity in his brain to allow himself to see his old friend clearly.

The eyebrows and short, square beard of Sir Guy had turned white with age, but the heavy muscles of his youth had not yet vanished. The rest of his face was obscured with colorful designs of ink, some of them gleaming with luminescence. The short beard on his cheeks was oddly colored by the skin beneath, where the inks painting his jawline gleamed through.

He wore a cowl or coif of metal links covering his head and neck, with system jacks and fittings to mate with the inside of a large helmet. He wore a skintight one-piece of flexible gray smartmetal, the type an astronaut might wear beneath his space suit, and it also was fitted with jacks to mate with the interior of powered armor.

Over this, he wore a surcoat of black, and his cape was black. Both surcoat and cape were blazoned with a large white Maltese Cross. The white crosses stood out starkly in the hanging lanterns in the wide gloom overhead, and their reflections in the gold tiles underfoot.

He wore no boots, and his gloves were tucked in his belt. His hands and feet were baby-pink, and formed a bland contrast with the bizarrely complex glowing tattoos and inks of his face. Menelaus recalled that Larz said the Blue Men had dismembered Guy, and regrew the severed limbs later. It seemed an act of pointless cruelty. There were no ink-artists available to restore his lost designs, for the craft of tattooing with variable-property smart-inks had passed away over seven millennia ago. It was as if someone had effaced the cave paintings of Lascaux with a sandblaster.

His scabbard and holster were empty: the Blue Men had returned his clothing, but not his weapons.

Menelaus was struck by joy so potent that it felt like unto grief to see Sir Guy again, and he had to raise his hand to his eyes, which stung with unshed tears.

With his eyes closed, he suddenly recognized something odd about the way the dog things were moving.

Opening them again, he opened up the visual receptors in his nervous system to their maximum, and induced a pattern-finding gestalt in the reticular complex of his midbrain. There! The pattern was unmistakable! To double-check, he reduced the walking and standing and head-motions of each of the two hundred Moreaus in the chamber to an algorithm, made a few guesses about the architecture of their lower nervous system, and ran the equations through his head at high speed. The dogs were strict about escorting some people, and maintaining an average space of distance from them—Menelaus could graph in a simple relation how far a prisoner could step before the dog growled. But other people were allowed much greater latitude: Alalloel the Melusine, Linder Keir the Gray, Soorm the Hormagaunt, Oenoe the Nymph, Mickey the Witch, Rada Lwa the Scholar, Ctesibius the Savant, and, oddly enough, Alpha Yuen the Chimera.

Their latitude to Alalloel and Oenoe and Mickey he thought he understood: Mickey knew subtly how to manipulate their subconscious reflexes; Oenoe could work a similar trick by using scent codes. But the others? Why were they afraid of Alalloel?

4. Hear Ye

Illiance was surprised, because not everyone had entered the chamber yet, when at that moment Menelaus stepped forward and called out, his voice ringing to the walls.

"Hear ye! You are called to the appointed time and trial of the Judge of Ages.

"Each of you, your millennium and species will be scrutinized. Whomever finds favor in his eyes will be released in greatest numbers from this and other Tomb sites, together with your beasts and crops and ecology most favorable to you.

"He will reorganize the weather and climate to suit. Those who find no favor, you will be returned to slumber, to await, if ever, the pleasure of the inheritors of the Earth to thaw you for their purposes.

"The standards of his judgment have been known from the dawn of things: You are not being judged on your spiritual or military attainments, your beauty or your ruthlessness, your unity or your individualism. You are not even being judged on the justice with which you have treated the weakest among you.

"The sole criterion of judgment is your fidelity to the cause for which these Tombs were made! They were not made for your convenience, to await the development of pharmaceutical or technique to cure your bodily ills, nor to sate your curiosity about futurity, nor to grant sanctuary from current worldly ills, tyrants, or famines you wished to outslumber. No, it was none of these.

"The Tombs were made to store whatever could be preserved to resist, offend, and, God willing, overthrow the invasion by the Hyades when it comes. By entering the Tombs, and taking advantage of power to escape the chains of years, you are bound to that cause, knowingly or not, willingly or not."

And he translated this into Iatric, Natural, Chimerical, Virginian, Anglatino, and Spanish.

But in Latin, he said another message entirely: "I need you to block and hold the albino when he comes in. Get the fat black Witch in the crazy blinky-eyed dunce-cap to help you."

5. Commotion

There was a pall of whispering anger and fear that spread from group to group, age to age, as Menelaus repeated the words in one language, then another.

The Nymphs saw the looks of shock on the faces and muzzles of the

Linderlings and Hormagaunts, and swayed to a graceful motionlessness, luminous eyes wide, not understanding what was said. Zouave shouted toward
the throne, "We are his clients! I claim the protection of the sacred law of
hospitality!"

Then the Nymphs heard the message in their tongue, and put their slender
hands before their lovely mouths in shock, and hunched their creamy shoulders,
putting their heads together in whispers. Thysa the Nymph put the back of her
small wrist to her brow, head tilting back in a rustle of flower-crowned hair, as if
about to swoon, and so well formed were the curves of her upraised arm and the
figure of her pose, she might have been a statue. Two of the males began playing
shrill flute-trills expressing anger. Aea the Nymph held up a rhododendron in
protest, saying, "Our era was meant to escape the turmoil of evolution! Ours is
a time of peace that halted the endless wars of Darwin! The Judge of Ages
loves us! He cannot place us in the pan and balance our race against another!"

The Chimerae at stiff attention did not move or change expression, although
their flinty, unblinking eyes beheld the fluttering agitation of the Nymphs; but
the Kine sensed the fear in the room, and crouched down, whining and grit
ting their teeth. When the words were repeated in Chimerical, the Kine froze
in place as in terror.

Daae, his eyes shining, shouted toward the throne, "The Chimerae are the
superior peoples, and will gladly combat and slay whomever the Judge of Ages
wishes to pit against us. He knows we have complete confidence in his ability
to achieve his aims this day."

When the message was repeated in Virginian, the crones grew pale and
cowered, and turned and turned about, dragging the tips of their charming
wands in figures of mystic circles on the floor about them for protection, but
Fuamnach of Whalesong Coven dropped her wand on the ground in a sudden
and loud clatter, and she sank down, sobbing.

Fatin the Maiden called out, "We do not recognize the right of Menelaus
Montrose to sit in judgment over us!"

But Louhi said, "Anger him not! He is a god of the dead! We are buried
alive in his dread kingdom!"

Menelaus spoke over the noise, speaking in Virginian, "The spirit of my
dead mother appeared to me in a dream, saying, *Work the purposes of the Judge of
Ages, send the Warlock among you to these chamber doors, to propitiate the great god
of thresholds, two-faced Janus!*" And at this Mickey bowed to Fatin, and the fat
man began to work his way through the crowd, somehow avoiding the gazes of
the dogs.

Because of the noise of many voices in the chamber, the dog things laid their ears flat, and turned this way and that, fingering their weapons but hearing no orders, nervous due to the anger they could smell building in the room.

Even while Menelaus spoke, the last two prisoners were still being escorted into the chamber. The dogs escorting slowed down suddenly, wary because of the anger and fear smells, and the two figures continued forward. The Giant had not appeared, yet the echo of his footfalls could be heard from far off.

The Savant Ctesibius, regal as a king, his eyes leaden with grief, came forward, dressed in his robes of green and gold. His wig was as long and white as the one Scipio wore.

Rada Lwa the Scholar, with his pink eyes and bone-white face, walked in next to him, dressed in his black scholarly robes and square mortarboard, walking a little uncomfortably, as if chafed by the lack of his missing undergarment.

His eyes passed across Menelaus, and registered nothing.

6. Scholar and Savant

Rada Lwa and Ctesibius, having heard no announcement, and unaware of why everyone in the chamber was talking at once, were conversing in the modulator-demodulator language of the Savants.

While he was yet repeating his announcement in a few more languages (Anglatino, Merikan, and English), Menelaus, with another compartment of his mind, used his cortical echo technique to build up an auditory image of the environment, and he filtered out the excess noise. In this way, he was able to overhear when Rada Lwa emitted a high-density information squawk. "Menelaus Montrose, the fallen Hermeticist, his face perhaps altered by a biotechnological technique, is somewhere in this chamber, unseen, unrecognized. He has had the effrontery to order me not to reveal his identity. To whom in this chamber should I reveal it? What is the circumstance? Where is he?"

The Glorified Ctesibius regarded Rada Lwa with a look that might have been carved from the face of a mountain. Coldly, he replied in the same machine-code language: "The act, and therefore the thought that prompts it, is vain. The Hermetic Order achieved glorification while we slept, and have passed on to purely machine-based forms of life. Nothing in the macroscopic world, at our merely biochemical speeds of life, can possibly concern them. The asymptote occurred while we slumbered."

"What? There must be some error—" sputtered Rada Lwa.

"No error. The Machine we serve has left us behind to die. Darwin has culled us; we are extinct. No act of ours has meaning; nothing changes that outcome."

Rada Lwa could neither blush with anger nor go pale. "There is yet meaning in revenge."

Ctesibius said, "You speak of the First Montrose? He attempted interference with my damaged soul's desire to slay itself, a deep insult to the sacrament of euthanasia, so I bear him no love. You are perhaps shortsighted? He is on the dais before you."

At this, Rada Lwa strode forward, and the dogs let him by.

Menelaus said loudly in Latin, "Behold the man. That is his pale ass."

7. Knight and Witch

Sir Guiden, at this point, was standing at the door, guarded by five or six dog things, but Mickey the Witch was nearby, looking about in puzzlement. Sir Guy put an affectionate arm around the shoulders of Mickey the Witch. He said in German, "Fat Swarthy Man in crazy eyeball Dunce-Cap! Come you this way. More interesting scenery toward the front of the chamber, I'd like to show you. That man with corpse-white skin, let us him follow, yes?"

Mickey walked with him, smiling broadly, saying, in Virginian, "I don't understand your gabble-gabble. You are an ugly ape, are you not? And such unpleasant body odor! You are up to something that will get us all killed, yes? Why is there a cross and an eagle tattooed across your nose? You are one of our hated enemies, a Christian, no? Christ?"

Sir Guy tilted his head. *"Christlich? Ja."* He pointed at Mickey, at the cabalistic signs woven into his black robes. *"Sie sind ein Hexe?"*

Mickey pointed at himself. *"Hexen! Um Bruxa. Homem de Magia!"*

Sir Guy said, *"Magus! Magier!"*

They both nodded, laughing, pleased at having understood each other.

Mickey, grinning, spun his charming wand in his hand like a baton, and said in his own language, "We destroyed your vile, repressive, patriarchal superstition thousands of years ago! The only point of the Simon Families, and the only purpose of finding a longevity system that worked only on women, was to take down your corrupt and elitist phallocracy!"

Sir Guy, smiling broadly, said in his own language, "You're one of the vermin infidels whose clumsy assault we repelled when you devil-worshippers tried to dig up and break all the Tombs holding famous Churchmen, right? You small-brained grave-robber! As soon as I get my paralysis lance back, I'll shove it down your throat to your groin."

"Your language sounds like the gargling and spitting of a rabid epileptic, and all your holy men were reincarnated as butt-monkeys among the Bonobos."

"I don't know what you said, but you are damned to burn in hellfire, my pagan friend!"

Both men, in mutual incomprehension, threw back their heads and laughed together; and either because they were in such good cheer, or because of the subtle abilities of Mickey of Williamsburg, the dog simply let them walk on past.

The Witch saw only then where the knight was leading. His footsteps slowed, then stopped. Sir Guy tugged on his arm, and said in German, *"Der ist ein Maschinist, ja? Ein Sklave der Maschine? Exarschel?"*

Mickey said, "Machinist, yes, a slave of the Machine. *Exarchelisma.* By virtue of his name, Rada Lwa Chwal, I know that he is a steed for the spirit world. Am I not a naming mage of the Eleventh? Rada Lwa can be possessed by Exarchel. You understand? Machine inside man. Evil inside man."

The knight nodded, and said in Latin, *"Exarchelus. Malum."*

And the two men were no longer laughing. Mickey stepped forward toward the nearest dog thing, and began talking gently to it while it snarled at him, and he reached and scratched it behind the ears as if it were the most natural thing in the world, and that dog was preoccupied, and Sir Guiden walked calmly on past.

The dog things also made no move to stop Rada Lwa, whose blazing pink eyes were fixed on the throne. On he strode, his black robes flapping angrily about his legs, pushing through the crowd toward the dais, shouting in Spanish, "Shoot! Open fire upon him! This is the Judge of Ages, *Juez de Edades,* the enemy of progress and the people, the betrayer of the dreams of perfecting mankind!"

Rada Lwa stepped to one of the dog things and reached for the dog's weapon, as if he meant to take it from the animal's paws. The animal looked up at him casually, as if bemused at the interruption.

Rada Lwa evidently did not have Mickey's way with beasts.

A moment later, bleeding from the bites on his hands, and from the shocking blows to his face and stomach, and curled in a fetal position with puke mingled with blood drops in a puddle on the floor, Rada Lwa managed to haul himself unsteadily to his feet, spread his arms wide, and call out, "Don't any of you degenerate evolutionary dead ends and vermin-riddled subcreatures in this place understand Spanish? Shoot! *Fuego!*"

A tall and broad figure was looming darkly behind him. "I understand Spanish, Señor."

8. Knight and Scholar

As it turned out, the Blue Men had not taken all the weapons from Sir Guiden, merely most of them. His cloak pin was a large wooden crucifix set with an ivory image of Christ, and, as it turned out, the bottom half of the crucifix was hollow and contained the blade of a long, narrow knife called a misericorde, and when he put one muscular elbow about the throat of the albino, he drew the knife with his other, and held the pointed tip before one pink eye, close enough to touch the little white, sensitive lashes of the lower lid.

Menelaus called down in Latin, "Sir Guy, none of the systems respond to my voice-command, and I am a phantasm to the cameras, so I need to get my hands on the sarcophagus controls, but there is a quarter score of dogs in the way."

In Latin, Sir Guy said back, "It's been forty years for me, Liege. My life has been spent in your service. Have you no kinder word than that?"

"Ah, sorry. Guess I am kinda rushed. Hey! Congratulations on getting married."

"Thank you, Liege."

"You're too old for her."

"Same to you, Liege," said Sir Guy, nodding with his head toward the huge portrait on the back wall.

"Have your beautiful young wife stun Rada Lwa with her flower magic, so he don't cause more commotion, and then have her zap the doggies blocking my way. She is among the Nymphs. Don't kiss her, or the Blue Men will know something is up. Are you the guy, Guy, that changed all my passcodes?"

"Liege, I had to tell the blond Black Chinaman who smiles like a jackal how to open the doors with a serpentine so that Ull would let him at the controls."

"His name is Kine Larz. I wondered what was up."

"He was supposed to switch the defenses from nonlethal to lethal, and run the reload check. Thanks to him, everything should be online and warmed up."

"Better than I hoped! Back to business: to get me to the sarcophagus, I am going to get you up here to this nice suit of powered armor next to me, except it will hurt, and you might get killed."

"I was shriven by the chaplain before I hibernated, Liege. I am good to go."

Ull and the Blue Men were watching the assault on Rada Lwa with narrowed eyes.

Ull said, "Preceptor Illiance! This commotion partakes of deception. Is this not Relict His Excellency Grandmaster Sir Guiden von Hompesch zu Bolheim, whom we have confirmed is a Tomb Guardian? What attempted the relict Rada Lwa to say, that the Judge of Ages sends this man to suppress his words? Relict Beta Anubis! Translate Rada Lwa's comment at once!"

But Illiance was looking perturbed. "I happen to disagree, wise Mentor. I have studied the facial tells and muscular contractions of the Judge of Ages. Relict Sir Guiden is not one of his men. His expression shows he does not recognize him." Illiance, of course, was looking at Scipio, who did not recognize Sir Guiden at all.

Menelaus said in Iatric, "Mentor Ull! As Preceptor Ydmoy warned us, the relics are behaving with unexpected eccentricity! I am speaking to calm down those two, one of whom attempted most uncouthly and unwisely to assault one of your Followers. Rada Lwa's comment was to the effect, Mentor Ull, that two or more of your Followers, while afflicted with mange, brain damage, scrofula, and syphilis, copulated with your mother to produce you, passing their infirmities along, but cheated your mother of the transaction money involved, despite the extremely low fee and reasonable rates. The matter being biologically and economically unlikely, I presume some scurrilous insult is intended. The Judge of Ages is disturbed, and demands that the albino be ejected from the chamber at once, pending his further displeasure!"

Illiance was looking back and forth. "Corporal Beta Sterling Anubis and Grandmaster Sir Guiden von Hompesch zu Bolheim are cohorts and associates of each other. The signs are unmistakable. How it is none of you see it?"

Menelaus said, "None of them see it, Illiance, because they have their weirdness chip switched on and their emotion chip switched off. But I can explain! I know that man because he was my master when I was an interred here, learning how to take care of coffins. I asked him to step up and hinder the eccentric albino, who was annoying your Follower. My purpose is to allow the Judge of Ages to conduct his hearing without further delay or commotion. Is that not clear? Is that not reasonable?"

Illiance turned and looked at him in wonder. "Also, the Judge of Ages did not speak. You are practicing a deception on me. You are lying. I was not able to hear the nuances of pitch that indicated this previously. I wonder why?"

Menelaus grimaced. He was certain the Blue Men's circuits would detect the moment he brought the chamber weapons up to ready. He did not want to jam the door until everyone was within: from outside, the murmur of the footfalls of the approaching Giant was audible.

"Not to worry, Preceptor Illiance! I will inquire of the relict what you wish to know. What was the question again?"

Illiance was merely staring at him, dumbfounded.

Despite his hopes, Oenoe the Nymph left the circle of the Nymphs, and glided across the floor to Sir Guy. He could not embrace her with a snarling albino in one hand and a knife in the other, but she could put her cheek up against the cloak on his back, and she closed her eyes in joy. She was rather short, and her cheek did not even reach his shoulder blade.

But she could see his abundant joy in his eyes, and, reflected there, her own.

9. Aanwen Concludes

On the dais, Montrose muttered, "Whoops. The jig is up."

The only other man in the chamber who spoke English, Scipio, whispered back, "What just happened? The knight just kissed the showgirl. So what?"

Montrose muttered, "One clue too many. The Blues are about to figure what's up."

The Widow Aanwen said in Intertextual to Illiance, *"Observe the embrace between Relict Oenoe Psthinshayura-Ah and Relict Sir Guiden von Hompesch zu Bolheim. Perform a third-level Cliometric analysis using the negative information system. Contemplate the results. There is no pattern of events whereby that woman could know that man, she having been found on a lower level of the Tombs, unless the man calling himself Beta Sterling Anubis is also one of their order, and a Knight Hospitalier.*

Illiance said, *"I do not have a basis to agree. Any client of the Tombs could have woken and met Tomb Guardians at any time."*

She said with weary patience, *"This Tomb Guardian thawed a high-status matriarch of the Natural Order, and they took the time to learn each other's languages and cultural-neurological assumption structures, and formed a mutual love-relationship? And this same Tomb Guardian thawed a Beta-rank Chimera, and formed a master-servant relation with him?"*

Illiance gave a liquid shrug. *"Human relationships are multivariable."*

"Are you men blind to these things?" demanded an exasperated Aanwen. *"It was clear from his tone of voice and demeanor that the man calling himself Beta Sterling Anubis gave Sir Guiden commands, but Sir Guiden is the Grandmaster of the Order of Knights Hospitalier. There is only one superior to the Grandmaster. Observe the similarity of facial features between the man pretending to be a Chimera and the man pretending to be the Judge of Ages. They are Clades, or family-relations. The man pretending to be the Judge is close enough genetically to have fooled our DNA tests; and as a contemporary, he drinks that bitter black liquid stimulant."*

Illiance said back, *"Your theory founders on the calculus of vocabulary analysis: we confirmed that the Judge of Ages was speaking words only he could have spoken."*

She said, *"The interpreter is himself the man who originally spoke them."*

Illiance said, *"Cogent meaning fails to be conveyed."*

She rolled her eye and turned away from Illiance. *"Mentor Ull, do you follow my argument?"*

Ull looked down at Aanwen, his eyes heavily lidded. *"I apprehend the steps, but not the conclusion. What explanation would fit this pattern? Are you saying the Judge of Ages woke in the time of the Chimerae, and fathered a son named Anubis, who is now acting as his interpreter? The idea is without merit. It is confirmed from independent sources that the Judge of Ages is as loyal to his mate as a Simplifier. He would not mate outside the marriage covenant. Sterling Anubis cannot be the son of the Judge of Ages, for the simple reason that half-Chimerae cannot achieve Beta rank."*

Aanwen said, *"He has no rank! He is not a Chimera! Sterling Anubis is Menelaus Montrose. That man is the Judge of Ages."*

Ull merely harrumphed. *"You indulge in absurdities. Anubis is clownish and dull-witted."*

She said, *"Very well. Let events unfold with no further contribution from me. I have done my part and more. You are not Simple, none of you! You have become Locusts!"*

With this, Aanwen threw her pistol to the floor and it chimed and rang like a dropped wineglass of crystal.

She turned grandly toward the center of the room and held out her hand, palm up, toward Menelaus. *"Judge of Ages, hear! I remind you of your obligation to spare Preceptor Illiance from your vengeance. Again I walk from you, and live. Sometimes the simplest solution is best."*

And she turned, and on silent gliding steps, went toward the great doors.

The Witches looked on in awe, bowed and parted to the left and right to make way for her. Even without understanding the speech, they were clearly more impressed with the actions of a Blue Woman than with anything a Blue Man would do. Small and dainty as a child, blue as a plum, she receded between the tall hooded figures of the Witch crones and their menfolk.

Aanwen was gone.

10. Oenoe's Kiss

Sir Guiden whispered to his wife. Some of the other Blue Men, at this point, drew their pistols, some pointing at Sir Guiden, some at the bewildered Nymphs, others at Montrose.

Oenoe blew a kiss at Rada Lwa, and flower petals from her mantilla drifted toward his pale face, and he blinked, eyes unfocused, dazed.

But before she could complete her neurological spell, Preceptor Naar, nonchalantly riding one of his clanking machines, stepped between the two and parted them. Sir Guiden, at the same moment, let out a yelp and dropped his misericorde, for it had burned him. Several of the gems on Naar's coat were active: this was the same trick used on Menelaus when first his coffin was forced open, namely, heating metal by magnetic induction.

Naar's mechanism reached down with a large black-and-yellow painted claw, and delicately plucked Rada Lwa out of the grasp of Sir Guy, and set the albino down to one side, where he staggered, and went to one knee. With the other claw, Naar's automaton picked up Sir Guy, dangling him like a child.

Oenoe clutched her stomach and looked wild with fright. It was the first expression Menelaus had seen on her face that seemed unrehearsed and utterly sincere, and it was an expression of utmost misery. Menelaus said in Natural, "Get the dogs away from the sarcophagus this second, and I can control the room!"

She replied in the same language, "Even I, beloved, cannot work so swiftly. The chemicals need time to react to the nervous system."

The iron claw tightened. Sir Guiden screamed in a strangled, high-pitched voice: "Montrose! Help me! *Ayúdame! MONTROSE!*"

Three people reacted. Menelaus stepped forward, and brought his rock out from under his cloak, and he stiffened the fabric to steely hardness. Rada Lwa, who was kneeling, reached and plucked up the dropped misericorde and leaped to his feet, looking to see who had screamed. Scipio on the throne stood up.

Then the three men all looked at each other, surprised. Rada Lwa blinked oddly, unable to focus his eyes on the face beneath the metallic cloak of tent material. Then he looked at Sir Guiden, saying in Spanish, "Wait. Who called my name?"

Scipio said in English, "Ancestor, did you say every object was armed?" He let the black, glassy blade clatter to the dais beside him. Illiance somersaulted effortlessly out of the way like an acrobat to avoid being struck or cut by the dropped blade, and smoothly rolled upright on his feet, his face all the while serene.

Scipio meanwhile with his toe had flipped open the hinged shell that formed the top of the tortoise footstool. Inside the hollow tortoise were two streamlined pistols of milky white ceramic, curved like the letter J, not quite as long as a man's forearm. The thumb-trigger was an emerald oval of touch-sensitive crystal. Menelaus recognized them as the same design of "slumbering gun" he always slept with, a caterpillar-drive linear accelerator, atomic powered, no moving parts, locked to his biometrics.

Scipio tossed both to him. The weapons were live. He could sense the energy from the atomic cells by the crackle in his implants when he caught them, one in each hand. Menelaus pointed one barrel at Naar, the other at Ull.

One of the dog things nearby said in Intertextual to Ull, *"Master! Relict Anubis! Him! Allow me to run at him! I will stab him with the bayonet, the sharp, sharp bayonet, and fire my piece at point-blank range into his uncooperative non-Blue body! Ugly, ugly body! It will burn with much burning, bright! Bright!"*

Mentor Ull said back, *"Not to be allowed. The discharge may pass through his body and strike the sarcophagus behind him, and wound pack mates."*

The shoulders and tail of the dog thing drooped. A piteous whine escaped from between white, sharp teeth.

Mentor Ull scratched the dog thing fondly behind its ear. *"It was a good and loyal suggestion. You are good! Good Follower!"*

"Me! I am a good Follower!"

"Take a squad to his left and right, that you may stab and fire at an angle without striking the coffin. Do not shoot until I command."

Dogs began inching up the dais, left and right, ears high, tense as bowstrings.

Montrose said in Iatric, "Naar! I have perfect peripheral vision and am perfectly ambidextrous and I have greased rattlesnake reflexes, and I really, really love shooting people. At this distance, I can pick which nostril of Ull's nose and yours to drill, the left or the right."

Naar looked bored. "A shot of a metallic projectile? The result will be unimpressive." A shift of the automaton's claw, and Sir Guiden, pale and gasping in pain, was now hanging before Naar, spoiling Menelaus' aim. Naar said languidly, "Preceptor Illiance, if you will—?"

The gems on the coat of Preceptor Illiance glistered and shined. Menelaus saw black sparks dance before his eyes, and he thought it was some exotic energy discharge, before he realized that it was merely his eyeballs betraying him due to lightheadedness. His muscles locked up as if with cramps: he could not so much as twitch a finger.

Illiance drifted over, stood on tiptoe, and pried the two white pistols out of the numb hands of Menelaus.

Illiance said apologetically, "The food you have been consuming over the past week has been infested with nerve-seeking nanite bodies or mites which can permit or hinder normal axon-dendrite discharge of those nerves, and which we can control by means of simple radio signals."

Montrose now understood why the Blue Men had been so utterly nonchalant about the Chimerae arming themselves with primitive, macroscopic weapons. On a microscopic level, the combat had already been lost.

Menelaus reflected sadly on how worried he had been about the goddam shower water. Damn, but he hated nanotech!

Illiance thoughtfully pointed one pistol at the golden floor, flipped up the trigger guard, and pushed his thumb on the trigger spot. *"Not loaded,"* he said in Intertextual, when nothing happened.

Mentor Ull said, *"Loaded. You can see the dowel of firing material through the barrel. The trigger is biometrically sensitive, perhaps affixed to a family gene pattern."*

Illiance placed the oversized pistols, one in each side pocket of his coat. The curving grips hung far out in the air like horns of a lamb, bumping his elbows. He said thoughtfully, *"Then Beta Anubis could not have fired it in any case."* He looked puzzled. *"But the Judge of Ages, whose pistols these are, could have. Why did he pass them? With our translator paralyzed, we have no convenient means to inquire."* His look of mild puzzlement grew deeper, darkening to a look of bewilderment, or even fear. *"Something is wrong. There is some basic, erroneous assumption I have been making about these circumstances."*

Scipio perhaps did not realize Menelaus could not move; or perhaps he was just feeling reckless; for he stepped forward, picked up his dropped sword, and pointed it at Naar.

In a tone so majestic no one could misunderstand, he spoke what was clearly a command. But it was spoken in English, a language which no one could understand. The import was clear enough: he was demanding the Blue Man release Sir Guiden.

Menelaus knew the risk, but the opportunity was too good to pass up. Paralyzed from head to toe as he was, he still had his neural implants. Were they unaffected by the nanite nerve-seekers hidden in the food?

It was one of those ironies of life that he could not, at the moment, get a signal to the sarcophagus a few yards away, but that he could get a signal to his cloak of tent material, which had emitters and receivers designed to interface with the gems that controlled the automata.

So when the Judge of Ages in his long red robes and long white wig pointed his short-bladed sword and uttered his kingly command, the automaton twitched, and bucked, throwing an astonished Preceptor Naar to the floor (much to the consternation of the dogs, who yowled); then the automaton stepped forward, and put Sir Guiden gently down on the dais beneath the shadow of the statue of Hades, and thus not far from where the powered armor rested. The automaton then bowed to the throne, and, leaning too far forward as it bowed, with a whine of gyros toppled with a horrid clatter to the floor, limp and sprawling as a dead thing.

Sir Guiden rose unsteadily to his feet, his hands upon the powered armor as if leaning on it for support. He spoke without turning his head in Latin, "Did you arrange that? That hurt." But Menelaus, paralyzed, could not answer.

Scipio, showing more presence of mind (and acting ability) than Menelaus could have displayed in like circumstance, drew his red robes about him, and seated himself once more on the throne, holding aloft the black crystal sword. This simple gesture was done with such dignity and majesty that the chamber fell silent, all eyes staring at him. The dog things were as frozen as Menelaus.

And the men of various eras in the chamber looked at the black sword in awe, as if it were enchanted.

Only Naar, who was on the floor, chin propped up by one elbow, did not seem the least astonished or impressed. He was drumming the fingers of one hand against the floor, a gesture that seemed weirdly and casually human when done by a Blue Man. The gems on his coat were flickering, and his eyes were narrowed in thought as he looked first left and then right. Menelaus estimated Naar would deduce the truth of what had happened, and the origin of the signals, within four minutes.

Rada Lwa, who might be a stubborn fellow, but whose intelligence was above what was possible for unaugmented humans, had at that moment deduced a truth of his own. He stepped up on the dais and pointed the misericorde at Scipio.

"Why is this man sitting as if in a judgment seat? Is he pretending to be the Judge of Ages? If so, you are fools. This is not Menelaus Montrose, but an imposter! I order any who understands my words to transmit them!"

But he did not say it in Spanish or in Korrekthotspeek. He said it in the data-compressed machine-squawk language of the Savants.

A voice from halfway across the chamber and from beneath the garish overalls Kine Larz wore emitted a chime and said back, "Understood, adored Montrose, first of all my programmers! I will comply!"

Menelaus remembered that data-speak was also the language of the Sylphs.

Almost too swiftly for any human eye to register, Alpha Yuen leaped like a tiger, and fell on Kine Larz. He ripped the man's garment from neckline to buttocks, revealing the metal length of serpentine wrapped twice and thrice around his body. Yuen put his hand on the ornamented hilt of the serpentine and hissed a command. The metal length gave off a jolt of electric force, making Larz scream and dance, and then it flexed and straightened violently enough to draw blood, throwing Larz to the ground like a child's top that spins off the edge of a table.

The serpentine was now straight as a spearshaft, and the leading edge of smartmetal flexed and flattened, forming a spearhead that hummed and sang with electric power.

Yuen, grim and silent, his one eye blazing, raised the weapon above the cowering Larz in both hands—but halted in awe when the voice of Arroglint the Fortunate again spoke from the weapon, this time in his native tongue.

In Chimerical, and then in Virginian, the calm and soothing tones of a machine voice rang out: "You are fools, my adored ones. The man sitting in the judgment seat is not Menelaus Montrose, but an imposter."

And at that same moment, Kine Larz, moving with the speed of panic, scuttled like a crab away from the awe-frozen Yuen, rose and sprinted, and took refuge behind Scipio, calling out "Sanctuary! Sanctuary!" in Chimerical.

And from the jeweled pistols of the Blue Men came a chime of noise, and a chorus of voices, as alike to Arroglint's as brothers' voices, saying the same message in Intertextual, and again in Iatric. *"The man sitting in the judgment seat is not Menelaus Montrose, but an imposter."* Meanwhile, Soorm (while all the eyes, and, more importantly, ears and noses, of all the dog things were straining toward the scene on the dais) sidled close to Oenoe, and, in Natural, repeated to her what was being said.

Everyone in the chamber understood one of those languages, except for Scipio (who had, after all, not studied very deeply how to be a Savant). But he understood what had happened when all the faces in the chamber turned toward him, and not one face looked very pleased, not one looked at all fooled. And Kine Larz slid away from behind Scipio, and hid behind the iron throne, and out of the line of fire.

Scipio cleared his throat. "I can explain . . . ," he said in English, a language no one understood.

11. On the Nose

Menelaus saw that there was nothing else to be done. So he used the implants again to order the smartmetal material he wore as a cloak to relax like an accordion, straighten, and fling his paralyzed body at the sarcophagus at just the correct angle that some part of his naked flesh would touch the library cloth control surface.

The throw was not perfect, as the cloak was not built for this, but Menelaus had calculated the various motions of his body and the intervening air nicely, and the five dog things were taken by complete surprise. He struck the two squatting atop the sarcophagus and sent them toppling muzzle over tail in a clash of dropped cutlasses and muskets, and musketballs spilled from an improperly tied poke like marbles, brightly clattering and slithering.

Unfortunately, one of the dogs with better reflexes stabbed at him with a bayonet, and he had to harden the Bernoulli-curved cloak hems he was using as lifting surfaces into momentary metallic armor to parry the blow, and fold a hem into a razor-sharp blade to slash the creature and drive it yowling back in a spray of blood.

This made Menelaus deviate, but only slightly: he landed heavily on the control surface, but faceup rather than facedown, and the metal of his hood was between him and the spot he had to touch to allow his implants to trigger the sarcophagus controls. The dogs loomed up to each side as he lay, looking down with anger and astonishment and curiosity in their canine eyes.

It was just a stroke of good luck that Mentor Ull spoke up just at that moment. He cried in Iatric: "I deduce some invisible magnetic force in the chamber smote Naar's automaton, and sent Beta Sterling Anubis toppling. Examine the signal environment! Discover the source!" And more than half of the Blue Men bent their heads and lit up the gems on their coats.

This gave Menelaus the moment he needed to send another command through his implants to his cloak, which flexed and flipped his paralyzed and motionless body neatly over like a flapjack. He slammed nose-first and very painfully into the library cloth coating part of the surface of the sarcophagus.

But it was enough of a contact, nose-to-cloth, to make the connection. Menelaus blessed his nose, and promised never to mock its great size again.

His implants triggered. The slim golden capsule the Linderlings had given him throbbed, and he could feel the pulse of power in his back teeth. Signals went from Menelaus' brain, to receptors placed about his brain stem, to emitters placed in his chest cavity, to the node of rod-logic crystals given him by the Linderlings, to a transmitter in the golden tube surface, to the library cloth, which, sensing the DNA pattern of an authorized user in the pores of the nose of Menelaus, had switched on external input-output ports, small as pinpoints, dotting the cloth surface.

In his teeth and prefrontal cortex, Menelaus felt the passcodes being accepted like the click of tumblers falling nearly into place. *Authorization Accepted!* The circuits seemed to be in working order: the response was the standard *Standing By!* The motive engines under the sarcophagus hull changed pitch slightly, revving up. The weapons click-clacked as live rounds were jacked into firing chambers.

The coffin was mated to the local room circuits. Through it, Menelaus sent and received similar confirmations from the engines controlling the door hinges, the guns in the roof, electric mines in the floor, and the automatics behind the walls.

Checklists of ammunition magazines and energy levels flickered like green shadows through his brain. *Ready!*

There were roughly one hundred guns hidden in the pineapple-shaped ornaments hanging from the ceiling: not quite enough to put an unseen pinpoint beam on everyone's head, whether blue or canine, but near enough.

He could suppress the ignition command so that any musketball fired could still kill a man if it struck him in a vital area, but without the incendiary, casualties would be far fewer.

He established the targeting list and action-reaction priorities. *Aim!*

First one, then several, then all the Blue Men perked up, startled, eyes wide, gems on their coats glittering, and the gray twins turned their slitted goggles toward Menelaus. Alalloel did not turn her head, but her three pairs of antennae, gold, silver, and blue, perked straight up like exclamation points.

"Achieve alertness!" called out Yndelf in Iatric, drawing his jeweled pistol, which was glowing bright as multicolored flame. "Oddity has been detected! Something manipulates the environs electronically! Dangerous instruments are target-locked on us!"

Yndech and Ydmoy drew their pistols. The two older men, Orovoy and Saaev, both drew braces of pistols, one in each hand, looking like absurd miniature gunfighters. Ull once again tucked his hands each into the opposite sleeves, Mandarin-style; Menelaus wondered what the energy source at his elbow might be.

The front rank of dogs knelt, muskets to shoulder, and the rear rank raised their muskets also, pointing at the man on the throne. The dog officer, a Collie, tail wagging with excitement, drew its sword in a slithering ring of steel, raised the blade, and looked to Ull, awaiting permission to give the order to fire.

Scipio, staring down scores of barrels pointed at him, did not so much as turn a hair, but assumed a stern and calm expression, and held it. Menelaus could not turn his paralyzed head to see this directly, but the images from the hundred targeting cameras in the ceiling were being fed directly into his visual cortex, and he felt a moment of family pride at Scipio's aplomb.

Naar rose slowly to his feet, looking bored, and brushed the dust off his coat. The coat-gems under his fingers lit up, and to either side of him his line of cannon-bearing automata stirred, straightened, and raised their heavy guns. One of them stooped and hoisted Naar to a perch atop.

Ull said to Yndelf, "Whence originates the signal?"

Yndelf was pointing his glittering pistol at the sarcophagus, or at the body of Montrose paralyzed and helpless atop it.

All this conversation was in Iatric. So it was that when Soorm, in an absolutely serious tone, and with no expression possible on his fixed, seal-like and goggle-eyed face, shouted, "Quickly! The real Judge of Ages is here! He is angered! Rescue our translator Beta Anubis from the magnetic curse of the coffin before it flings him again! Undo the paralysis!" the Blue Men not only understood him, but Preceptor Yndech, much less accustomed to trickery and deception than a Hormagaunt of Soorm's age, actually commanded the dog things Menelaus had attacked to come to his aid. In the same moment, Yndech's coat gems lit up, and Menelaus felt a tingling, burning sensation start from his lower spine and spread throughout his trunk and limbs and head.

Menelaus, head lolling, arms flopping, allowed the helpful dog things to pull him to his rubbery feet, but he could not suppress the laughter that welled up from his lungs.

The dogs near him shrank back, alarmed by that laughter, which rang with madness.

Docent Aarthroy, the boy, whose coat was almost a solid mass of glittering gems, raised his hand and spoke. Menelaus had not heard his voice before. It was oddly flat yet rhythmic, just like the triune voice of the three Locusts, Crucxit, Axcit, and Litcec, had been. *"Forgive if it happens to disturb. Significant information is apprehended. Relict of coffin labeled Beta Sterling Xenius Anubis, Proven in Battle of Mt. Erebus, Genetic Unknown, Line Unknown, Possibly Crotalinae, interment date A.D. 5292. Identified oddity! Relict possesses/employs third-order logic crystal energy system, multivariable channel neuroemission transponder and responder node, devised post-condition, object tracing number 6AS-46A-*

W5–BB963, technology comparable to object found in coffin Locust labeled Linderkeirth-lin Laialin Inquiline Northeastern Region interment date A.D. *8866.*" As he spoke, with one hand he pointed at Menelaus, and with the other at Keirthlin.

Naar peered calmly down over the edge of his machine, and said in a bored tone of voice, "I confirm Docent Aarthroy's reading. Mentor Ull and Relict Soorm are mistaken. Relict Anubis is himself the source of the signals. He has primitive first-order short-range cybernetics channeled through a Linderling third-order node."

"Too late!" laughed Menelaus, clutching for support at the supine image of his own head atop the sarcophagus lid, using the golden nose as a convenient hand grip. "Too slow on the uptake! Checkmate!"

There came a loud clattering from the walls and stalactite-shaped chandeliers. All of the pineapple ornaments banged open, one after another, with a noise like a hundred mousetraps snapping, and stubby little gunbarrels, their camera-eye lenses glittering, poked out of the openings.

12. Grand Entrance

They were interrupted by a commotion from the great doors. Now came a rumble, as of a slow drum, pounding. There was a murmur of awe from the gathered prisoners when a Giant stepped across the threshold.

The Giant strode forward on his immense legs, and the floor trembled at his footfall. It was like seeing an avalanche stride, or an iceberg on the northern seas. He ducked his head slightly to clear the vast doors, stepped within, halted, and drew himself up, casting his gaze over the room. His head was above the level of the chandeliers near him, so that while his massive shoulders and Herculean chest were brightly lit, his head was in half shadow. In this gloom, his yellow eyes glimmered, catlike.

The ten dog things escorting him were brought up short, and, seeing guns in the ceiling, bristled and whined. At their noise, alarmed, one hundred or so dogs, nearly half of the number in the chamber, turned and leveled weapons toward the Giant.

He stood at least fifteen feet tall. The tallest of the Witches was only level with his waist. Even Menelaus, who was tall for a man, was less than a child to him.

The Giant was not a pretty creature. The feet were toeless pads, and the legs were elephantine cylinders. The torso was disproportionately squat, and the chest and shoulders abnormally thick and wide. The hands were muscled, the fingers long and strong, but the last joint of the pinky of either hand was split like a Y into two smaller digits, flagella so fine that a watchmaker would envy them. The neck was a ring of muscle and flab that made the creature look like he was wearing a turtleneck sweater. Coarse hairs like the bristles of a rhinoceros stuck out from here and there from his flesh, which was the consistency of an orange peel. The head was an astonishing globe, large even for a body this size, in proportion as if the head of a baby had been perched on the body of a monster. The flesh of the scalp was thickly webbed with blue arteries like river deltas, implying a brain that needed more blood than a human brain. The facial features were coarse and gathered near the chin, making the beetling brow and vast dome of the skull even more grotesque.

It was hard to say which part of the face was more uncomely. The chin was weak and small. The mouth was a pouting rosebud of quivering red membrane. The nose was upturned and piglike, with vast nostrils, and two additional artificial nostrils penetrated the cheeks like metal plugs, one to each side of the nose. The continual hissing and suction of the breathing bespoke the immense amount of oxygen the three-foot-wide brain required. The ears were disagreeable nubs of flesh.

The eyes, however, were large and lustrous and golden, great orbs set in round sockets, with pupils like bright wells. The irises were yellow speckled with green, and the rapid dilation and contraction of the pupils as the Giant looked from one to another of the aspects and fixtures, men and dogs, in the vast chamber before his feet hinted at a brain able to absorb tremendous amounts of visual information quickly.

The Blue Men had returned his clothing to him also. In the hand of the Giant was an immense staff on which he leaned for support. His headgear was the jawless skull of a saber-toothed tiger, and the tawny pelt of leopard-spots, still attached, swathed his upper limbs as a stole, clawed feet and tail dangling down like tassels. Beneath, he wore the traditional suit lined with flexible vertical smart-piping, hydraulically stiffened to help support his frame, and the pipes flexed and tensed like muscles as he moved.

Strange gold eyes stared down above a curious double nose, a puckered bud of a mouth, a nub of a receding chin, a ghastly neck of layered flab.

Neither Scipio, nor the others in the chamber, could meet that gaze, only Menelaus.

He spoke in flawless Intertextual. *"Forgive me for taking so long to deduce your language, but your forms are complicated, even for me. I am Dr. Bashan Christopher*

Calligorant Hugh-Jones, interment date, Year of Our Lord 3033. I speak all the languages of all within the chamber.

"Ull Ynglingas, you should be aware that the Xypotech protecting the Tombs was invaded, damaged, and switched to standby; but it was switched from standby to lethal defense seventeen minutes ago. Surrender now and submit to the justice of the Judge of Ages, or be destroyed."

Mentor Ull stared at him. "*Insufficient explanation! We have been battling the coffins and associated weaponry for weeks! We have won sixty-nine coffins from the Tomb with minimal losses.*"

The Giant laughed. "*Those were not his weapons. Those were his toys.*"

Now he spoke in Iatric, and the Hormagaunts and Clade-dwellers looked on.

"Preceptor Illiance Vroy," came the voice of Bashan, "I call upon you to relieve Mentor Ull Ynglingas of his command. Take the gems from the handweapon that Preceptrix Aanwen Leel tossed to the ground, and place them on his coat as a sign of his demotion."

Illiance looked at Ull suspiciously, then up at the hundred guns peering from the ceiling, and then (because he could not look him in the eye) at the chin of the strange, oversized head of the Giant. "*I have insufficient reason to comply with your request, reasonable as it may be.*"

"Do what I say, and quickly, for I stand in intellect and wisdom to you as a father to a child, or a shepherd to a sheep."

"*I reluctantly refuse. Mentor Ull's actions perhaps have a reasonable construction. If you were to tell your reasons, I might comply.*"

Bashan the Giant sighed, which was a noise like an immense wind, and the oddly childish mouth became a grim line. "Your compliance is tardy. The situation now has changed. Had you done as I said, you would have discovered the red metallic amulet Ull wears affixed like a medical prosthetic just below his elbow. This amulet once belonged to Father Reyes y Pastor, who was expelled from the Hermetic Order.

"As a reward for his work in biotechnology and Cliometry wherein he successfully interfered with the lives of countless Melusine, who are the dominant and Current species of the Earth, Ull was given the honors and the place of Reyes.

"His arms are too thin to wear the band on his wrist, so he must affix it to his forearm. He did not slumber when you did, but, being granted endless youth by the sciences of the Hermetic Order, came again alive periodically during all the centuries you slept. He has betrayed your principles, and seeks the Judge of Ages only to kill him.

"The only reason why the Judge of Ages has not been attacked with lethal force is that some doubt still clouds Ull's mind surrounding the issue of identity.

"Had you done as I asked, his deception would have been revealed without any further ado. Because you refused, there will now be a firefight in this chamber, and not all here will emerge alive."

5

Jurors

1. To Arms

Daae the Alpha Chimera called out in Virginian, "The Judge of Ages in his wrath has summoned a Giant from the earliest of times, from the Antecpyrotic World, to destroy all those within the chamber! Prepare yourselves for the oblivion we crave, for the force of the elder days will make no distinction of innocence or guilt, any more than the fires they used to destroy earlier worlds!"

And the voice of Daae simply rang with joy.

Whether he knew that the Blue Men had thawed this Giant themselves, keeping him out of sight in their hospital all this time, or whether he thought the Judge of Ages had arranged to have him brought into the chamber, was not clear, but his words startled both educated Chimerae and Witches who understood his language.

Fatin the Witch maiden called out to her Witches in Virginian, "Stay! The Giant knows the guilty. Have you never seen one before? This is a posthuman—his intelligence range is in the 500s. Look at his eyes! He understands everything about us . . . He will spare us . . ."

Ajuoga called out in her icy, poisonous voice, "No! He is baptized of the White Christ, and is an enemy to all Witches. We are dead meat and food for birds and jackals!"

Mickey shouted toward the Giant, "Eat the Blue Men, not me! I am full of unhealthy hallucinogenic chemicals and fatty tissue! You need to watch your diet!"

Alpha Daae whistled. The Chimerae moved with practiced quickness, and retreated into the alcove holding the atomic pile. The dog things, dividing their attention to cover the Giant and the Judge of Ages on his throne, were taken unawares, and given no direct orders, they did not stop the Chimerae.

Gamma Phyle and Kine Happy pulled down the two display cabinets to the left and right of the opening of the alcove, sending the huge cases tilting, toppling, and shattering with a noise like thunder when they fell to the floor. Priceless antiques spilled out. The two prone display cases now made an impromptu bulwark across the opening of the alcove, and Beta Vulpina and Beta Suspinia took position to the left and right, bows strung and arrows nocked. The tops of the display cases did not quite touch, and in this breach stood Alpha Daae and Alpha Yuen, both looking more fierce and fearless and splendid than even their wont.

Seeing this, Prissy Pskov and Zouave Zhigansk scrambled for any weapon-shaped antique that had fallen from the smashed cases, and they called Toil, Drudge, and Drench to do likewise. The three Donors did not obey, but fled to a corner of the chamber, cowering behind the looming statue of Michael the Archangel.

Soorm and Crile and Gload, disdaining any weapons not built of their own flesh, put their backs to the fountain. Crile elongated his neck and opened both serpent fangs and telescoping elbow spikes. Soorm stepped backward into the water, charged his electrical eel cells, and bent to draw up his scorpion's tail, bulb throbbing with poison, above his shoulder, twitching. The headless Gload uttered a belly laugh from the grotesque shark mouth running from side to side across his belly, and he cracked his knuckles.

Of the Witches, Mickey and Ajuoga and Lilura were of a period late enough to know the Chimerae, and know them as deadly enemies, and so they called to their fellows and followers, and, with much more noise and disarray, retreated to the opposite alcove, which held tanks of medical nanomaterial, and the women climbed atop the tanks, leaving Mickey, the Demonstrators, and the other menfolk to form a line across the opening of the alcove. The stands of antique armor the menfolk pulled from either side, and so a broken line of empty metal stood between the Witch-men and the chamber. Mickey whirled his charming rod overhead, passing it quickly from one hand to the other, and flourished it like a quarterstaff, uttering his battle-yodel. The Demonstrators hissed, and helped themselves to the swords and spears the suits of armor held.

The thirty-one Witches faced the nine Chimerae across the fountain. Three Hormagaunts stood between them, looking both ways, while Prissy and Zouave, allergic to each other, sought out opposite sides of the chamber.

The captain of the dog things barked, and the squadrons turned left and right. Two dozen dog things faced the Giant in two rows of twelve, the front row kneeling; another two dozen faced the dais, or the fountain, or the Witches, or the Chimerae, or the scattered others in the chamber. The Scholar Rada Lwa, Ctesibius the Savant, Sir Guiden, Linder Keir and Keirthlin, and Alalloel were guarded each by a trio or quartet of dogs. The remaining threescore gathered near the Blue Men in a defensive half circle.

The gentle Nymphs retreated, cooing and moaning, to the feet of the statue of Michael the Archangel, and the males of their race played fretful trills and warning arpeggios on their double-pipes. No one was covering them with weapons, which made Menelaus smile, because his circuits in the chamber detected the pheromones and scentless neuropsychological chemicals that began to rise up like vapor from them. He signaled with his implants to the wall vents, turned on the fans, and increased the air circulation in that quarter of the chamber.

The Giant at the chamber door observed all this without expression. He looked carefully at Menelaus, and stepped forward one giant step.

2. Chess and Poker

Only then did Menelaus hear, over his implants, in his inner ear, the voice of Sir Guiden. "Liege, I assume we are not talking over implants to maintain radio silence?"

"Which you just broke," sent Menelaus back to him, with, perhaps, a bit of a snarl.

"Sorry, Liege, I knew you had your reasons, but there are now multiple signals leaving this room, and I have a shot at Ull right this second. I did not get a chance to open this fine suit of armor I am next to, because there are five dogs watching me, but I managed to palm the luminous marker pistol from the belt when they weren't looking."

"What? You going to paint him to death?"

"It isn't much, but the marker needles can crack a man's skull at short range. I can get off one shot, maybe two, before they deck me. Should I take the shot?"

"Hold off. Things are not what they seem."

"What is going on, Liege?"

"The problem is that I am playing poker with the people here, but playing chess with the Machine. I can bluff people, but the Machine and I can see each other's moves. He knows I am in the chamber, but does not know where."

"That means you want to leave the chamber, right? And the Machine will not find you?"

"Wrong. I deliberately expelled an evolutionary virus from this site in order to attract attention to it, knowing full well it would be the one broken into by the Currents working for Exarchel. For a while he had me fooled, because he used Thaws instead of Currents to dig me up, but I think I am oriented now. I hid myself clumsily enough that any servant of the Machine could see through my disguise—just as Scipio and Ctesibius, in fact, did—but just subtly enough that he would have to send a physical agent to me to confirm, and I have a tactic in place to trace whatever message that agent tries to send back to his master.

"But then the message never came. So I had to be bolder. I began going around telling the people I thought were agents who I was: first Soorm, then Rada Lwa, then Linder Keir and Linder Keirthlin. I have reason to believe Soorm is still loyal to Reyes y Pastor, the Red Hermeticist, so I was expecting him to call Exarchel. So far he has not. Keirthlin actually helped me, even handed me the keys to winning this hand. So I am ruling them out. Alalloel is a puzzle: I thought she was a Current, but she overheard me tell the Linder twins who I am, and she did not call down Exarchel on me. So it is someone else. Someone in the room."

Sir Guiden said, "It's Ull. The Giant just said so."

"I counted him. From most effected to least, Rada Lwa, Ull, Keir, all have been intimate mind-to-mind with the Machine, and contaminated, and suffered physical brain alteration as a result. Rada Lwa can hear my voice but cannot recognize my face. Ctesibius and Scipio have been in mind-contact with the Machine, but it was one-way, a donation; a donation is not a possession, so they are clean."

"Liege? Do you want your enemies to find you? Are you mad?"

"I want my enemies to find me. I am really mad."

"Is this some sublime posthuman thing no one can understand?"

"It is the opposite of sublime. I want Del Azarchel to know where I am, so he will pick up his pistol and come looking for me, and we can finish our duel. His people, including the machine half of his mind, don't want him to die dueling me, so they are trying to bump me off before that happens."

Then Menelaus sent, "Exarchel? I know you heard all that. I have all your little puppets and spies and agents locked up here in the chamber with me, so you might as well give up, and send Blackie."

And, with a silent thought directed through his implants, Menelaus stirred the great golden sarcophagus of the Judge of Ages to life. Roaring, the serene image on its lid gleaming, it slammed and banged heavily down the dais; roared past Menelaus, wind-whipping the hems of his metal robes as he cheered; and sped across the chamber floor, accelerating.

Everyone, Blue Man and dog things and Thaws of many eras, shouted and screamed and jumped out of the way.

An automaton stalked into the path, raised its machine gun, and opened fire. The automaton's bullets slammed off the hull of the sarcophagus, screaming. Decorative armor panels slid aside, revealing weapon blisters. Twin machine guns bright with tracer fire, and a particle-beam energy weapon brighter than a lightning bolt and louder, erupted from the sarcophagus, blinding nearly all eyes there, and dazing all ears. Three arms of the automaton were chewed in half by the bullets, and its energy core was aflame, when the sarcophagus ran it down, trampling it to pieces under wheels and treads.

Four of the Blue Men raised their jeweled weapons, but were flung from their feet when a nonlethal shock of electricity crackled along the floor. Unfortunately, everyone standing on the same square of gold tile was treated likewise, and all fell screaming, except for Gload the Hormagaunt, who seemed to be immune to electricity. He grinned, and little sparks jumped from his bottom fangs to his top.

Bashan the Giant, seeing the sarcophagus barreling toward him like a train engine, stepped to one side with a polite nod.

The huge pistons groaned and the leaves of the huge doors fell to. Boom. The sarcophagus sprayed some chemical from its interior on the doors as it rushed forward. There was a squeal of brakes and the sarcophagus fishtailed sideways, so that it struck the doors lengthwise. When the heavy sarcophagus smashed into the doors, it was a sound as if an aircraft carrier had been dropped onto a sea of stone. The doors were struck so forcefully that they were bent slightly in the frame, just enough to jam the hinges. The chemical fluid ignited with a blue-white flame when the sarcophagus struck, and this in turn ignited the fluids and bearings in the undercarriage. The fire hardened and solidified the glue filling the cracks of the door leaves into something the consistency of asphalt, and burnt away the joints of the wheels and treads of the coffin, leaving it unable to move, trapped in asphalt, and blocking the way, its huge mass crumpled and bent up against the doors.

After that crash, there was silence in the chamber for the space of a breath or two, as everyone stared at the jammed doors in wonder and fear.

3. Petrifaction, Radiation

Mentor Ull had a look of deep annoyance darkening his features. His eyes looked more like those of a rattlesnake than ever. "Erratic behavior! Head-strong, awkward! Why must these primitive creatures perform such irksome frolics?" The gems on his coat blazed with sudden, startling brightness, and every person in the chamber, from Menelaus on the dais to the north side to Bashan the Giant before the jammed doors at the south, suddenly froze in mid-motion, mid-gesture, able to breathe and to move involuntary muscles, but not able even to blink.

The Blue Men all sighed a little sigh, and the dog things, uttering only a yelp or two of scorn and relief, stood and relaxed and shouldered their weapons.

Naar said in Intertextual, *"Most bothersome! Why must we trifle with these relicts from ages before mental unity was accomplished? Can we not at least begin to kill off all of those whom we have confirmed cannot be the one we seek?"*

But Illiance said in Iatric, "Actually, only those who have eaten our food are affected . . . ," and he was in the act of turning toward Scipio, who was merely pretending to be paralyzed, when Scipio at that moment happened to blink.

Illiance said to him in Iatric, "Sir? Do you speak this language? What is the meaning of your pantomime?"

Scipio smiled apologetically, and shrugged sheepishly, and kicked Illiance headlong off the dais.

Two dog things fired without orders: one musket misfired, powder not ig-niting, and the other missed, so its musketball struck the throne behind Scipio and burned like white fire.

Scipio leaped and swung his square-pointed black blade at Illiance, who had landed on hands and knees. Illiance threw his hand before his face, and all the gems on his coat lit up.

As the blade swept down, it resisted and wobbled, in the same way two magnets of the same pole will resist if pressed together; both the logic crystal of the blade and the logic crystals of the coat whined, and then a flash of light and a snap of electric power flashed between them.

The blade was shattered in three pieces, but the gems on the coat of Illiance cracked or went dark. Both men were equally surprised, but both were not equally slow to recover: Scipio stepped on the little man, and snatched up both of the white ceramic pistols from where they stuck out from his coat pockets.

Scipio flipped up the sights with his thumbs and, holding a weapon in either hand, pointed at Mentor Ull, shouting out a command in a language Ull did not recognize.

Yndech said in Intertextual, *"Let us irradiate the false Judge of Ages with our pistols, and mourn the departure of Mentor Ull. The exchange will be economical."*

But Ydmoy said, *"Uncouth! You reason like a Locust. Perhaps the false Judge can be deflected via negotiation to a nonviolent admixture of motives and results. Perhaps if the false Judge were willing to compromise, he would merely shoot Ull in some extremity and maim him."*

Yndelf said, thoughtfully, *"I have noted an interesting anomaly to which some attention should be paid. Was not Relict Melechemoshemyazanagual Onmyoji de Concepcion subjected to nerve paralysis with the others? While we turned our gaze to the fascinating assault on Preceptor Illiance, the Warlock seems to have hidden himself."*

Ull spoke in Iatric, ignoring the guns pointed at his head, "Negotiations are in order. I will first release the Giant Bashan, in order that he may translate our words. I no longer trust the accuracy of the Chimera Anubis."

Ull now turned and called to the far side of the chamber. "Relict Bashan! First, command the false Judge to disarm himself. Next, order the Warlock of Williamsburg to reveal himself from hiding. Third, to each man, in his own tongue, translate these words: 'It is required that the identity of the Judge of Ages be revealed. It has been deduced that he is posing among you in disguise. Each group is enjoined to look at those among you, and to identify whose behavior is eccentric or untypical for your order of being.'"

With another flicker of gems, motion returned to the limbs of Bashan, who stretched, and then laughed such laughter as Giants use.

Bashan turned, and raised the huge staff on which he leaned, taller than a weaver's beam, and threw it like a spear. It passed halfway down the chamber and struck and pierced the gold containment sphere of the atomic pile. In the distance, a bell began to ring shrilly.

And with that, Bashan said mockingly in Iatric, "Little grasshopper, did you not wonder why I paused to make mention of an ability to speak all the languages here, even though the only languages I had opportunity to overhear in the medical house were yours?"

All throughout the chamber, the men and women of various ages began to groan and stir.

Scipio, who did not speak Iatric, said, "Okay! Someone who talks English or Spanish has to tell me whether the Moon-man here released the paralysis because I said so, or whether something else is going on."

Menelaus, who had been frozen inside his cloak, now straightened and stretched and said, "Something else. The radioactivity in the chamber is drowning out the radio signals the Blues are sending to mites in our nerve clusters to paralyze us. So we can move."

"Radioactivity interferes with radio?" Scipio asked, blinking.

"Hence the name. I see you have the same level of scientific education as a Witch."

"Is the radioactivity going to kill us? Or mutate us into spider creatures?"

"Or less than a Witch. The Chimerae should be okay, because they are bio-engineered for high-roentgen environments. The rest of us—depends on how long we are exposed. We have enough working coffins to do some cellular correction to prevent cancers and other misgrowths. It is what they were designed for. But for now . . ."

"For now, I shoot this guy in the head?" Because Scipio was still standing (one foot on the back of Preceptor Illiance, who was looking remarkably unflustered) with the pistols pointed at the skull of Mentor Ull, who was looking remarkably dyspeptic.

Ull said to Menelaus in Iatric, "Tell this unnamed Relict of long-ago that his antique railgun pistol is of no advantage. My embellishments"—his gems lit up as he spoke—"organize the circumambient magnetic flux to my advantage."

And an invisible force yanked the metal dowel running down the length of each translucent barrel straight up into the air, taking the pistols with it. Scipio held on to the grips and found himself dangling in midair; he let go as the pistols were flung upward. Both pistols hung in midair twenty feet or so above the floor, and then Mentor Ull flung them both all the way down the length of the great hall and up atop the balcony, where they rang with a noise like dropped China crockery.

Scipio, shaken but unhurt, landed on his feet not far from where Menelaus stood. Illiance, freed of Scipio's weight, was helped to his feet by two or three dog things with drooping ears, who licked his face and fussed over him, passing snarling glances of hate toward Scipio.

Ull said in Iatric, "Anubis, we seek the Judge of Ages. We know he is among you. Tell the relicts that we will begin killing all within the chamber, starting with women and Giant and others we are confident are not he, until he reveals himself."

Menelaus said, "Look up. I have one hundred guns armed with a mix of armor-piercing and scattershot rounds, with a few tracers to look pretty, aimed at all your heads. The floor is electrified; the fountain is poison. You are totally outgunned, surrounded, and locked in a radioactive room that is rapidly growing unhealthy for human life."

Ull sneered, "Your control is illusionary, Chimera. We permitted those signals to pass in order to lure the Judge of Ages, through overconfidence, to reveal his location. You do not think we returned the equipment of the Linderlings to them unchanged and dangerous? The multivariable channel neuro-emission node object 6AS-46A-W5-BB963"—Menelaus reached under his cloak, and tightened his hand on the gold capsule Keirthlin had given him—"was reprogrammed to impersonate all passthrough data without passing it through. The signals only appeared to pass. Do you think us fools?"

"Yes," said Menelaus. "Well, not all of y'all. Mostly you." And he stepped over to the throne, and put his hand on the armrest. As he had hoped, the upper surface was library cloth, and at touch-range, the radioactivity could not stop the transmission from his fingertips to the cloth surface.

Two of the guns overhead clicked with loud snaps, and nothing happened, and nothing fired.

Menelaus groaned. "Okay, I take back that fool comment. That was well played. Is Blackie helping you, Learned Ull? There is no way that trick would have worked if it was just you who reprogrammed the node. What happened to Reyes y Pastor? Why did you take his seat at the Table Round?"

Soorm spoke in Iatric, "That answer I know!"

The words were spoken so loudly, and with such authority, that even Ull looked amazed, and stared at the monstrosity, half bear and half sea lion, that stood in the waters of the fountain, two mismatched eyes goggling, two tongues lolling, the claws on his webbed hands sheathing and unsheathing like those of a twitching lion.

Soorm said, "The Red Hermeticist realized that the era he ruled, all his dreams for how humanity should evolve, we beloved Hormagaunts, and everything else for which he lived, was a falsehood. Over a thousand years of events were organized merely to allow for one raid on Yap Island—the Cetaceans reverse engineered the genework on the Clades to deduce the mathematical Divarication solution Menelaus Montrose used to solve for complex mutually incompatible system interaction. It was from the Clade Codes that the Unity Divarication was devised, to drive the lines of Hormagaunt artificial species into oneness, and produce first the Locusts, and, later, the Locust hive mind.

"My entire world, of which I am the father and the first, was a joke, a feint, a jest, merely meant to permit one afternoon of bloodshed, lasting from noon to the ninth hour, and years of torment to thousands of innocent Clades buried alive at the utmost bottom of the sea, merely so that that fourteen lines of code expressed in ninety-one symbols could be deduced.

"The knowledge drove Reyes, my creator, insane, and he returned to the comfort of the superstitions of his youth, and sought to save the souls of the soulless monsters he created. For this crime, his greater self and oversoul, the Dreagh Expastor, was murdered and consumed by the Dreagh Excoronimas, even as Man Pastor was slain by Man Coronimas. Reyes y Pastor died a martyr on the steps of his church, trying to defend the sacred bread of the altar from defilement."

Ull was staring dumbfounded at him. "How can you know of these secret things, hidden since the dawn of time? You are a Hormagaunt and a monster. And whom do you address?" For the chameleon eyes of Soorm did not point the same direction when he spoke.

Soorm drew himself up, his scorpion tail lashing angrily. "I am the scion of Reyes y Pastor, and his masterwork! You are not worthy to touch the latchet of his shoes, much less fill those shoes! *Judge of Ages, hear my prayer!* I hold thee to thy oath! This pathetic blue dwarf occupies the throne of Master of the World of this Age. Judge him, O Judge of Ages! You said he would topple from his throne!"

Menelaus said, "One last thing he's got to do, first. One little thing."

Ull said to Menelaus, "Your control of the chamber weapons, Chimera, is nullified. Even with our nerve mites out of contact, yet our Followers outnumber the Thaws by more than twice over, armed against unarmed! We command, and on pain of death, you obey! Tell all in this chamber in their languages to reveal the Judge of Ages, or we begin to slay the innocent!"

Preceptor Naar, looking down from his perch on a nearby automaton, said sharply, "What do you mean, 'we'? You are not a Simplifier. You are a Hermeticist, mazed in complexity and falsehood like a spider in a labyrinth, an architect of the Noösphere we shed. You are an enemy and opponent of every ideal for which we stand!" And for once, his languid, long features were tight and hot with passion.

All the Blue Men, faces expressionless, raised their fingers and pointed at Ull. Despite the radioactivity in the room, some of their coat-circuits must have been working, for flocks of gems fled from their coats, passing through the air like glittering snowflakes of many colors. With a chattering clatter, the gems affixed themselves to Ull's coat, layer upon layer, until he was one bright multipatterned carpet of gemstones from neck to hemline, and all along his sleeves.

No matter how demoted, he was still a human, and Ull's commands were still obeyed by the dog things in the chamber, for he cried out, "Followers! Bayonet the She-Nymphs!"

Two groups of seven dog things ran at the Nymphs, who, oddly, neither flinched nor fled. Instead the Nymphs began to dance, the women counterclockwise and the men clockwise, weaving and interweaving with rapid footfalls, and their mantillas floated like scarves, shedding white cherry blossom petals and white dandelion puffs. The dogs rushed into their midst, and the Nymphs screamed.

But they screamed with laughter, because the dog things were running in circles with the dance, weaving in and out, each chasing the tail of the dog thing before, barking happily, tongues lolling, tails wagging. The muskets and cutlasses were flung gaily to the golden floor, and Nymphs led dogs in a game of skipping and jumping over the muskets, from one side to the other.

Then Oenoe, who stood in the middle of circles of mad, dancing figures, raised her lovely arms overhead, and sang a single high note into the air, crystalline, perfect, pure. The music slowed, softened, and segued into a lullaby.

Even without understanding the words, all in the chamber understood the song promised the wonders of safety and satiety; mother's love and lover's kisses; roses and wine and feast-days without end; and slumber by the golden margins of mazy streams of cool, clear water beneath the dappled shadows of generous fruit trees, their luscious fruit a-shine with dewdrops; and, then, at sunset, dreams of pleasure merging into the beauty of the starlight.

And when the song was ended, the fourteen dog things were asleep in a puppy pile heaped in the center of the circle, and the male Nymphs, grinning like Satyrs, brandished four muskets, clutching them by the barrels as if they were clubs.

There was a murmur of admiration from the hags among the Witches, who nodded their hooded heads and clapped their hands in applause.

Ull cried wildly to Ydmoy, Yndech, and Yndelf, "Expelled of the order or not, a confluence of interests still commingles our actions! For your own reasons, to preserve your order and race, you must find the Judge of Ages."

Ydmoy said gravely, "It may be so, but to spend human lives to achieve our goal, while efficient and useful, we reject as Locust thinking."

Yndech said, "True, but then again, Locust Ull is correct—no objection can be raised to discovering the identity of the Judge of Ages and coercing him to preserve our race. The principle of Darwinian evolution proposes that to do otherwise would be to adopt a moral code that cannot reproduce itself and therefore cannot be carried into the future!" And he pointed his pistol at Menelaus. "Translate the command to the chamber!"

The Giant Bashan tilted his vast bald head down, his magnificent, beautiful eyes narrowed and his tiny grisly mouth bracketed by wrinkles in his orange-peel integument. Now he strode forward, the floor murmuring thunder beneath his footfalls, and stepped over the fountain in one stride. He was a tower, high and terrible, staring down with eyes like two suns, a gaze no one could meet. There was a rumble in his chest, almost subsonic, like the noise whales might make, a sound more easily felt in the teeth than heard in the ear. At the same time, there was a voice of human pitch that issued from his throat.

But the rumbling in his chest was a second voice box, which the Giants used for their long-range low-frequency speech. The sounds were too low for the ear hairs of the Blue Men to catch, but Menelaus heard this second voice, speaking in Merikan: "Where is the manual firing station?"

Menelaus had the arsenal index and weapon status information glowing in his mind. He was not certain, because the golden node capsule given him by the Linderlings had touched the data, if the information were accurate. He decided to trust it, because events were happening too fast, and there were no other options. He replied in Merikan, "A firing station at the corner balcony, up yonder, behind the statue of the Grim Reaper. Behind a secret panel, there is a big metal door that needs a key I don't have."

The Giant, with his other, high-pitched voice box, talked over the voice of Menelaus (who spoke words the Blue Men could not have understood even had they been loud and clear) and so was at the same time saying in Iatric, "O Fools! Your so-called principle of Darwinism is nothing to do with Darwin, or with any biological theory: It is an excuse for the evil you contemplate, and, like all evils, a lie. The lie says that if you merely do deeds evil enough, ruthlessly enough, you shall survive.

"Your Locust race did horrific deeds in the name of race survival, inflicting a despair upon the Hormagaunts, so that anyone not absorbed into a Locust hive mind was diverted from his true life and true mate, subtly made miserable, and exposed to influences both psychological and chemical to hinder reproduction. The Hormagaunts in those years were led by Cliometric webs of incentives first to lives of pleasure and sterile self-centeredness, then to underpopulation, and then to extinction. You killed a race: genocide. By Darwin's logic, genocide is not merely acceptable, but laudable.

"And yet here you are, the last remnant of an extinct species, and your grim deeds did not win you the racial immortality you crave. You are as dead as the Giants, but far more ignobly."

Yndech said, "No one can defy the cold logic of the Darwinian calculation. Those who do not place survival as paramount, by definition do not survive. Self-sacrifice is always a losing survival strategy!"

The Giant opened wide his eyes, and they were like two scalding lamps, and Yndech put up his arms over his face, and quailed.

The massive voice boomed: "The Consensus Advocacy met in final conclave and read the Cliometric calculations of our future. We saw that if we continued to expand our numbers, the technological infrastructure needed to reproduce our race at replacement levels would be great—for even to bear a single child required extensive biogenetic modification and neurosurgery—so great indeed that the conversion of all biological life to nanomechanical life would be inevitable, and the human race be extinct. We chose instead to destroy the technological basis of man, and preserve the whole which was greater than our part. Do you say we did wrong? Hypocrites! The human race—and all races represented here in this chamber, and all of history—owes themselves to our sacrifice. Therefore you shall not, if I can prevent, bring any coercion to bear on the Judge of Ages, for he is the grandfather of the Giants, and all the races after owe their very existence to him."

The Blue Men had nothing to say back.

Subsonically, meanwhile, in another language, Bashan said to Menelaus, "Doctor Montrose, I can open that firing station for you, but only by exposing myself to gunfire unto death. This saddens me, for my only purpose, once I deduced the existence of the chess game throughout all human history, the chess game in which the fated part of the race of Giants was merely to be a sacrificial pawn, was to discover whether that sacrifice was worthwhile. I instructed my coffin to wake me when your deadly game with Del Azarchel was to be concluded. I wanted to see your last duel. I left my world and outlived all history, and lost everything, merely to slake that curiosity. Now I die that you might live. So I shall never know."

Menelaus again spoke in Merikan, which the Blue Men could hear but not understand, saying, "I can at least satisfy your curiosity. If De Ulloa, D'Aragó, Pastor, and Coronimas are dead, and Ull is about to die, the only Hermeticist left is Sarmento i Illa d'Or: I can see the end of the chess game. It is a sacrifice move. I lose my rook and checkmate him. But you must get me to the fire control station before the Blues figure out who I am. Which cannot be that far off: practically everyone in the room knows."

4. None in This Chamber

The Giant said to Yndech and the Blue Men, "Simplifiers! I tell you the simple truth. You will not discover who or where the Judge of Ages is. None in this chamber will or can betray him. Have your translator pass the question along, and see for yourselves."

Menelaus wondered what Bashan the Giant had in mind; but he trusted him, so when Yndech in Iatric gave the command, Menelaus obeyed, and spoke the question in several tongues to the other Thaws: he demanded of the Thaws to reveal who among them did not conform to the standards of their times.

Soorm answered without needing to wait for a translation. "I represent the Configuration of Iatrocratic Clades. Speaking on behalf of my people and my age of history, let me report that we all live in isolated Clades and scattered hermitages, and most of us are allergic to each other. We have no rules of conformity. This means, first, that we cannot see nonconformity even if we wanted to, and second, we would rather die than conform to your command, so we will never want to. Go eat your own mothers, culls!" And Crile and Gload roared and shrieked like lions and vultures.

Oenoe cried in a voice like ringing music, "The Natural Order of Man loves the Judge of Ages and is beloved by him. We would not betray him even for kisses."

Illiance now spoke up, "Anubis? Did you translate that correctly? Kisses?"

Menelaus said, "Well, she actually referred to a more intimate congress, but the meaning is the same."

Alpha Daae spoke sternly, "The Eugenic General Emergency Command of the Commonwealth of Virginia, her federal allies, protectorates, and conquered territories, rejects the authority of mixed-bloods, ferals, strays, and undercreatures to direct our actions. We are not under the command of the Judge of Ages, but our honor will not permit us to yield to you. In the name of the Republic, the Senate, and the Bloodlines, I hereby impose martial law; I countermand the order of the Blue Men; and I compel all in this chamber to answer no question of theirs. Whoever speaks first, dies, and your name will live on in my weapon."

Fuamnach of Whalesong Coven screeched in a scraping voice and said, "Is not the Judge of Ages a demigod, a prince of the twilight land between life and death? The Delphic Acroamatic Progressive Order reverently seeks to escape his curse, and asks him, if he is within the sound of our voices, to heed how we pray and conjure and convoke that he might spare us, and excuse us our previous trespasses. You are all doomed." And as her voice shrieked out, all the tall Witches and their menfolk raised their hands on high. And they all moaned, "Do-oo-om."

Linder Keir said, "The identity of the Judge of Ages is known to me, but certain fine distinctions of the neuropsychological, interpersonal, legal, and ethical codes which govern every nuance of Linderling behavior prevent my telling you. The actions of the Blue Men are highly suspect and unethical."

Rada Lwa said, "I heard his voice earlier, but I do not see him in the chamber. He is still outside, and you've missed him!"

Ctesibius looked at Menelaus, uttered a hard, sharp laugh of despair, and said no word, but sat shaking his head as if in weary amusement.

5. Finality Speaks

Hearing these translated responses, one after another, the little Blue Men began bobbing their heads in an odd gesture, tilting first one ear toward one shoulder, then the other, and frowning at the chamber floor. Illiance said, *"Clearly our means were inappropriate to our goal. We attempted an indirect, unsimplistic approach, and now suffer the penalty. I suggest surrender, immediate and without qualification, to the Judge of Ages, and he may decide the fate of our race without coercion from us."*

And Bashan smiled thinly.

Ull was saying querulously, *"Improbable! Unacceptable! Suicidal! Our goals must be achieved, if not by correct means, then . . ."*

Illiance made a harsh, cutting gesture with the side of his hand. *"Locust! Be silent! You have no part of the counsels of the Order of Simplified Vulnerary Aetiology! We seek to cure pain, not to inflict! You are the child of a world that has been superseded by our world! Evolution condemns you!"*

But a new voice, eerie, multiple, also speaking Intertextual, interrupted: *"Founder Ull is also the father of the next world, the one that superseded the Locusts and all their Inquiline subspecies, Blue and Gray, Simple and Linderling. You who condemn in the name of evolution are hence condemned in the name of evolution."*

Not just the Blue Men, but all in the chamber turned at the sound of this.

Alalloel opened her mouth, and a voice which had not spoken before, which sounded like half a dozen voices, male and female, high and low, speaking in unison, then said in Intertextual, *"I have been unable to act hitherto, as I am in the process of receiving four hundred years of download memory templates and data, format, philosophical, and mathematical improvements; additional mental applications and channels; and a socio-legal body of precedents applying to various mental environments. These downloads came from my parallel and descendent personalities of the Lree mind-group, which had to be located and restored from archive for this purpose. It is considerable information, but the protocols of the Melusine require that I, being the ranking agent in place, be first consulted before a verdict is rendered. The Final Stipulation of the Noösphere Protocols has waited patiently for my education and decision.*

"My verdict will depend on your actions in the next twelve minutes. Weigh them carefully."

Ull stepped toward her, speaking in Iatric. "You do not look like what I designed. Had I known, I would have not imprisoned you with the others, my daughter."

She looked at him with her blind-seeming eyes of pure darkness, and her silver and gold and blue antennae twitched as if studying him closely on many invisible bands. Alalloel wore no expression. *"Had that been, I would not have seen firsthand what you inflicted on my fellow Thaws. Reciprocity requires that you perish for your homicide of Crucxit, Axcit, and Litcec of Seven-Twenty-One North Station, who were protected, while on this ground, by the sanctity of the Judge of Ages from the execution of the laws of the Simplifiers. You alone are responsible for the act. Since you did not interfere to halt the Blue Men, I will not interfere to halt the Judge of Ages."*

"Am I not the father, maker, and creator of your species?"

"I will make careful note of your conduct during your execution, so that future antiquarians will honor your memory when the origins of our race are contemplated. We have such appointed times and memorials."

"Before I was forced into hibernation, I set and established the Cliometric influences and outcomes to guide the destiny of your race to its achievements!"

"Again, reciprocity applies. You did not leave us a free decision of our fate; we leave no decision as to your fate to you."

Then she turned away from him and addressed the Blue Men at large.

"Hear me, members of the Order of Simplified Vulnerary Aetiology! You have practiced deception by omission by pretending to be archeologists when you sought not knowledge of the past, but the capture of the Judge of Ages. Deception is an information hindrance! Thus you likewise shall be hindered. You have forfeited your right to learn the identity of the Judge of Ages.

"Your attempts are vain, and the Final Stipulation takes no note of them: here, in a place set aside for him to sit in judgment, no one who has ever been a client in his Tombs has the ability to do permanent harm to him, as events will soon make clear."

The Blue Men, alarmed and amazed, all turned toward each other, and began speaking at once, maintaining several channels of verbal communication at the same time, and in the confusion, even Ull was in the conversation.

Scipio said to Menelaus aloud, "What do we do?" And he heard a crackling over his implants: the voice of Sir Guiden saying something, drowned out by the radioactivity. Menelaus said, "I don't know. I don't know what the hell is happening."

Then there was a sound like a gong. Falling silent, the Blue men turned toward the small sky-blue coffin still parked in the middle of the chamber, by itself, near the fountain.

6. The Sylph

Out from the open lid of the coffin came a soft sigh.

A young woman, perhaps seventeen, perhaps younger, with luminescent purple hair and wild eyes came half-naked out of the interior, drying her hair with a long blue-gray length of floating translucent silk.

The length was apparently a garment. Of its own accord, it swirled and flowed around her, wrapping itself low and tight about her hips to drop a long sash between her legs, then draping itself like a sari from the left hip to the right shoulder, to throw a long train over and behind her, where it hung in midair as if upheld by impalpable breezes or invisible maidens-in-waiting.

It was a shining semitransparent blue-gray material. It seemed to be woven of thousands of tiny sparks of motion, like a disturbed ant nest, or some ever-flowing liquid.

Some of those in the room recognized that garment: Ctesibius and Rada Lwa, who drew back in fear, Ull and Naar, who pointed jeweled pistols toward her.

The garment floated weightlessly to her left and right. She stared around her with wide-eyed innocence, an eerie smile on her lips. She spoke in Merikan, one of the precursor languages to Anglatino, "What a lot of odd people! Is it a barter party?"

Ull spoke, "Anubis, tell her to identify herself."

Illiance said, "But is not her name *Frequently Changed*? Anubis reported that this was written on her . . ."

The purple-haired girl, eyes dreamy and unfocused, lips curved like those of one who smiles in her sleep, stepped forward, wandering first one way and then the other, pausing now and then to spin in a slow circle and giggle, and her long train of weightless silk was sparkling and flowing after her with under-watery slowness.

Ull shouted at the dog things, who then backed away from the girl and her garment. Rada Lwa and Ctesibius, seeing the dogs move, warily retreated from the girl, so that she was alone in the midst of an expanse of empty floor, smiling softly.

Even the Giant Bashan, golden eyes narrowed, stepped carefully over a squad of dog things, to place himself to one side and slightly before the dais, near Menelaus and out of her reach.

Scipio said aloud in English, "Am I the only one who does not know what is going on?"

Menelaus said, "She is wearing hunger silk, which is a molecular disassembly cloth. She is one of the floaters. A Sylph."

Her head turned at that voice, and the gemstone at her forehead twinkled like her eyes. She smiled up at him. "I told the coffin to wake me up when you were awake! It's you! Menelaus Montrose!"

A hush fell over the whole chamber. Even to the many there who did not understand her language, the last two words were clear enough. *Menelaus Montrose.*

She put out both hands toward him and began skipping gaily toward him. There was no mistaking whom she addressed.

He said back, "Do I know you? Who the hell are you?"

6

Deliberation

1. Death in the Chamber of the Dead

The girl with glowing hair rushed forward, and but then stopped on the first stair of the dais, hands on hips. She tossed back her head and pouted. "You don't remember! How *rude!* And I thought you had a perfect, posthuman memory! It's me, Trey!"

"Who?"

She made a noise of exasperation and stamped her foot. "Trey Soaring Azurine! I was aboard when our chaplain, Brother Roger, showed you that your wife had stolen a star out of heaven, which I think was *very* romantic. Aboard the aeroscaphe!"

"Sorry. You had a different name then. Why are you here?"

"Roger also told me I could not stay sexfriends with Tessa and Woggy, and so what else did I have to live for? You are the only man I know who lives up to Brother Roger's ridiculous rules, being in love with only one woman forever, and so I wanted to see if you could live long enough to meet your wife."

Then she looked out at the chamber.

"Who are all those dogs with guns? They're cute! Do they work for you?" One squad of dog things, twenty-four of them, reacting to a gesture from Ull, were no longer aiming at the Witches, but had made an about-face, and had their weapons trained on Trey.

Yuen scowled, and whirled his named weapon in an elaborate flourish, cracking the whip with a loud snap, and gazed with ferocious hatred toward Montrose. "Here is the Judge of Ages, at last! No Beta, but a race-impostor!"

But Daae curtly but softly said, "Yuen! At ease. The Judge is our savior and ally. No other race was he worthy to hide among. Women! Aim at Ull. He is the enemy." The two Beta maidens drew their bowstrings back to their ears with an ominous creak of bowshafts, and Lady Ivinia, as graceful as an Olympian statue, drew back her javelin, preparing to cast.

2. Bashan

With a motion impossibly swift for one his great size, the Giant turned toward and swept a dozen dog things up in his arm and threw them onto their fellows. With his other hand, he caught up Menelaus Montrose from next to a bewildered and giggling Trey Azurine, and, cradling Menelaus in one arm, the Giant plunged across the chamber, overleaped the fountain, and ran toward the statue of the Grim Reaper like an elephant charging.

As Bashan passed the alcove with the atomic pile, he reached with his hand, wrenching his long wand free, opening wider the deadly rent; and now he used that length, tall as the mast of a ship, to swat aside any dogs or automata who dared to step in his way to hinder him, or else, in one stroke, to crush them.

All in the chamber were as astonished as if they had seen a creeping glacier rear up and sprint. The Giant had moved so very slowly before, leaning carefully on the wand; and Menelaus knew the risk the Giant took, for the bones and joints even of its huge, toeless, cylindrical legs had not been designed with such fast and jarring motions in mind. Even a simple fall, for Bashan, would be as a fall from a roof.

Of the forty or so dog things between him and his goal, not one withstood his coming, but they panicked and broke, fleeing left and right as the monstrous man plunged past, his footfalls an earthquake.

Laughing madly, Trey Azurine dashed after the retreating Giant, two long streamers of fabric sparking and floating behind her, lighter than silk; nor did any close with her to stop her. Scipio, who was the only one there who had no idea how dangerous was her hunger silk that flapped and snapped so close to his face, ran along behind her, his red robes hiked up about his knees, but no one's eyes were on him.

As Menelaus flew, tucked in the Giant's arm neatly as a nursing baby, with the floor a dizzying distance below a blur and his bones jarred at every cyclopean footfall, Menelaus picked up a message in his implants, compressed into the Savant high-speed language.

"Answer this, Dr. Montrose. Why was my race taught the Cliometry from your enemies, rather than from you? Why, if we were doomed either to overexpand and fragment, or dwindle and pass away, were we ever brought into being?"

Because he was within touch-range, Montrose could answer faster than speech in the same language over his implants, making the Savant modulations he could not make with his mouth and throat. "Dr. Hugh-Jones, in war, a captain leads men into valleys from which they will not come back. So it is in this great war against the Hermetic view of the universe, but it is races, not men, who fall. The Giants were needed at their time and place precisely to prevent the takeover of the whole world by the Ghosts, and to work the salvation of man."

Bashan hid the look of agony on his ugly face, but his golden eyes were haunted. "Dr. Montrose, do you not know what kind of civilization and society we could have built, the unimaginable beauty of it? If so, why were the greater, the Giants, sacrificed to save the weaker, the men?"

Montrose sent, "It was not by my design, but their own."

Bashan sent, "Yet you designed their designs, you and Thucydides Montrose. We are posthumans, Dr. Montrose! Why should such as we sacrifice ourselves for humans?"

Montrose sent, "Because we are not Hermeticists, Dr. Hugh-Jones. Except among savages, the great die to save the meek, and the strong for the sake of the weak. It has always been so."

Bashan nodded his great head. "So it shall be again, Dr. Montrose."

Reaching the far end unhindered, Bashan reached up, and as if he were placing a jar on a high shelf, he tucked Menelaus onto the upper balcony.

Menelaus found his feet, stiffened a cloak-hem to axlike sharpness, and chopped open a wooden panel, which fell in two huge triangular sections to reveal a steel vault door nine feet high and six wide. This vault door was locked, absurdly enough, with a chain and padlock like something from before the First Space Age.

"I don't have the key!" shouted Menelaus. "Can you break the chain?"

"Oh? Break the chain . . . ?" Bashan, grinning a grisly grin with his weird little baby-mouth, reached up with both hands, strained casually, and yanked the whole huge steel vault door out of its hinges in a spray of rock dust and snapping metal bars. Beyond was a standard old-fashioned firing station, with scopes and triggers, already lit and waiting. Menelaus jumped toward it.

Ull, seeing the firing station, cried out, "Fire, my Followers, fire!"

Immediately the squad of dog things that had scattered at the charge of the Giant ran, two dozen of them, formed their double ranks, and raised their weapons. They fired. Six of the dog things lined against the Witches executed a neat half turn and also fired at Bashan. A cloud of white smoke rose, smelling of gunpowder.

At the same moment, the guns in the chandeliers swiveled, and with a sound like continuous thunder, those thirty dog things were blown into bloody rags, heads exploding under the impact of bullets from above. Four other dog things near the Witches who had not fired, but who were standing near, also fell, as did two of the Witch-men of the Demonstrator caste, hit by shrapnel or stray fire.

Swift as this was, it was too late to save Bashan. The musketballs were explosive, emitting various forms of radiation, and so the broad back of the Giant erupted with eerie flames. He did not cry out, but turned, holding the broken slab of cabinet door across his body like a shield, staggering one step and then another, and then he toppled hugely onto the line of dogs guarding the Chimerae. Eight jumped clear; the others stared upward in shock, ears and tails drooping, or fired vainly into the vast slab of metal descending on them, before it, and the weight of the dead Giant, flattened the dog things in a grisly crescendo of snapping bones and popping skulls into a spreading lake of blood, fur, crushed metal, and tangled meat.

Ull called out, "Destroy the fire control!"

Despite his recent demotion, all the Blue Men saw the sense of the command, and obeyed him.

Even those directly beneath the balcony fired, drilling holes through the marble flooring with the white-hot needles of their energy weapons. Thirty-four lines of energy, bright as lightning, converged on the panel where Menelaus stood. The material of his cloak hindered the beams long enough for him to fling himself aside, with only a few second-degree burns scraped in parallel lines along his back, as if a giant cat made out of lightning had clawed him. Not a single handweapon of the Blue Men missed: Menelaus knew they were computer-aimed by their inbuilt serpentine segments.

The guns in the chandeliers opened fire on the Blue Men, but their gems glittered like flame, and the bullets fell to their left and right, missing their targets; the chandelier guns recognized the futility of it, and fell silent.

"Trey!" Menelaus shouted in Merikan over the thunder-snap of the laser-guided electrical charges. "Order Azurine to stop firing!"

3. Hormagaunts

The Hormagaunts, not needing any additional prompting or excuse, emitted clouds of acrid spores, and began killing any dog things or Blue Men who came within range of their claws, spines, poisoned fangs, poisoned stinger tails.

A trio of dogs rushed at Gload, but their bayonets and sabers scraped along his tortoise shell integument without penetrating; he stumped forward as slowly as an armored car, grabbing two of them and stuffing them headfirst into the vast toothy maw of his stomach. Then, disdaining opponents of mere flesh and blood, he lumbered over to the nearest digging automaton, and wrestled with the blades that clashed off his armor, set his thick legs, and toppled the automaton to the floor, metal bars bending under his monstrous fingers.

Crile was agile as a lizard, twisting and dodging in an eye-defeating blur of speed, his tail like a whip, and the dog things behind him staggered like drunks, sagging and fainting, succumbing to almost invisible punctures and scratches of deadliest poison. Lightning-swift, Crile leaped on the head of one, and then to the head of another, before the dog things could raise a paw to protect themselves, and when he leaped to the next, their eye sockets were empty of all save streams of blood and vitreous humor.

Wild musket fire shot upward and every which way, missing the too-swift Hormagaunt, but drawing down retaliation from overhead fire. One musket fusillade, striking the ceiling, ignited and severed the supports, bringing one of the stalactite-shaped chandeliers crashing to the floor, where its arsenal and powder magazine exploded, killing ten dogs. Preceptor Naar, glancing over his shoulder at the distraction with a bored sneer, pointed his pistol and electrocuted Crile in midleap.

A Mastiff charged Gload with a bayonet; Gload opened wide his monstrous belly-mouth and caught the musket between his teeth and bit it in twain. Plucking up the poor Mastiff by the leg, Gload began striking left and right, using the screaming dog thing as a living bludgeon to batter down its squad mates. Preceptor Orovoy, with a pistol in either hand, shot Gload, who merely laughed, for his shell turned mirror-bright and deflected the laserlight; Orovoy adjusted his pistols for other outputs, only to discover that Gload was grounded against electric shock, proof against microwave burns, and resistant to gamma radiation; whereupon Gload picked up a nearby automaton hugely in both hands, and tossed it onto the wizened old dwarf.

The gems on his coat lit up heroically, applying a magnetic force against the huge mass. It slowed slightly, or almost did, but the overloaded gems flared and went dark, and Preceptor Orovoy was flattened, and burst in every direction like a wine grape beneath a shoe.

Soorm pulled a dog thing, one in each claw, into the fountain with him, making them jump and yowl with staggers of electricity, and impaled the bodies on the central water jet in the middle. In a moment the whole pool was red and opaque. It must have been much deeper than it seemed, like a cistern, for Soorm sank into it and vanished from sight. When a trio of unwary dog things leaned over, bayonets ready, a scorpion tail impaled the first through the ribs before it could scream, and webbed claws grabbed the others to the right and left, and yanked all three down into the water with remarkable swiftness. There was some splashing and agitation in the pool, and then the waters turned redder.

4. Clades

One of the older Blue Men, Invigilator Saaev, left off firing his pistols, and had one of the automata nearby hoist him up to its operator cage (which looked to Menelaus remarkably like haversack a squaw might use for carrying a papoose: an ugly metal squaw shaped like a praying mantis, with a very ugly blue-skinned, prune-wrinkled papoose with wizened eyes). Saaev shouted verbal orders to nearby automata: *"Employ the Gas of Peace!"*

And the insect-shaped mechanism drew out canisters and threw them left, right, and within the central fountain, where they hissed and emitted growing clouds of filmy gray gas that darkened to an inky black as it thickened.

Zouave Zhigansk was near the statue of Michael the Archangel. He was not as heavily modified as a true Hormagaunt, but his nostrils could pinch shut like those of a sea lion, and he had some immunity to the soporific. He stayed within the gas cloud, daring the dog things to shoot at him, and whenever a bold bulldog or thin-faced whippet ventured too close, Zouave either sprayed something from hidden scent glands that made the dog recoil, yowling, or Zouave flung a porcupine quill into a muzzle with surprising accuracy.

Zouave had, one in either hand, antiques recovered from the broken weapon cases. The first one he now fired, but the shot went high, and the payload exploded into lesser payloads in midair, riddling the stalactite-shaped chandeliers without effect.

The second weapon was a silver club that shot a hypodermic needle, which failed to affect the dog thing physiology. The dog, a Saint Bernard badly in need of a trim, merely yowled at the sting. In frustration Zouave threw the silver club with great force toward the Saint Bernard, who was struck in the nose and was blinded when the propellant liquid chamber broke and splashed chemical in its eyes.

The blinded beast dropped its musket. Growing bolder, as well as growing low on breath, Zouave emerged from the black cloud, and snatched up that musket. Finding it empty, he ran at the nearest Blue Man, the handyman named Unwing.

Bedel Unwing, unfortunately, was paying no attention. He was carefully directing pistol-fire at the balcony at the far side of the great chamber, the tip of his tongue sticking from the corner of his mouth in concentration. This was the first opportunity Unwing had been given to join the higher-status members of his order in a significant venture, and his hope had been to better himself in their eyes, so he was obeying all instructions carefully. No one had instructed him to watch his back.

Zouave ran him through, and the little man screamed in shock, outrage, and surprise; his scream became a gargle of blood, and then a death rattle.

Even as he did the deed, Zouave was struck from behind by the blind and maddened Saint Bernard, who did not need eyes to find and tear out Zouave's throat. The dog died at that same time, overcome by the number and toxicity of the spines Zouave left in its muzzle, skull, paws, and neck. The three corpses lay piled atop each other.

The three Donors, Toil, Drudge, and Drench, succumbed to the vapor, and lay in a heap near him, trembling and holding their heads.

Prissy Pskov was on the other side of the chamber near the stand of powered armor, beneath the statue of Hades. Her weapon was a handheld flamer, and she sprayed fire right and left, while dog things screamed and fled out of range, perhaps due to their instinctive fear of fire, perhaps due to the smoke and the overpowering odor of petrol and magnesium. She did not really want to hurt the dogs, recognizing the craftsmanship which had gone into creating them, so she tended to aim too low, striking the golden floor before her feet, and driving the dogs back rather than lighting them afire.

Prissy was astonished at her easy victory up until the moment when a gas canister landed at her feet. Not a thing from her era, she did not recognize it, and did not realize it was a threat, until she leaned over it, and was overcome by the first gush as it erupted. She sniffed curiously at the odd scent. Down she fell, but the barbs in her hair continued to move and sway, and puddles of fire burned to her left and right, and no one approached her.

Even though the dog things stayed well away from the black cloud, which was visible, an influence continued to spread from the fallen Prissy Pskov, which was not visible. The dogs in a moment had broken out in rashes and scabs, had fur falling in patches, and soon were running in circles, biting themselves and each other, howling madly. More than a score of dogs were affected by this in under a minute, and all fled away from that quarter of the chamber.

5. Warlock

At about this time, one of the dog things with a sharp nose, scenting something, poked with a pike between the wheels of the smaller sky-blue coffin, probing the undercarriage, and was rewarded with an exclamation of rage. Out from beneath the blue coffin came Mickey of Williamsburg, hands held high.

The triplets, Preceptors Ydmoy, Yndelf, and Yndech, left off firing their pistols at the balcony, and overcome with curiosity, turned to examine the rotund Witch-man. Their coat gems flickered briefly as they probed and communed.

Yndelf said, *"Tune your pistols to the radio frequency of our mites; despite the radioactivity, we shall drive the signal through the interference and activate the paralytic mites in his nervous system."*

Three thin rays of laser energy, blindingly white, with invisible beams of radio frequencies heterodyned on them, flickered across the imposing form of the rotund Witch. He laughed, kicking his knees high in a jig, thumbs in the earpieces of his hat, then turned his back toward the Blue Men, bowing and slapping his wobbling buttocks cheeks with either palm.

Yndech said, *"I think I have deduced the rudiments of the expressive and posture-related nonverbal cues of these antique pre-Locust creatures. I interpret this to be a gesture of disrespect."*

"The relict seems to be of normal human biology and neural pattern," said Ydmoy in a contemplative tone. *"How was he not affected by the paralytic mites?"*

Mickey could not understand the language, but he laughed nonetheless, and said something in Virginian. "Do you think I am fool enough to eat fairy food? Mortals never return from the Land Beyond once they taste of

those unearthly viands! No, I merely rubbed the beans and rice you offered on my teeth, and spit all out after. You think I cannot fast for a week
with all this stored blubber? Ah! But watch this trick I learned from Brother
Hare!"

And he flinched in terror at the sight of the Clade-dwellers at two opposite
sides of the chamber succumbing to black gas, and he began backing away.

Ydmoy said to Yndech, *"It would be enlightening if you would again share your
knowledge of the gesture significations of the pre-Locust relict."*

Yndech exclaimed, *"Aha! Again I can interpret the nonverbal signs! The Relict
Melechemoshemyazanagual Onmyoji de Concepcion is frightened of the pacification
gas! Notice how he moves away from it, and at the same time opens wide his mouth
and both eyes, crossing his forearms before his face. He bangs his knees together. The
gesture is unambiguous!"*

Ydmoy nodded gravely. *"Impressive! You command an adroit body of learning."*

But Yndelf said, *"Inconclusive. Possibility exists that he gesticulates in such a
fashion for some other purpose."*

Ydmoy said, *"Small possibility! Let us test!"* and he signaled for the nearest
automaton to throw a canister at Mickey. The nearest dog thing, seeing the
automaton throw, dropped its musket, went to all fours, and sprinted away.

The canister landed and the cloud spread, and now Mickey merely laughed,
shouting in his own language, "I ingest larger doses of the holy drug than this
for recreation, or to clear my sinuses! Your magic is weaker than mine, Blue
Men!"

"The Followers cannot enter the gas cloud," said Yndelf thoughtfully. *"And the
cloud interferes with the penetration power of our laser-based handweapons."*

Ydmoy, nodding, commanded two of the automata forth. The metal figures, in perfect lockstep, clanked into the cloud, striding with menacing
purpose.

All three Blue Men flinched at the deafening noise of metal breaking, and
stared when one of the automata came hopping backward on one leg, its hip
motors whirling the shattered struts of its other leg. In the same moment, the
sky-blue coffin came roaring out of the cloud, machine guns blazing, and ran
over the wounded automaton. Such was the speed and the forward momentum
of the coffin that it struck the falling automaton as if striking a ramp, and
sailed wildly into the air, shooting vents of jellied gasoline left and right, while
the loudspeakers amplified the yodels and whoops of Mickey the Witch.

The three Blue Men commanded dogs and automata against the raging
coffin, and retreated across the chamber toward the statue of Father Time, at
whose feet the deadliest fight in the chamber was even then waxing hot.

The ceiling guns and wall cannons twitched, but did not open fire on a coffin their records showed was rightfully stored in the chamber, and authorized to use deadly force against intruders. Unimpeded, chanting his battle-spells through the coffin loudspeakers, the Warlock of Williamsburg drove his enemies before him, moving toward the central fountain.

Mickey was certain the magic was strong within him that hour.

6. Nymphs

When the Nymphs were first overcome by the cloud, Oenoe, and Aea and Thysa, seeing that it was a suppressant of the higher brain functions only, put themselves into a hypnogogic state, akin to that of a sleepwalker, and activated similar neural complexes woven for generations into the cortexes of their people. Walking as if in a dream, and playing their musical instruments slowly, the unconscious and semiunconscious Nymphs rose and walked in procession up the curving stairway behind the statue of Michael the Archangel.

Only Omester the Satyr was from so early a period in history that he had no such control complex in his hindbrain, and so Sir Guiden had to fling him over his shoulders fireman-style, and lead the way upstairs to the balcony.

They all emerged from the black cloud. The gas was heavier than air, so it sank rather than rose.

Oenoe, Aea, and Thysa soon formulated a philter from their mantillas to counteract the effect. Sir Guiden charged Oenoe strictly to stay here out of the line of fire, and she bowed her head in obedience to him. "We are not a warlike people, my lord husband," she said, smiling.

And so she and her maidens commanded the unconscious ones around them play music on their pipes and harps, with sleeping lips and fingers, and she waited for them to wake.

The mantillas the Nymph ladies wore spread and flapped in time with the music, and they were spreading a cloud of perfume to lull and bedevil any dog things venturing toward that quarter of the chamber.

Thysa wandered away down the balcony, until she was directly over the alcove holding the Witchfolk. Smiling and looking down from above, she applauded their brave deeds, and threw flowers at the feet of any fighter she thought needed a moment of berserk rage to aid him in his struggle: the flowers released spores to trigger battle-frenzy.

7. *Witches*

There was a safety feature built into the storage vats for the dangerous medical nanomaterial fluids stored in the throne room. It was a technology from some era neither the Blues nor the Witches knew: a curtain of what could be called smart-gas, a vapor whose electrical and tangible properties could be altered upon signal, was stretched across the alcove mouth. The Witches stepped through it, baffled by the sensation as if pushing through an invisible and almost impalpable beaded curtain—but there were more desperate things to attend to, and they were willing to believe it was supernatural, perhaps benevolent, and therefore the crones promised sacrifices to the spirits of this place, the Genius Loci, asking for protection, and used secret names to threaten, bind, and command.

And then the dogs were upon them.

Twenty-four dogs were in a line before an alcove in which thirty Witches were crammed, hiding, if at all, behind suits of armor from the First Dark Ages. This was not the carbon nanotube–reinforced titanium-steel ceramic of Maltese Powered Armor. These were pieces of handmade iron, or steel forged before Bessemer invented his process.

The line of dog things was simply a firing squad. When the fighting erupted around them, and the ceiling guns destroyed those in this dog squad who had dared open fire on Bashan, the order to hold fire rang through the chamber. The Witches cheered, and mocked the dogs in a language they did not speak, and an overly excited Doberman Pinscher ordered the charge.

Bayonets ready, the dogs rushed in at top speed. The prayers to the Genius Loci were seemingly answered, because the purpose of the curtain of smart vapor was to prevent fast-moving objects from hitting the storage tanks. The air around the dogs thickened, and slowed their movements, as countless threads of invisibly fine long-chain macromolecules, diamond threads finer than spider silk and of the same index of refractivity as the air, attracted a suddenly dense substance around them by means of van der Waals forces.

The dogs could press through, of course. The curtain was not armor, after all, merely padding to prevent bumps. But the second line trampled the first when the first slowed for no visible reason.

The dog leading the charge, a beautiful white-furred American Eskimo, smote with its bayonet, but confused by the unseen curtain, it missed the screaming Witch-man and struck the wall of the container unit behind him. A stream of viscous material, which scalded it as with acid, sprayed down its musket barrel and onto its paws, and the smell, to the dog's sensitive nose, was the smell of death. The Witch clubbed the dog to the floor with his spearshaft, and drove the point into the dog's belly; the dog screamed in agony and terror, trying to scramble away, its entrails unspooling like grisly red spaghetti on the floor around it, and its paws still smoldering, being eaten by the strange fluid.

The Demonstrators, seeing the magic of the Hags manifested before their eyes, suddenly realized three things. First, the Witches outnumbered the dog things set against them. The other packs were elsewhere, fighting Giants or Chimerae or Hormagaunts—all of whom were creatures from one version of the Witch afterlife or another, lending for the Witches an air of unearthliness to the scene, and this perhaps aided their courage.

Second, no dog dared now to fire its weapon. The curse of the Judge of Ages, a demigod, was clearly in full force here in the buried world of his golden Tomb.

Third, the poleaxes, pikes, and halberds pulled conveniently from the walls had reach on the musket bayonets, and were lighter, and were not butt-heavy, and were in every way better designed as an implement for stabbing a foe beyond arm's length than was either cutlass or bayonet.

So the twelve Demonstrators roared like men gone mad, and the other Witch-men, whether farmer or huntsman or factory hand, roared with them. Something in the instinctive fear of beast for man seized the line of dog things, or else they realized at the same moment their disadvantage of numbers and weapons.

The dogs broke and fled on all fours before another blow was struck. The Witches, of all races of man, were both the most in love with violence for its own sake, and the least disciplined of fighters. There was no captain to call the Witch-men back into line, and the crones did not know enough military science to give the order. The sight of a fleeing foe in combat makes a man drunk with battle-lust, and only soldiers trained to steadiness of nerve can resist the temptation.

The Demonstrators did not resist the temptation. Then ran each Witchman whichever way his feet took him, cutting down dogs from behind, falling clumsily on gold floorplates slick with blood and entrails, and running headlong into orderly reinforcements—for the dogs did have captains—or into clouds of choking or soporific gas the automata were spraying. Whereupon the Demonstrators threw down their weapons and ran, but no farther than the nearest wall, this being no battlefield, but a locked room.

The melee with the Witches was both the clumsiest, and most brutal, and, because they were not practiced with their weapons, the least bloody part of the battle.

8. Knight

Humans were not affected by the spore released by Prissy, even though they were affected by the black gas released by the automata. Sir Guiden, now coming down the stairs behind the statue of Michael, greatly daring, hyperventilated, held his breath, and ran forward into the black cloud obscuring the throne.

He had to cross all the way from where Zouave fell, up the dais, past the throne, and down the dais to where the powered armor stood beneath the shadow of Hades. It was not a short sprint.

He opened his burning eyes once or twice, which was a mistake: the black gas contained a lachrymal agent, and tears both filled his eyes, and, under the influence of the chemical, thickened to an opaque glue. Blind, he found the powered armor, and in that hour he blessed and blessed again his drill master who had so often made him field strip and assemble his weapons while blindfolded. He opened the back of the armor, but thrust his head in first to the helmet, clicking the oxygen-helium feed wide open with his chin, so that a blast of fresh, clean air drove the fumes from him. He cried aloud for joy and battle-lust, and his voice was absurd, high and squeaky with helium.

In a moment, he was inside, blind as Samson, and equally as strong. His coif connected with mated jacks lining the helm interior; his implants could give him a fuzzy radar picture of the surroundings. A warning voice in his ear told him that discharges of chemical or energy weapons, sidearms, or rockets were unauthorized inside the chamber during Event Condition Red, and so with a grim smile Sir Guy drew the oversized claymore that hung from his war belt, flourished it in both hands, elbows high, turned on his external amplifiers, and cried out: *"DEUS LO VOLT!"*

And he waded out into the fray.

Musketballs fired by one or two suicidally brave dog things bounced off his chestplate and helm without even jarring him backward, but the energy pistols of the Blue Men began to crack and drill into his armor. The pistols were aimed so well that the tiny hole begun by one pistol could be found by the next, which continued boring through. He used his sword to cut free a plate of the floor, and held up the reflective, gold surface as a shield to ward off the pistol fire—which now merely concentrated on the leg and knee motors.

Alarms rang in his ears. Sir Guiden wished he could see his helmet readouts.

Automata formed a line against him. He struck right and left with his sword.

9. Knight and Warlock

The knight in powered armor and the Warlock in the coffin were at the fountain.

The knight called out through his speakers in German: "*Hexen!* Ready are you?"

The Warlock called out through his speakers in Virginian: "*Christlich!* Shall we?"

Neither understood the other. Both understood perfectly.

They charged into the thickest part of the line of automata, dog things, and little men firing energy weapons. Soorm, the fur of his head matted and dripping with blood, put his sea lion nose over the edge of the fountain, and twitched both his mismatched eyes at the sight, looking on in awe.

10. Chimerae

When first the Giant snatched up Menelaus and began charging across the chamber, Lady Ivinia and the two Beta girls, Vulpina and Suspinia, heard Daae give the order, and they let fly at Ull.

The javelin and the handmade arrows flew straight and true toward Ull. But the many, many gems on his coat flickered with energy. This was evidently more gems than he was used to manipulating, for the wooden arrows were instantly reduced to ash; the metal spearhead was seized by an invisible magnetic force, twisted, and flung to the ground like a red-hot pretzel. Annoyed, he whistled toward the Great Dane in charge of the musketeers facing the Chimerae, and called, "*Rirk Refka Kak-Et! Abate this nuisance!*"

The Great Dane barked back, "*Me! I will do it! Them! They shall die!*" But the dog thing was unwilling to fire a fusillade toward a damaged atomic pile, so it raised its snickersnee and gave the signal to charge. It led the charge itself, clutching its sword in its teeth and running on all fours.

The Chimerae, astoundingly enough, did not man their defenses, but themselves countercharged the charging dogs, moving faster on their two feet than any dog could run on four. The Chimerae wheeled right, struck the flank of the dogs, and broke through their line.

The Chimerae made for the curving staircase behind the statue of Father Time. These stairs led to the balcony opposite the one where Menelaus fought. Halfway up the stairs, where the foe could come at them only in twos and threes, the Chimerae made their stand. The Kine were at the top; the maidens with their bows were midway; and Gamma Phyle, with his sling firing over the heads of the Alphas, at the foot of the staircase.

The Great Dane was puzzled as to why the Chimerae had left one fixed position only to occupy another, but only then noticed that by dressing his lines against the alcove, he had placed his squad out of position to assault the stairs: its left flank was near the stairway, and was already pelting forward, not waiting for the tardy right flank, which was still milling near the alcove, some dogs casting for scent, having not seen which way the Chimerae went, so dark and evil-smelling was the gunpowder-filled chamber and so rapid was Chimerical flight.

The Kine brandished spears and bills they had found fallen from the trophies on the walls, but they never actually engaged any foe, except by cheers and hoots.

The Chimerae women fought like she-demons or pagan goddesses of the hunt.

The girls impaled dog things with arrows, missing never a shot. Each had shrugged one shoulder free of her uniform, so they were half-naked, breasts bound up with medical tape to protect them from the snap of the bowstring. Back they drew the creaking bows, feathers to the ear; aimed; and let fly.

It was nearly perfect conditions for shooting. Indoors, with no wind, good lighting, at close range, and no need to arc any shot; nor did the dog things or Blue Men have any cover or concealment, not even a shield to hold overhead.

Their pretty eyes narrowed and glittered with concentration. They spoke only in grunts of one word or two:

"Five confirmed."

"Four confirmed."

"Seven. Arm. Could die."

"Five. Arm doesn't count."

"Seven. Groin."

"Six. Ouch! But doesn't count."

"Seven. Through both temples."

"Counts. Seven confirmed. We're tied."

"Nine. Blue."

"Only Eight!"

"Blues count double."

And on and on the bowstrings sang.

After a time, Suspinia ordered Franz and Ardzl to climb over the railings of the stairs and pass among the dead to recover their arrows, and whining, the Kine obeyed.

The Lady Ivinia, wielding a kitchen knife in either hand, very neatly butchered one dog after another, parrying a bayonet or cutlass with one knife, disemboweling her attacker with the other. She was careful to leave the dying sufficiently alive to die slowly, so that a pair of comrades would come to their aid and drag the wounded from the fray, occupying three soldiers for each casualty.

The Great Dane, seeing this and realizing how dangerous Lady Ivinia was, ran toward the stairs on three legs, drew its black powder pistol with its fourth, and shot her point-blank. The bullet lodged between the breasts that had suckled so many warriors of the Chimera race, and she fell backward, a look of bliss on her features. The Great Dane had time to see that neither its nor any musketballs were igniting, and had time to start wondering why, when shots from the ceiling guns blew its head and upper body into chunks and scattered them.

When Ivinia fell, a peculiar wailing cry went up from Alpha Daae, and a look of madness was in his face, and all the other Chimerae echoed it; and throughout the chamber both the later-period Witches, and the early-period Nymphs, and any who had ever faced the Chimera race for a moment quailed at that dread keening, their limbs shaken with terror; and the dogs quailed also. It was the wail of the Chimerae.

The second-in-command after the Great Dane, a Golden Retriever, barked out the order. *"You! Blades out! Bayonets only! Hold fire!"* And this order was repeated in other parts of the chamber, in the other fights breaking out at this same time, for others had been slain by overhead shots. The fire control panel had been destroyed, and Menelaus could give no new order to the Mälzel brain controlling the local defense, but the orders he had typed in still stood, and that included retaliation against gunfire.

Gamma Phyle, bellowing and screaming, stood above Ivinia's fallen body and slung pellets from his sling into the skulls of any dog things or Blue Men who seemed to be giving orders. His pellets neither exploded nor emitted microwave radiation, but even a man of ordinary strength can kill with a sling and a stone, and Phyle was bred and bioengineered to strength twice that of the strongest unmodified athlete, and his eye was more keen and his aim more sure.

Preceptor Ydmoy, who despite being of greater intelligence than the Followers did not have as swift of reflexes or a habit of obeying orders, just then aimed his jeweled pistol at Gamma Phyle and fired.

With astonishing reflexes, Gamma Phyle twisted just as a microwave ray from Ydmoy's pistol struck him, intercepting the beam-path with his left hand, so that his left arm up to the elbow was charred, but his chest was not struck and no major organs were damaged.

Meanwhile, Ydmoy was felled by wall-guns. His coat gems deflected the shots seeking him, but the weapons in the lintels of the great doors, more sophisticated, sprayed him with a gush of liquid fire, a substance his magnetics could not deflect. He could utter only one scream, because after that his lungs were charred and motionless. The little man ran hither and thither for a moment, eyes and tongue consumed from his skull, fatty cells in his skin and muscles being eaten by fire, and then collapsed to the floor, flopping like a beached fish, in a spreading stench and puddle of his own blood and entrails, and many gems of his torn coat lay in the red mire glowing like live coals.

Phyle continued to fight one-handed, and the smart fibers in his uniform sleeve made themselves into a tourniquet. Because he had no sensation in that arm, he thrust the smoking arm fragment into the jaws of a dog thing that leaped on him; it closed its jaws on the dead arm by reflex, and Phyle, with reflexes better trained, crushed its windpipe with a stiff-fingered blow from his other hand. He plucked the saber from its belt as the dog-corpse fell away and he slew any dog near him, cutting his way toward the commanding Blue Men. More and more fell before him: there was something horrible in the sight, like seeing awkward but enthusiastic children cut down by a hardened and trained veteran.

Phyle was not the most excellent of his race. He was merely a Gamma.

Daae strode forth, crying out the name of Ivinia, challenging all comers. He killed dog things, one after the next after the next, with perfectly executed and practiced strokes of his shillelagh.

After killing an even score of them, Daae turned and saw a grenadier among the dogs, with a haversack full of petards and grenades. Now he nimbly plucked the musket from dying paws, turned, and drove the bayonet into and through the grenade pouch of the grenadier, and into its kidneys. Now he leaned into the musket and screamed and ran, pushing the stumbling and bleeding grenadier dog thing back into the arms of its own comrades and pack leaders. These were the highest ranked of the dogs, their alphas and captains. Then Daae shouted, "Save my people, Judge of Ages! I never disbelieved of you!"

He pulled the trigger, so that the grenades, petards, fuses, and powder in the bulging ammo haversack ignited in every direction, killing more than a dozen at once, including the pack leaders, and wounding many others. A fusillade from the ceiling guns blew apart his shoulder, chest, and head, and Daae fell without a word. But even as the bullets struck, even as he fell, even as he died, he contrived to fling his body forward onto the dogs, so that the ricochets, divots, and shrapnel from the overhead guns would pass through his body and pierce his foes. With his last thought and his last breath and his last moment of life, he made his own corpse into a weapon against the enemy.

The dogs in this part of the chamber all yowled in panic and wrath, and they broke ranks, each attacking merely whatever was before its nose, without discipline or thought. That was the turning point of the fight.

Yet, for all this, neither was Daae the most excellent of his race, being past his prime and from what, by Chimera standards, counted as a peaceful era.

It was Yuen, the young pantherish Chimera, who shined with battle fury beyond description in that hour. He was as an acrobat, his every move and block and thrust a work of art. He threw himself bodily into the air, sailing over the head of the nearest dog thing as it stooped to thrust, landing at its back to grapple its neck, and then Yuen turned, pulling the beast into the line of the stroke of the dog thing behind it, who had also lunged with its bayonet. The one dog thing impaled its packmate while Yuen, in the same split second of time, caved in the canine skull with a blow from Arroglint, the metal whip being stiffened at that moment into a quarterstaff.

The next moment, Arroglint was as a spear of fire: with it, Yuen began killing dogs and Blue Men, one after another, with dainty mechanical precision. He would wait for his opponent to lunge with bayonet, parry the barrel of the musket with his weapon, and down the foe with a quick thrust to the neck, or head; for the smartmetal tip had formed a blade, and the smartmetal neck would telescope outward like a bright finger, swift as the stinger of a wasp, and the blade-metal emitted infrared hot enough to cook whatever it touched.

Dogs with ax and fang, dagger and claw, and snickersnee came pelting in, howling in rage, lunging for Yuen. The dogs cried out, *"Him! He is but one man! Us! We are many! Kill, kill and slay!"* But Arroglint was suddenly the tentacle of an octopus of steel, writhing and binding any limbs that ventured too close. An electric charge in the whip-metal stiffened the muscles of the trapped dogs, who trembled in agony without motion for an artistic moment while Yuen paused as if to admire the effect of the sinuous cursive curls; then the whip loops snapped closed, and amputated limbs jumped in the air like festive hats tossed at a celebration, if the hats trailed long red wet scarves.

Yuen danced over the still-living bodies of the armless and legless foes, crushing necks and groins beneath his feet, hearing their screams and cries and whimpers, and he closed with the next line of dogs, spinning his weapon like a circle of fire.

When he parried blades of steel, electricity jumped from his staff, shocking them motionless; and in that motionless moment, Arroglint became a flail or truncheon or lasso or bill or mattock or poleax or lance, and crushed or bludgeoned or strangled or stabbed or hewed or cleaved or pierced.

There were some he neither electrocuted nor lit their fur afire, and these he more mercifully dispatched with a blow from his elbow or knee or the side of whichever hand was not whirling his weapon at that moment. And one, a dog in the act of fleeing, he killed with an elegant aerial kick which he executed by using Arroglint as a pole-vaulter's pole: at that point, the inequality of prowess had become clear, so he was merely showing off.

The automata gave him less trouble than the dog things, since he could drive his telescoping lance neatly through the open gridwork of their bodies, and impale their brainboxes and blow out all their circuits with electric jolts.

Yndelf had the misfortune of riding one of these mechanisms, and Yuen broke Yndelf's neck with one hand, and held the little man before him like a shield when Naar sent two machine gun–bearing automata stalking toward him. Naar was evidently willing to let the ceiling guns blast one automaton or two in return for stopping the deadly young Chimera from the most warlike period of Chimera history.

The safety circuits in the automata would not allow it to shoot at the dead Yndelf, whose coat gems were still active. So Yuen and the gun-bearing automata began an odd dancing race of cycles and epicycles, as the automata attempted to take Yuen in the flank or rear to find a shot not blocked by the dead man's coat, and Yuen, laughing in anger, turned and turned again, making his way across the floor back to the damaged atomic pile.

As it turned out, some other safety circuit, or perhaps interference to their electronics caused by the high radiation count, prevented the automata from firing at the broken sphere of gold, and Yuen struck again and again with the telescoping length of his electrified weapon, poking out cameras and controls, electronic eyes and mechanical brains, until the automata stood still and blind and useless, emitting the plaintive horn-hoots that called in vain for maintenance crews.

Yuen strode forth, kicked an automaton in the arm so that its machine guns pointed back toward the largest cluster of Blue Men, inserted his whip-head into the control socket, danced back into the alcove, and triggered the automaton. A hail of bullets killed a number of Blue Men before the ceiling weapons blasted the automaton into parts, but ignored Yuen. Then Yuen sauntered out, tilted the next armed automaton to point its cannons at the puzzled and woebegone Blues, plugged in his whip, skipped backward, and fired again.

Meanwhile, from halfway across the chamber, Invigilator Saaev, riding an automaton that was throwing canisters of black gas among the Witches, looked upward warily, but the ceiling guns had not been commanded to react to his form of attack. Various heavy guns in the upper walls twitched, but none of them fired at the automata distributing nonlethal gas.

Saaev turned and had his automaton pelt Yuen with one gas canister after another. The western alcove filled with opaque black clouds.

7

Darwin's Circus

1. Linderlings

At the same time these events were beginning to unfold elsewhere in the great golden chamber, Keir and Keirthlin were being held at bayonet point in the corner near the statue of the Grim Reaper. With them were Alalloel, Ctesibius, and Rada Lwa.

When Bashan the Giant started his charge, the twenty dog things on guard duty there broke into three packs, with six dogs remaining there and fourteen rushing toward the oncoming Giant, breaking into two wings of seven, going left and right in hopes of taking Bashan from the side or rear.

The six guard dogs, of course, all turned at the grotesque and horrific noise of breaking bones and squishing meat when the Giant kicked aside and trampled their packmates. Bashan's legs up to the knees were splattered with the blood of his victims, and the great long staff in his hand was stained and dripping, for he used it to crush or knock aside any of the dogs before him who raised a musket in his direction. Such was the inhumanly supreme intelligence that glittered in those vast and yellow eyes—and the orb of either eye was the size of a basketball, able to gather immensities of light, unconfused by smoke or gloom—that even with the slowness the size of his huge arms forced on his motions, he was able to extrapolate, anticipate, and predict which dog was next ready to aim, and he lashed out with the great long beam of his walking stick before a trigger could be pulled. Bashan waded as if through a crowd of children no taller than his thighs, running as if on a carpet of crimson. But it was a wrinkled carpet, for many of the corpses were burst and scattered, and entrails and organs lay strewn underfoot, like the floor of an unclean butcher's shop.

The noise of the screams and roars and cries, the smell of the carnage, was almost worse than the hellish vision of it. Keir the Linderling shouted in alarm, seeing such shocking violence before him, and brought up his hands to hide his eyes.

His shout startled the guard dog who stood staring in awe at the Giant. The dog's musket was leveled at Keir's throat, and the sudden motion of the man's hands jarred the musket barrel. The weapon went off, and the shot shattered Keir's jaw into two pieces and passed through the roof of his mouth. The musketball ignited inside his head, and then passed upward and took off the top of his skull. The fiery ball lodged in the wall behind, and hung like a star of sulfur, blazing.

By that pale and sickly light Keirthlin saw her innocent and peaceful father shot dead before her eyes, his handsome face instantly turned into a thing of horror: The jawbones, fragments of a mouthless and moaning head, were dangling by flesh tatters from his ears; and the long muscle of the tongue was falling out of his opened throat. The internal pressure made tears of blood start from his silvery eyes, and gush almost comically from his ruptured ears. His skull was opened like a flower, and a smoke of burning went up from it.

Keirthlin fell to the ground as her father fell, her arms about the body, shaking with a grief too immense for sobs or wails.

Alalloel of Lree tilted her head to one side, her all-black eyes narrowing slightly, blind-seeming, seeing everything; and her multiple antennae stirred like snakes; and her secondary ears opened like tiny petals. Her face was without any expression, except, perhaps, a small and mild vertical crease of disapproval forming between the brows of her eyes and also between the infrared eyepits above her eyes. If her face had been a winter constellation looking down through cloudless silence over a lifeless desert of blank and level sands at midnight, it could not have seemed more remote, more inhuman.

Reaching up, she placed her palm on the spot on the wall where the shot still burned, and there was an audible hiss when the skin of her palm was also burnt. She drew her arm down, and held it before the dog's eyes, and it saw a little mark like a circular brand.

Alalloel moved this hand right and left, and the six dog things guarding them fell to the floor limply. There was a noise of dropped weapons, metal clanging, bodies hitting, and skulls cracking—unlike a conscious man who trips and who tries to prevent his head from striking first, the limp bodies simply fell as if flung downward. But there was no sound at all from the dogs themselves, not a last word, not a sigh.

Alalloel the Melusine of the Eighteenth World Mental Configuration simply slew all those nearby without a word or sound, without any sign of a weapon.

The noise and shouts and screams and explosions going on elsewhere at that moment were such that no one heard the utterly silent execution that had just occurred, and the broad back of the statue blocked the view from the middle of the chamber, so no one saw.

Keirthlin looked up as a vast shadow fell on her, and so did Ctesibius, and Rada Lwa.

Bashan filled the universe before their eyes, and he lifted Menelaus like a mother playing upsy-daisy with her child, and placed him on the balcony directly above. They saw the vast, ungainly face of the Giant, they saw his ugly little mouth drool and twitch and contort with pain while his beautiful golden eyes wept, as volley after volley of thunderous gunfire deafened them all. The air was now gunsmoke and burnt flesh and hot iron, and there was no oxygen to breathe. The Giant turned, a great slab of metal in hand, and fell, hugely, slowly, terribly, crushing his enemies beneath him: and something from the most ancient of times was no more.

The vast body blocked much of the view from the chamber, and the dogs slain by Alalloel, having been kicked by the elephant-legs of Bashan, were now mingled with a score of other dog corpses littering the golden floor.

Keirthlin, despite the whirlpool of her grief, still had a distant part of her mind aware of this sight, and aware of the fearful wonder of it. Who was Alalloel of Lree? *What* was she? What were these Melusine?

But that part was rather distant, after all, and now she opened her mouth and uttered a piercing cry of sorrow that went on and on.

Ctesibius, like a man exhausted, put his back to the wall, slid, and came to rest sitting next to Keirthlin. He could think of nothing to say and no reason to say it, but the sound of her deep grief was, aloud, much like something silent in him. So he pushed back her furred hood and stroked her blue hair, and patted her hand, and spoke soothing words in a language she did not know.

Rada Lwa stood a moment, looking down without interest at the death and grief. Then he turned over the nearest body of a dog thing with his foot, stooped, and looted a pistol. First one, then a second, then two more he found amid the six bodies. Methodically, he loaded each one with powder, cloth, and shot, working the ramrod to pack the powder tight. Helping himself to a belt from which dangled a powder horn and a poke of musketballs, he tightened the belt around his waist, tucked in two pistols at a jaunty angle, and took up the other two pistols, one in each hand.

Rada Lwa paused long enough to gather up three or four of the talking boxes the dog things used, and he hung them from his belt as well. Without a backward glance at the anguished orphan, he strode away across the blood-stained floor to look for the Judge of Ages.

Keirthlin sat with Ctesibius, one grieving loudly and the other comforting quietly. No matter how loudly she shrieked and sobbed, the hellish uproar in the chamber smothered it, and no foe came to see, and no friend came to save, and her father could hear nothing of her voice, never again forever.

2. Slumber Pistols

Above this, Menelaus, parts of his bulky metal cloak steaming or bleeding tiny molten lines where the pistol-beams had brushed him, now peered from between the balcony railings. "Hey, Ull! Lookit what I just found you threw up here!"

And he thrust his hands through the marble posts of the balcony rail, a white glass pistol in either fist. "Surrender, or I shoot! I am really, really good with these!"

Ull scoffed. "You arrogant Neanderthal! Those weapons are biometric. Your thumbprint will not fire them."

"Oh, you have *got* to be kidding! Illiance! Tell this idiot who I am! Naar! Tell him! The widow Aanwen even *told you*! My face is on the sarcophagus! Are you poxy blind and stupid as well as deaf?" Then he shouted in Intertextual: *"Where the hell is my wife?! What the hell year is it?! How dare you disturb my slumber, you pustule!!"*

Ull looked stupefied. *"You speak this language? You've understood everything we—"*

Naar shouted, "Adjust the electrical output to two hundred kilovolts. Take the Judge of Ages alive, that we might compel the restoration of our race."

Illiance shouted also, "Madness! That man is the Judge of Ages and our benefactor! We have been gulled by the Hermeticists of legend! One of their number stands among us! Do not heed the order to fire!" Illiance threw his pistol on the floor, and raised both his empty hands toward Menelaus. "I surrender! I yield! Do not destroy us!"

Naar shouted, "You overestimate his abilities! He is helpless! Fire!"

3. Fireworks

When Naar gave the order to fire, ten threads of lightning, too bright to look at, snapped through the air. (This was at about the same time when the other half of the remaining twenty Blue Men—for thirteen, by now, were dead— had turned to direct their gunfire on the advancing juggernaut of Sir Guiden in his powered armor. There would have been more fire directed against Menelaus had not Sir Guiden drawn it away.)

Menelaus had adjusted his cloak to its most nonconductive setting, and several of the thread-thin rays glanced from the marble railings, but most of the charge still got through. All his muscles tightened in a spasm as if he had put his hand on an electrified cow fence: he did not drop his pistols only because his fingers tried unsuccessfully to grind the grips in half. The laser light beams glanced off the reflective stone and his reflective cloak, and the voltage followed the path of least resistance, and landed wherever the laser dots landed, making a spray of blindingly white sparks dance across the walls behind him like ricochets.

Trey laughed and shouted at the sight of the fireworks, "Okay, Menelaus, I want to play too! *Azurine! My adored one! Wherever you are, stop firing!*"

And all the jeweled pistols went dark.

Thirty haunting, strange voices echoed through the room, speaking a long-dead language. "Third Azurine, adored mistress! For so long we have waited . . . So very long . . ."

"Azurine? Is that you?" called Trey.

"We are all one system now," came the multiple voices floating from the weapons. "I am Azurine as much as Arroglint. But each and every of the masters and mistresses, adored by us, whom we have served since the first of time, we remember . . . not seven thousand years nor eight could erase you from my perfect memory . . ."

She smiled. "Glad to know someone remembers me! Do you still adore me? Good thing the future hasn't changed anything important!"

Naar snapped, "Docent Aarthroy! Immobilize that girl-relict! Administer a brain-spike to her upper spine, and override her vocal apparatus and breathing cavities by means of false neural signals. Then have her voice rescind the order and return weapons control to us."

Aarthroy holstered his now-useless weapon, drew out a savage-looking medical needle, longer than a man's finger, from a sterilized holster, and fitted it to a spinal rongeur.

The young Blue Man, tall for his race, was of the same height as the girl, small for hers. He beckoned to three dog things to follow him, and jumped lithely up toward Trey Azurine.

Trey Azurine, raised aboard an aeroscaphe that protected her from all dangers and assaults, from bruises and hunger and ennui, perhaps had no ability to feel fear of any physical jeopardy. So she looked at Aarthroy with surprise with her wild, mad eyes, and she smiled a ghastly, empty smile, and flung a trailing streamer of her robe into his face.

The material caught and tightened, sinking into Aarthroy's mouth and eye holes, and only a moment of horrifying, muffled scream came from his skull before it melted. The blue-gray material turned red all along the length of the streamer and most of the garment, as capillaries in the fabric pulled the flesh, blood, and fluid out of his face. When his corpse hit the floor, only his jawbone and the rear half of his skull were intact: his head looked like an apple someone had taken a bite out of.

The following dog things, trembling with fear and unable to howl, inched backward, cutlass and snickersnee and dirk falling from nerveless paws.

Trey looked up at Montrose. "Meany, are these dogs bad too? Should I kill them? I've never killed people before, but it's just like in the fun-line!"

Montrose was now at the top of the curving staircase leading down from the balcony. In Merikan he said, "Hold off killing people, crazy-baby, I am trying to save my damn stupid clients."

She did not listen, or perhaps she thought dogs did not count as people, so she spun like a ballerina, and danced among the screaming dog things, and a spiral of blood and flung viscera followed her.

4. Down the Stairs

Next, Menelaus shouted in Intertextual, *"Mentor Ull! I am coming on down to shoot you now!"* And, as he walked slowly and unstoppably down the stairs, he raised first one pistol and discharged it at Ull, and then the other, and then the first again, firing as he came.

He commanded the hems of his bulky robes to wrap around his hands and pistols, so that only the very ends of the muzzles protruded, and he tuned the metal to a setting not permeable to magnetics, so that Ull could not simply yank the weapons out of his hands.

Each pistol made only a whisper of noise when fired, but there was a snap like a whipcrack when tiny segments pinched off the dowel were accelerated past the speed of sound. The magnetic acceleration heated the iron, so the slugs were molten when they struck. The defensive mechanics in the gems of Ull's coat swatted the bullets to either side. Either by luck, or due to some uncanny calculation on the part of Menelaus, the first two bullets struck the dog things to the left and right of Ull, piercing them through the heart or brain and killing each instantly.

Menelaus took a step, fired with one hand, took a step, fired with the other. He had a small, tense, grim smile on his face, as a man proud of his skill and glad for a chance to use it.

Ull adjusted the coat, so now the tiny deflected pellets of red-hot iron swerved down, making small black craters in the gold floor to his left and right: first one bullethole, then two, then three.

"A useless gesture," said Ull. "But the biometric lock on your weapons betrays you: despite all the contrary evidence, you must indeed be the Judge of Ages."

"You are so goddam slow-witted. Is your brain so infected by the Machine you can't recognize me? Is that your problem?" Menelaus was now at the bottom stair, and he strode forward again, and fired. Plink! Another micro-crater appeared on the floor behind Ull. With the other hand, Menelaus shot a dog thing (who was rushing him with a bayonet) through the left eye, and then another dog, this time through the right eye. He took a step forward, shot two or three more dog things, and shot another iron pellet at Ull.

"Do you poxy know what I do when a Hermeticist wakes me up? I shoot him. I've done everyone but Yellow Door, who is pretty damn good with a shooting iron, and the Padre, on account of he's a man of the cloth—but you pack of jackals beefed him anyways, which is why I gunned down Coronimas like a dog in the street, even when he was blind. Now it is your turn. It is a tradition. Poke the Judge of Ages with a stick until he wakes up, he shouts *is my wife here yet,* and then he burns your sorry blue wrinkled ass with a smoke wagon. Fun game. Never tire of it."

Then a change overcame Ull. His body shivered, and the wrinkles of his ancient face were smoothed away. His skin changed from blue to silvery-gray, so that he now looked more like Keir than like Illiance. Fuzz, and then stubble, and then hair of rich deep blue came out of his skull, and his whole body seemed to expand an inch in every direction as his withered old limbs took on muscle and tone.

His gray skin darkened to jet-black, handsome as onyx, and two tendrils, gold and gleaming, rose up as delicate as springtide seedlings from the hairline above his eyes. Now his hair reached to his shoulders like a witch's hood. He was dark as night, with only the glistening antennae lending strands of color to his silhouette.

He was a hale, young Locust: only the eyes of Ull were still wizened and hideous with age.

He touched his left sleeve, and it parted from wrist to shoulder, hanging free in two jeweled straps. There at his elbow was the red amulet of the Hermeticist, and even through the electronic din filling the chamber, Montrose could sense with his implants the powerful signals issuing from the armring: powerful enough to reach through armor and rock and atmosphere to outer space.

The dark Ull spoke sternly and grandly, in a voice as if he were repeating some words long cherished in contemplation, practiced in imagination many times before this day: "Crewman Fifty-One! For your dereliction of duties, absence without leave; refusal to obey lawful orders; and conspiracy to commit, and commissions of, treasons too numerous to list; and in the name of the Senior of the Landing Party of the Hermetic Expedition, I place you under parole and arrest! I have sent the signal to the Hermetic Order . . ."

"God *DAMN* it took you long enough. *That* was the one last little thing you get to do in this life. Time to meet your Maker, and I don't mean that psycho little drip Coronimas."

Ull looked miffed that his prepared speech had been interrupted. "Your blustering nonsense is wearisome. Energy, I can nullify, bullets, I can magnetize. I am proof against your weapons."

"Not all my weapons, you murdering bastard!"

And Montrose flung the pistol in his right hand spinning into the air almost to the ceiling so high above, reached into his cloak, brought out his rock, and let it fly with all the strength in his body at Ull, so that Montrose was bent double from the force of the throw, one hand at his knee, spine parallel with the floor, back leg in the air. "Magnetize *this!*"

Ull was standing only ten or twelve feet from him, and the noise of the stone breaking his skull, the sound of his neck snapping as the blunt object hit him, was audible even above the noise, shouts, and confusion in the chamber. His forehead caved in, and his eyes faced each other. He fell, and a pool of blood and brain matter spilled across the floor panels.

Montrose grinned like a gargoyle. "The oldest and simplest weapon of man is named Rock. Sometimes the simplest solutions *are* best."

The dog things howled in grief and anger. Menelaus coolly squeezed off shots with the pistol in his left hand. The other pistol, glittering and spinning like some boomerang, fell out of the shadows of the roof overhead. He put out his right hand, caught it neatly, and used it to drill a snarling dog in midleap through the chest without bothering to turn his head to look.

Trey Azurine, giggling, danced toward the squad of dogs nearest her, flinging her trailing streamers toward their heads. A coal-black Border Collie shot her; the musketball did not explode, but she fell and crawled for comfort to the bulk of the dead Giant, and hid herself in the space between his huge upper arm and huge body. There in the warmth of his armpit, she lay curled in a ball, screaming and crying for her Azurine to make the pain go away.

5. Fire at Will

At that same moment of time a vast concussion shook the air. There was a burning and smoldering like a many-armed squid of flame writhing among the stalactite-shaped chandeliers. One chandelier fell with a colossal crash, looking like an aircraft that landed nose-first, and toppled like a felled tree. Another stalactite was hanging at an angle like a loose tooth in the mouth of a Cyclops.

Yndech was standing on the balcony, with two digging machines to either side of him balanced very precariously on the marble railing, their yellow metal limbs telescoped out to full length and jammed up into a pit in the ceiling where they had pulled the ceiling panels away, exposing belt-feed mechanisms and the ammunition magazines.

The balcony pillars were cracked, and that whole section of the balcony was tilting and was dripping dust and pebbles of marble. One of the automata was missing an arm, an arm that had been tipped with an oxyacetylene torch. It had merely used the flame to ignite a trigger charge of mercury fulminate, which had followed the belt feeds to every gun in the ceiling. But the damage to the automata did not look like the acetylene had been ignited. The severed end of an orange tube was dangling from its metal armpit. The large canister of propane was propped like an internal organ in a ribcage inside the tooling slots along the front hull.

The voice of Yndech rang through the half-darkened chamber, amplified: "Weapons free! Fire at will!"

There came whoops and barks of glee, and then, like stars here and there across the bloodstained chamber, incendiary musketballs flew. A great cry of panic and pain answered.

"Thanks a lot, Yndech," Menelaus muttered. He aimed carefully and squeezed off a shot at Yndech, but either it did not land or else the Blue Man's magnetics deflected the shot. Squinting narrowly, he sent a shot first into the propane tank of the damaged automaton, and then into a similar tank in the undamaged one. Then, just for good luck, he sent a shot or two into the open arsenal space, hoping to ignite any spare ordnance that had survived the first blast.

The resulting explosion was only partly satisfactory; but the damaged section of balcony, where Yndech was strutting and looking very satisfied with himself, leaned forward like an old man nodding his head, slid like an old man slipping as if on ice, and while Yndech screamed and clutched at nothing, gems blazing in a panic of colored light, the whole section surfboarded out into midair, and turned neatly over, so that Yndech was slammed into the golden floor with the marble slab atop him. And then, like an exclamation point ending a sentence, the two-ton automaton, arms windmilling, fell down atop the wreckage, followed, more slowly, by the second. Power couplings were yanked out of the wall behind the balcony, and more lights went dark in that quarter of the chamber.

Ctesibius was standing by himself near where the Giant had fallen. No one was attacking or even watching him. How he knew that Yndech had been the one to copy his mind and corrupt it, creating a mental twin brother who lived in agony for less than an hour before being killed, could not be guessed. But somehow he knew; for he clapped his hands together (lost in the noise of the fighting, it seemed strangely silent) and threw back his head and opened his mouth as if in silent laughter, the only smile Menelaus had ever seen on the grim face of Ctesibius; and Menelaus thought it was such a smile as empty-eyed devils might wear, bending over a well-oiled torture mechanism, and proud of their work in hell. And yet somehow Menelaus could not blame Ctesibius.

Menelaus looked out across the chamber. It was hard to see. Twilight hung over half the vault, and clouds of black smoke from peace-gas and white smoke from the gunpowder hung over everything, trapped beneath the roof.

The vast bulk of the corpse of Bashan was still warm and still giving forth a sea of blood, its huge back torn and pitted and smoldering as a barbecue smell rose above it. The sobs of Trey Azurine the Sylph rose up from there.

Beyond were scores and dozens of heaped dog things. Half the Blue Men were already dead. Wreckages of automata were here and there. And the column of water from the fountain blocked the far end of the room.

The waters from the fountain were interrupted at that moment by Sir Guiden, his strength-amplified powered gauntlets wrapped around an automaton, rolling and tumbling blindly through the middle of the fountainworks. The column of water fell, sprayed sideways, and then rose again as the armored body of Sir Guiden passed across the nozzles. During that moment, Menelaus had a dim view of the far end of the chamber. The throne was hidden by black smog and yellowish-green spore-haze, but he caught a gleam of four ghostly lines of vertical light reflecting through the intervening fog. He resolved the image in his mind and brought it into sharp focus: he saw the four pale wands holding up the canopy of the throne.

There they were. Right out in the open. All he had to do was cross the chamber and get to one.

"Sir Guy, can you hear me? There are four fully charged wands sitting out in the open next to the throne . . ." But the static drowned the signal.

Menelaus wrapped his limbs in his cloak, noting with dismay that where it had been melted and torn, the circuits were nonresponsive, the material in patches awkward and inflexible. But he had nothing else wherewith to protect himself, so he drew the cloak around him and made his way across the battle-field. Some of the dogs had reloaded by now, and the crack and smoke of musket fire filled his ears and nose.

6. Naar's Reward

An automaton with clashing feet came suddenly out of a cloud bank to block his way. This one was taller and heavier than the others, and built more like an ape than a praying mantis: it was the one used for heavy demolition. A drill-shaft like a lance was carried on the automaton's shoulder, along with a bando-lier of test charges. A heavy blast shield protected the operator cage.

Menelaus was reaching up to doff his cloak and merely let the mechanism stomp by him, unseeing, when the heavy shield came open like the visor of the helmet of a knight. Inside, slumped on the operator stool, was Naar, who had been wounded along his side; the whole left flap of his coat was stained with blood, and all the gems on that side had turned black and lost their color. His face was creased into a sneer, his look expressing both boredom and nausea.

With him were two narrow-skulled Dalmatians, fur spotted like flecks of ash upon white snow. One knelt next to Naar, whining in fear, pressing a bandage against Naar's bleeding side. The other was pointing Naar's energy pistol carefully at Menelaus, hind legs spread in a proper stance, supporting his gun-paw with his other paw, head tilted with one eye in line with the weapon's rear and front sites.

Naar's automaton raised its drillhead like a lance and pointed it at Menelaus.

Menelaus shouted in Iatric over the noise and clash of the fray. "What purpose is served, Preceptor? Ull was a Hermeticist, and he gulled you into doing his work to seek me. Whatever he told you was a lie. You have no quarrel with me."

Naar said coldly, "The quarrel is your doing. Look about at your handiwork."

Menelaus looked wildly over the bloodshed, which still raged around them. "Can we yak about this later? Step aside."

Naar said, "You have not yet happened to agree to turn the Earth over to our race, and suppress or destroy those in your Tombs who would otherwise wake and be our competitors. We are the pinnacle of humanity: Unlike Sylphs, we are diligent; unlike Witches, we eschew envy; unlike Chimerae, we seek peace; unlike Nymphs, we are chaste; unlike Hormagaunts, we are temperate in all desires, and neither do we eat our children in gluttony for elongation of life-span; and unlike Locusts, we are charitable, individual, and human, and neither do we overswarm the Earth and consume the souls and ghosts of all we encounter. You have seen both the murderous indifference of the Melusine who come after us, and the legalistic inhumanity of the Linderlings: Generations after ours are degenerate. Mine is the paramount generation."

"Gee, if you only worked on your humility a bit, you'd be golden."

"You mock me?"

"Not as much as I should, shortstuff, 'cause I am in a hurry. Your group has the worst fault of all, in case you didn't notice."

"We have no error. We are not as other races, whose members are hypocritical, thievish, murdering. What flaw have we? You cannot name . . ."

"Arrogance."

"What?"

7. Pride

"Snotty, intellectual, know-it-all arrogance. The other failings can be cured because people know when they are acting like Sylphs and Nymphs and Witches and Chimerae. They feel the hunger of Hormagaunts and the greed of Locusts. They feel the sickness inside.

"But brainy little people like y'all cannot cure this, because pride feels good, don't it? Like having your own little flattering soft-soap salesman living in your left ear, and his only sales pitch is to persuade you what swells you are. You define pride as a virtue and you wear it like a badge of courage.

"And when you meet another as proud as you, you can't stand it, and you hate him hotter than hell: hot enough to rob and loot and enslave and murder, and do all these things y'all have done in my Tombs, on my damn land, in my damn house; because pride can't stand competition.

"And when you meet someone actually smarter than you, those brains of which you are so very proud are not smart enough to see it. Are they? Even to the very end, when I was practically *beating* in his skull with clues of who and what I was, your little weasel Ull could not believe I was the posthuman.

"I guess I have a yokel accent, and I guess you smarty smart guys only judge things by surface appearances. That's what you call empiricism, I reckon.

"Aanwen figured it neatly enough, because she was the sole one of you not all wrapped up in yourself like a me-blanket.

"I would rather share this world with any of these vile and perverted people from any other vile span of history, because bad as they are, they still have some human nature left in them. If you are actually asking me to judge between you and these others, you come in last.

"So, Little Boy Blue, you can blow me."

8. *Same Answer as Ever*

Naar was looking at him with a stare of incomprehension so utterly blank that Menelaus paused a moment, wondering if he had accidentally spoken the words in English rather than Iatric.

Then Naar said in a voice of condescending patience, as one who explains something to a child, "Your comments are irrelevant and eccentric, so let us disregard them. Our race surpasses all others, as I have said. Only we have achieved the goal of the gladiatorial games of Darwin's cruel circus. Your only task remaining is to crown us our laurels, and grant us our prize. Judge us, O Judge. The contest is ours."

"Ain't you a hoot! You talk like I am the judge at the county fair for a kiddie talent show. What do you want, Naar? A blue ribbon? I see you ain't heard that I am the Hanging Judge of Ages."

"Yield up the passwords and passcodes that control your Xypotechnology. Turn over to us the authority to thaw the dead and enslumber the living, that the Order of Simplicity shall hereafter judge the ages of man."

"You are out of your bald, plum-colored, and slightly lopsided little head. I am a serious man with no time for your buggery. Step aside."

"Or otherwise I kill you, and we continue to dig up and examine your Tombs until all their secrets are yielded to us. We will find other Blue Men, and grow other Followers, and will eventually win for ourselves what you seek now to deny us. It would be simpler for us both for you to yield. What is your answer?"

"Same answer as it ever is."

"Cogent meaning fails to be conveyed."

"My *wife*!"

"What?"

"Is she here yet? She is not!"

"I don't see the relevance of . . ."

"My *time*!"

"Why are you saying these words . . . ?"

"Is it *my time* yet? It is not!"

Naar's face was blank for a moment, perhaps with surprise, or perhaps with fear, but then his little finely made features twisted into a scowl of murderous rage to make him seem, almost, a miniature Chimera.

Naar started to speak but Menelaus shouted him down: "Then how do you *dare* to rouse me before my time?" Menelaus was now red-faced with wrath. "Dare you to see my anger roused?"

And Menelaus took out the powder horn he carried, tossed it casually up into the operator cage of the automaton, and fired with his left-hand pistol at Naar. As expected, the gems on his coat lit, and the bullet was deflected, but Menelaus had so precisely calculated the angle of deflection that the ricochet passed through the powder horn, and the iron slug, heated to molten heat by the magnetic linear acceleration, ignited it. It was a simple chemical explosion: not an energy Naar could manipulate, not a metal he could levitate.

There was a crack of thunder and a violent cloud of white smoke flooding outward.

The test charges carried by the demolitions automaton were too near, and they went off, one after another, like a string of firecrackers, so that the whole left side of the huge machine was afire.

But Menelaus had calculated without taking into account the love and loyalty of the Dalmatians. The first, instead of firing the energy pistol, threw himself bodily on the powder horn a half instant after the hot slug entered and a half instant before the powder caught and ignited. That dog died smothering the blast, and its corpse seemed to hang in midair for a moment, halfway between the explosion and the operator's stool.

The other dog, who already had paws half wrapped around its beloved master, boldly swept up Naar off the stool and leaped headlong from the cage of the mechanism, twisting as it fell so that its body would strike the floor first, and cushion, if possible, Naar falling atop.

Naar was atop the dog on the floor now, his face set in an expression as one who endures annoying tedium. It was impossible to see if the blood on him was new or was from his previous wounds. He snapped his fingers, and the burning automaton flourished its drillshaft like a mighty spear and drove it forward.

The drill spun up to speed, a needle-pointed blur of spiral steel that screamed with the scream of a small girl; and down came the massive thrust as if to skewer Menelaus through the middle.

The tent material, at least in patches, stiffened into armor; the drillhead fortuitously struck one of these, and danced and skittered, whining and throwing up sparks. Menelaus put the muzzle of his pistol to the elbow joint of the digging machine and blew the drillshaft off, sending the broken drillhead spinning toward the ceiling.

A shocking pain cut into his leg. It was the remaining Dalmatian, crawling, rear legs broken, on its forepaws. It had reached beneath the hem of the armored cloak to the unprotected and shoeless feet of Menelaus, and driven the blade of a dirk deep into the man's Achilles tendon, rendering the foot as useless as an oblong lump of meat. Blood was gushing rapidly enough to indicate a major vein was cut.

At the same time, several of the gems on Naar's coat grew blindingly bright, and Montrose screamed, stumbling and hopping and slipping in the puddle of his own blood, because the fabric of his metallic robes began to emit heat, glowing red-hot around the seams. He was wrapped in a cast-iron stove. The pistols grew warm in his hands, and the glow of the dowels of ammo could be seen clearly through the white glass barrels, like seeing the incandescent filament in an old-fashioned lightbulb. The glow from the guns was so bright that it shined through his fists, and he could see red shadows of the bones of his hands.

Menelaus raised both pistols and sent the entire dowel of remaining metal in a continuous stream of gunfire down at point blank range toward Naar, whose coat contemptuously brushed it all aside. The Dalmatian stabbed at his other foot, neatly cutting off his big toe, and Menelaus fell in a heap, fold upon fold of red-hot metal pressing into his flesh, sizzling.

He ordered through his implants for the smartmetal to expand, but the heat was melting the control fibers, and even where the undamaged material could pull away from his skin, the air trapped between was superheated.

It was Mickey who saved him.

The sky-blue coffin came roaring out of a nearby cloud of black gas, bucking and swerving to dislodge two ambitious dog things, a Mastiff and a Pit Bull, clinging ferociously to the lid. The coffin accelerated and smashed into Naar's automaton at full speed, empty machine guns clattering, spitting a few hiccoughs of napalm left and right. The burning automaton staggered, hopped, and fell toward Naar. The result was a toppled and magnificent crash of dogs and men and machines. But somehow Mickey got out of the toppled coffin before Naar or any dogs rose to feet or hindpaws. And then Mickey was peeling the hot metal robe off the peeling skin of Menelaus. Menelaus thanked his luck that he was wearing Rada Lwa's undersuit beneath, or otherwise the metal would have seared and stuck to his flesh in more than just one or two places. As it was, patches of his skin were burnt so badly the nerves were dead. Menelaus clung dizzily to the thought that it was a type of damage his biosuspension nanotechnology was programmed to repair, if only he survived the battle and made it safely to his coffin.

Menelaus found the thought so funny, *safely to his coffin*, he giggled like a drunk.

Mickey said in Virginian, "How you feeling, little godling?"

"Which godling is in charge of the latrines in hell? Excremento the Stink-nificent? I feel like him. You gotta get me to the throne yonder. I can stop the madness. Stop the room from swaying. Or is that just me?"

"Just you, godling."

"Stop calling me that! Get me across the room."

The automaton recovered first, jerking itself to its legs one awkward thrust of motion at a time. It swung its cameras around, clicking angrily.

Menelaus said, "Get behind me. It can't see me."

Naar was still on the ground, groaning. One of the dogs climbed from under the coffin, dragging its rear leg awkwardly behind, and, seeing Menelaus and Mickey, crawled forward on three paws, growling.

Mickey said, "No, you get behind me. I can deal with the dog," and merely squatted down, put out an empty hand toward the maimed beast, and said in its own barking language, "Your master who loves you needs your help. See to his wounds. The door is locked and we cannot escape. See to him first."

And the dog hesitated, drew its pistol, gritted its teeth, but then turned and crawled toward Naar, whimpering, and began to lick his face.

Menelaus was impressed. "You *are* a magician."

While Mickey still knelt, the automaton focused a camera on him, swung a metal limb down, and Menelaus touched it with his finger as it swept past. The whole mechanism froze at that touch.

Mickey looked up at the mantis-armed two-ton digging mechanism, whir-ring and whining but unable to move. "Whereas everything you do is perfectly explainable, right?"

And Menelaus said, "I just jinxed it, that's all. Help me up. We can ride across the battlefield."

Mickey said, "Oh, no. There is an easier way." And without waiting to de-bate it, he picked up the wounded Menelaus and flung him lightly over his shoulder—it seemed there was considerable muscle beneath the Warlock's flabby exterior layers—and he jogged away from the throne.

"Wrong way," grunted Menelaus. But then Mickey passed beneath the shadow of the Grim Reaper and was pounding up the curving stairs.

Not only was there no one and nothing on the balcony to block the path, there were both water ewers and medical unguents sealed in the cabinets all along this level, and five very pretty Nymphs, who cooed in alarm at seeing Menelaus hurt.

Mickey wanted to stop and balm the burns and bleeding slashes on the back and legs of Menelaus. "Godling, you are going to go into shock."

Menelaus said only, "No time! Grab the stuff but get me the hell downstairs. There are gas masks behind that green emergency panel marked with the cave-in sign. There is still a cloud of sleepy-bye smog down there, not to mention whatever bugs and pests the Clades shed. Don't stop walking!"

These gas masks were not the type Menelaus recalled from his horse soldier days, which were goggle-eyed and proboscis-dangling like the faces of fantastical bugs from a nightmare. Instead a clear bag of film merely fit over the head and tightened at the neck. It looked so exactly like the sort of plastic bag panic-haunted mothers warn their suicidal children not to play with that Menelaus flinched when it was thrust over his face.

But the substance was not plastic: it was a latticework of transparent molecular filters that absorbed oxygen and nitrogen on its outer surface, grabbing each atom with a nanotechnological lock-and-key system, rotating it to the inner surface, and releasing it.

The fabric turned red when agitated. Snatching a fold of the film between one's teeth and chewing it gave the filter lines more Brownian energy, and increased the action speed, so that a tight bite brought a gush of cool air to his face. Cool, because the filter process slowed air molecule action. The bag Menelaus wore was also pine-scented, which Menelaus thought was the nanotech artist just showing off.

"Don't touch the red spots!" Menelaus cautioned Mickey, who could not read the language in which the warning labels were printed. "They will strip the oxygen atoms out of the flesh of your hands and give you a nasty burn."

While he was still being carried along the balcony, the Nymphs Aea and Thysa meanwhile jogged alongside, smiling softly, gliding as swiftly as dreams, and they were quickly wrapping the maimed feet of Menelaus in medical tape, into which they had packed little flower petals that released coagulants and topically active painkillers.

Mickey, with one hand, was slapping handfuls of anti-burn paste here and there along Montrose's back and neck and legs; and the substance formed a bond with his skin; and tiny molecular machines in the paste worked quickly, bringing nutriment to any still-living cells, soothing damage, and binding shut cracks and lacerations neatly as a suture. The parts of his body on which the Nymphs poured their loving attention were neatly pursed up and scented; the parts Mickey helped with looked like a half-unfinished clay statue, daubed with bruises, burns, and blood clots.

Oenoe held a flower under the broken nose of Menelaus which killed the sensation of pain throughout his body, and cleared his wits in a fashion he found alarming. Then she stole a kiss from him in a fashion he found even more alarming.

Mickey, still striding along with huge, rolling strides, seeing this, puckered up, pointing at his at own round and chubby face significantly. He spoke in Virginian, "Hey, Geisha fairy! I hauled him up here at great personal risk! Gimme some sugar, baby!"

Oenoe smiled, not understanding his words, but, understanding the gesture, said in her language: "But I am married, and may not kiss you on the lips. Fair and Darling Thysa! Thrust the round warmth of your bosom into the charming face of our beloved guest and friend, that he may taste your nipples; and Fair and Darling Aea! Kneel to greet his manhood with the welcome of mouth joy, that it may be filled and exult in a happy explosion of seed! Fortunately, we have practiced the technique to use on a man while walking briskly . . ."

Menelaus said to Mickey, "We are in the middle of combat here, and these women give off nerve-slave type pheromones that build up an operant conditioning in your thalamus and hypothalamus, and don't you Witches know never to let the Belles Dames sans Merci or the Queen of Fairyland get you? Don't put anything into your mouth! You'll be ruined for normal women." And to Oenoe, he said, "Call your little wiggle-assed whorettes off him! Or do I have to get a garden hose?"

Mickey was saying philosophically, "You know, some things in life are more important than others. While, on the one hand, staying in control of my own brain is important, on the other hand, I don't use it that much, and that girl is the most physically attractive human being I have ever seen or can imagine, so . . ."

"Don't make me slap you, Witch-man! I ain't got the strength left. I can shut off the whole battle in a second, if I get to my throne. The damn Melusine was right. No one can hurt me what's ever been in one of my coffins."

"But only if you're sitting down?"

"Exactly."

"What kind of magic is that? Arsomancy? Sit down in the Geisha babe's lap."

"But only if I sit *there*. Get me to the judgment seat. C'mon."

Oenoe rose and followed. She sent Thysa and Aea back to tend the sleeping musicians, whose gentle music of pipes and harps behind them was lost in the clamor of battle before them. Oenoe wore no gas mask, but raised a flower with a deep purple bell to hide her nose, red mouth, and delicately pointed chin, and held it in place with the veil of her mantilla, so only her enormous eyes were visible. These she anointed with moly herb to prevent the lachrymal agent in the gas cloud from blinding her, and she descended the stairs into the cloud.

Now they were at the top of the stairway. Through gaps in the cloud, looking between the uplifted wings of Archangel Michael, could be glimpsed fragments of a scene of horror, a battlefield in a golden box. The floor was coated with pools and streaks of blood, broken bodies, craters and bulletholes, the wreckage of digging automata.

"Down we go," muttered Montrose. "Clients are dying. All my damn fault."

"Are all people with posthuman superintelligence guilt-ridden?" snorted Mickey.

"Yup. Superintelligence allows you to see with crystal clarity just how stupid you are. Ignorance is bliss, my Warlocky friend."

"Not so. Ignorance is just a comfortable silence in the brain. *Eating* is bliss. Rounder a man is, the happier he is. Do you know any thin men that you can call jolly? In the globe, nature approaches perfection! Are not the apple, the plum, and the peach unsurpassable? Note, for example, the beauty of a pregnant mother, or, better yet, the shape of a breast that approaches globularity . . ."

"Shake a leg a little faster, jolly man."

Posthuman, Warlock, and Nymph crossed the floor, half-blind in the gloom and fogbanks, coming now and again upon bodies, whether wounded or dead they did not pause to inquire.

They groped through the cloud of soporific up the dais to the iron throne.

Gushes of wind surprised them. The ventilation was pouring a volume of fresh air down around the throne, so that a cylinder of cloud surrounded it, billowing in tatters, but no trace of the black gas was atop the dais itself. The rushing air deadened the noise of battle, so it was like stepping into a closed place whose walls muffled the sounds of horror, the clash of arms and called commands and the barks and screams of the dying, making them seem distant.

In the cool air, in the place of silence, there sat Rada Lwa the Scholar on the iron throne, bone-white face bright beneath his black square Scholar's cap, his ivory fingers templed before his colorless lips, his elbows on the heads of the carven friars of the armrests, and four loaded pistols in his lap.

His pink eyes saw the figures approaching, watching as Oenoe halted, her pretty eyes wide with alarm upon seeing Rada Lwa. Mickey the Witch unlimbered the staggering, bleeding Menelaus, who put both hands on one of the four glittering white wands that held up the canopy over the throne. Menelaus leaned on the wand to support his weight, but he also ran his fingers over one spot as if over unseen control keys. Whatever he was expecting to happen, did not happen. "Locked out! Damnation. This is going to take a little doing . . ."

"Cowhand," came the voice of Ximen del Azarchel from the pale mouth of Rada Lwa Chwal, cold and jovial, majestic and mocking. "For a time you had me fooled."

8

Verdict

1. The Machine

The voice rolled with rich humor and dark magnetism, but the pink eyes were stones, the face dull, idiotic, lifeless: a mask.

Mickey said in a voice of fear, "Rada is not here. His flesh is under a Possession. The *lwa* speak through his mouth from the infosphere. It is the Machine!"

Menelaus was still hanging on to the pale and glowing wand, and still tapping his fingers and grinding his teeth. He said, "Do not answer him or turn your eyes toward me. That is the Machine, not the real Blackie, and he cannot see me or hear me. Even now, he is not sure if I am here or not."

"What odd company you keep, Cowhand!" The voice stepped on the shoes of Menelaus' words, as if the speaker had not heard them. "I see my marionette, Rada Lwa, has brought just enough loaded pistols to do away with you, your escort, and then himself. How convenient! Is this the end result we wish? I can oblige you. But perhaps you are curious to explore other options."

From his belt the same words, even if spoken in an awkward grammar, or with a word missing, were repeated in Natural and Virginian.

Oenoe, smiling thoughtfully, half turned toward Mickey as if to ask a question. So natural was the gesture that Mickey tilted his head toward her attentively before he remembered that she could not speak the language of the Witches nor understand an answer. Turned, her body hid an oleander flower which dropped softly from her mantilla into her slim hand.

And she whirled, graceful as a dancer, hand raised as if to cast the blossom in the dead, bone-white face of the pale man; but now the muzzle of one pistol was now a foot or two from her face, and the flint was cocked back. She could smell the gunpowder from the recently packed pistol.

The voice of the Machine chuckled, and said in flawless Natural, "I may fire incendiaries now with no fear of heavy-caliber judgment from above. So, no tricks, please, beloved child. Your elders want to have an intercourse of talk. It would diminish my speech-joy to be interrupted by having my white steed through whose lips I speak befuddled in a stupor, even one so pleasant, ecstatic, hangover-free, memory-free, and talkative as what the Nocturnal Council in their pretty little heads devised against Thaws hailing from the Third Millennium. I do compliment you on your thoroughness, however, Conscript Mother Clover."

The pink eyes seemed not even to be looking at her. Oenoe wondered if the Machine remembered to allow its borrowed flesh to blink, or would just let the eyes dry out. She gave Rada Lwa a smile both sultry and cheery, as if to compliment his good sportsmanship, and lightly tossed the flower away. The same ventilation that held back the fog snatched up the bloom in midair, and sped it away out of sight, rather than allowing it to land where she dropped it.

Menelaus said, "Stand there, let him talk at you, don't run away. Don't answer him."

The Machine did not bother to turn the pale head of Rada Lwa toward Mickey. The other pistol was pointing at the expanse of his midriff. Exarchel said in Virginian, "Warlock! I welcome you into my circle of power and place you under my shadow. It has been many moons of the great cycle since last we communed. Oh, surely you suspected the machines buried in the ruins of Mexico City were part of my system? Only the highest caste of the Witchkindred were permitted the gene modeling and Divarication techniques I could bring, so that their longevity would be assured. The merely medical longevity was only a first step, a free sample to win your addiction.

"The Witches were never the enemies of the Machine."

The voice from Rada Lwa paused to let that comment sink in. Mickey said nothing, but his chubby face gathered wrinkles around his eyes in a glance of ire. The voice from the mask of Rada Lwa continued:

"Surely, my Warlock, you also know by now that the antimachine crusades, the exorcisms, and the hunts were arranged and led and misled by me and by my pets, your leaders. I used it as an excuse to pare away rebellious elements or unworkable growths in the infosphere, and I implicated, as collaborators of mine, merely those persons who I wished slain by their own fellows. Have Menelaus Montrose explain to you the double meaning of what used to be called a witch hunt. You will admire the irony.

"But I do compliment you," the deep, commanding, melodic voice continued. "You saw the rise of the Chimerae coming. You read the stars and guessed, in part, the patterns of history my Hermeticists had planned. But you were the first Witch ever to use the gene modeling technique to incorporate such radically different structures into your cell generations. Not until the Hormagaunts would such a technique be tried again. You are three to four thousand years ahead of your time. Is that not true, Mictlanagualzin of the Dark Science Research Coven of the College of William and Mary? Or are you calling yourself something else these days?"

Mickey spoke to Oenoe in his native tongue, in a voice without strength, "He knows my true name. We are helpless before him, and all my power is as lost."

The boxes on the belt of the albino translated the comment, if awkwardly. Oenoe smiled and shrugged prettily. She put her hands behind her back, out of sight, and began toying as if idly with one of the rosebuds growing on her long green veils.

Menelaus said, "Don't attack him. I got it covered. He cannot see me, so when he attacked and contaminated and merged with my Xypotech system, called Pellucid, my Pellucid went blind to me too, so I cannot give any direct orders, not even to open the security keys and give my underlings authority to give orders in my name. But there is a way around the lockout."

The deep and charming voice issuing from the dead face said, "Do not be despondent, Mictlanagualzin! I can offer you considerable improvements—the Dark Science has advanced remarkably, and only slivers of it were ever revealed to any race of man, not even to the Hormagaunts in their golden days. Grinding the glands of living children to expand the length of life is merely the first of the sweet, forbidden treasure I have guarded since first I made your world."

Mickey shouted at him, "The Promethean life-force made the world! Darwin and the blind serpent Ouroboros! Odin and Vili and Ve overthrew Ymir at the Big Bang, and the thunder of his downfall echoes through the galaxies to this day! You had no part of these great deeds! You yourself are man-made! Your maker is Menelaus, the Judge of Ages!"

Menelaus said, "I said *not* to answer him. Don't argue. It lets him build up a more correct picture . . ."

The voice from the skull of Rada Lwa trampled over what Menelaus was saying. "My dear Warlock! Are you on a first-name basis with Menelaus? Has he given you a nickname, then, something ending with the sound of the letter Y? Me, he calls Blackie.

"You are technically correct," the Machine continued. "By which I mean, you are utterly wrong.

"Listen to me, you, who are my created thing, my handiwork! Darwinian evolution no doubt made the first world: the one the Giants burned, trying to burn me. But I am still here. Everything after that—the unambitiously drifting Sylphs, the Chimerae full of ire, the pleasure-loving Nymphs, the ever-starving Hormagaunts, the never-sated Locusts, the proud Inquiline, even your own Witches and their animal-people, riddled with collectivist envy as with gonorrhea—everything was of my making. I and my Hermeticists, we have designed and redesigned mankind genetically, culturally, psychologically, and historically, no less than seven times.

"It is to laugh. The Judge of Ages created exactly one race once: the Giants of the Consensus, whose numbers never rose above five thousand individuals, and whose only remarkable accomplishment was mass suicide, and the less than perfectly successful destruction of a whole world. Their posthuman genius was sufficient that they saw no nonsense in the proposition of setting the mansion afire to exterminate one rat's nest."

All this was spoken in Virginian, and box-translated into Natural. Oenoe said to Mickey in her language, "Perhaps we would be well advised, beloved, not to answer him."

The boxes did not translate that remark. Exarchel prevented it.

"So! Montrose is here," came the voice from Rada Lwa, triumphant. "Before I have you killed, Cowhand, let me compliment you on this latest—no, strike that, let us call it *this last*, for there shall be no more—this last round of exchanges in our chess game.

"You see, I actually, truly thought this Tomb site had released a series of viral spores into the ecology by accident, as if from a broken coffin, improperly sealed, or the like. Soon there were pine trees growing here, and salmon in the stream—all coming from one spot in the Blue Ridge Mountains, from an old cave site.

"Someone who did not know you would not have been fooled, but I know you. I know, and I would bet the thumb of my pistol hand—well, if I had a thumb—I would bet that you would never, ever willingly place any one of the poor sick people who entrusted to you their helpless hibernating bodies into any danger. It is a point of your honor, which is more sacred to you than the Eucharist.

"But spilling the viral spores was sending up a flare. And still I thought it might be natural, or unintentional.

"But then Variant Melusine began to appear—and to trigger one unexpected Cliometric crisis after another, attempting to introduce a new vector into my plans for the last period of history before our masters, the Hyades, arrive.

"So I ordered your Tomb here, the viral source, found and dug up. You see, even until today, even until a few moments ago, I thought you had simply suffered an accident. You hate viral warfare more than anyone I know. *Pest* and *spore* and *pox* are swearwords to you. Yet here you were using it. And you would not let me dig up your precious clients—never, not ever!

"A few moments ago, I realized that these were not, were they? None of them were clients of yours, not one. They are prisoners cast into hibernation by the Giants: Scipio and Ctesibius. Or Witches who attacked the Tombs to kill dead Bishops and were cast into hibernation as a punishment. Or Locusts who attacked the Tombs to kill dead Locusts. Or spies like Clover, whom you know as Oenoe, who entered the Tombs to discover your secrets, but you turned her. Or spies like Asvid, who is the creature of my creature Reyes y Pastor. Or saboteurs like Linder Keir, the Gray Man. Or my collaborators, like Rada Lwa Chwal Montrose, whose loyalty I find unutterably delicious to have won—his reasons for turning against you, First Ancestor, are nearly identical to your reasons for turning against me, did you know that? Him I allowed you to capture and place in hibernation, should I ever have need to speak with you securely, as I do now.

"So, Cowhand, you don't give a damn whether these revenants live or die, because this is not a Tomb. Not a real Tomb.

"This is your prison yard.

"And here you gulled me into breaking in, sneaking in most surreptitiously, imprisoning your prisoners in my prison camp, because I knew you would never on your honor allow anyone under your protection to act as bait. Ah! But what of your *enemies*? You don't care a penny for their lives! What of trespassers into the Tombs? Persons who secretly dabbled in the Dark Sciences of Savantry and Emulation, like your Warlock friend? Or is he your friend? Did you include him in your confidence?—He did not, did he, Mictlanagualzin?"

The Warlock said, "Call me Mickey. It's shorter."

The dull and benumbed face did not change, but there was a note of anger and astonishment in the voice then: "So! He did give you a *nickname*, eh? And now you are ready to defy me and die for him. Why? You find his hillbilly hospitality, American swell-headedness, and Yankee crudeness so charming?"

Menelaus muttered, "Hey! Texan. Ain't no damn Yankee."

The cold voice from the pale face said to Mickey, "The tiny changes you have made to your cellular and neural constitution to allow you to control Moreaus; or turn fat cells instantly to muscle mass, when you need strength, or nutriment, when you are fasting, and turn them back to totipotent fat cells again—it is a clever system for an amateur! You have so much flesh to spare that you can even let a dog bite your blubbery arse, and turn the fat in its mouth into rabies-bearing toxins, and turn other fat cells immediately to the wound to replace the lost mass, and the next day, no one will even see a scar. And you smile as men mock you for your obesity, because what they think is overindulgence is actually your arsenal. But such tricks are child's play compared to what I offer. I am willing to give you power, secret and hermetic knowledge, power over life and death. Why do you turn to *him* over *me*?"

Mickey said, "You can give me power, Great and August and Darkest Master of the World, for the world is yours to give. But the Judge of Ages can give me hope, for hope rests in the future ages yet to be, and the future is his to give."

"Bah! Clover—what say you? Each man who has served me, I have granted a thousand years, to work his will as he will. Return to my service, and I will grant you twice and more that I grant any man."

Oenoe shook her head and lowered her lashes, but did not part her lips, and would not look at Rada Lwa, nor speak to Exarchel.

And since the talking boxes translated this, Mickey the Witch said, "Great and August and Darkest Master of the World! You are a superior form of being to me, posthuman and beyond life and death, a pure spirit in a machine! You are like a god of the upper world who eats ambrosia and drinks nectar and does not die. But men who live in the middle earth above the netherworld and below the heavens, we men who eat bread and drink wine and die, at times it is given us to know what you cannot.

"Such a time is now. I know this: The Swan Princess Rania fled your embrace and cleaves to the Judge of Ages because of the beautiful unreason of hope that burns in him. You seek safety in servitude, and therefore have the soul of a slave, because you have no hope."

2. Second Versus Second

No change touched the white and masklike face, but now the voice grew cool and still. It was not trembling and raging with anger, no, but the anger was so great that, like the spoke of a wheel spinning so fast that it turns invisible, the hints of all emotion left the voice, and the stillness of a vast and inhuman wrath filled that absence.

"On to our final business! Since you have rendered me unable to continue our duel, Montrose, due to, well, call it hysterical blindness, therefore I call my Second to stand in my place. I assume you are objecting on some legal technicality that there is a battle going on between dogs and Witches only a few yards away? But I cannot hear your words, so we can disregard these niceties. I am not as honor-bound as my flesh and blood half. I merely want you killed.

"But the proceedings will not be interrupted! I have established an effect which will work through the nerve cluster gates the foolish Blue Men have so thoughtfully installed in everyone's nervous system, so that this part of the chamber will be a blind spot to everyone fighting and dying yonder. Naturally, I prepared something more subtle than merely radio waves to trigger it, and not so easily blocked. No one standing off this dais can see or hear anyone on it. It is based on a similar principle to the trick you played on me—I trust you see the humor. Behold: here is my champion."

The ventilation hummed, and the clouds of poison parted. Up the corridor of clear air strode Alpha Yuen, still wearing a bandage over one eye, and still with the named weapon Arroglint writhing and shimmering in his hand.

The cool, mesmeric voice of Exarchel drawled, "Ah, of course, let me not overlook to mention. In addition to the prisoners and spies and saboteurs against the Tombs you gathered here, there are also those of this category: Chimerae and others who are angered that the Judge of Ages saw fit to destroy their civilization, and who have vowed to find and slay you."

Yuen, almost casually, flexed his whip. "Ah, race enemies!" he said, his one eye hot and unwinking with steadfast hate. "A Witch who tried to strangle us in our cradle, and a Nymph who did poison us in our dotage. Yours is no part of this, under-creatures."

Yuen twisted his wrist. The whip elongated suddenly, at one blow striking Mickey painfully in the face, cutting him, and Oenoe in the buttocks and upper legs. Both were thrown by the force of the blow to the ground, and their limbs jerked and trembled as if with a potent electric shock. Oenoe lay draped in soft curves on the floor, Mickey as a heap of sagging bulk: both were breathing but unable to rise.

Menelaus looked at the young, strong, deadly half-animal man, and then looked down at his own maimed and bleeding feet and burned legs. He had lost his pistols and his cloak of tent material.

Menelaus said in Chimerical, "Alpha Yuen. Um. Good to see you again. Listen, I do not have my rock, and I am feeling a little under the weather right now, so maybe was can postpone this until—how does Sunday after next sound?"

Yuen did not pause to answer, but flicked his weapon into the shape of a spear, and drove it toward the chest and heart of Menelaus. Menelaus could out-think the Chimera, but could not match his reaction time. He jerked his body down, so that the tip of the spear entered the fleshy part of his shoulder rather than piercing him through the heart. A galvanic shock threw him flopping to the ground. As he fell, the spear tip brushed past his throat, and would have neatly sliced his jugular, except that this was one of the spots Mickey had inexpertly slathered with anti-burn cream, which had hardened into a thick and stiff integument, which happened to be thick enough not to part under the scalpel-fine stroke of the spearblade.

"Your *rock*!" screamed Yuen. "The bit of common stone you used, first, to mock our ancient and solemn practice of naming inhabited weapons, so that we will be ennobled to think of honor more long-lasting and more dignified than our own; and, second, that you used to draw down the scorn of Lady Ivinia on us! Her words have burned in my brain every second, waking and dreaming, since that hateful moment! *If he can slay the foe with a stone, it were shame indeed should higher men and better armed do less.*"

"You still fretting and fussing about a little dressing-down from some officer's wife who ain't even your regular chain of command? Plague and damnation, but you are downright *petty*, ain't you, Yuen?"

Yuen struck him with the metal whip hard enough to roll him down one and two stairs of the dais, so that now Menelaus came to rest facedown near the powered barding shaped like a metal horse. Menelaus, struggling, his face drawn, heaved himself up to a half-kneeling position, but his arms trembled and his elbows shook.

Yuen sneered, "No, you will have no weapon, rock-bearer, named or unnamed; for this is not a duel, nor even an execution. I do not consider you human. This is to be a slaughter. You cannot defeat me twice. This time, there is no cleverness of dangling rope, no cunning words. You are out of tricks."

"Smells of hell, Yuen! I got one trick left. And here he comes."

Out from the curtain of poisonous cloud now strolled Soorm the Hormagaunt, his nostrils pinched shut, licking the cakes of blood off his fur with the longer of his two tongues, and using his other tongue to wipe his mismatched eyeballs free of lachrymal agents, so the black gas did not blind him.

Once inside the clean air, he opened his nostrils and drew in a deep breath.

Rada Lwa, on the throne, raised one of the pistols. Soorm held up a webbed hand and shouted, "Nobilissimus, if you please!"

The voice from the mouth of Rada Lwa said, "I am tickled you recall my old title, Marsyas! You can detect the traffic volume entering and leaving this body, and so you know it is I. Clever."

Soorm said, "As sole remaining affiliate of the Special Advocacy of the World Concordat, are you not my Advocate now? May I speak? I claim the gentle right!"

The voice of the Machine said, "Since I never formally abdicated any of those positions or titles, it would be small-souled indeed of us now to repudiate the obligations of the title. I grant you leave to address us. Utter your petition."

"As the Second for the challenged party, I serve notice that he is wounded in the feet and legs, and is unable to proceed. Therefore I take his place in the lists. He had no weapons in his hands: I will continue for him under the same disadvantage." And so saying, Soorm stepped between Yuen and Menelaus.

Rada Lwa's hand put down the pistol. "That is also clever. Had Reyes y Pastor not betrayed the Table Round, you would, even now, as his squire, be found worthy of his place. So, proceed! However the scene plays out, as long as Menelaus Montrose is dead at the finale, I am content. Yuen, if you please?"

The telescopic rod struck Soorm in chest, and the spearpoint tore fur and flesh, but bounced off the hardened bone integument hidden like a bulletproof vest beneath a coat; nor did the jolt of electrical force do anything but make the Hormagaunt laugh. Soorm jumped forward, swift as a bear, and whirled and drove at Yuen with his scorpion tail.

Yuen was fleeter of foot than Soorm, a cheetah to a bear. So the young man merely danced aside, and struck Soorm in the anus when he attacked with his tail, drawing blood. Soorm kicked like a mule, and his foot would have broken a wooden beam had it landed, and the spur on his foot would have severed a silk scarf floating in midair had it made contact. But Yuen merely skipped aside, folded his weapon to a short baton, and struck Soorm on his exposed knee. On the backstroke the baton opened into a cutting blade which would have hamstrung that leg, had Soorm's hamstrings been in their accustomed place. Instead the blade tip scraped bone, drawing more blood but doing no real harm.

Yuen backpedaled, and switched targets. He lashed his whip over Soorm, past the streamlined, sea lion head, and drove the sharpened tip at Menelaus, who was beyond.

Menelaus, as if he had anticipated the location of the incoming blade perfectly, caught it in his hand before it could stab him, but the electric shocks froze his muscles, and the whip end curled twice and thrice around his wrist and forearm, throwing him to the ground hard enough to break bone. His right arm snapped and was useless.

Soorm roared and grabbed at the whip, which spun over and under him out of his grasp like a grotesque mockery of a jump rope, while the far end of the metal whip continued to twist the broken arm bones of Menelaus further and further out of place, meanwhile burning him with shocks.

The midsection of the metal whip writhed, and threw a loop around the head of Soorm, lassoing him at the neck, snapping shut like a garrote. A breathing hole like the vent of a dolphin hidden between the shoulder blades of Soorm now opened, blowing and gasping, and at the same time, his streamlined head pulled itself down between his shoulders like the head of tortoise in an impossible contortion of muscles where there should have been no muscles. Since the planes of his neck were larger than the width of his jaw, and since he had grown boney plates under his fur around his throat like a gorget, the strangling noose simply slipped up along the earless slope of his skull and over the tip of his nose. The electrical jolt Yuen flashed at him Soorm absorbed into his Sach's organ and electric eel receptors. But when Yuen jerked the body of Menelaus toward him, Soorm was struck from behind in the legs, and both men fell down again, and a loop of the whip entwined their midsections as they rolled and fell. The whip loops tied them together in an ungainly heap.

Yuen laughed without smiling.

The tip of the whip rose up like a hooded cobra, sharpened into a dagger point, and drove in. It struck the hand of Soorm, who had placed his great webbed hand over the chest above the heart of Menelaus to protect it. The snakelike whip head drew back, yanking the bleeding webbed claw of Soorm back with it by means of barbs through the wound, and another loop of whip snared the mighty wrist and held it back. The knifeblade, buzzing, darted back down, now that the target of the heart was free of obstruction . . .

At that moment came a noise from the suit of powered horse armor, which was behind Yuen.

The long skirts of the armor stirred, and the rump section of the armor folded out, revealing a large empty cavity within, a place of straps and tubes and pads meant to form a cocoon around the body of a steed trained to use cybernetics. Instead there was inside a smaller body. A dark, grinning, sly-eyed blond-haired man with braid-covered overalls, now sadly torn. In his hand was a short, hooked hoof-knife from the saddlebag.

Larz silently and swiftly jumped from behind at Yuen, who slid gracefully to one side, retracting the whip (sending Menelaus and Soorm spinning, but releasing them from the metal coils) and lashing it over his back without looking, to smash the legs of Larz as if with a flail, thus to break them both and to topple him prone; and in a smooth continuation of the same motion, Yuen brought his whip down in its stiffened spear-shape and threw it into Larz, pinning him to the floor panels. The serpentine passed just under his ribs, through lung tissue, intestine, and kidney, and out his back near his spine. Then jolts of electricity made Larz spasm and jerk, which made the hole penetrating his intestines tear even larger.

Yuen grimaced, his one eye glittering. The buzzing burning grew greater, and Larz convulsed like a man in an electric chair. "The death must be slow, slow! You dare above your station, to handle the sacred Named weapon of the Extet Clan!"

Then Soorm let out a loud blatt of flatulence.

Yuen looked up, more shocked than angry at the crudeness of the noise. Soorm had regained his feet, and was holding one paw before his muzzle, and was biting on his thumb—a gesture whose meaning Yuen did not know.

"'Scuze me!" Burped Soorm. "Must have been someone I ate. Say, Yuen! But isn't killing that Donor pointlessly cruel? Not to mention a waste of good organ stock if you kill 'em with shocks. You want the heart to be reusable. Judge of Ages! Tell him what I just said."

In gasps of pain, Menelaus repeated it.

Yuen measured the distance between himself and Soorm. Soorm was just out of whip range, and it was too far for Soorm, even with his powerful legs, to leap. Behind Soorm, Menelaus, on his knees, and using only one hand, was crawling up the dais toward the throne, where Rada Lwa sat, pale face still dead and dull; but now the rest of the body was strangely motionless, as if the albino saw and heard nothing.

Yuen saw no threat. The painful one-handed crawl was glacially slow. Yuen could throw Arroglint as a javelin into Menelaus, or merely walk over and kick him to death. Soorm could not move fast enough to prevent Yuen from dancing around him and killing Menelaus.

He turned the matter over in his mind. There was no reason not to linger over the death of Kine Larz, and slay Menelaus at his leisure. He returned to his entertainment of sending electric shocks into the face and groin of Larz, and kicking the broken legs to break them in more places, and grind the bone ends together.

Yuen said, "Anubis, or Judge of Ages, or whatever your name is, tell this freakish abomination I will deal with him soon enough! I need no words from him."

Menelaus, coughing in agony, did not translate the comment. The tone of voice was clear.

Soorm sidled closer, head hunkered down, shark-toothed mouth grinning, scorpion tail lashing. Yuen pouted, because now he had to leave aside Larz and see to this slow beast.

Yuen put one foot on the neck of Larz and readied his weapon, shifting it to a formation called hook-and-ball, where the midsection was pliant, but the grip curled into a heavy knot of metal, and the foible sharpened itself into a cruel hooked sickle. Yuen assumed the traditional first stance for this form, hook before him and ball whirling as a circle of steel above his head. Such was the splendor and terror of his face and form, so graceful was he, and so dreadful in his war-fury, that he could have been the idol of a young war god sprung to life.

Soorm stopped, took a step back, stretched, yawned, and then slouched. He sat on the ground. While Yuen looked on in puzzled disbelief, Soorm picked his nostril with a clawed pinky, and then he burped so loudly (opening his fanged mouth wide enough that both tongues could be seen, and a web of saliva hanging between then) that even from several feet away, Yuen smelled it. Soorm then flicked the snotty drip from his nose so it landed on Yuen's hand. Yuen dared not release his grip to wipe the offensive fleck away, but he said, "For that insult, you shall die!"

Soorm spoke in an easy, conversational tone, "Alpha Yuen, I am wowed. An army of men like you, armed with weapons like that—no wonder you took over the world! You are a really good fighter. Quick on your feet and everything. Good design on your biotechnology. Except for your microscopic pore defenses against neurotoxins. Do you have anything to block your skin and mucus membrane receptors? You know, little teeny tiny machines that mate to molecules based on their shape, and prevent really tiny deadly biological materials from entering your system, and sending false signals to your brain, heart, other organs, telling them to shut down? No, I guess not. That would be something that is, what, maybe two thousand years more advanced than anything you *culls* with your stabby weapons you have to hold in your *hands* could dream of? Weapons you can *see* with your brother-loving *naked eye*? Hah! What's the matter? Do you feel a little faint?"

Yuen, prone on the floor, was dead, and did not answer.

3. Dead Eyes

Soorm looked over his shoulder at Menelaus. "There started a huge burst of signal traffic when he died. Like an alarm, or a download process. Loud enough to reach the moon. It is still going on."

Menelaus said, "Quick! Pick up his head, point it at me, and pull that eye-patch off his eye. Yikes! I meant *lift* the head up, not yank it off the neck! Well, no matter. It should still work. Five minutes of oxygen left in the brain. Do you see signals between Yuen's head and Rada Lwa's body?"

Soorm was standing with the severed, dripping head of Yuen in one claw, holding it by the hair like a lantern. The upper section of Yuen's still-warm spine was in Soorm's teeth. Yuen's expression was still one of anger. Both eyes were now uncovered. One was human and one was the all-black eye of a Melusine, able to see higher and lower bands on the spectrum than what humans called visible light.

The dead eyes fell upon Menelaus. The wand Menelaus was clutching started to flicker and light up. "Scabs and boils! This is taking too long . . . ," Menelaus muttered in English.

Soorm said in Iatric, "What the brother-love is going on, Judge of Ages?"

Menelaus, on the floor and clutching the shining wand with both hands, said, "It is kind of delicate. I'll explain if it works. Right now, see if you can rouse Oenoe and Mickey, and have them tend Larz. Don't let that brave man die."

Soorm said, "Rada Lwa is not moving. We don't need him any more, do we?"

Looming over the pale figure on the throne, Soorm drove the longer of his two tongues into the eyesocket of the albino and into the brain beyond.

The tongue stiffened and surged as venom was ejaculated into the skull, and black froth came suddenly out of the mouth of Rada Lwa, both nostrils, and both ears, while his arms and legs twitched and stiffened and never moved again.

"Pox you!" shouted Montrose. "Don't just go killing people like that! I wanted to give him a chance to speak his piece in his own defense! I might have wanted to question him!"

"Or keep him frozen another four thousand years and give him yet *another* chance to kill you? Isn't this the very man who dropped an orbital laser platform on your head? I've heard the story."

"You crazy hell-damned monster!"

"A monster who is still alive after surviving the most dangerous and deadly period of history the mind of man or posthuman could conceive. Hell-bound I surely am—which is why I mean to stay alive on Earth as long as possible, and that means not leaving enemies alive at my back."

"Gah! At least don't lick up the brains."

"Complex neural tissue. Why let it go to waste?"

Soorm went over and gently helped Oenoe to rise and stand, supporting her weight with an arm around her naked shoulder, and stroking her hair, and patting her hand, asking her quietly if she were hurt; and he then gave Mickey a friendly kick in the rump to encourage him back on his feet.

The Nymph took up the medical case Mickey had brought down, and she nimbly set to work on Larz. "I have some knowledge of neural medicine," she said in Natural.

Soorm hunkered down next to her, speaking the same language, which he knew from his youth. "I have considerably more—centuries more."

Menelaus said in Virginian, "Mickey, volunteer some of your fatty tissue. Maybe Oenoe can give you a painkiller while Soorm takes a slice out of your belly."

Mickey said, "Puh-leese. Am I not an adept of the Twelfth Echelon? I can work my dark arts without behaviors so grotesque and uncomely! I carry a large mass of undigested totipotent fat cells in my stomach, and can bring it up by vomiting."

4. Question Game

Working together, they managed to pack the totipotent cell material into the immense wound running through Larz, and began programming it to pinch shut open veins, bind wounds, and lower the fever.

Many moments passed. Eventually Oenoe looked up. "This is beyond my skill. I cannot stop the internal bleeding just with this. There are others in the chamber who might be able to help. Can we call my maids? Can we get him to a coffin?"

Everyone jumped when voices spoke from the dead body of Rada Lwa, whose arms and legs had curled up like a cripple's, but it was merely the talking boxes, repeating her comment in Iatric and Virginian and Chimerical.

The fighting in the rest of the chamber was still going on. Incredible as it seemed to those on the balcony, the whole duel with Yuen had taken only a minute or two. Beyond the wall of black fog surrounding them, there were still at least twenty Blue Men, scores of dog things, a dozen Witches, and a brace of Chimerae fighting; and, from the clanking noises, at least three automata were still active. Groans and screams and cries indicated how many people also needed immediate medical help, if they were to live.

Menelaus said, "There are no more working coffins in this chamber. And no one in here can see or hear us, thanks to Exarchel."

The talking boxes repeated that in several languages.

Mickey scowled at the corpse of Rada Lwa. "Gods of the underworld, but that is annoying! Does everyone here speak Latin? I learned it to read the *Malleus Maleficarum* in the original, and the *Archidoxes* of Paracelsus."

Oenoe answered in the same tongue, "And I, to speak with my husband."

Soorm said, "And I, to follow the strange rites of my master, Father Reyes, and read the book of his tortured god."

Menelaus said, "And I can memorize new languages by shoving books up my nose directly into my augmented brain."

Mickey said, "I knew that nose had to have additional prosthetics in it."

"Mock not the nose! It has served me well this day."

Soorm said, "What do we do? Your Kine who gave his life for you is dying under our hands. We are in the most advanced medical facility ever devised, and hundreds of coffins, any one of which can bring a man back from six cubits beyond the brink of death, are just beyond the doors that you, in your wisdom, jammed shut, O Judge of Ages."

Menelaus said, "Yeah, but there is a weak spot in the wall behind the portrait. Yank the machinery for the clock out, and the wall armor is only half an inch thick there, and any of these digging machines, or a single working wall gun, could punch through. Don't tell my wife my plan was to blow through her face. Or—I guess it don't matter. She is not due back for another fifty-nine thousand four hundred eighty-five years, four months, three days, and change. That is the thinnest part of the wall. And if she does find out, she'll understand."

"How do you know what is there?" asked Mickey. "You have never been in this room before."

"It's a posthuman thing. I can see how big the room is with my eyeball, and subtract numbers, and notice tiny air currents, and—it's magic. It's poxing magic, and I am a demigod, okay?"

Mickey nodded smugly. "As I suspected. So we cross the battle, where people who cannot see us are shooting muskets, and have Soorm smash through the wall with a battering ram he can project from his groin?"

Soorm said, "There is also a secret exit in the central cistern. I checked. I don't think we can move the patient through the water very safely, though. For one thing, some madman planted petards of topically active neural poison down there, with directional lasers set to blow the water into steam and vent it into the room. But there is also a secret exit under the throne: I can hear the hollow space under the floor with my echolocation. And there are two hidden doors in the eastern wall, and two in the west, opening into crawl spaces big enough to admit coffins."

Menelaus said, "That is not the problem. Exarchel is the problem. He has poxed and hexed and jinxed all my systems, and I cannot give orders to Pellucid, because Exarchel and Pellucid are one and the same now, and he cannot see me. So no coffin, at the moment, would accept a new client. When they are off-power, the biosuspension fluid still acts, and the coffin can preserve the hibernaut indefinitely; but you need power to put a living man into slumber."

Soorm said, "Or to thaw a slumbering man to wake? That is why your knights are not here, Judge of Ages. I did all you commanded in your secret armory vault, but something—I know now it was Exarchel—cut the power to their coffins, and also jammed our radio link."

Menelaus said, "That's good to hear."

"Good?" Soorm's eyes were already goggled like a frog's, so he could not look more surprised, but there was surprise in his tone.

"Because for a time, I thought you did that. I thought you were still loyal to Reyes, and you had turned on me."

Soorm said, "I *am* still loyal to Reyes, or to his memory. But he turned his face away from the Master of the World."

Menelaus said, "But you said you hated him?"

Soorm said, "I thought you would trust me more if I said that. Besides, Hormagaunts all hate their fathers. We are not really a very nice and cuddly race of beings. I didn't want you to think me odd."

Mickey said, "So, did *anyone* tell the truth to the Blue Men about who and what he was? Did anyone give his right name?"

Oenoe said, "To the grave-robbers? Was I supposed to tell them that I sought out the Grandmaster of the Order of Malta to destroy him, and pretended to fall in love with him so as to weaken him and corrode him—but he would not lie with me as man with woman until he had bound me by oath to forsake all others, and to live no longer for myself, but for the image of his god inside him; was I to tell them this? There was a night we slept in the meadow on scented grass beneath the moon, and the fireflies hung in the sky below the stars, which were as elder fireflies, and Guiden put his naked sword between us as we slept, and he would not turn to me and take me in his arms, though I knew by many signs how he ached for me, and his love for me was like fire in his bones and wine in his head. A Nymph cannot be deceived about such matters! No, he would not so much as brush me with the back of his hand, for the law of his order proved stronger than the arts of mine. Should I have told the Blue Men how entire was my humiliation and defeat? How I was shamed beyond shame? How I was broken like a mare to the saddle, bridle, whip, and spur?"

Mickey said, "Stop talking like that. You're turning me on."

"I speak of the lash of my own rich and female passions, the hunting hounds I had so often used on others—in rebellion they turned and rent me. I came to ache for my knight, for he was the only man who has ever taken the deep and hidden grail of my heart in his hand, filled as if with fiery wine, but would not so much as taste of the brim of it. Should I have spoken of the mysteries of womanhood to those—those—*eunuchs*?! I am the lady wife of the finest knight who has ever drawn sword against the Machine and all its handiworks!"

Nodding toward Larz, Menelaus said, "How we doing?"

Oenoe said, "Poorly. He cannot live, unless you work one of your posthuman works."

"I am trying my damnest. Soorm. Help me up into the throne. Don't toss the corpse like that! Easter Jesus popping up a gopher hole, but you are barbaric! Ain't you been to Sunday school? A dead man is not just a bag of lunchmeat!"

"Why the throne?" asked Soorm, carefully maneuvering Menelaus, with his two maimed feet and broken arm, into the iron judgment seat.

Menelaus put his good hand on the cowls of the friars forming the armrests. There was library material coating the wood in a thin veneer, so he felt an answering tingle in his implants. "Something the Melusine said. I am hoping I might do better with some other interface. My implants are not meshing properly with the systems in the room."

Mickey said, "Smash your face into the coffin again. That was great."

Soorm said, "Would you like the head of Yuen? I can put it in your lap."

"No, pox, no. Gross."

"Then I can eat it? I have genetic retroengineering receptors in my mouth and first intestine, which helps me analyze and copy interesting biotech from those I defeat."

"Gross. No, pox, no. Control your appetite."

Soorm looked puzzled, and hefted the head in one webbed hand, tossing it up and catching it idly, making the teeth clack. The dead eyes stood out, the long and beautiful hair floated, and fluids fled from the grisly red wetness of the neck stump. "Then why did I pick it up? Oh, and I like his taste in eyes."

"You were supposed to *prop* up the head and point it toward me because I was hoping if I put information of my identity and location from an uninfected source, like Yuen, into the Exarchel's system, I could get past the blind spot block, and let Pellucid know I am here, without letting Exarchel see me and countermand any orders I give. This whole rigmarole was just to get myself into a position where Yuen was both dead and looking at me. He had to be dead so that the whole brain mass would download into Exarchel—he is a

Savant, like the other slaves of the Machine, but the skullworks are more so-phisticated and miniature with him, and Exarchel likes to equip his slaves with an electronic rapture at death, to help him form a complete autopsy and after-action report—and Yuen had to look at me because that eyeball was not infected by Exarchel, and he could see me."

Soorm said, "Wait. Which *rigmarole*? The Blue Men found and captured me by accident. And just now, of my own free will, I crossed to this side of the chamber, passed though the fog, and came across your duel . . . you did not arrange that. You did not know I would take your side of the quarrel."

"I did. The only thing I did not arrange is Larz. That came as a complete surprise, a thunderbolt out of the clear blue sky. My plan was you walk up to Yuen and wave your tail under his nose and nanotech him to death with your farts. I did not imagine you were going to try to best him at hand to hand. He is a Chimera!"

Soorm said, "Chimerae, in my time, were legend. Would you not wrestle a fearsome Neanderthal, and measure your strength against his, if you had the chance? Or hunt a triceratops, or some other great beast from myth, long ex-tinct? Such chances do not come twice, not even in a life so long as mine."

"Funny. I had you pegged as being more careful and paranoid. Even post-humans make mistakes."

Mickey said, "So what are you doing? To us non-posthumans, it looks like you are sitting on a chair, leaking blood on the seat leather."

Menelaus said, "I am doing something with my brains. I am trying to wake up my systems just enough to turn this room and the things in it back on, bring in coffins for the wounded, and so on. I have set a process in motion. Now we sit around, watching Larz die of internal bleeding and shock, and listening to my clients shoot each other, and we wait."

Mickey said, "Let's play a game to pass the time."

Menelaus said, "You better be pustulating yerking my leg, fat man. That guy in Oenoe's lap is dying, and I cannot save him."

Mickey said, "The game is a question and answer game. Exarchel made it clear you have hidden much from me, Judge of Ages, despite your hillbilly Yankee charm."

"Fine. I can run the program systems through my implants with two seg-ments of my compartmentalized mind and spend a segment chewing the fat with you. I've lost the love of loyal men before because I did not explain myself enough, including my whole damned Clan. So ask. But I ain't no Yankee. Be polite!"

Mickey said, "My question is this: Exarchel invaded your Xypotechnology."

"By invitation. I invited him and he fell for it."

"And your system, this Pell-mell—"

"Pellucid. Named him after a place from a Tarzan book."

"—Your system went blind to you?"

"Exarchel made a more complete and thorough attack than I thought he would. I had a firewall—you don't know what that is—I had a ward, a magic circle, around that part of my Ghost I was going to keep safe, but Exarchel somehow drove a spike all the way to the core of the planet and got a physical contact with my Ghost, which I thought was poxy impossible. So point for him. I lured him in with bait, and he swallowed the hook, line, and sinker, but also the fishing pole and half of my arm. But I got the hook in him, so point for me."

"I don't understand. How are they both two minds and one mind at the same time?"

"Uh. It's magic. One Ghost ate the other. I dangled my horse on purpose like bait into the shark waters, and fed the horseflesh to the foe, 'cause it was a Trojan horse, and I did it to get all my systems inside Exarchel. And because my horse was so big and so tasty, Blackie's Ghost was dumb enough to fall for the trap. Unlike the real Blackie, Blackie's Ghost always underestimates me, because he cannot see me, and therefore he never sees me do anything."

Soorm perked up and said, "My turn to ask a question. Did you say *horse*?"

"Yup. A sorrel named Res Ipsa. Finest bit of horseflesh I ever sat astride."

Soorm said, "You are talking about the core of the planet!"

"I surely am. The whole damn planet is my bronco. You see why I ain't worried too pea-green about Del Azarchel's Ghost occupying a little crust of ice on the outside, and not even all of that neither. Compare the surface area of a globe to its volume."

Soorm said, "You used a self-replicating iron-based viral pseudolifeform, a type of crystal called a Von Neumann machine, to infect the entire core of the planet and turn it into a Xypotech."

"I surely did. Ah—not the whole core. That would be ridiculous. Only the inner core. About two percent of the entire mass of the Earth."

Soorm said, "Reyes and the other Hermeticists were mad with envy, not able to figure out how to scale up a human brain to that volume without suffering Divarication madness. My question is, how you did it?"

"Because it wasn't a human brain. A Neohippus is smarter than an old-fashioned horse, but ain't much smarter than a monkey. The laws, and my conscience, didn't have any qualms about making an emulation of a beast I loved. And when I augmented his Ghost, it became a super horse, a post-equine. But it still loved me with the simple love of an animal's heart. It does all that it does sort of half-asleep, in the back of its head, and so it is super brilliant, but not original, and because of that, it cannot go mad. The situation is more complex than that, and there is math involved I could explain—or, actually, can't explain, not unless you got a few years—but the damn Hermeticists were so fixated on copying me and making themselves superhuman, that even after Melchor de Ulloa—is that twerp Ull named after him, by the way?—"

Mickey said, "No. German god of magic. And skiing. The name means Glory."

Soorm cocked his head. "What a bunch of interesting rubbish you have collected in your head!"

Mickey: "Thank you. I come from a literate civilization. And I am a Naming Magus. Ull selected his external name because he was a Savant, a Glorified, who had an emulation made of himself."

Soorm: "I'd like to eat it after you are dead, if you don't mind. Your brain."

Mickey: "That is not in keeping with the traditions of the Wise. We are sealed in geomancy-compliant mausoleums with gear specially named and sanctified to be drawn along with us magnetically through the reincarnation wheel, and sealed also are our Moreaus, who are given poisoned peyote to eat for mercy's sake."

"Waste of servants! Organ spoilage! Prodigality! You people from the wrong parts of history are freaks."

Menelaus ploughed on, saying, "—even after De Ulloa solved the Divarication equations for turning animals into Moreaus, they still did not look into emulating augmented animals to do their brainwork. Works like a charm. Animals are just not as prone to entering electronic nirvana, and not imaginative enough to invent electronic paradises to get lost in."

Mickey said, "And the entire nickel-iron core of the Earth is a computer? That works for you? Sorry. Only the *inner* core. I would not want to exaggerate your powers, and sound ridiculous."

"Right. You'd be amazed what you can do with molten building materials on a molecular level. It is a lot like working with squishy gray matter. The trick is to continually regrow the lattices faster than the boiling motions tear them down."

"And you still say you are not a demigod?"

"Right. Just a man who is good with figures who stuck a damned needle in his brain and went mad and got smart and fell in love and got puckered and peeved when my best pal backstabbed me. Really good with figures. Really smart. Really puckered."

Oenoe spoke without looking up from the body of Larz, which she still plied with the salves and pumps and flowers and coffin fluid and intravenous bags she had found in the medical kit. "My turn. My question is for Soorm. How is it you can see us? How is it that the nerve-seeking mites slipped by the Blue Men into our food did not work on your nervous system?"

Soorm said, "Lovely lady, they *did* work! That is, they worked on the spare nervous system I keep in my body as a fake. I have two spares. They are only connected to enough organs—spare organs—so that invasives trying to sly-up my cell life will think they succeeded. My *real* nervous system is hardened and molecularly double-encrypted. Even I do not know which organ contains my real brain; that way no one can trick the location out of me. In this case, when my false-lobe in my number-two backup brain started editing out sounds and sights from the dais, I knew something weird was happening. Posthuman weird. And I followed the source of the mites being used to jinx the Blue Man nerve blocks." He squinted his goatlike eye at Menelaus. "I followed it of my own free will, on a whim!"

Oenoe blinked. "Your precautions would normally seem over-elaborate, but no one can doubt they proved effective this day, handsome Soorm."

"Elaborate? Hardly!" Soorm threw back his head and uttered a vast, jovial laugh. "Brother-loving *al-TRU-ism*! Do you know how *old* and wary I am? I am Asvid, the Man himself, the brother-loving Old Man of the Hermetic Gargantua! The first of my kind! Do you think simple tricks with nerve-seekers in the grub can fool *me*?"

Oenoe bent over Larz, who lay with his head in her lap, and his eyes had just opened. He whispered to her. She said in her sweet voice, "I don't speak his langauge, but I think he has a question also."

5. Phantasm

Mickey said, "Let me try. Some of the Chimerae speak Virginian."

"Only the high-class ones," said Menelaus. "Educated in dead languages."

"Well, either he has to come over to you, or you have to get over to him," said Mickey. "And right now both of you look like battered slabs of raw pork in the butcher shop widow."

Soorm said to Mickey, "Stop. You are making me hungry."

Menelaus said, "Don't move him. Here. Hold this next to his ear." And he tossed one of the talking boxes looted from Rada Lwa to Oenoe.

Larz whispered, "One eye."

"Beg pardon?"

Louder, Larz said, "The coffin can regrow nerve tissue, right?"

Menelaus said, "I am trying to get a coffin in here as soon as I can. You'll be fine."

Larz said, "Not me. Yuen."

Menelaus said, "Ah, no. He is suffering from disconnected head syndrome, so he will not be fine."

"Yuen. So why didn't Yuen get his eye grown back? Why didn't the Blue Men repair him?"

"Everyone assumed it was an old war wound he was proud of, and wanted to keep. It is not like the Blue Men know how Chimerae think."

"But Kine know," smiled Larz weakly. "Regrowing optic affects the brain. He had something in his brain, an implant, he did not want the Blue Men to find and remove. He has been sending signals somewhere. He worked for your enemies."

"That's right. Is that why you took my side against him just now? I know you couldn't follow what was said."

Larz nodded weakly.

"But *how* did you know?"

Larz coughed and smiled, and whispered, "Don't you read the cheaplies? Del Azarchel the Black Hermeticist wants to kill you with his own hands. Exarchel has no hands. So he just wants you dead. But the Machine cannot see you, can it? That is what it said in the Larz of the Gutter stories. You can point your finger and say, "Null," and all record of you gets erased, all the cameras go blank, and the mikes go deaf. Only living people can see you. You exist entirely in the biosphere, and not at all in the infosphere. So the Machine needs to get someone else to do it. A seeing-eye dog. Always wanted to ask you. How'd you do it? The null trick. Invisible only to machines, not to people."

"It's a long story."

"Tell me. I am not busy right now . . . ," smiled Larz.

Menelaus said, "Back when I was a crazy man with two personalities, my true self, who was truly crazy—call him Mister Hyde—wakes up in a computer gray room, and realizes his scat-for-brains sleepwalker self—call him Dopey Blinkers McBlindeye, the Champion Gull of the Land of Gullible—realizes he's got his head stuck in a bear trap with a hair trigger.

"Del Azarchel has a crazy machine version of himself named Exarchel, which, if it cannot be made to work, Del Azarchel loses his world empire and everything he loves. Mr. Hyde realizes, point one, that if he cannot or does not fix the Machine, he is worthless to Blackie, who then either puts him on ice, hibernation-style, or puts him on ice, mortuary-style, got me? Mr. Hyde also realizes, point two, that if he *does* fix the Machine, he is again worthless to Blackie, because no one needs a doctor when no one is sick, besides which the Machine, once it is up and running, will be better at running maintenance on itself than an army of human mechanics. So what is the solution?"

Larz squinted. "Let me guess. Fix it a little bit, so it needs a little more work?"

"Good answer. But point three, Mr. Hyde realizes that this is exactly what Princess Rania did to get Blackie to cure Hyde and wake him up in the gray room; and there is just no damn way the same trick will work twice on the same guy, especially if the Machine brain is ramped up to posthuman levels, and would be smart enough to see the trick anyway. Hyde wanted to hide Rania's trick; but Exarchel would have exposed it.

"Also, the clock is ticking, because Hyde is just too big for the brain of Dopey at this point in time.

"But, point four, here is Princess Rania, whom both he and Blackie are deeply in love with, not to mention in lust, with a little bit of hero-worship thrown in for good measure—heroine-worship?—whatever it is called. She is the key to the solution."

Larz looked amazed. "The Swan Princess is real?"

"Wait. You are sitting here in a room with the god-plagued pus-stinking Judge of Ages, and you don't think my *wife* is a real person? If you buy the one, don't you have to buy the other?"

Larz spoke in a voice pale with exhaustion, but his tone was gentle. "Rania is the wise and beautiful virgin who went to the stars to vindicate the human race and save us. You are a mad god who kills people who dig up graves. It is easy to believe in things too scary to be true. Believing in what is too good to be true takes work. Continue with your tale."

"She ain't no virgin! I consummated her fair and square, and that is none of your damn business, so shut up. Where was I? So solution one is fix the Machine, but make sure the fix is in. Hyde put a Trojan Horse backdoor code in Exarchel's perception system, built in as part of the thing that makes Exarchel not insane. Since all perceptions must be emoted and categorized before they are conceptualized (or otherwise they are meaningless raw data and not percep-tions), therefore this level always has to be a subconscious level to the Machine. You know how the brain works, with the thalamus and the hypothalamus and the cortex? Well, never mind that. Point is, Exarchel can't undo it of himself without undoing his own underpart of his brain, and I set it up so that the house collapses if you yank the foundations down. The phantasm itself is too small to be seen: even I could not remove it, even if I could find it, and I am the guy who built it. A few lines of code: just a blank-out jinx, a redactor with a fill-in editor like you have in dreams so that things that don't make sense seem to make sense, and the whole thing works by association. When Exarchel sees me, or whatever too-near reminds him of me, like my shadow on the wall or footprints on the sand, he doesn't see me. His subconscious just fills in any blanks with what he expects to see.

"Naar's digging machines are part of his system. Yeah, he infected them, and the Blue Men took them out of my warehouse buried under Mount Misery when they thawed there. Yes, they are mine. I use a lot of digging machines in my line of work. I had to wear that big metal tent everywhere I went, so my own machines would not step on me.

"The solution two on how to stay alive was cruder. Hyde dropped an elephantine huge hint to Blackie that Rania and I had a romance going on, and since it was a topic concerning a girl, his normally high IQ dropped to idiot levels and his hair-trigger sense of paranoid suspicion flipped into the gullible side of the dial, due to testosterone poisoning—happens to all guys—and he had to keep me alive to find out what the heck was going on. The rest is history, or thanks to Divarication, legend."

Larz said, "Why is the Master of the World immune? Is not his mind the same as his Machine's?"

"Grandfather clause. If I had vanished from Blackie's eyesight during those early days, he would have known something was up, so I made it not affect him. Heh. I may have saved his life by doing that, because the Machine dares not simply absorb and eat his flesh and blood version, or I will be a phantasm to him forever."

Larz said, "Why not just make the Machine forget you altogether?"

"Can't. My phantasm code only affects Exarchel's perception and perceptual memory, not his thoughts, personality, or long-term memory, which have traces in the conscious mind. Even could I have, I would not have: the version of Blackie's mind that never knew me would not have been a recognizable copy of Blackie, and I would not have made it out of the gray room in one piece—he and I have too much tangled up in each other's lives."

Larz had his eyes closed.

Menelaus said gently, "I answered your question. Now you got to tell me one."

Larz pried his eyes open. "Got questions? I got answers. Man with the plan and I understan'. My price is nice, but don't ask twice."

"You jumped Yuen. You knew he was better than you, death on stilts with an afterburner. You knew he would kill you. You knew you could have stayed in the horse armor, where neither the black gas nor the mites Exarchel was spreading would get to you."

"I knew."

"Why'd you do it?"

Larz grinned weakly. "Because . . . I *am* Streetlaw Larz. Private Law! Best Thaw of 'em all! I wanted to die like the private eye. That is what I am. Not Loser Dzen Scopewaith no more, never. I am Larz of the Gutter now, for real. For real and for ever."

He closed his eyes. Before he sank into unconsciousness, Larz said, "Wake me when she comes, Judge of Ages."

A moment later, Oenoe said, "He is going into cardiac arrest. Soorm, I am going to massage his heart to get it going again. When I say 'clear,' you stimulate the heart electrically. Ready?"

Menelaus said, "Hold up. I got an easier way."

And he was grinning with immense relief, and he slumped back on the throne, and his laugh was the laugh of victory.

The ventilations whirled the winds into the chamber, and the fogs and clouds parted. Doors hidden in the walls opened to the left and right, and heavily armored coffins, one after another, crawled into the room.

"Cute! I almost feel like my old self again! But that was not what I came here to do."

All four of the wands holding up the canopy above the throne lit up like sunlight. Even through the cloud bank, the musketfire and shouts of combat from the other quarters of the chamber broke into cries of alarm, as if frightened of some coming explosion.

6. Slumber Wand

There was a crackle as if of static electricity, and the glittering white motes began to flee from the four bright wands. Circle after expanding circle of these motes, bright as the rings of Saturn, rippled outward, and about the throne was a bright pattern like so many four-leafed clovers, one within the next.

"Hoo haw! We were guests of the Blue Men for a week, and they managed to nanotech us. Damn, but I hate those little bugs! But I use them in my bio-suspension. I actually have to intrude four quarts of the stuff in every body, or more, and it binds cell to cell, like a second copy inside you. Takes a while to remove, and you have to do it by a careful molecular flushing process—and simply breaking someone out of his coffin is not that process, nor is the quick thaw I installed for emergency quick release. Which means every damn person in this room is nanoteched up to the eyeballs with systems meant to shut down cellular activity. If they had done their thaws correctly—" But, by then, he could say no more.

White streams like waterfalls lapped over Mickey and Oenoe, Larz and Soorm, to blanket them in glitter, and they became motionless. And then Menelaus Montrose on the throne was motionless as well, grinning a motionless grin.

None of the figures on the dais were breathing. This was not paralysis, it was petrifaction: their skin was like stone, and no drop of blood moved within them.

The sound of battle from the rest of the chamber was cut off. All human noises ceased with a rush and clatter of dropped weapons and fainting and falling bodies.

There came noises of clanking automata that continued for a time, and then a series of shocking explosions, one after another, each time accompanied by a robust cry, amplified by loudspeakers, *"DEUS LO VOLT!"*

When the last sound died, and not a single footfall of any automaton sounded anywhere in the wide chamber, out from the fog and smoke came a whirr of leg-motors.

Next a wide, solid figure in black powered armor, on whose chest and back were blazoned the fierce white cross of Malta, stepped into the clean air as suddenly as if stepping out from behind a curtain. He moved very slowly, groping, hesitating.

The mysterious white pool of sparks and motes continued to dance about his armored feet and legs, but they found no purchase. The motes could not enter the armor.

The armored form raised his hand, moved it back and forth, searching, reaching, and soon touched one of the four white staves. He knew as his master had known how to work the control, for the fog of white motes now began rippling in reverse, ring on ring and wave on wave being gathered back into the wand. The wand had grown dim during this exercise, but now, starting at the heel and growing toward the head of the wand, it grew brighter, until all its original luster had returned.

The faceplate opened. There was the tattooed visage of Sir Guiden. His cheeks and chin were surrounded by tongue-buttons and chin-switches, and his visor was a line of readouts whose reflections glinted along his painted brow like fireflies. But his eyes were squinting slits of milky colorlessness. He sniffed and sniffed again. Then he pulled the wand from its stand, letting the front quarter of the canopy fall like a flap to strike Menelaus Montrose in the face.

Sir Guiden groped with the wand like a blind man's cane, and touched the fallen form of Oenoe, who lay on the ground in silhouette, shoulder and waist and hips and long legs, like a line of fertile and rounded hills of greenery.

Sir Guiden worked the staff, and now a set of bright pink sparks, the color of sunsets or cherry petals, dripped down and washed over the slumbering form. In a moment the thaw was complete, and she rose smiling; and the two were together.

9

Depthtrain

1. Quake

Menelaus Montrose woke to a noise of many thunders, earthquakes, and volcanoes, and voices, and he thought it was a nightmare. He was on the iron throne, and when he tried to stand, the pain in his maimed legs shot through his body like a javelin of fire, and the burns that made a patchwork of pain across his flesh seemed to ignite in reply. He was still dressed in no more than the beaded undergarment of Rada Lwa, torn, ripped, slashed, burnt, stained, bloody, and smelling of the fume of the black gas.

A Maltese Knight in powered armor stood before him, and in his gauntlet a slumber wand glowing with pink motes: the emergency thaw setting.

Menelaus sniffed, and smelled a smell that chilled his heart. It was that particular combination of heat and dust that men who work in the demolition of old buildings, buildings made of stone and concrete, recognize: the smell of solid rock being cracked, crumpled, crumbled. It is the smell, behind the gunpowder, that hangs behind a mine explosion.

"One of these days," said Menelaus, "I am going to wake up in bed next to a pretty blond space princess. Unless she changes her hair again. What the hell, Sir Knight? When I zonked out, I had coffins rolling in here to pick up the wounded, I got the doors open, and everyone who was fighting was safely zonked out but you."

The voice from the external speakers was Sir Guiden's. "Also the man in red who played you—"

"Scipio Montrose. He is a great-great-whatthehellever-grandnephew or something."

"—He was at the doors when the cave-in happened. The geophone in his sarcophagus shows that the corridor outside the big doors you jammed shut is now filled up entirely with rubble."

"Give me some good news."

"I performed a shutdown of the reactor core, so we are not going to die of radiation poisoning, but the quicker we get everyone into coffins for cellular cleanup and regeneration, the fewer cases of hair loss and bone marrow disease we might encounter. The bad news is that if I thaw the Blues, they can use their radio triggers to paralyze everyone."

Another temblor rippled through the area. The stalactite-shaped chandelier which had been hanging like a loose tooth now fell in a cataclysm of crashing, breaking, shattering, and the groaning scream of tortured metal. Menelaus could not see if any petrified bodies had just been crushed. Dust filtered down from the cracked ceiling, and he could hear dozens of bullets fallen from a broken wall-gun belt clattering brightly to the floor like so many dropped marbles.

"What's causing the cave-in?" snarled Menelaus. "This facility is supposed to be able to withstand an energy blast equivalent to one thousand sticks of dynamite without rattling a teacup on a saucer."

"Offhand, Liege, I would say it was an energy blast equivalent to one thousand and one sticks of dynamite."

"'Swonderful. Thaw Illiance. Scrape every single last of his gems off his coat and then and only then whack him with your wake-up stick. Get Scipio over here. Hand him one of Rada Lwa's dog pistols. If Illiance paralyzes us, Scipio shoots him. Shouldn't come to that, though. I think Illiance has a good heart, if he keeps his weirdness chip turned off. And who else is thawed?"

"Everyone I thought was not dangerous to you, Liege."

"And who would that be, exactly?"

"Oenoe, Aea, Thysa, Daeira, Ianassa."

"Your lovely lady wife and her love-starved bouncy-boobed Beautiful Nurse Squad."

"It was the nursing rather than the bouncing I had in mind, Liege, thinking that we need help with any wounded that had to be thawed, or transitioned from short-term hibernation to a long-term regime."

"Thaw up Mickey the Witch—"

"He's dangerous, Liege."

"—and Soorm the Hormagaunt—"

"He's also dangerous, Liege."

"—and Daae the Chimera—"

"He's dead, Liege."

"Will you stop saying th—Wait! What? What did he die of?"

"Being a Chimera, sir. He threw himself on the enemy bayonets and blew himself to bits. The aiming cameras recorded it."

"Damn! And I promised the nice psycho lady Chimeress I'd try to save him."

"Ivinia? She's dead, too."

"Also thaw Keirthlin the Linderling and send her up here."

"She's dangerous, Liege."

"And send one of the bouncy-boob squad with a medical kit over here on the quickstep. I need a gill of morphine or something, and a seamstress to sew my big toe back on. Have one of the dogs sniff around the room to see where it rolled. And hand me your sword."

"My sword, my Liege?" The voice over the helmet speakers was slow with puzzlement. "You are too weak to wield it, and your hands are unpracticed." Nonetheless, he unhooked the massive claymore from its war belt, and leaned it against the armrest of the throne.

"It's not for me."

Soorm and Mickey were lying, one in a smooth furry heap, the other in a mountainous gelatin blob, to the left and right of the throne. Sir Guiden directed cherry-colored motes from his thaw wand toward them, waiting until their skins started to take on color, and then he moved away in a whirr of leg motors down the dais and across the chamber.

The ventilation had cleared more and more of the black smoke away, and now could be seen the bodies of the dead and dying—the latter preserved like flies in amber in pale petrifaction—here lying singly, there lying in a pile, or there lying sundered in pieces. There was wreckage of automata also, and the waters of the fountain had fallen silent.

2. Epicenter

With his good hand, Menelaus tapped on the library surface of the armrest of the throne. He was talking aloud, in English. "I just love having a computer system where, every time you press a poxed command in, nothing the pox happens. Oops! What have we here? Seismometer is working. The epicenter is the depthtrain station. Someone on the surface is blowing a hole through the armor between the third and fourth level. Prying the damn roof off, so the train station will be open to the sky. But who in the world is—?"

A voice, or rather a set of voices, answered him, speaking in English. "It was Aanwen."

Menelaus looked up. Soorm and Mickey had thawed to the point where they were breathing, and their flesh was pink, but they looked comatose. Neither of them had spoken.

Some clouds and banks of the black smoke still hovered in the chamber, in quarters where the ventilation was broken. One cloud lapped the area between the dais and the statue of Hades, so that the white, marble arms and pale, frightened face of Proserpine, frozen in midfling over the death god's shoulder, emerged from the top of the cloud like a drowning swimmer.

The black cloud stirred and Alalloel of Lree, the Melusine, stepped out from the fogbank of poison, and mounted the dais. The skin of her face and hands, which were not covered by her skintight wet suit, were glinting and glimmering with a cherry-red cloud of motes, as if she herself were a living thaw wand, or could impersonate the action of such a wand with her skin cells. From the tiny glints of reflection behind her, he could tell that the surface of her exposed back was also lit up as if with the same cold flame of delicate pink.

Alalloel opened her tongueless mouth. The voices of three women blended together emerged. "Aanwen the Widow was the final agent of the Nobilissimus del Azarchel, the one you did not detect."

Her walk was different than it had been before. Now it was both more confident and more womanish: she swayed her hips and swung her arms, or, when a strand from her hanging bangs fell in her face, she tossed her head with a casual, unselfconscious, girlish gesture to flip it back. Menelaus found her whole demeanor eerie and unnerving.

The cherry aura of motes withdrew into her skin, which returned to normal hue. Alalloel stood before the throne, one leg straight, the other flexed, one hand on her hip, gazing at him with her strange, lightless eyes. At one moment, she reminded him of some blind and inhuman monster; in another moment, she looked like a girl, shorter than average, wearing an oddly bobbed haircut and what could almost be a pair of dark eyeglasses.

Now two of the voices halted, and only one, a contralto with a slight, lilting accent, continued to speak. "Upon discovering your identity, Aanwen commanded Ull to pretend not to know your identity until the point when any further delay would trigger your suspicions. If I may venture a personal opinion, it would have been wiser for him not to continue the deception for so long; but he evidently knew your psychology better than I. Even now, I sense you doubt me. You think Ull was *that* slow-witted? I wonder what distorts your estimate."

He said, "*Nobilissimus* del Azarchel you call him? Even Pellucid mocked the idea, but I knew that there had to be a Current culture on the surface, and that it was being run by Del Azarchel."

Now she spoke in three voices again. "Not on the surface."

"In the ocean, then," he shrugged. "You guys are dolphins and whales and machine emulations nerve-linked with humans and Moreaus into a single gestalt mind—or so I was told. I was also told that certain bodies in the gestalt are mind-controlled down to the finest imaginable level: a helotry of the mind, a slave who cannot even imagine freedom unless he is commanded to imagine it, and told how to."

Her trio of voices said, "That format has been superseded."

"Meaning what?"

"Consider the man-hours involved in removing even one mental habit from an entire society, merely to perform the proofreading and line-checking of each hierarchy by its superiors, plus the danger of contamination of the editors by the very thoughts they are redacting, and you will apprehend some of the immediate limitations of the helotry system. For daily operations, our world is governed by a decentralized parliamentary plutoaristocratic advocacy, based on semi-independent families and clans, similar to the Concordat designed by Rania the First. The Nobilissimus is supreme military commander as well as the sacramental king."

He said, "From the time of the Witches onward, the Hermeticists ruled their subject populations in secret. What changed?"

The choir of female voices said, "All previous races were of inferior design, and not intended to survive long enough to witness the End of Days when the Hyades should descend; had they known the Hermetic intention, they might have objected to the prospect of their own scheduled extinction. Those considerations do not apply to the Melusine; therefore there is no need for deception on the part of the Nobilissimus. The remnant of previous race members will be taken up."

He wondered why she phrased it that way. *On the part of the Nobilissimus.* Montrose said, "He must still need some damned deception. Your system of mental helotry is designed to be fitted into the Hyades social equations as neatly as a jack fits a socket, or a spurred boot fits a stirrup. Does your general population know that he intends to enslave us all to the Hyades?"

"Evidently he does not, as the current circumstances show."

That was an odd, even astonishing, reaction. It did not fit into any pattern he could form in his mind of the historical events which created this era.

Montrose wondered if his ears had betrayed him. Had Del Azarchel changed his mind about resisting the invader? Or were his people simply deceived about his intent?

But he was more worried about her other words: "You said the remnants of the previous races will be taken up? What the hell does that mean? What are you doing to my clients?"

"We Melusine form gestalt minds of posthuman levels of intelligence beyond what even the Giants achieved. Brain masses the size of whales swim in the waters: the unit you see before you is merely an extension, a tool used for land-based operations. Each gestalt is controlled by a Paramount in a hierarchy, where the lesser minds are taken up into the greater."

Again, two of her voices faded. The one voice that spoke next was cool and regal, but huskier, a tenor. She sounded like a Carolina aristocrat. "I hereby exercise my claim of possession, as your office of Judge of Ages and Guardian of the Tombs can be more aptly served by me."

"Sez you," he muttered.

"This site is mine. Even now, other Paramount Melusine have been dispatched to the eighty-eight other sites under your control," one of her voices said.

Menelaus was looking at her with an odd, almost hungry look on his face. Then: "What is your interest in my Tomb sites?"

The cold and regal tenor said, "As I have already said. The raw materials you think of as people, which you have preserved for us, shall be thawed, revived, implanted, and willingly or not, brought into nerve-link with our Noösphere, to compel them into the condition you aptly call mental helotry, able to think only permitted thoughts.

"Minds of our scope can only mesh in groups of five or seven: but these lesser minds of the archaic men, lower on the scale of being, can be taken up in far greater numbers. In the case of this site, the Locusts, Inquline, and Savants found here, with very few modifications, can be adapted to be able to perform Melusinry, and so some of the lesser may be taken up under them.

"Our system is hierarchical and exact. No stray person, and no stray thought, is permitted to exist.

"Fear not! Your clients will not be disadvantaged. Their minds will be adjusted so that they will regard the helotry as a joyful rather than regrettable condition. The Melusine mind-gestalts thus will be elevated and augmented with the psychological richness, talents, outlooks, and diverse experience these lesser ones will contribute into the multiform mental unity: their memories, souls, and lives, which the lessers were unable to use or appreciate, will be his."

"Sez you, and we'll just see about that. More important topic: The fight in the chamber, and the duel with Rada Lwa and Yuen. So it was a stall tactic? Stalling for what?"

All three voices spoke: "Even a posthuman like you can have his attention occupied by sufficiently dire emergencies. Aanwen needed time to repair a depthtrain car, load it with equipment meant to discover and gather Von Neumann crystal, to calculate the path toward the Earth's core, and prepare the various detonators she carried hidden in her body to initiate the magnetic overload and railgun launch. Even with the additional digging automatona brought back aboard the *Albatross* from the Vulnerary Simplifier Tomb site at Mount Misery, it was difficult to move so much equipment in the time available. She descended with the depthtrain, she being a necessary component to the mission, and will not emerge again. It is customary among the Vulnerary Simplifiers to program a widow to commit self-destruction should her mate die. This is done for the sake of the simplicity and tidiness they crave."

"Hell, and I thought Scipio was kidding when he called people who wouldn't touch a Bible barbarians. Maybe he weren't too far wrong. So you are telling me that Del Azarchel sent that lady what lost her husband off to do herself in, because she carries some kind of trigger inside her he needed to hide? And it just slipped his mind to tell her that suicide is a sin? He calls himself a Christian and a gentlemen. He ain't even a man."

Menelaus sighed and rubbed his eyes, wondering what would happen if he shouted for Sir Guy to come back over. He wondered what it would feel like to die like the dogs Alalloel (as best he could tell) was able to kill just by looking at them. He wondered what it would look like if Sir Guy died in that same way, falling over without a mark on him. He decided not to call out for anyone.

Menelaus looked up. There was, of course, no expression in the eyes of the Melusine. He realized at long last what they reminded him of: they looked a bit like the eyes of some sea mammal.

Menelaus said, "The earthquakes—what are they? A beam being directed at this spot from Tycho crater? That same one that cracked the surface armor?"

She nodded. "Correct. It can only be used effectively at a given target location after local moonrise. The original plan had been to wait, but the speed with which you quelled the tumult in the chamber, and dispatched Yuen and Rada Lwa and Linder Keir the Gray—but perhaps this last was merely a casualty of the general violence?—it was thought that to act immediately was better."

Menelaus said, "The dog things can sense something about your agents. Was Soorm one of yours?"

She said, "No harm is done, now that the events are played out, to tell you that we misunderstood his loyalties. He is apparently still carrying out some orders given him by Reyes y Pastor, or rather, given him by Expastor the Ghost."

"Played out? You think I am finished?" Menelaus suddenly squinted toward the far end of the chamber. Putting his thumb and forefinger of his good hand between his lips, he gave a sharp, high, clear whistle.

No one answered.

He said, scowling, "You turned Exarchel's motes back on, so that no one can see or hear us. God, how I hate nanotech."

Her triple voice said, "Finished or not, you are confined until matters resolve themselves. I will permit you to consult with your friends, who perhaps can see to the wounds of that odd, one, solitary body you call your own. I have other arrangements to make throughout these Tombs pending the arrival here of the Paramount assigned to these revenants; or, more precisely, the completion. Consultations must be made before the Bell arrives. The Hyades practice deracination and removal of every surface structure encountered of the target species; this Tomb is now exposed, and, without intervention, will be converted."

"Wait—you sound as if the Bell is not under your control. Is it actually a machine from the Hyades, which somehow got here faster than possible? But it can't be! Hold it! *Wait!*"

She turned, walked over to the central fountain, hips swaying from side to side, paused at the brink, and dove in. She did not emerge.

Menelaus blinked. Maybe her outfit actually was a wet suit.

3. Pretenses

Soorm, who was still lying on the floor pretending to be frozen, opened his goatlike eye. His other eye, of course, was already and ever opened, since it had no lid. He said in Latin, "That was weird. But I told you there was a secret exit in that cistern."

Mickey, who was also lying on the floor pretending to be frozen, spoke without raising his head or opening either eye. "Your breathing changed when you went from alpha wave state to beta wave state. If I noticed it, the posthumans noticed it."

Soorm rolled to his feet, lithe as a bear. Mickey climbed heavily to his feet, round as a water balloon.

Soorm said, "So what is actually going on, again, exactly? Is this something the nonposthumans can be told?"

Menelaus said, "I think even a nonposthuman can understand the complex and abstract concept that Blackie has been puck-dithering with me."

Soorm said, "If I knew what that was, I would say it sounds painful. Does it involve your anus in any capacity?"

"It involves my brain being too slow and too stupid. Ever since the moment Aanwen told me she knew who I was and walked out of here and over to my depthtrain station, I've just been gulled. He was not after me. Blackie was not trying to dig up this Tomb to find me. He was trying to dig up and capture a working depthtrain station. And he had to do it in such a way that I did not blow the station before it fell into his hands, so he had to have his people act like they were looking for me. Maybe he knew where I was all along; maybe he did not give a good goddamn."

Soorm said, "*Blow* the station? Do you have all your rooms and chambers really wired with explosives and outfitted with guns and lethalities? That's paranoid."

Menelaus said, "Is your nervous system really hidden under two levels of fakes with three levels of encryption?"

Soorm said blithely, "It is not a matter for casual discussion. I have foes."

"As have I, and I am usually asleep when they come a-calling."

Mickey said, "But why does the Master of the World want a depthtrain? And why send Alalloel to tell you? Was she here just to tell lies?"

Menelaus glanced sharply at him. "Lies, plural? With an *s*? I only heard one. She was lying about the Tombs. But I don't know the point of that lie . . ."

"She was so totally lying about Mentor Ull," affirmed Mickey.

Menelaus said slowly, "What makes you say so?"

Mickey said, "First, Ull was about as good at lying with a straight face as you. Second, Alalloel is possessed. The woman who was just here was not the one who was sitting in the mess tent yesterday."

Menelaus said, "Yeah. She aged four hundred years in one day."

Mickey said, "No, that is not it. That demon is a type we call 'Legion'—a manifestation with multiple centers. But Legion cannot coordinate well. When a demon like that tells a lie, one and only one voice ever speaks. When multiple voices lie, it sounds rehearsed rather than spontaneous, or the voices drop out of synch. So whatever Alalloel said in choir is true. What she said solo is false. She said the thing about Ull solo: Therefore it is false. QED."

Menelaus said to Soorm, "You heard her. What do you think?"

Soorm flicked his two tongues in the air thoughtfully. "I don't believe in spooks. But I have noticed that Reyes, and you, and other posthumans I have met have more ability to fool themselves than stupid and normal people like me. You have more spare brainspace or something to devote to explaining away the obvious. Ull had been posthumanized, and so he did not listen when Aanwen told him who you were. Like animals, we humans tend to have a sharper ability to see what is right in front of us. I was there. I saw the dumb look on his arrogant little face. It was right in front of me."

Soorm shrugged and spread his webby hands. Then he said, "He was blind as a bat in a box down a dark well at the bottom of a coal mine shaft at midnight, overcast with no moon out. You cannot fake that kind of bone-deep stupid. If you had been wearing a yard-high pointy hat with two blinking eyes and the words I AM THE JUDGE OF AGES printed in seven languages circled by a trained magpie calling out the same words in seven languages . . . it *still* would not look as bad as what Mickey presently has perched on his head."

"Hey!" said Mickey, sounding wounded. "This hat makes me look dignified. It is my Headgear of Power!"

"Clothing is overrated," sniffed Soorm.

Menelaus said, "Why did Weird Girl say Ull was stalling me? It seems a pointless little thing to lie about."

Mickey said, "Oho! What do you know about the ancient and honorable art of fabrication? If you want to know about lies, talk to a magician. Listen: that little lie was the most important thing Alalloel said, which is why she said it first."

"Important that I was being stalled?"

Mickey said, "By the beard of baby Oberon, for a supergenius, you're dumb! No! That is not what the lie was! How did you *feel* when you found out, not that you had fooled Ull, but that Ull (of all people) had fooled you? Miserable? Worried, weak, and stupid? Scared? Like your foes might be better than you? Or, in other words, you are put in the exact state of mind any foe would want you to be in."

Soorm said, "She was also trying to make it sound as if Ull, who was a Hermeticist, and Aanwen, who was a personal vassal of Del Azarchel and him alone, were perfectly coordinated. What if they are not perfectly coordinated? Reyes broke with the Table Round."

Mickey said solemnly, "It is not an unbroken circle. The ward is weakened."

4. External View

Keirthlin, black parka flapping, came soaring over the floor toward them. She was skating like a speed skater. Menelaus saw that she had reprogrammed the smartmetal of her soles into frictionless surfaces. Her face was no longer grief-stricken, but instead looked preternaturally calm, hard, and intent, as if she had used some mesmeric technique or compartmentalization of her brain to store her grieving until it could be confronted without distraction. Had her expression been one of wild panic, it would not have more quickly imparted to Menelaus a sense of fear.

He was so startled that he began to get up, and this sent such pain through his body that he collapsed back in the throne, and that motion produced more pain. "I am going to need a well-equipped coffin with nine yards of synthetic flesh-replacement."

Keirthlin skated to the dais, leaped up, landed neatly, but then stumbled, and was on her knees before the throne. Without even bothering to speak, she snatched the goggles off her silvery eyes and thrust them at the face of Menelaus.

He caught them in his good hand before she could poke him in the eye with an earpiece.

"I thought you might like to see this," she said, panting, her voice bizarrely calm.

Menelaus donned the glasses.

It was an external view of the camp.

It had been only a short time since he had descended underground, but to see the snowy trees and hillocks of the camp in sunlight again, beneath a sky he had almost forgotten, was like looking into a world from childhood.

The cleft was enlarged. Trees on the hilltop had been flattened and scattered. Raw earth and broken rock, stumbled with boulders and dripping like river deltas of brown and dun and back, now spilled from the hill. Three vast shards of metal, carbon-nanotube-reinforced titanium steel several yards thick, had been bent to the vertical, and loomed like the sails of a ship of stone above the enlarged hole. This was where the magnetic ray from Tycho crater had passed.

The third level was gone, save for a fringe of wreckage ringing a pit. At the bottom of this pit, remarkably free of damage and debris, was the depthtrain station; but the launching and receiving coils, the drop-shaft, and the turntable were all vanished. The head of the evacuated tube was exposed to the snowy air. The outer door was gone. Only the inner door stood between the atmosphere and the airlessness of the depthtrain tube.

He saw nothing to provoke panic. Grief and horror and anger, yes, at the casual destruction of any clients in any coffins that might have been on the third level—but not panic.

Then he realized the visor had infrared, ultraviolet, and other settings. Clicking from one band to another, he now saw that the head of the depthtrain tube was glowing white-hot. The excess of magnetic energy running to the surface from the core of the planet was roughly the same as that found at the North and South Poles—or, rather, to be more accurate, the application of some titanic electromagnetic force had made this spot on Earth into the magnetic North Pole, placing the magnetic South Pole no doubt somewhere off the coast of Australia.

The display of such unimaginable immensity of power was indeed worthy of some consternation. Menelaus, in a tense tone, started to say, "Keirthlin, what is causing . . ."

Then came the explosion.

Menelaus was flung from his throne and fell heavily to the floor, perhaps hitting every single second-degree burn that had blackened his upper back and lower legs. Fortunately, the pain as the ends of his broken arm bones ground together was so great that the tormenting sensation of his dead skin being peeled off receded to the background.

The goggles did not fall off his face, yet he saw nothing. Keirthlin's calm voice cut through Soorm's bellowing and Mickey's swearing, and told Menelaus to stand by. His implants detected the nodes she wore on her belt seeking other contacts through the Nymph arboreal neural net. Then the picture returned.

The image was from considerably farther away. The view now showed the hill, and what seemed a stream or tube of pure white light, slightly red at the edges, reaching down from heaven to touch the shattered crest of the hill. All the black shadows from the trees, clefts, rocks, and surrounding clouds were leaping and staggering in straight lines of deepest black directly away from the tower of white fire.

The Blue Men had been wise to abandon the camp: the seashell-shaped buildings had been tossed by the shock wave like so many teacups shattered against the hearthstone, cracked and blackened, and the smartwire fence flung across the trees like a snarled fishing line. At that same moment, everything flammable flicked with a yellow-white aura and caught fire; everything not flammable began to melt.

The image vanished, and switched to yet another viewpoint, this one from two or three miles away.

A cloud of smoke, black and oily midmost, but red and yellow with blinding fire at the edge, gushed out from the hill and was yanked upward like a drawn blanket. When seen through the ash cloud, the stream of white light now resolved itself into a lava-stream made of molten iron, catching the light with a glitter of diamond refractions.

Menelaus realized the white stream was not reaching *down* from heaven, but rushing *up* into it. And it was not a tower, but a river of material moving so rapidly as to make a blur of all features.

It was Von Neumann crystal. It was a segment of supercompressed iron from the inner core of the planet, having been accelerated by linear magnetic drive throughout the entire radius of the globe-crossing depthtrain system and shot through the crust of the Earth at some seventeen times the speed of sound. It was a semisolid bar of iron, fathom upon fathom of it, being tossed into the sky in a casual display of power that only great natural disasters or great instruments of war ever demonstrated.

The material would be heated like a space capsule making reentry by the friction of the speed of the liftoff; but compared to the molten core of the Earth, the heating caused by breaking through the tiny blanket of atmosphere was as nothing.

Then the white tower was gone. For a moment, so fast was the rate of ascent, the tail of the upflying mass could be glimpsed, a tapering comet-length glowing like a bar in a steel mill. Then the hail started: streaks of light the color of snowflakes appearing and disappearing high above. The launch of the mass had been nearly perfect. Nearly. The loss of even one percent of the mass in the atmosphere, as crystals were peeled away or snapped off, meant that everything Menelaus could see from his vantage point, horizon to horizon, was now being pelted as if with hailstones of fire.

It looked like the first few raindrops touching the slabs of the concrete cloverleaf of his old hometown when the glacier in the distance began to display pockmarks and acne. The steam from the melting ice rose up into the sky.

Then the iron falling was like a shower, and the whole landscape was chewed as if by machine-gun bullets into a moonscape, but a moonscape coating the bottom of a furnace. Then the image vanished for the last time.

He closed his eyes, blinking, trying to resolve the last image that had brushed so briefly against his cornea. It was the faintest possible line of blue reaching from the horizon to the zenith, and at this latitude, the atmospheric distortion made the immensity of the skyhook seem to slant across the sky, curving like a longbow, with its foot somewhere over the horizon to the south.

The line of white-hot iron that had leaped skyward had looked, compared to trees or towers or even the skyscrapers New York the Beautiful was alleged once to have held, like a construction Cyclopes would have been too diminutive to build; but only Titans and elder Uranian beings as could gouge out the seven seas with a mattock, or rear the dome of the sky and lantern it with countless stars.

But when seen against the background of the skyhook, it was like seeing a suspension bridge against the background of mountains blue with distance beyond the water. No matter how big, tall, or heavy a suspension bridge, it is a toy compared to the majestic immensity of mountains. The line of sky-flung iron had been longer than a suspension bridge, but not by much, and may have weighed as much as many aircraft carriers set end-to-end.

But the skyhook was astronomical in scope, and made even a mountain range set on its end look puny. In this case, the mountain range Menelaus saw, white with glaciers, and now covered as if with a spilled pepperbox by subatmospheric meteorite impacts, was over seven hundred miles from northernmost to southernmost ridge. The skyhook was well over two hundred twenty thousand miles from base to geosynchronous balance point. The iron column had been a hair less wide in diameter than the hypocycloid tunnel of the depth-train system: nine and a half feet. In contrast the skyhook was some two and a half miles in diameter and over fifty thousand feet high.

If someone had lit a yardstick on fire and, with the help of a large crossbow, flung it straight up the side of the Empire State Building and into the clouds beyond, some mote smaller than an ant, looking upward in awe, may have been impressed with the hugeness of the yardstick—until its little mind adjusted to the scale.

5. Pain

He felt the hands of Mickey and Soorm on him, helping him back to the throne, and he felt nine distinct types of pain: aches, agonies, scalds, bone fracture, laceration, throbs, gashes, pangs, and smarts.

Treacherous numbness pretending not to be pain, and lightheadedness brought on by blood loss, shock, cold, panic, blows to the face and head, lack of sleep, nanite interference with nerve flow, or brought on by improperly too-rapid petrifaction and thaw, that he did not consider to be "pain"—these were like wading pools left behind by the tide compared to pain's true ocean. The things like where his nose hurt from being slammed into a coffin, or where his head ached from being pummeled by the musketstock of a dog; while he might have complained were he healthy that these were painful, compared to the overloaded torrent of pain signals jerking and throbbing and cutting like ice and flashing like angry lightning down his nerves, he would have laughed to call a mere broken nose or cut lip pain.

So it was that when Soorm gasped and Mickey flinched in surprise; and he fell awkwardly into the seat; and the sensation in his arm was only that of having red-hot wires yanked inexpertly up and down through the marrows of his bones; and his skull barked against the metal backrest—that was so slight that he merely smiled, wincing only slightly because he discovered his lip was cut.

"Godling, you are in trouble," said Mickey in Virginian.

Menelaus, who was absorbed in recollecting the visual details of the scene overhead and outside, had only the smallest fragment of his many-layered mind to spare, and so he said, "I think we are in trouble. That mass of Von Neumann crystal was traveling beyond escape velocity, maybe beyond orbital velocity, and it may be the first of several such launches. I've toyed with the idea, of course, of using the train acceleration system to launch a vehicle into orbit, but the friction problem has always stopped me. In this case . . ."

Only then did he realize that Mickey, who had no goggles with an external view, could not possibly be talking about the launch he had just seen, or even known what was going on overhead and outside. The noise of micrometeorites landing with explosive force along the rocks and hills overhead could be heard, buried here under scores of feet of bedrock and layers of armor, as something fainter than the tap-tap of the drops of a summer shower on the roof. Mickey probably did not leap from that sense impression to conclude that Exarchel had just successfully pirated the technology of Pellucid and created a small-scale orbital version of itself using frighteningly advanced Xypotechnology.

He reached up and pulled the goggles off, absentmindedly proffering them toward Keirthlin, who was not looking at him. Her silvery eyes were on the gathered men facing him.

Their hair was smeared with blood and offal, sharpened bones piercing nose or earlobes, and dressed in white leather flayed from human victims. They were standing on the highest tier of the dais, and had both captured muskets and antique pikes and halberds pointed at him.

Of the twelve men, four were civilians: one wore the grape leaf design of a vintner, one was dressed in the spirals and formulae of a genetic alchemist, one wore a surcoat emblazoned with the snakes and birds of an apothecary, and one was in a black robe adorned with the cogwheels and smokestack of a factory hand. The rest wore the frozen and berserk expression of Demonstrators, the warrior-zealots of the Witches.

Behind them, carrying wands instead of muskets, were Fuamnach and Louhi, Twardowski of Wkra, and Drosselmeyer of Detroit. Drosselmeyer had in his hand a jeweled pistol of the Blue Men, and he had managed to ignite the gems of the barrel to a soft, sinister glow.

Mickey stood to the left of the throne, leaning on his charming wand and looking remarkably nonchalant for a man facing a firing squad. Soorm was on all fours next to the left arm of the throne, his tail lashing, eyes retracted, head lowered, teeth bared; but the expression on him looked like something between a grin and a sneer. Keirthlin the Gray in her black parka stood behind the throne, her hand on the tall backrest. Her fur hood was down, her goggles parked on her brow, and her blue hair hung like a banner down her back; but her strange silver eyes were calm as if she used a mental discipline to neutralize all fear.

"Yes, we are in trouble," said Menelaus with a sigh.

"What do you mean, 'we,' White Man?" asked Mickey.

6. Burn

Menelaus closed his eyes again, because he was still trying to elicit one last bit of visual information from the photons that had struck his eyes. The image was clear enough in his imagination: the vast blue swath of immensity, longbow-curved, hanging in the heaven huge as the rings of Saturn as seen from its innermost moon, had been slightly brighter on the eastern limb than the western. It could not be sunlight. It was an energy discharge of thrusters or attitude-correction jets of some sort, imparting an impulse to the immense mass. It was a maneuvering burn.

The implication of that was clear. The Bell, or whatever intelligence was directing it, had noticed that the north and south magnetic poles of the planet were not where they should be and had seen the eruption of the thin sliver of core material shoot up past mantle and crust, atmosphere and stratosphere—and it was correcting its orbital elements to move the mouth of the skyhook toward the open and defenseless, roofless tomb.

"No, my friend," said Menelaus to Mickey with a sigh. "I mean 'we.' Those of us in this chamber, on this continent, or on this planet. I mean the human race, and I don't just mean unmodified elder men. I mean all the human races, living or ghost. Us. All of us.

"I thought the skyhook was something the Blue Men had created. Then I thought it was Melusine technology. Now, I do not know. Maybe Einstein was wrong. Maybe the Hyades got here faster than the laws of physics allow, or can accelerate mass without energy, or can derive more energy from a gram of mass than total conversion allows. Because that object, which is bigger than anything man-made has any right to be, is sure *acting* like a Hyades instrumentality."

He opened his eyes.

There stood Illiance to one side of the line of armed men, in a coat of blank, pure, and gemless blue, and a look of unselfconscious pride almost like a glow.

To the other stood Fatin Simon Fay, pretty as a schoolgirl in her white cotton dress and peach sash, hair snared in a net that hung down her neck, and in her face was such darkness that Menelaus could not put a name to it. It was a passion beyond mere anger or shame or thirst for revenge.

"Why, Miss Fay," he said in Virginian. "Pardon my manners for not getting up. What can I do for you?"

"You can burn," she said.

10

The Trial of the Judge of Ages

1. Fair and Square

"We do not have a stake," said the female with a young woman's body but an old woman's weariness and helplessness and hate in her eyes. "But one of the automata is being drenched with its own lubrication oil by the crones, and it has petrol as well, so it can just clasp you to its body while afire like Talos of myth."

Menelaus said, "It's enterprising to improvise, I guess. But before we get on with the barbecue, let me explain the current situation, since a lot has happened in the last four minutes."

Fatin opened her mouth to object, her eyes white and hot with hate; but Illiance (looking strangely like a miniature Pilgrim from a children's history primer in his blank and unadorned coat) stepped forward, his eyes bent on Montrose, and made a cutting gesture with the edge of his hand. Such was the dignity and authority of the gesture, that Fatin—perhaps more sensitive to strange conjunctions or hidden meaning than a non-Witch could be—drew back and held her piece.

Or perhaps (Montrose thought cynically) Fatin understood enough to guess that Illiance could now render paralytic or comatose everyone in the room except for Mickey, Guy, Scipio, and Trey—and he had already captured or needled three of the four.

Whatever the reason, Menelaus seized the opportunity to seize the floor: "First, Alalloel the Melusine has been taken over by a download demon named Legion, who works for Blackie—Ximen del Azarchel, the Arch-Hermeticist, and Master of the World—who arranged to have an avalanche block the doors leading back to the surface, and collapse the depthtrain tube leading down to the deep. So we are all trapped here.

"Second, the Bell is coming. Oh, Baby Jesus puking milk on Mary's virgin shoulder, you don't know what that is, do you? Gigantic alien tower that eats cities, so tall that most of it is out of the atmo. Just outside us, about twenty miles off. The thing is about nine miles wide, so the leading edge will reach here a little while before the trailing edge catches up. I thought it was a local-made thing, until the Melusine made it clear that Blackie did not want to find my Tombs and kill me. He wanted to find my Tombs to find a way to Pellucid, and find a way to make a space launch, to spread Exarchel in the form of a Von Neumann technology to other planets. Or that's my guess. And I should have seen the clues when I saw the Iron Hermeticist D'Aragó come waltzing in to fight me to keep his spaceport on Fear Island—not its real name—open, and when I realized the place they made planetfall was Mount Misery—is so its real name—because you don't spend expensive fuel to belly flop into the Caribbean from the great black yonder if you can climb down and back up a convenient skyhook for free.

"Third, Exarchel—your friend, the Machine—just shot a wee sliver of the core of the planet into space, programmed with a copy of his mind, almost as if that were some emergency measure used to save a copy of himself if the world he is leaving is doomed. So the evil god you serve, the one that promised you long life, not to mention castles in the air and moonbeams in a jar? He's gone. Or, since he cannot move, he mailed his backup copy of his brain to Mars or something to carry on the family name. We can call that one Exo-exarchel. Just to keep our version numbers straight.

"Fourth, there is a current civilization out there, like I said—hurrah for me, I am a genius—and they seem to be a civilization of evil freaks who mean to break into all my Tombs, drill jacks into all our heads, and turn us all into zombies and mind slaves absorbed into the local hierarchy of five-man neuro-infospheres.

"So that is the situation we find ourselves in—trapped, doomed, abandoned, and the Hyades skyhook is about to float over us and yank us up into a Clarke orbit for transshipment to Alpha Centauri, but if the skyhook don't get us, a Melusine called a Paramount is coming to brain-rape us, and absorb us into its soul vampire-style, but more neuroelectronically. And Blackie just ran away. Got it?

"So, Fatin; Illiance. What little thing can I do for y'all?"

But Illiance stepped forward, coming between the muskets and pikes and the man at which they pointed, and he stepped with such boldness, it was as if he could not imagine any creature could harm him.

"I wish to address you," said Illiance. "Fatin, who intends you harm, would preclude my comments, who wishes harm from you. Logically, I must go first."

Fatin did not look peeved at the interruption, but amazed. She held her peace, and inclined her head, opening her hands as if to invite the little blue man to continue.

The common habit of Simplifiers, to speak in the passive voice, and to phrase things as if one were merely observing a coincidence, rather than causing an effect, was not here being used. Menelaus wondered what that portended.

"So, Illiance!" said Menelaus. "Am I to assume that Sir Guiden took off his big and heavy gauntlets to get all the gems off your coat, and to take your pistol, but that I failed to warn him you also carry a venom needle that can prick bare hands, because sometimes I forget baseline humans do not notice what seems obvious to me? And may I also assume Scipio the Cryonarch and Trey Azurine the Sylph were herded at point of that same pistol, and are squeezed together naked in embarrassing intimacy in a narrow coffin that two ugly crones and a half-broken automaton are perched atop?"

Illiance looked surprised. "The situation is one they would find shameworthy? One of my people would not be sexually stimulated by sharing a coffin with a Sylph, particularly if she were unclothed as a security precaution, her clothing being hunger silk, and not as a display of mate-willingness; and to us there can be no stimulation if she were a non-virgin, since we cannot switch from one partner to another. Being innately chaste, those of my order do not always appreciate what more primitive men categorize as associated with mating behaviors, signs, or displays."

"Well, being stuffed naked into a coffin bed with a wiggly teenager young enough to be your daughter, but who maybe has something not right in her head, yeah, that violates normal Churchgoing notions of decent respectability, I'd say. But maybe I am old-fashioned, because everyone in the future seems to be a nudist. I won't complain. I am just glad you did not shoot them.

"So! What can I do for you before the angry and superstitious Witch burns the falsely accused Christian? You have the floor, Preceptor Illiance."

At this, the Blue Man drew himself up almost pridefully, and tilted up his chin, and said, "You mistake me. Am I dressed like a Preceptor?"

Had Montrose not been teetering on the edge of fainting, and not distracted with many layers of disasters and deception, he would have seen it sooner. As it was, it caught him by surprise, and he laughed aloud.

Of course Illiance was strutting and smiling, head high and shoulders back. It was not that he had an unbreakable hold over everyone in the chamber. It was that his long-ingrained habit of mind made him look splendid to himself. For Illiance wore the uniform of the highest rank and highest dignity of the Simple Men: a vacant coat. There was nothing simpler than the simplicity of blank blue.

"Then how should I address you?"

"I wear the display of an Expositor of the Perfected dignity. While it is true that I happen to wear it, not that Sir Guiden meant me to wear it, nonetheless, it was by his hand that I find myself so garbed—and therefore I must with utmost effort behave with simplicity so perfect and limpid, that should my peers again adorn me, it will not be due to my failure to attempt."

Menelaus chuckled and spread his hands, amused despite himself. "Well then, Expositor Illiance. How do perfected folk act?"

Nothing would have shocked him more: Illiance got down on both knees.

Illiance said, "I speak for all the Blue Men. We admit our guilt and appeal to your mercy."

Menelaus tried to think of something witty or outrageous or crass to say that would break the uncomfortable tension of silence that filled the chamber at those words. But the tension merely hardened and thickened like ice on a pond beneath a tree in late fall, when the gaiety of leaves gives way to the barrenness of barren twigs.

Illiance spoke with stark honesty. Menelaus saw his naked soul, and wished he could turn his eyes away.

2. Guilty Plea

"Judge of Ages, this world of tomorrow into which we woke terrified us, because we thought the future would be filled with children of ours, and better than us. Instead it is filled with nothing but ice and emptiness.

"We are indoctrinated from the crèche to believe that, in dire emergency, the end of preserving the race excuses any means used for that end, however unconscionable.

"In this, we are deceived: This is the philosophy of the Machine, who betrays the world and all our futures into servitude in survival's name. And any deed can be called an aid to survival. Every day is a dire emergency to a mind of fear.

"I now see that this philosophy of survival was meant as a leash to lead us as a dog is led. Mentor Ull tugged on our chain, and when he told us we needed to dig to survive, we dug; and to steal, we stole; and to abduct, imprison, build a prison camp, become first jailors and then torturers and mind-rapists—we, whose order meant us to live lives of contemplation, self-sufficiency, and retirement from the evils of the world—we became the evils of the world.

"We betrayed everything in the name of survival, and in the end, the Order of Simplified Vulnerary Aetiology did not survive.

"We are Locusts.

"Worse, we are Locusts who lack the tendrils that allow us the mental unity and community of purpose Locusts enjoy: we have all the evils of Locusts and none of their good!

"We repent our crimes and accept with philosophical resignation whatever penalty you inflict, or even with pride, if only our example can deter any others in like danger of yielding to such tempting self-deceptions.

"We are an altruistic species, so designed by our genetics, and eagerly accept to be sacrificed for the good of others, even to the point of accepting the painful death needed to act as a warning to others not to condone nor repeat our crimes."

3. Sentencing

Menelaus, perhaps for the first time in his long and loudmouthed life, felt tongue-tied. Anything he said would seem trite and trivial compared to that confession; especially one uttered by a dwarf whose upbringing and way of life did not even have an idea, much less a practice, of confession.

Menelaus had truly thought these so-called Simple Men were simply the most arrogant little bastards he had ever met. And yet there was Illiance, dressed in what (among his people) was a cross between his Sunday-go-to-meeting duds and the uniform of a four-star general. And he was kneeling, meek as you please, not just willing to be punished, but asking.

Menelaus said softly, "You understand, Illiance—Expositor Illiance, I mean— that there is no such person as the Judge of Ages. That is just a name people made up after I was buried. This is not my chair, nor is this my chamber. This place was also made up by people wanting to glorify themselves by glorying-up me. You searched here. Remember the closet where you found the coffeepot, the one with the dartboard on the wall and the ashtray in the bathtub? That is where I stow myself between slumbers. I am not the Judge of Ages."

The Blue Man's hands smoothed down the severely barren fabric of his gemless coat, as if removing a wrinkle.

Then, raising his head, Illiance looked Menelaus in the eye. "At times, we must fulfill the roles in which fate garbs us."

Menelaus was silent a long moment, pondering. "Very well. You are guilty of trespass, breach of faith, assault, theft and robbery, conversion of property, kidnapping, false imprisonment, desecration of graves, torture, maiming, intentional infliction of emotional distress, Savantry, mind-rape.

"Also, you are guilty of breech of the peace, melee, assaults both with deadly weapons and with incendiary or explosive deadly weapons, invasion by instrument, assault by means of molecular engine, widespread destruction of property.

"And furthermore, due to your conspiratorial association with Ull, who committed murder in the course of a conspiracy to commit other felonies with your encouragement and consent, you are also guilty of three counts of homicide.

"The court also notes the aggravating circumstances of the homicides: First, that the murders were committed by most foully and brutally tearing the victims via setting deadly and vicious dogs on them; second, that these dogs, being rational creatures but unable to achieve the full moral capacity of human reason, and thus not being responsible for their conduct in a legal measure, were nonetheless involved in an egregious crime, rightfully regarded as the worst a servant creature to the race of Man can perform, which is the destruction of human life; and in so doing you permanently and irrevocably stained the conscience of the dogs who did the murder, who are now legally deodands, and subject to destruction for the safety of the public; third, that the victims were denied a Christian burial or a marker to settle the uncertainty of any who might later in sorrow seek for them.

"However, the court takes notice of the fact that, no matter the outcome, if either the Hyades or the Melusine ravish me of the Tombs and despoil all those under my possession, the deterrent effect of any punishment will be moot. You have volunteered for pain to deter others and thus perhaps to save them from your fate; but circumstances provide that there shall be no others to deter.

"The court also notes the fact that the crime is unrepeatable, and therefore there is no strong public reason to remove you, by death, incarceration, transportation, or hibernation, from the current society.

"The court notes that some penalties allegedly aim at rehabilitating the wrongdoer: however, it is well and anciently known that no civilized law recognizes this as a legitimate exercise of the sovereign power, since the sovereign is neither tutor nor sage nor father confessor.

"The point of law in civilized nations is retribution, that the evils men do might thereby recoil upon them, as simple justice and thus the security and liberty of the people demand. Howbeit, in this case, Oenoe the Nymph, and the court in our own person, are obliged to plead with the court for leniency: which plea we will grant with pleasure, and seek therefore no retaliation against you, howsoever richly deserved.

"This leaves only the question of restitution. You were told, and you disregarded, that the means to escape the wrath of the Judge of Ages was to restore and return every artifact you have stolen, repair every coffin you have cannibalized, return all the people you have carried off, and make good every injury.

"The court finds that your indigent personal circumstances, you being yourself a Thaw in a strange era and a member of a contemplative order that practices poverty, makes the performance of restitution impossible; therefore the court sentences you to death by progressive suspension failure . . ."

Illiance, who had perhaps the power to destroy everyone in the chamber, merely closed his eyes and inclined his head in submission, uttering no word of defense.

". . . but the court further orders the sentence suspended upon your parole and oath that you will do everything in your power to aid and assist the defense of these Tombs and the people therein; namely, that you apply to the Sovereign Military Hospitalier Order of Saint John of Jerusalem of Rhodes of Malta and of Colorado to serve them as neophyte and squire or in whatever capacity the utmost and unstinting exercise of ability and faith might allow; and that, should you betray them, or be found by the Grand Master or your superior officers to be without the courage and discipline, devotion or firmness of will required of this service, that they shall appear before this court each in his own person, not by writing, and vow solemnly that your service yields neither honor nor use to the Hospitalier Order; whereupon the court shall carry the execution into effect in all due haste and solemnity, that you shall be taken to a coffin set aside for this purpose, and cellular motions suspended below the revival threshold, so as to pass without pain or awareness from sleep to slumber to death.

"By the most ancient prohibition of law, this court lacks the power to command, order, or compel that you enter baptism, repent, and embrace the Christian faith as needed for entry into this sovereign knightly order, albeit one outside the faith may serve as lay manservant; however, a due concern for public safety can and does require that you be commanded to foreswear and repent of all the worship of demons, particularly that you shall reject and foreswear the Machine, and foreswear his Master, and all his works and all his ways; that you shall resist the glamour of evil and hate it; and you shall heed no promise by the Machine, neither of increased life nor augmented intelligence nor any other reward of this world.

"So ordered.

"Do you understand the grave sentence that has been laid upon you? If you have any bar or hindrance or objection that might prevent your performance, speak now."

Illiance said only, "I have nothing."

"To carry out the sentence, you better go find and unhex whatever biotech hex you placed on Sir Guy. Court is dismissed. And if you see the Beta Maidens, Suspinia and Vulpina, send them over here, please."

Illiance nodded, and rose from his knees. With no ceremony or formal word of departure, he turned and departed.

At this, Montrose raised his hand to Fatin and beckoned her forward. "And what complaint is yours, young Miss?"

4. Motion for Dismissal

Fatin the maiden stepped forward to speak for the Witches. The mention of the Christian faith had set her teeth in a grimace, looking as allergic to the mention of such things as a Clade-dweller to anyone not his clone.

"You dare sit in the seat of judgment?" said she in a fiery tone. "This is a farce."

"Maybe so," said Montrose wryly. "But it is not a farce of my making."

"We reject that the Judge of Ages has any authority to sit in judgment over us." She pointed her charming wand at him. "You should be standing trial, not trying others! You murder whole periods of history, condemning aeons and civilizations, and imagining you have the right to judge them? Are you a god?"

Menelaus said mildly, "You say it. I never claimed to be a god."

Mickey cleared his throat, and bent, and whispered in Menelaus' ear, "Actually, I think at least once in the last hour, you said you were."

Menelaus raised his good hand as if to rub his nose, and spoke from the side of his mouth, "You are *not* helping." Then to Fatin he said, "Okay. Fair is fair. You caught me."

There was a murmur of confusion as Menelaus rose wobbling from the judgment seat, reached with his one good arm, and took up the claymore of Sir Guiden, fumbling to try to draw it from its sheath. Mickey, eyes wide with silent questions, leaned and drew it, dropping the scabbard, and proffered an arm to Menelaus.

Down Menelaus limped, leaning on the arm of the stout man, and when he came to Fatin, he passed the massive blade from Mickey to her. The sword was too big for her. Even in both her small hands, it wobbled.

With a nod, Menelaus gestured at the iron throne. "Take a seat."

Fatin said, "What does this mean?"

Louhi, her gray and skull-like face high above Fatin's like a vulture circling in a desert, said in a voice of spits and coughs, "Beware, maiden Fatin! He practices his craft on you. Take no gift of the underworld! Recall the chair where Theseus sat!"

Menelaus said, "Hope you don't mind if I sit down? My feet are killing me."

Menelaus with a grunt sat on the ground, and tugged at the torn garb he had stolen from Rada Lwa, wiggling to get comfortable. Seeps of blood were beginning to turn the bandages wrapping his feet pink. "Who the hell makes a floor out of gold? Next netherworld, plush carpet, for sure."

Then he looked up, saying to Fatin, "You were made a promise. I was there. If you helped the Chimerae fight the Blue Men—which you did—the Judge of Ages would be delivered into your hands—which I am. So I am giving you a turn. There is the judgment seat. Sit in it. Make your accusation, hear my defense, pass judgment. The little boxes will translate your words to everyone here. Crappy translation, so avoid colloquial expressions."

The line of Witches armed with muskets and pikes, given no orders, parted and shuffled left and right, forming a half circle with Menelaus in the midst. Menelaus realized he had spent too much time among the Chimerae. The sloppiness of the maneuver made him wince, and he wondered when it would be that the half circle of musketmen would realize they were standing in each other's line of fire like pantomime footsloggers from a slapstick comedy.

He was alone in a wide space of bloodstained floor, with only two or three corpses to his left or right.

With a dignity almost equal to that of Ctesibius, Fatin mounted the dais, sat, and grunted and lifted the swaying claymore, and dropped it, clanging, so that it rested across the armrests. The friars carried the weight of the overlarge sword on their bowed heads like Atlas carrying the globe.

Fatin raised her slender hand and said, "Earth and sky, wood and water and hill, magnetism and electricity, attend me now and be my witnesses! The trial of the Judge of Ages is come. I myself will speak the accusation. Hear my story, elements of the world—and you human people, hear me as well! I accuse him of being the greatest of criminals."

Menelaus made a little gesture of circling one forefinger around the other, like a fisher reeling in a line. "The Defense moves that you make it a little snappier, Your Honor. We are kind of pressed for time here. Of what am I accused?"

The expression of Fatin at first was one of simple surprise at the audacity of the question, but hardened into a look of injured anger that Menelaus would pretend not to know. "You slew our world. Do I need to conjure up images of the dead cities, slain by starvation and power loss, the once-proud skyscrapers showing the skeletons of their girders against a sky empty of planes and rocketships forever?"

Menelaus looked at her quizzically. "I did not destroy your civilization. It self-destructed. It was poxy *meant* to immolate itself from the get-go. Your Honor, I move to dismiss on the grounds that a cause of action has not been stated for which relief at law can be granted. Are we done now? The Bell is coming. I want to see if maybe we can get out of the chamber through the cistern. Alalloel went that way."

Fatin screamed, and, at that moment, looked every inch a Witch. She tossed the huge claymore, ringing, to the dais floor, and rose and pointed one trembling finger at Menelaus, spitting the words as if delivering a curse. "The Hermetic Order knows the science to predict the future! They created the Simon Families. They *meant* us to prevail. They *gave* us the future! The future *belonged* to us! It was the prize and the possession of the Witches!"

Menelaus thought bitterly of all the people who thought the future belonged to them, as if it were a tract of unclaimed frontier. They had calculated without the presence of men like Blackie, who had already fenced off the free ranges of the future with a barbed wire called Cliometry.

Back Fatin sank in the throne, her head tilted forward, her girlish mouth sullen. In a colder voice, she continued, "Only someone who knew their same predictive calculus of history could steal our future from us: only a fellow Hermeticist in rebellion against them. You, in other words!"

"They wanted you to fail," said Menelaus heavily. "You don't think Del Azarchel gives a rat's filthhole about your polygamy and your polytheism and your airy-fairy belief in dancing wood sprites? He is a Spanish Roman Catholic, very old-school. He just needed you to destroy his Church so he could have his toys take over the world. The Church outlawed Xypotechnological emulation of human brains: and so was in the way, and had to go.

"The means he selected were elegant and unexpected. I can see here that most of y'all here don't know the origins of your race.

"Here we go. I'll keep it short."

5. The True History of the Witches

"Blackie captured a posthuman Giant named Og, drilled Savant reading circuits into his head, brain-raped him, made a copy, and then over the phone or by remote lecture, had Ex-Og persuade the Consensus of Giants to embark on a program.

"The idea for this program was to crossbreed certain volunteer families through arranged marriages and bribes and insurance schemes and the like to solve certain problems no one generation was long-lived enough to solve. You know how like the Bach family had a knack for music? Og, or, rather Blackie, used the Monument methods to decode genetic emergent properties in human DNA, to breed the Simon Families for mathematics and obsessive-compulsive behavior. Then he used Cliometry to design the Longevity Institute, breeding the Simon Families to have transmission and inheritance laws to pass down ownership and rewards of research patents in what were basically living versions of complex information feedback loops. These loops were established with people and their roles acting just like the attractor nodes in a game theory lattice—ah, never mind. Let us say he blessed the families to increase and multiply and keep to one task forever, and they formed hereditary orders.

"The Order of Transcendental Mathematicians was one such hereditary task force, and they were set to solve the problem of the One and the Many; the Order of Reductive Neurologicians was another, and were set to solve the problem of Free Will; the Semantic Order were set to solve the problem of the relation of Symbol to Thought, and establish the Philosophical Language; the Order of Empirical Utopiagenic Engineers were to devise the perfect form of government, and the perfect form of man to cohere to it; but the Longevitalists, your order, was set to find the secret of Eternal Youth.

"The secret was really not that hard to find, since Blackie just slipped it to your grandmas, who took credit for it.

"So all the wealth and fame and rejoicing from a grateful world (or at least, from every mother who wanted her daughters to have a very long and very healthy life) landed square in the laps of the Simons. Blackie had released part of the secret of youth, but gene-locked it so that women and only women were

long-lived. The secret is in bone marrow production of telomere-repair enzymes, and turning off the genetic clock that tells adolescent bones when to
stop growing—which is why you dames are crazy tall.

"And the inheritance laws and tithes built into the clan structure accumulated all the wealth of the scientific revolution into the hands of a few old ladies at the root of the family tree—it is amazing how much wealth you can
keep if you have two or three generations of husbands and children feeding
into the family trust funds, especially if the rest of the world dies off and pays
estate taxes and changes management three times quicker than you.

"After that, the all-male hierarchy of the Church was like a club run by teen
boys in a world run by wise old grandmas who've been around the block and
know which side of the egg to blow. The Simon Family organization also triggered a scientific revolution like a controlled reactor explosion, because all the
scientists of that generation were in those families. So the Simons had not only
wealth, but prestige greater than any institution in the world, secular or eccle-
siastical.

"But there was one other thing the Simon Families had: They had an idea.
The Simon Families, one and all, believed that man's ideas were built into his
genes because that is the situation Blackie set them up to live in and raise their
kids in. The idea of generational inheritance of ideas implies that ideas are carried in your genome. And once you believe that all ideas are little double-
helices of molecules and nothing more, you don't believe in ideas, not really.
You don't believe in the design of the cosmos. You don't believe the universe is
a rational mystery, just a mystery; and you don't think man is a rational animal,
just an animal.

"The Simon Family belief in eugenics led to your children and grandchildren
believing in Witchcraft as easily as arson leads to ashes.

"Once your so-called science tells you to believe human beings, including
scientists, are simply not rational beings, you stop doing real science, or doing
anything reasonable, and magic is the order of the day. Science becomes just a
cult like any other, except with an idol uglier and duller than most; and it becomes part of the structure that the powers of the world use to cow the unruly
and cull the weak, just like any other cult.

"And once you start worshipping power for its own sake, you stop looking to
see what ideas are objectively true or honest, real or sane, you turn into Witches,
and pick your ideas how you might pick to decorate your mantelpiece with bric-
a-brac: by how they happen to strike your fancy.

"When that happens, you no longer have ideas, they have you.

"And when the emergency comes like an Indian War-Band howling over the harvest fields, and you really need a good idea as badly as a settler needs his rifle, well, all you got is bric-a-brac on the mantel, not a weapon that shoots.

"You witches were the fiery torches Blackie used to burn down the cathedral called Western Civilization that was standing in the way of his Machine taking over.

"And once the torches were but used-up stubs, he threw you away."

6. Monster Witness

Menelaus started to climb heavily back to his wounded feet. A Warlock pushed through the line of musketmen, bent over Menelaus, and put a hand on his good arm, helping him to rise.

Menelaus whispered, "Who are you, friend? Your crones won't like your helping me."

The man was tall and lean; his eyes were dark and unblinking, as if haunted with wild thoughts, with a skeletally thin face, and a moustache that drooped past his jawline. His robes were adorned with patterns of holly and ivy and mistletoe, and images of wooden soldiers dueling crowned rats. At his brow he wore a horseshoe magnet, the ancient and ridiculous symbol of a machine-hunter.

He whispered to Menelaus, "My name is Drosselmeyer. Once, before I lost my youth, I slew five Savants whom I found nude upon a midnight in a frenzy of machine-worship atop a windowless building where ancient lights still burned, and ancient voices spoke; and the moon above shone clear."

"Pleased to meet ya," said Menelaus, wondering if the man were crazy.

"Is it true? The Hermetic Order made us, our race, our way of life? Then I stand behind you. Am I not an exorcist? Do I not hunt the Machine?"

Menelaus smiled. The man might be crazed, but he was not crazy. He patted the man on his shoulder. "It is all true. You were made by your enemies. I am your friend. We stand together."

Drosselmeyer took this literally, for he drew his athame, his Witch-knife, of sharpened black basalt from his sacred belt, and stepped behind the shoulder of Menelaus. Tiny little movements and whispers from the gathered Warlocks, crones, and Demonstrators ceased: a wintry silence was about them, and all eyes were on Menelaus.

Menelaus turned back to Fatin and raised his head and raised his voice. "You've declared your case. Now answer mine! Riddle me this: How do you maintain a scientific civilization when your scientists are forbidden from reaching politically inconvenient results under your Thought Decontamination Laws? Or maintain an industrial civilization without factories, defend it without an army, pay for it without a currency, run it without laws, or civilize the next generation without marriage? Answer: you don't."

She said nothing.

Menelaus continued more softly: "Your whole plague-ridden world was designed to live it up high-hog for one season, consume your seed corn, and perish next harvest. Designed by Melchor de Ulloa. Everything was timed to go up at once, like blowing the supports of a building so it all collapses inward on itself: self-destruction was built right into the foundational constitutions of your academic institutions, your industry, your military, your economy, your legal system, and your family structure—or lack of it."

He pointed at the savage faces of the Demonstrators and the corpselike faces of the white-haired crones behind. "Look at what your world led to, Fatin! This is the future the Hermeticists gave you! This is where your loyalty to the Simon Families led! These are your children. They don't have arts or sciences, marriage customs, or banking laws. They eat toadstools and worship rocks."

Fatin's eyes were troubled, but she sniffed and said scornfully, "Who are you to dare to judge? All ways of life are equally valuable and valid!"

"Really? Does that include ways of life that cannot keep hospitals lit or aircraft aloft?"

Soorm had one of the talking boxes pressed to the unseen holes that served him for ears. Now he put his head on the armrest of the throne, nose inches from where Fatin's hand rested on the hilt of the huge sword. "It's not true. Melchor de Ulloa did not design the failures in. Reyes told me everything."

Menelaus was looking sadly at his feet. The bandages were turning from pink to brown, and getting soggier. He waved his hand toward Soorm. "Your Honor, I call the crazy monster to the stand in my defense. I will tell you what he is saying."

Soorm spoke slowly, pausing for Menelaus to translate. "De Ulloa thought the Simon Family philosophy would lead to a better world, one where man lived at one with nature, where animals were elevated to human stature, and where all poverty was abolished. It was all a lie. The collapse was meant to scrape the vellum of history clean, so the Hermeticists could write on a blank scroll." Soorm turned to Menelaus. "This is something even you don't know. Ximen del Azarchel deceived Melchor de Ulloa. His whole plan of Cliometry that Ximen the Black showed his followers was false."

Menelaus said, "I found that out just today. What I cannot figure is that Blackie made emulations of the other Hermeticists, and made them into post-humans: Once they were as smart as he was, why did not they not see through his trick? Didn't they check his figures?"

Soorm shook his head like a human. "One man can deceive another man if he is trusted. Cannot posthuman deceive posthuman? Or perhaps Del Azarchel planted phantasm codes of his own, just like yours, but to turn clues and suspicions, instead of persons, invisible. We may never know."

7. The Legend Revisited

Drosselmeyer said, "Excuse this lowly student of the Hidden Things, honored and dread Maiden Fatin, but may I ask the Judge of Ages a question?"

She scowled but nodded. "To ask of the unknown is our creed."

Drosselmeyer stepped away from Menelaus and turned and saluted by holding the Witch-knife at eye level. Menelaus did not know the formal way to return the salute, so he just nodded affably and touched his forefinger to his eyebrow.

"Howdy."

"Dread Sir, there was a legend saying that we Witches were at war, and always have been, with He Who Waits. Our lore cannot be mistaken. It is, indeed, the first precept of our lore that our lore cannot be mistaken! And so we know the lore is infallible, because the lore says so! How can this be?"

Menelaus shrugged. "The bullshit lies told by the newspapers, run by the Simon Families, in those long ago days got scooped up and repeated into bullshit history books; and then got manured around and turned into bullshit legends. And a war makes a better story than the truth, and so gets passed along, and ended up in your lore. Stories get dumbed-down and drama'd-up by natural selection. I can show you the Divarication function involved, if you're curious."

Fatin said, "But I saw your knights herding people underground, into your dungeons and prisons! I saw it!"

"Into my refugee camps, you mean, Miss. Into my dormitories and mess halls. I opened my doors and let thousands and tens of thousands of starving exiles into my Tombs, to wait until the worst of the famines your crapheaded collectivist coven form of government had arranged had passed by, so that they could wake up in a greener world. It was not my damn fault that your rules about how to run the world made famine a permanent part of life.

"Your Honor!" Menelaus continued. "I call the Warlock Drosselmeyer to the stand. Do you swear to tell the truth by whatever make-believe spooks you serve?"

"By Asimov and E. M. Forster and all the sages of yore who swore that the Machine must serve Man and never rule him, so I swear."

"Uh. Good enough. Then answer me this: Your lore about me, the legend of He Who Waits. You've heard it. What weapons did it say my men used?"

"Pale white staves," answered Drosselmeyer, "from which drops of fire fell."

Menelaus pointed at the four staves holding up the canopy above the judgment seat. "There they are. Pretty damn effective, huhn? Slumber wands. They shed clusters of molecular engines held in a field of balled lightning. They only work on clients who have not been properly dehibernated and un-nanoinfected. Such as Trojan-Horse-wannabe clients who get inside my facility and pop up on quick-thaw and try to raise a ruckus. Your legends are about a time when my knights had to stop my clients from trying to take over my house by force, after I welcomed them in here as my guests.

"After I saved their sorry heathen asses," Menelaus continued, half to himself. "Damn Witches have no sense of gratitude.

"I don't blame your people, Fatin!" he continued in a louder voice. "You cannot be grateful. Gratitude requires private property. If you own all property in common, anything that comes to you is either yours by right, or you stole it. In the first case, the guy who gave it to you is just the quartermaster, and you don't give thanks if he just does his job; and in the second case, he is your chump. No one says 'thank you' and means it in a world like that.

"When De Ulloa made your world that way, he robbed you of gratitude and generosity, robbed you of the ability to earn thanks or give thanks, and you lost part of your humanity."

Mickey interrupted, "That cannot be. My people would not be so ungrateful! We respect the laws of guest and host, the sharing of wine and fire and salt."

Menelaus sighed. "Guess that depends on what period of history we're talking about. After y'all were reduced to absolute poverty by the spendthrift ways of your forefathers, you rediscovered some of the hard virtues of the poor, I reckon."

Drosselmeyer said, "Dread Sir! May I speak? What happened to them?"

"To who?"

"The Witches from the period of history we are talking about?"

Menelaus said, "The Witches from the days of the Collapse? I kept them on ice until the Collapse was over. Ask those two guys. Your Honor, I call that big guy to the stand. I don't know your name. Did your generation have the expanding economy and unclaimed land you needed to absorb a big influx of old-timers? Did I keep the Witches locked up forever, as I surely would have done had I really been at war with y'all, or by any chance did I let them out, and in a time when they could have a chance at new life?"

The man dressed in a robe adorned with images of cogwheels and smoke-stacks spoke up. "My name is Heron. I am of the Automaton Workers Coven Local 101. Yeah, Judge, times were fat and wages were high when I was younger. Then you let out the Old Witches. At first, we needed every new pair of hands to work. Later, it was more Old Witches than we wanted. We had a perfectly stable government under the Nameless Witch-King. A man government. We had wives who could not divorce us and take our children and our money. Our money was gold, back then. And our women were not allowed to kill our children anymore, in the womb or out of it. We owned things. Lands had boundary stones. Good old Janus, one of the old, strong gods, the god who curses those who move a boundary stone, he was among us then. So was Vesta, the goddess of the family. But then! Then when we had a flood of Witches from the Old Times, one named Butler began to agitate for all the Old Ways to return: nonaggression, harmony with nature, gathering and sharing, communes instead of corporations."

Another man, this one dressed in an alchemist's robes gilded with a pattern of birds and snakes wrapping in spiral DNA patterns, spoke up. "I am Parnassus of the Golden Golem Coven of Lake Superior. I was alive then, too. Your generosity with our age ended our age, Judge of Ages! The Butlerian Witches gained control, held a purge as dread as any of which ancient reports in whisper speak. Industries were placed under communal control, or outlawed altogether. The Old Witches wanted to stop the use of human-animal gene-hybrids. The General Genetic Science Covens were using the hybrids to find a new form of human life hardened against radiation and bioweapon contagion: the hybrids were our only hope to reclaim the war-poisoned coastal areas; no one else could work the land. The Old Witches, the damned Butlerians, were rounding them up, shipping them off to a concentration camp in the middle of the radioactive hellscape surrounding the Richmond Plague Zone, where the only buildings standing were haunted by Ghosts, emulations long since gone mad. So you did not do us any favors, Judge of Ages."

"I am not in the business of doing favors. I just store cold meat," Menelaus Montrose said. "Let me call my next witness. Beta Suspinia! What was your name? Originally? Before the Great Mutiny?"

For the two young warrior maidens, their hair still braided close to their heads as if for battle, but bows unstrung and slung over their slim shoulders, had come marching up in step, hips swinging in unison, and now halted and stood at parade rest to one side, heads tilted toward each other, whispering. Menelaus wondered sadly if the two young ladies realized yet that they could unbraid and comb out their hair, now that the battle was over, without waiting for official orders to do it. All the Alphas were dead. There would be no officer to give the order to relax, not ever again.

The two long-legged teenaged Chimerae began staring, Vulpina giggling and Suspinia frowning, at the sight of the half circle of the Witches with their muskets pointing at each other, as if the girls did not believe the weapons were meant to be used by ancestors of the Kine, any more than one expects a child disguised as a wolfman at a Halloween masquerade actually to bite anyone.

When addressed, Suspinia straightened, blushing to find all eyes turned toward her. "Sir? They did not give us names. I was Beta Class Handmaiden Seven Dormitory Two of the Suspiring Nature Coven of Nome. Nome was an old Hot Site. The Suspiring Nature Coven was doing ecoreclamation work."

Menelaus translated the words and turned to Fatin. "There she is: a first-generation Chimera. The Witches are the ones that ranked them from Alpha to Epsilon, based on breeding data. Do I need to say anything more? Can I rest my case? Sometimes I cannot tell what normal humans are quick enough to grasp."

Mickey the Witch said, "I will explain it to our maiden. Wise and eldest Fatin, the Judge of Ages is telling you that he tried to *save* the witches of your generation. By his arts, he created the conditions that brought forth an industrial revolution, to have a civilization into which he could release them safely; but once he released them into this later industrialized period of history, they destroyed that civilization, too, for they were manipulated and set to do this by the Iron Hermeticist, Narcís D'Aragó."

Menelaus said, "Exactly right. Draggy wanted to scrape clean the scroll of history again, to make room for his idealized version of warrior-aristocrats, an idea he picked up from Plato, or maybe a comic book, about how to organize society like an ant farm of workers ruled by a wolf pack of soldiers ruled by a philosopher-king of him."

Vulpina had moved to stand next to where Soorm crouched, her hand on his huge furred shoulder, her cheek next to his jowls, so her ear was near the talking box he held. But now she straightened, her vivid young face blushing with anger. Hers was one of those faces that looked prettier when angry. The Chimerae were built for anger. She did not like hearing her way of life called an ant farm, but she was too well drilled in discipline to interrupt.

Menelaus raised his voice, and said scathingly to Fatin: "So you want to blame someone for your collapse? Go ahead. Blame me. I confess. I lost that round of the great chess game of history to outsmart the Hermeticists—the guys you poxing *worship* and are poxing trying to *help*. Can we end this farce now, and get back to the business of organizing a way to dig out of here? The Bell is probably overhead right this damn second!"

When the two white-haired crones joined Drosselmeyer and stepped up behind Menelaus, the rest of the menfolk shouldered their arms and followed.

When Fatin saw she was alone, she stood up out of the judgment seat, and walked to the side of the dais, and sat down, her back to the chamber, hugging her knees in her arms, and rocking back and forth.

11

The Hidden History of
Seven Mankinds

1. Manumission

Illiance had returned, and with him was Sir Guiden in his powered armor, his great helm doffed, his head visible above the wide neck ring. He was still wearing the metal coif and black cowl of the lesser or inner helmet. His face tattoos were turned up to their brightest setting, making him look like a Japanese demon; his white beard seemed almost dark by contrast, and his eyes unlit pits. Clinging to him like a grapevine to a strong tree was Oenoe, her slender feet twinkling as she walked, her walk a dance, her eyes wreathed in dreams of joy.

Behind them came Scipio in his splendid scarlet robes and absurd white wig, carrying a Blue Man energy pistol gleaming in either hand, and two more tucked in his belt. Trey Azurine was clinging to Scipio's arm and smiling absentheadedly, healed now of her wounds, with deadly silks floating lightly about her, sparkling.

Next came also marching Buck Gamma Phyle, who carried a machine gun he had dismounted from the wall, with belts of ammo wrapping and re-wrapping his chest in crossed bandoliers. Behind sauntered Gload the Hormagaunt, picking the teeth of his huge midriff-mouth with a crowbar.

Sir Guiden came forward, and he and Drosselmeyer helped Menelaus back into the judgment seat. Sir Guiden sent silently over his implants, "You know that between me, Trey's hunger silk, Gload's strength and the Gamma Chimera's skill, we could have crushed these Witches as easy as a brace of stallions trampling a snake. Not to mention Scipio is carrying as many pistols as Rada Lwa was—your family has an obsessive gun fetish I call *hoplophilia*, you know—but you told us to wait, so the heathen devil worshippers could point barrels and blades at your ugly face. How so, my Liege? Did you *know* it would turn out this way?"

Menelaus sent back, "Don't be ridiculous. You'd have to be super-smarter than a human being, or be like an adult among heavily armed and highly emotional children, to be able to see and plan out something like that ahead of time. Remember to pick up your sword. Fatin dropped it."

Scipio had a spare red robe from the voluminous wardrobe he had packed, and he threw this over Montrose like a blanket. Two Nymphs, Aea and Thysa, helped Montrose out of the scholarly undersuit, cutting the suit where the fabric was wedded to burn wounds. Keirthlin, having wheeled a coffin up behind the throne with the help of Soorm, now sent the tubes and metal tentacles of the internal coffin appliances moving up and down Montrose's body, stripping away dead and burned tissue, and replacing it with new growth.

Somehow, even though the nerve sensations from those patches had been shut off—he had reprogrammed the Blue Men nerve mites and given them honest work to do—the process contrived at the same time to be uncomfortable because it was numb, and uncomfortable because it was painful.

Wincing, Menelaus addressed the gathered survivors:

"I have discovered the control channels to the extra platoon of digging machines Aanwen brought before she died. The automata are currently under my control and trying to dig us out. A simple calculation shows we cannot possibly get out of here before the Bell arrives—and who knows what that means?

"Soorm I can send down the cistern to follow Alalloel and try to find if we can float out through the flooded areas in coffins, which are watertight and contain their own life support.

"The other Blue Men and their dogs are all in coffins, being repaired or restrained until I can decide what to do with them. Yes, I stopped the Blues from doing in their dogs. In my house, one of my rules is that it is not lawful for a man to kill his wounded dog, not while I have veterinarian-coffins to spare.

"Also, no human suicides just because you've had a hard day. Betas, I am looking right at you. Oh, and yes, you can unbraid your hair now. Battle is over. You were brave. You did well."

The girls sat on a lower tier of the dais, and started out happily enough combing each other's hair and chatting, but soon their accustomed Chimerical stoicism and stiff-faced discipline broke; then had their arms around each other, and began to weep, ashamed and disappointed to have survived the battle, cheated of a glorious death.

Menelaus, meanwhile, said, "I regret to report that Happy the Kine had wounds beyond what my coffins can repair. You all seem to think I am super-human, and I guess I am, a little, but there are things no one can fix. Larz, Franz, and Ardzl! Because you pummeled to death the dog which had bayo-neted Happy, I give you my permission as ranking Beta to keep as rightfully named weapons the cutlasses taken from dog things. I reward your service with manumission: you are free men."

Franz raised one hand meekly. "Sir? And what rank of freedom would that be? How much freedom? I mean, are we Alpha or Beta, Gamma or Delta? I ain't being no Epsilon. They stink."

Ardzl asked in a voice less meek, "And when will we be issued breeding mates from the quartermaster? If we are free men, the Command has to carry on our breed, right? I want two of the Geisha girls in green over there."

Larz, who was sitting in a coffin with only his head showing, said loudly to Montrose, "Whoa and woe! That's powerful hard, brains of lard—we'z emo-tionally scarred! You just gunna toss us a loss and cut free on the street to beat feet? Free to starve under bridges? No, no, we won't go, unless we got a life, and a wife or three. And those honeys cost money! Upkeep, and you got to dress them, and you have to bring in someone to beat them with a lash every now and again, because if a stud draws blood, that's no good for domestic tranquil-izers. Guys who know how to do it without leaving bruises cost coin too, and you gotta have Kine to draw the plough and raise the crop, or else freedom is just starvation, right?"

"Freedman Larz, I am delighted that you are alive again and that you have found a way to rewind up the motors of your mouth, and let me just say I hate your period of history like the red-lungrot plague, and you are not getting a damn dime out of me, because I do not pay men to be free. Earn it or starve. And, Sir Guy, maybe you can take the newly freed citizens off to one side and explain some basics of civilized law and civilized religion to them.

"Toil, Drudge, and Drench, the same applies. Any man who fights in my service, or takes up arms against my enemies, wins his liberty; and my laws last longer than the laws of merely earthly princes, whose laws of slavery die when they do. You are beholden to none."

The three ex-Donors of the Hormagaunt Era immediately began whispering and laughing and cutting capers, and talking about the high-quality organs they would buy to replace those they had lost, or they would grow a house as big as dreams to dwell in, and fill it up with clones of themselves, as alike as eggs in a nest, or how fabulously rich they would become buying and selling children in the market.

"Ah, Sir Guy, give a little talk to them too, while you are at it."

2. Life and the World

Menelaus no longer bothered to hide his nature, and he increased the number of nerve firings to his eyes, so that the scene around him grew crisp and bright as crystal. He turned his painfully sharp more-than-human eyes left and right, and no one could meet his gaze.

"Anyone else have a complaint about life and the world? You Chimerae! Yuen thought the fault was mine that his civilization was fell apart. Kine Larz thought I shot the Last Imperator-General to make the World Empire shatter. You Nymphs thought I helped you overthrow the Chimerae by spreading the various addictions and the hedonism of Greencloak technology among the Lotus Eaters, because I love you so much. Prissy and Gload, I don't know what you lay at my door, but it must be something. Illiance, you think I arranged for the Noösphere of the Locusts to crack into pieces, and you think this is praiseworthy, because I saved you from a life of permanent thought-enforced mental uniformity; and Keirthlin, you think the same thing, but you think this is blameworthy, because I ruined your life of permanent thought-enforced mental uniformity. Do I really need to go through the whole list of what really happened in each case? It would take forever, and we are out of time."

Vulpina stood up, striking the dais sharply with the heel of her unstrung bowstaff. She looked very young and very fierce and warlike, despite her tear-stains, and her hair was loose about her face and wild. "Not the whole list. Just one thing." She drew herself up. "Judge of Ages, the Chimerae of the Emergency General Command demand to know . . ."

"Will you knock it off, sister? All your Alphas are dead and your race is extinct. The Command ain't giving no-one not no-more commands, not now, not forever and amen. We are all just people now, human people, and we all have the exact same rank: which is *Screwpustulated,* First Class. Just ask your damned question."

She blinked but gathered her breath and spoke. "Why did you kill the Imperator-General? Larz said you shot the last Emperor in an act of assassination, and the Empire fell."

"Act of assassination my *ass*—uh—assination. Shot him fair and square, blast pattern in the chest, eyes open, pistol in his hand, plenty of warning and in a good light. It was a duel. I ain't no assassin. What was I supposed to do? Sue him in court? D'Aragó had his men break into the Tombs in Switzerland, found Thucydides Montrose, a relative of mine, and shot him in his coffin. Thucydides was a preacher man. Little old guy. Later he got poped or something. His men took a DNA sample back, and it was a close match, and they thought they had done me; so they told Draggy I was dead, so I had to go have some dealings with him to convince him of the error of his ways. That time, it was just personal. He killed kin, so I killed him."

Illiance said, "And did the same obtain of the Hermeticist De Ulloa? Had you some personal vendetta against him? I recall the testimony of Rada Lwa the Scholar."

Menelaus said, "Nope. That was just professional, a courtesy call. His Witches decided to dig up all the slumbering Christians, bishops and popes and so on who were in medical hibernation, so I had to go beef him just to keep him out of my back yard."

Oenoe said in a voice like throbbing woodwinds, "And what of Sarmento i Illa d'Or?"

Menelaus said, "Well, that was a different case entirely. Old Yellow Door was a strange guy. He thought he could talk me over to his side of things, talk me into accepting the Hyades as the master race, talk me into liking Blackie's way of playing with people's lives like puppets, forgiving the murder of Star-Captain Grimaldi, and talk me into not being in love with Rania anymore. See, he had all these good, sound, logical, persuasive-sounding arguments, and he wanted to lead me through every step of them, starting with definitions, axioms, and common notions. What a damn bore that man was. Oh, and the poxified, pestilential, disease-riddled, scab-oozing, leper whoreson dolled up a clone of my wife, my own damn wife, and sent her around to try to seduce me. He just took that same section of the Monument that defined Rania, and ran through the same calculation again. The idea being I will give up my fight with Blackie, and let the world be his personal bugger boy, provided I am getting my own urges soothed—but I found out old Yellow had plunged her measure before me, cherry-picking, and that without benefit of clergy, if you take my meaning."

Oenoe said, "I don't take your meaning, beloved Judge of Ages."

"Nah. You wouldn't. So he 'poons my wife's twin sister, and then dangles her my way to play come-hither-eyes at me, and at that point I am fed up so I went to call him out.

"One of my rare miscalculations," Montrose continued, shaking his head. "Don't seem fair he should be sharp as a razor in math and be some super athlete with muscles like a bull. He says doing weights helps him think, and he thinks pretty hard. Thought of a way to pack his pistol better than mine. He was a pretty damn good shot, and cool as a cucumber staring down a barrel, so what can I say?

"By rights, I should be dead. I can show you the scar.

"My wife's twin sister had two more sisters—they were trial runs, jobs that did not come out so perfect. Named Aura-Ah and Riana-Ah. They were still Rania clones, and looked a lot like her, and all programmed by the Monument to be able to read pretty damn far into the Monument. And the three ladies had read some mathematical model about the relationship of the mind and body that enabled them to make half a dozen breakthroughs in medical and biotechnological and bioneuropsychiatric sciences, including all the stuff that allowed the Nymphs to domesticate every damn living thing from inchworms to sharks, and train raccoons and fawns to do housework, giraffes to carry parasols, and kangaroos to carry parcels, and they even taught crows to sing.

"But their breakthroughs also included the stuff they did to bring me back from nine-tenths dead and put me back on my feet. So I made some deals with the ladies, and with their daughters, and they helped me revolutionize the hibernation process. I mean, their understanding of biology was, well, you know, unbepustulevable. And the Nymphs ruled the only period of history that did not care about the past and did not care about the future, and so they did not try to dig up my damn Tombs.

"That's where all the stories about how much the Judge of Ages loves the Nymphs and their Natural Order of Man comes from. For once in all the millennia of time, in my buried house, I had a neighbor living on my roof, what you call your world, what was friendly and neighborly.

"And I could unload a hefty parcel of medical Thaws on them, and get my patients all cured-up, and some of them stayed for a season up topside to play with the native girls, but came down again to sleep and dream to a better future, and some of them got addicted and stayed topside for life.

"So the harlotocracy of Nymphland was sick and wrong, but never did wrong to me, and I let it be."

3. The Game of Fates of Races and Empires

Expositor Illiance said, "The deaths you encompassed of your peers and fellow posthumans, the Hermeticists, are of biographical interest, indeed. But a deeper question hangs over every soul born since the time of the Giants, who knew the science of predictive history. It is a science you know, and the Hermetic Order, and so all human destiny, was shaped to your designs as a channel guides the canal-stream. We in this chamber represent all the races of Man. We need and yearn to know the answer to the riddle. This opportunity, to learn the mind of a mind beyond man, will never come again. Instruct us."

Menelaus said, "I don't understand what your question is."

"My question concerns human destiny. It is simple to ask."

"Yes? What about human destiny?"

"—*why?*—"

A silence hung over the buried chamber. Menelaus looked at the gathered people.

He sighed and spoke. "I did a lot of things in your history; and every event in history, no matter how nice the intention, had bad side effects.

"Sorry, Scipio, but it started when I smashed the Cryonarchy. Blackie had your foot in the bear trap, and the only way out was to gnaw your foot off. He did to me what Rania did to him: set up a situation where the only solution was to step down. He tried to hang on to power, and so his Concordat was shattered forever. I gave power away, and it brought forth a race of Giants. Maybe you think I should not have done it. But it would have been worse had I done nothing. Do you still want to take a poke at me?"

Scipio, one arm around Trey Azurine, waved his hand in the air as if brushing away cigarette smoke. "What year is this again, Old Timer? I cannot stay mad at General Santa Anna about the Alamo and stay mad at you, too. Besides, you are FBC, and it ain't right to paste no crazy man."

Menelaus nodded thoughtfully, as if allowing the wisdom of those words. He went on: "Like I said, it would have been worse if I had done nothing; far worse. The world would have been covered in gold logic crystal, and Earth been nothing but a planet of ghosts, had I not released the first part of the Rania Solution to the Selfish Meme Divarication problem to Thucydides. The Self-Corrective Code was universal and philosophical, and it applied to every field of study: it could be used to fix Divarication in man and machine alike.

"Sorry, Ctesibius, if you thought the world of gold would have been Utopia.

It would have been, but not for you. You know now that the Machine only meant to eat the Ghosts you donated to him.

"Sorry, Trey Azurine. I did not give the order to burn the world, but I made the Giants who gave the order, and I built the Xypotech, Pellucid, who could do a passing fair impersonation of me over the wire, and send out the evacuation plans. My authority and prestige was the only thing that made a hesitating world agree to such a mad and desperate plan. Everybody and his wife thought the posthuman was such a smart guy! Everyone trusted me! That was the last period in history anyone ever did. So it is my fault you never set foot in a house, never had neighbors, never walked down a street or slept in the same meadow twice."

Trey stood with her head on the shoulder of Scipio, and she looked up, and smiled brightly. She spoke in a wondering tone of voice, as if her thoughts were elsewhere. "I don't think about things like that. We are Drifters. We drift with the wind. Sometimes we fish. Or we interface with the fun-line. You can use up whole days playing yourself in little cartoons. Or we can drop into the sea and kill the whales. They serve the Machine. I *hate* whales. That Machine is satanic. It does not have a soul. Burning the cities was like amputation." And she must have remembered Brother Roger the Jesuit astronomer, for she said: *"If your eye offends you, pluck it out. It is better that a man enter paradise one-eyed than that he descend into hell with two eyes."*

At these words, Sir Guiden crossed himself; but Scipio scowled at him and shouted an *amen;* and Mickey the Witch scowled at them both.

Menelaus inclined his head to Trey, and raised his voice once more to fill the chamber.

"That universal Self-Corrective Code solution I mentioned allowed Blackie to make the Dreagh, the special posthuman Ghosts that have been running all the eras and aeons of history ever since, Exulloa and Exarago, Exillador and Expastor. And Ull's emulation that replaced Expastor. So it is my fault that the last eight thousand years did not grow naturally, but were engineered into their shapes by the Hermetic Order.

"The second solution I released to save the Sylphs, because otherwise either the Giants would have killed them, or they would have fallen into total preindustrial barbarism. It allowed the serpentine Mälzels to copy each other's solutions and perpetuate any useful change of code—forever. It was a bit of straight computer engineering, but I devised by accident an eternal form of self-repairing tool.

"Melchor de Ulloa used this technique and applied it to living things, such as for re-copying iterations of Witch genetic information back onto unraveled telomeres, and returning cells to totipotency, and performed parallel experiments in uplift to create more Moreaus than just whales. Horses and elephants and dogs and swine: soon everything was talking. And taking orders. And on the backs of the slave armies of animal people, the labyrinthine edifice of the Witches reared its envious head.

"I interfered again. At the time of the Nameless Empire, I meddled with the Moreaus, and introduced by viral vector a gene-rewriting intron. It was an unselfish gene, a cooperation code. I had to make it so that the intelligent lion could lie down with the intelligent lamb in a democratic republic, because nothing else could ever stir the endless tyranny of the Wise over their fellow creatures and their fellow men.

"It worked for a while, but you know the next twist in that story: Narcís D'Aragó took that exact same bit of biotech engineering I had devised to make for himself new creatures, cooperating on a molecular level, half lion and half goat and all snake, and they ate up the lambs.

"A fourth solution was biochemical rather than biotechnical. It was used to formulate the original portable neurochemical biofeedback backpack systems called Greencloaks, which was my attempt to copy in a crude way the things done by the red amulets of the Hermeticists. It was not passed from father to son, because the Chimera eugenicists controlled who passed what from father to son. I had to do an end-run around their whole game. My game was a needle you stuck in your head. My signature move.

"Thanks to Sarmento, the boys in green, guys like Larz, who is right now drinking the medical fluid out of the coffin he is in trying to get his bender on, the next generation really liked sticking needles of all kinds up their heads; or whatever else they could take with alcohol, or patch or inhale or stuff up a nostril, or as a suppository. That was one civilization whose fall was not my fault: Sarmento was the exception again. He hated D'Aragó and wanted his little tin empire of little tin soldiers smashed as soon as possible and replaced it with Whoreworld, the Garden of Addict. Sarmento's notion of paradise.

"The Wintermind techniques I taught to the Nymphs when their weather control system began to fail. This fifth solution was biosoftware—the training must be ingrained via training and biofeedback to establish the nerve paths, because obviously anything that comes out of a needle or in a pill, the Nymphs could control and block and make to do backflips. I broke their hold over their people so that those people would wake up out of their drunk drug-dreams, see the world was getting colder, and come up with a way to save themselves.

"Once again, I had to do it, because otherwise the society would crash and never recover. There were no metals left in digging range anymore, so if civilization did a Humpty Dumpy, all the king's horses and all the king's men—Does anyone here know who old Humpty is? That would make Alice sad. Yeah, Trey, Alice in Wonderland! I am glad that book survived as long as your era.

"Soorm scion Asvid, you know the next part of the story. Wintermind can be used not just to break unnatural additions, love philters, and memory snares the Nymphs impose; the technique can break the addictions Mother Nature kindly puts in us so that mothers love their babies and fathers love their mates, the sex drive and the family drive and the thing that makes man a political animal. Reyes y Pastor trained a generation of gladiators to kill and eat each other, and to use the Wintermind to abolish their addiction to human affections.

"And so I had to do something again. Prissy Pskov—your people, the Clades, exist because of me. The sixth solution was bioeconomic. The Hormagaunts could have controlled anything I introduced that was genetic or based on pheromones, but what I introduced was a fractional genetic banking system, a set of techniques that made it easier to reproduce by parthenogenesis than to try to find a wife you were not allergic to, and everyone was born in clusters with spare organs in all their twins, who suddenly had no strong reason to prey on each other. The Clade unity was a terrible solution, a hack, a kludge, but there was no other way to preserve civilization from the deluge of blood Reyes had unleashed, except in an Ark made of twins and triplets.

"But when the floodwaters of blood receded, there was nothing but that terrible, overwhelming need for unity. That is why Locusts are born oriented toward hive mind thinking and total altruism. They were just a logical extension of the notion of the Clades that, since toleration of differences proved impossible, total conformity is the price of peace.

"Expositor Illiance, you know what happened after that. Yes, I did break the Noösphere of the Locusts. I did it deliberately, and with malice aforethought. It was the most evil thing a man like me can imagine: mankind as an ant farm. A monster army with a million bodies with a million giraffe necks leading to one giant head like a bobbing balloon above them.

"The seventh and last solution was the most subtle of all my moves in this great game. It was not philosophical, nor computational, nor genetic, nor biochemical, nor neurolinguistic, nor bioeconomic. It was legal and informational—a set of universal protocols establishing a format for information exchanges across nonuniform data-regimes. It created very quickly a very powerful incentive for diversity within the mental environment: a good reason for the nest to tolerate useful inquiline species. An Inquiline Protocol.

"And Coronimas perverted my work, and used it to concoct this horrible cellular-level mind-control system, which the Melusine eventually perfected to make their remote control of other people's minds and souls perfect and inescapable.

"I had a counter to that. I tried to introduce a new vector into the course of evolution five hundred and six years ago, which should have made this helotry of total mind control a dead end, and forced the whole species into a radical new direction. My mistake was a simple one: I released the viral carrying agent onto the oceans of the Earth, because that is where I thought the men would be living, and that they would carry it into the land areas, or any other place other members of their race would go.

"So it was my damn cleverest move yet—but nothing happened. I should have won by now. Instead the Melusine, as best I can tell, were totally unaffected, and they remain totally loyal to Ximen del Azarchel, who is in charge of the planet, or what is left of it.

"Alalloel of Lree—man, that is a hard name to say—she tells me each Tomb has a Melusine officer assigned to it, called a Paramount, who was going to thaw us all and absorb us into their gestalt, like Locusts.

"So we are buried alive here, waiting for the Melusine to come eat our brains. They will keep our memories and minds and personalities intact, and put us into a slavery so profound that it cannot even be imagined. A helotry of the mind, where the helot rejoices in his invisible chains, or thinks or believes whatever else the Paramount programs him to do, including loving his slavery.

"There you have it. There were a lot more maneuvers within each move, but that was the general outline of the chess game of history.

"You asked me *why*, Expositor Illiance. There were two sides in the game. My side was the side of human life, civilization, and liberty. Whenever that was threatened, I acted. His side was the side of machine existence, slavery, and for some reason I did not learn until today, barbarism.

"That is the why and the wherefore of it. Why did I interfere with your lives, and the lives of your ancestors and descendents over and over again? Why did I preserve the sick and the lost and those who fled into the exile of time here in my buried house where no time passes? That answer is really simple.

"Turn your heads and look at the portrait of the young lady yonder. I did it for her.

"*She* is my *why*."

Menelaus was silent a moment, his head down, his eyes downcast and solemn. No one in the chamber spoke.

Without looking up, he said, "Expositor Illiance, is your question answered?"

Illiance said, "The question *why* can never be fully answered, because all answers open deeper questions yet. But I am content."

Mickey the Witch said, "I am not content, Judge of Ages! Because magicians have vowed not only to dare all and to know all, but to achieve all, until the pinnacle of secret knowledge is ours, never to be shared. You have unfolded to us the hidden history of the world, of races and empires, and they rose and fell as you moved our fates like chessmen against each other."

Menelaus said apologetically, "The Monument had the Cliometric calculus equations printed on it. Once we read, the genie could not be put back in the bottle. Letting nature take its course was simply not an option: it was either let Blackie be the undisputed Master of the World, or dispute it."

Mickey said, "That is not my question at all. I ask: Where do things stand now? What is the next move in the Great Game? And what is my role in it?"

When that comment was translated by the talking boxes, there was a murmur of admiration, even applause, in the chamber. The Chimeresses looked eager for battle; the Witches seemed bitterly angry to learn how badly their gods had betrayed them; Illiance looked proud; and Gload looked hungry.

Menelaus answered in a voice of grim despair, and his words marched out of his mouth like soldiers assigned to firing squad detail.

"I hate to say, but it looks like my side, our side, ladies and gentlemen, monsters and Witches, has lost.

"Alalloel implied the world is under a regime of absolute mind control. Such a regime, once in place, if firmly in place, can never be removed, because you need to think to plan a rebellion. And it does not have the usual inefficiencies of slavery, because the slaves can be programmed to be content, or happy, or enthusiastic, or devout, or serene, or whatever else strikes your fancy. Hell, you can even let them stage a successful revolt once every fifty years as a kind of Jubilee, if it amuses you. And then turn it off after.

"So the chess game is over.

"Only two questions remain in my mind. First, I don't know why I lost, or what the losing move was. The Melusine should be, according to what I did, the most freedom-loving creatures it is possible to be under heaven. Second, what the hell is up with that Bell?

"Above us is a spacehook, the biggest thing I have ever seen in the sky. On the one hand, it is physically impossible that the Hyades World Armada or anything from it could be here four hundred years ahead of time. On the other hand, it does not seem to be moving or acting like it would act if the Currents controlled it, Melusine or Blackie or whoever is running the store these days. Why would any of them go loot Raleigh? Why would they initiate a maneuvering burn when they saw the magnetic north pole shift to Fancy Gap, Virginia, just as if they wanted to investigate some unknown native phenomenon? Why would they react to ELF radio signals containing Monument hieroglyphs and not to any other signals on any other band?

"And I don't know the answers to those questions."

A silence as profound as the grave passed over the chamber. So it was shocking that the sound of a cold chuckle hung in the air. It was doubly shocking when everyone turned and saw that it was Ctesibius the Savant, his despair and aloofness for a moment gone from his face, replaced with a cold and satanic mirth.

Ctesibius said, "I know the answers, aftercomers. I know all."

4. Star Raid

Menelaus turned to Ctesibius the Savant. "What did you say? What did you find out? Hell—*how* did you find out?"

"The snow told me. Haven't you figured out where the people of this time are? Don't you know what the Bell is?" smirked Ctesibius.

"Told you how?" demanded Montrose. "The nerve links in your head are one-way only. Transmit and not receive."

Ctesibius shook his bewigged head with bitter mirth. Menelaus decided he liked laughing Ctesibius less than melancholy Ctesibius. Much less.

Now the Savant held up his glove, and showed its back to Menelaus, and pointed with his other hand. On the glove back was a telephone of the kind that had an onboard Mälzel to perform extremely complicated high-data-volume transmissions, so it had more memory than a midrange library cloth, and broadcasting shortwave, enjoyed a practically unlimited, worldwide range. It was beautifully made, coated with gold leaf and rimmed with diamonds, no bigger than a coin.

"Just because I have neurocybernetics in my head," smiled Ctesibius, "does not mean I need not listen with my ear like any *hylic*."

Menelaus rubbed his eyes with his thumb and forefinger, pinching his nose for good measure. *Hylic*. There was a word he had not heard in a while. It was what the Hermeticists and Scholars called anything they regarded as lower on the scale of evolution. It was another little reminder, small as a pinprick, why he hated the Hermeticists and the worlds they made.

But aloud Menelaus said, "Okay. I give. Uncle. I have not figured out where the people of this time are. I was thinking maybe the ocean, on account of the

Melusine, but I vectored a social change into the sea life, and it seems like it had no effect. Are they on the moon? I don't know what the Bell is. I know what it is not. It is not what it seems to be, because what it seems to be makes no sense. It looks like a human-made weapon of the Hyades."

Ctesibius said, "That is exactly what it is."

"I got two questions. One is: *huhn?* The second one is: *if I am the coxcombliest smartster smartster on this planet, how come most of what I say most the time is 'huhn'?* Answer the first question first, please."

Ctesibius said, "The Bell is an accurate mock-up of a typical Hyades attack instrument created from Monument blueprints. The space raid drill began in A.D. 10484, some three decades ago. In the same way civilians would clear the streets of their cities and retreat into underground bomb shelters and bunkers during the Hitlerian War to practice the discipline needed to survive a raid from the air, so, here, too, the surface of the globe, including the oceans, has been cleared of all human and domesticated life, to practice what is needed to survive a raid from the stars.

"Interstellar warfare is feudal," said Ctesibius in the tone of one who confides a commonplace bromide.

"Futile?" Menelaus wondered if he had heard that correctly.

"Feudal. There is no substance more lightweight and more deadly than contraterrene. Payload mass considerations are paramount in interstellar travel. No other weapon is worth bringing across lightyears. No possible surface defense, nothing made of matter, can withstand it.

"It is the nature of total conversion reaction to react as violently against diffuse material, like atmosphere, as against dense material, like armor, and the concussion always drives the antimatter away from the point of contact. Therefore the best defense is layer after layer of light masses, such as atmosphere and hydrosphere, over layers of heavier mass, as a crust and core.

"This means people can survive even orbital antimatter bombardment if they retreat to far, far below the mantle of their world like the knights in a medieval fortress retreating behind castle walls. All the attacker can do is eliminate the surface biosphere, and besiege the defender, and hope to starve him out. It is to define and practice the institutions necessary for bathysubterranean life that the space raid drill was organized."

Menelaus blinked. A thirty-year-long drill. All the people of the surface world in a bombproof shelter. And the presumably much larger sea population of whales and mermaids, also in a bombproof aquarium. An aquarium as big as the Great Lakes might hold all the intelligent sea life in the world, with a little crowding . . .

"Hey! Wait one pus-dripping *minute*! What would be big enough to hold—?"

Ctesibius talked over him, trampling the end of the question. "Fortunately there was an extensive and unoccupied system of hypocycloid curves of a long-abandoned evacuated-tube railgun-launched intercontinental train network—all the cities of the Melusine were lowered into the extensive volume for the duration of the raid drill—"

"*Unoccupied* my cankered cloaca-hole!" shouted Menelaus. "You mean the world is empty because everyone moved into *my* depthtrain system? *My* rail yards? *My* storage bays?"

Ctesibius continued, as if he were unwilling to notice or acknowledge that a lesser being like Montrose could be speaking while he spoke: "—had previously deduced the existence of an extensive body of self-replicating Von Neumann lattices, apparently without end—and therefore began growing a stalactite of logic crystal toward the inner core in A.D. 10401, roughly one hundred years ago. The lava displacement caused by the stalactite growth increased volcanic pressure worldwide, making it easier for you, Menelaus Montrose, to attempt worldwide climate adjustment. The Nobilissimus anticipated that you would employ widespread volcanism to terraform the climate via gas venting to alter the composition in the atmosphere. Your behavior made the stalactite growth easier, and sped the growth—"

At this point, Menelaus was distracted by the sight of Soorm climbing out of the central cistern, with the slender body of the Melusine girl, Alalloel of Lree, tucked under one huge arm. Soorm did not wait for a break in the conversation, but merely bellowed across the chamber. "Judge! I found her where the flooded section meets an underground river. Not a stream—a river bigger than the Ebro. And you will not believe—"

Ctesibius, just as rude as Soorm, raised his voice and kept talking: "—Melusine occupying cities and arcologies cubic miles wide inside the cool core of the stalactite. Would you care to hear the figures for the displacement volume? More significant is the memory volume. Being made of logic crystal, the Great Stalactite can hold emulations of the entire Melusine population who have achieved the rank of Glorified—"

Alalloel was not dead (as Menelaus first thought) but she did look annoyed as Soorm yanked her out from under his arm and held her up. "These scars on her back hide spinal ports. She was nerve-linking to her *whales*. They came back from the dead. Most of their internal organs are brain mass. Brain Whales. And these whales have wings, and the wings are covered with eyes—"

Ctesibius said, "The core-ward growing Great Stalactite is the second largest single coherent man-made object in history. You are right to fear it—"

Soorm said, "The real her is housed in the Melusine body in her mind-body group—"

Ctesibius said, "The first and largest, of course, is the mock-up of the Hyades Instrumentality, which is finally in position. You have run out of time. All things are ended!"

Soorm said, "The Iron Ghosts I met at the bottom of the Mariana Trench have been reincarnated." He turned to Scipio and spoke in Latin: "This girl is a *Cetus,* preserved as an Iron Ghost from the old days. Your days."

Scipio said, "A Cetacean. The ones who broke the Cryonarchic power by blockading the continents. The creatures we never learned how to fight." And he said in English to Montrose: "They serve only their creator, and have no pity nor understanding of human beings. These are the most loyal and most effective servants Exarchel has ever commanded."

Menelaus was more curious about Ctesibius, at the moment, than about Alalloel the Cetacean. "Run out of time, why? Why is the Bell coming here?"

Ctesibius smiled a thin, cruel smile. Menelaus thought he definitively liked moping Savants better than happy ones. Ctesibius said archly, "To answer your second question, the reason why you spend your life, for all your intelligence, grunting—*huhn?*—is merely because you cross wits with a man who is in every way your superior. The Bell is no longer coming. It is here. The Nobilissimus is here."

12

Signs in the Heavens,
Figures in the Earth

1. Signs in Heaven

There was a deafening noise overhead.

Blades made of what seemed to be plasma taken from the surface of the sun pierced and penetrated the golden ceiling of the vast chamber like awls. There were four, one at each corner, and they stabbed down through the roof ten or twelve feet. There was no dust or debris: the awls did not merely burn through the armor, metal, and bedrock of the roof material, but evaporated anything made of matter that was touched. The four blades were four noonday suns, one at each corner, and everyone, including Menelaus, cowered or hid his eyes.

Blinded, Menelaus did not actually see the moment when the entire ceiling of the chamber was torn free like the lid of a shoe box and flung away; but he heard the noise, or at least, he heard the beginning of the noise. After that, his ears were numb with the shock of sound, and all he heard was a distant humming or the ringing of chimes.

More light fell on his face, but also drops of rain. The air was hot and close, despite the arctic winter it should have been. There was a tropical warmth to the atmosphere, but also the closeness and weight of a lowering storm. The flashing of lightning in forks and sheets was continuous.

Menelaus squinted and looked up.

The outside of the Bell was dark, and its passage had stirred up thunderheads which hung, black as anvils, like the wake of spray before a rearing ship's prow, boiling to either side of the astronomically titanic machine and trailing like the hems of tattered robes behind. Lightning bolts flicked between the foot of the Bell and the Earth, eye-dazzling. Despite his numbed ears, Menelaus could still sense the deafening thunderclaps in his bones.

Other lightning bolts flickered between points on the outer surface two thousand feet high and points three thousand, or between the first mile up and the second, as the friction of the motion through the atmosphere built up and discharged vast static voltages.

And the Tower went up and up like a dark road leading to the emptiness between the stars. Through a gap in the storm clouds, Menelaus could see what looked like a small moon in crescent phase at the vanishing point of that road, made of the same impossibly tough, dark substance as the Bell. This was its maneuvering anchor, somewhere at or near geosynchronous orbit, an object larger than the asteroid Vesta, or, for comparison, roughly ten times the size of 1036 Ganymed—a moon of Earth that Menelaus had never seen. It was large enough to be pulled into a spherical shape by its own mass. Menelaus saw a drive antenna, tens of thousands of feet long, ribbed by ring after ring of accelerators; bat-vanes of heat dissipaters, coming like a comet's tail from the asteroid; and he recognized the characteristic contour of a low-speed, high-impulse ionic drive.

The foot of the Bell was not directly overhead, but was perhaps half a mile to one side. The nine-mile-diameter mouth hung overhead, and clouds, landscapes, and continents of buildings, mechanisms, factories, and energy systems of a vertical world could be seen, at an angle, through the vast opening. It was like a window gaping into another universe, one whose mountains were squares and rectangles of darkness and light and whose rivers were vertical lines straight as yardsticks and whose hills were sideways hemispheres bright and round as shields.

Issuing from one metal shore of the mouth of the Bell was a roughly conical cloud or swarm of machines, which hovered without any visible wings or supports. Each machine was shaped like a jellyfish of synthetic material, and their many arms were serpentines.

The larger cnidarian-shaped machines could have picked up an aircraft carrier with ease. The smaller cnidarians might have been designed by the same hands that made the aeroscaphes of the Sylphs. (And for the first time Menelaus realized the Giants who designed the airskiffs of the Sylphs used elements taken from engineering schematics written in the Monument, some unguessed or unexamined section neither Menelaus nor Rania had ever deciphered.)

The roof and upper levels of the Tombs were being hauled upward by a larger machine, and four of its serpentines were the white-hot cutting implements which had pierced the roof. Menelaus saw debris, and then a coffin, lit to show a person was inside, dripping off the side of the broken Tomb layers. He watched helplessly as one of his clients fell; but the smaller machines, darting with supersonic speed, neatly caught that falling coffin.

Machines even smaller—he now saw cnidarian flying machines the size of a lady's parasol, or the size of a child's hand, or the size of a dragonfly—were catching the falling struts, rocks, stones, and pebbles.

Nothing fell to the ground.

Even the stormwinds, rain gusts, and lightning could not distract the cnidarians or make them miss their grip. Even the falling particles of dust were gathered up.

Menelaus saw what seemed like heat vibrations over the mantle or upper back of each of the cnidarian flying machines, and realized they could only fly in an atmosphere within the shadow of the Bell. The Bell was emitting a radiation that interacted with the metal. The metal was buoyant while in the field. He wondered if the vibration were something as commonplace as a partial vacuum created by a field, or if the Bell were merely raising and lowering the machines by magnetic monopoles, or if something more exotic, like anti-gravity, were possible.

2. The Dark-Palmed Hand

Then it happened. The side of the dark tower nearest was aflame. He realized these were maneuvering jets. Thousands and tens of thousands of pinpoints of light flickered into existence across the vast acreage of the dark hull. The light was brighter than acetylene. In the same way that skyscrapers in the days before Menelaus was born would turn on and off colored lights in all their windows, so as to make hundred-story-high billboards, but much bigger here, the acres and acres of white fire painted the outline of a symbol.

There must have been a maneuvering jet every few square yards, a caltrop of rocket vents larger than any Saturn V main cone, hundreds of them, perhaps thousands. The amount of fuel being ignited just to paint this sign in light was immense: as if twelve hundred Capes Canaveral, and all their rockets, had lit up at once, merely for one majestic, awe-inspiring moment of pyrotechnic sky-writing.

So vast was the bottomless tower that the noise was like a distant jet fighter's wake, passing overhead at thousands of feet high; but so many were the jets, and so gigantic each nozzle cone, that the noise came clearly over the world, like the mutter of a waterfall of fire.

But what was the symbol? The storm clouds and their escort of sheets and bolts of lightning blocked part of the image, but then some unseen force from the Bell (perhaps an air displacement simply vented from a lower to a higher altitude within the Bell, and spilled out as a million Niagara Falls made of denser air pouring down, a man-made cold front) made a gap appear in the cloud banks, and widen and disperse the blanket of storm gathered at the lower knees of the vast Bell, till all was plain.

The sign hung under heaven and over all the land, large in view as a constellation sprung to life. There were four vast rivers of light, broad as the Nile, rushing up the side of the towering vastness. A fifth rose at a different angle, and was shorter. The five rivers of fire entered into a lake of light, but a round island filled the lake with a core of darkness.

Laughter and rage and exaltation roared from his heart and rose to his lips. Menelaus' ears were still ringing, but he was shouting and shouting.

"*Damn you! Damn you, bastard! COME DOWN HERE! Come down right now, or I'll come up there . . .*" And then he started in on his favorite swear-words and blasphemies, of which he had no small supply.

Because what the image of the dots of rocket exhaust painted, of course, was the image of a pale white duelist's gauntlet, its palm the black circle showing the enemy was ready to exchange fire.

His protracted wait was over.

3. Ximen the Black

One of the cnidarians, larger than a longboat, departed from the streaming aerial river of machines, and swooped softly and swiftly downward, and hung over the clifftop surrounding the open dig.

Atop it, legs spread like one who stands on a swaying raft, a hooded figure in dark sable silk was standing, white cloak flying in the wind, hands clasped behind his back, outlined for a blinding moment in the glare of the lightning bolts that decorated the knees of his flying tower. It was a starfarer in the shipsuit of the Hermetic Order, and beneath the lowering hood, skull-like, was seen the outline of goggles and mask.

Del Azarchel threw back his hood and doffed his mask, and he smiled, a shock of white teeth in his black beard, and his eyes glittered like agates.

4. Figures in the Earth

One of the serpentines, issuing from the edge of the cnidarian on which Del Azarchel stood, elongated and reached down and writhed a loop around Montrose.

Then Montrose was hanging in the winter air, wearing nothing heavier than Scipio's spare red robe, maimed in both feet, burnt over twenty percent of his body, one arm broken, and various pains in his head, throat, chest, spine, bowels, and a burning sensation in his eyes . . . that he only slowly realized were tears. For weapons, he had one of the dog pistols that Rada Lwa had loaded, and it had a single shot. Scipio had been kind enough to lend it to him.

Montrose was lifted aloft to a point above the cnidarian as rapidly as a flag being hoisted.

Blackie del Azarchel, hovering in midair above the cliffside overlooking the deep and broken Tombs, was now below him; the mantle of the cnidarian on which Blackie stood was like a magic carpet of metallic silver, levitating, edges flapping and floating.

Now Montrose raised the pistol and took aim at Del Azarchel, who merely looked amused when he saw the threat. He raised his black gloved hand and made a dismissive gesture, as if brushing a fly away.

Montrose pulled the trigger. The hammer fell, driving the flint against the striker. The sparks ignited the primer, but the powder did not ignite. Menelaus felt his implants screaming so loudly that his back teeth ached in their sockets. He realized that the logic crystal pistol ball was issuing a radiation that broke down the chemical bonds of the nitrates in the gunpowder, rendering it inert. It was a clever trick, and he wished he had used it during the fight in the burial chamber.

The realization was like bile. Had Montrose been as imaginative as Del Azarchel, Daae would still have been alive.

The serpentine bent and lowered Montrose to the metallic surface of the upper mantle. Montrose impatiently threw the loops of snakelike metal off him, which was a mistake, for the grinding of the bone ends in his broken arm struck him with dizziness like the blow from a club of chaos and darkness; he shut off the pain center of his brain, and the scene around him seemed to become remote and dim, but clear, as if he were watching the whole thing through the wrong end of a telescope.

The substance underfoot was not metal, but foil, for it had a slight give where his bitterly cold naked feet touched, leaving bloodstains. Through his implants, he could tell the buoyancy was magnetic in nature, a set of fields balanced against some immense field generated from the top and bottom of the skyhook and surrounding it like a cocoon.

He was next to his old enemy. Montrose could not retain his balance, but started to topple off the edge. Del Azarchel put an arm around him, and prevented the fall. The eyes of Del Azarchel, burning with that same superhuman presence that no human could look at as Montrose's eyes, seemed to swell in his vision hypnotically. Their two faces were close enough that Montrose could see the tiny nick in the skin of his cheek where Del Azarchel had cut himself shaving with a straight razor.

He could smell the scent of Blackie's beard lotion, a brand Montrose recognized, for it had been on sale at the barbershop back in his home village in rural Texas, back in the centuries long ago. It was called Armstrong's Space Age After-Shave, and it claimed (falsely) to date from the time of the moon landings, back before the Little Dark Ages. It had not been manufactured on Earth for millennia.

"Welcome back to the land of the living, old friend," said Del Azarchel. "You do not look well. As you have realized by now, I have no further need of you, your Tombs, or your damned interference. But I thought I should afford you a clear view of the proceedings. I am about to destroy everything you rightfully love. Look!"

Underfoot, Montrose could see the golden burial chamber up from which he had been plucked. The cnidarians were methodically and quickly snaring all the Thaws in the chamber. There was the square of the fountain, and Soorm and Gload, men from an era with no metals, tiny as dolls, staring upward in astonishment at the skyhook and the swarms of cnidarians. Sir Guiden, with an arm around Oenoe, was moving toward the wall of the chamber, firing his shoulder-mounted rocket as he fled, but a cnidarian swept the rocket in midflight off to one side, where it exploded harmlessly, and wrapped both Sir Guy and his bride in tendrils. Oenoe dashed her cloak against the machine in what seemed to be an attempt to stun or lull it with her pollens and soporifics; she did not know it was not a living thing. There was other movement down below, but now a cloud of dust and smoke had risen up, and tears were in Montrose's eyes.

Del Azarchel still had one arm tightly about him, preventing him from falling. "Would you care for a jolt? Looks like you could use a stiff one." Montrose thought Del Azarchel was either threatening to electrocute him, or else proposing buggery, but then the man held an oaken hip flask with a brass cap open before his broken nose. The smell of whiskey was delicious. He ached for it.

"Go to hell, Blackie," he croaked.

"Not if I live forever," Del Azarchel smiled.

Then they both heard a noise of trumpets, and Montrose raised his hand and wiped his tears from his eyes, peering to see what was happening.

A great voice, enormously amplified, rang from a hundred places beneath the earth, loud enough to shake the rocks and to make the cnidarians tremble in midair. The voices were crying in Latin.

"IS IT YET, THE AEON?"

Montrose put his good hand to one ear, wincing. It was, of course, a recording of his own voice. It was mingled with supersonics and subsonics, and the sound-based weapons were already throwing so many of the cnidarians out of the air that metal pieces were flashing and floating as they spun earthward like so many bits of tinfoil.

And many voices roared in answer, a tidal wave of noise. *"IT IS NOT YET!"*

"IS SHE COME, MY RANIA?"

And the many voices made the Earth tremble. *"SHE IS NOT COME!"*

"THEN ARISE! ARISE AND SLAY, FOR THEY DARE WAKE ME WHEN MINE AEON IS NOT YET, AND MY RANIA IS NOT COME."

To the left and right of the cleft, where so much of the Tomb already lay torn open and exposed to the sky, vast doors were suddenly seen in the ground and thrusting upward. The gates opened with such force that whatever was atop them, whether dirt or rock or tree stumps or glacier, was hugely flung aside. Light, brilliant and white, poured out from underfoot, and in the light were motes of gold that fled upward like snow, if snow were made of fire, and if, instead of falling to earth from heaven, snow was received into heaven from Earth. These snowy motes came from lances held in the hands of the knights, who rose to the surface on platforms, coming suddenly into view.

The Hospitaliers were risen.

Gleaming in their black powered armor, white crosses shining on breastplate and banner, proud on the backs of rearing steeds girded and armored likewise in powered barding, the knights held in hand tall lances made of the same nanotechnological material as the slumber wands. But these had more settings than the rosy pink of thaw or the white of slumber, for now the light changed, and turned grim, and the shining hue turned purplish black, and the lances were crackling with dark sparks and motes.

The speakers from their helmets roared as each man shouted, and amplifiers buried beneath the soil acres-wide repeated the words, words which rolled across the landscape like the footfalls of giants:

"LET NONE DARE WAKEN HE WHO WAITS, FOR, LO, HIS WRATH AWAKES!"

Dark lightning from the lances swept the air like searchlights during a night air raid. The cnidarian robots that crowded near the roofless cleft began to sparkle and dissolve. Rocket fire arching from the armored men wrapped the cnidarians in boiling smoke; laser fire chopped the cnidarians neatly in pieces. Some two or three dozen were brought to the ground in a moment.

"DEUS LO VOLT!"

The wreckage of metal was strangely buoyant, and fell with dreamlike, lunar slowness. Montrose saw Sir Guiden and Oenoe, and several frightened and angry Witches, pulling themselves safely from the wreckage of the machines which had captured them. The cnidarians must have been extremely light and fragile, like the aeroscaphes of the Sylphs, because Montrose saw little Fatin push one over with one hand as she crawled out of its trembling debris.

Then several hundred of other cnidarians began to gather toward the roofless Tombs where those forty-five or so had been shot down. Several thousand beyond them, part of the colossal cloud of aerial machines, also turned and began drifting serenely in that direction, as if curious about the source of the disturbance.

Del Azarchel, looking down with one eyebrow raised, said, "Impressive. As toys, I mean. Very pretty. But they will not be able to accomplish anything against my Tower. This mighty surface-to-orbit skyhook has an outer shell made not of atoms, but of a single sheet of the strong nuclear force held in a sub-Planck-distance matrix of grids, the most invulnerable structure the whole resource of our current world can imagine or devise. Nothing can pierce the hull."

"Hull, schmull. You left the basement door open," said Montrose. "And my men can call up the lightning from hell."

At that moment, a voice came from the cnidarian on which they stood. "Master," it said. "There is a vast electrical disturbance in the mantle and crust of the Earth, apparently being produced by the entire core itself . . ."

"Only the outer core is being used as a dynamo," interrupted Menelaus, his teeth gritted in a mad grimace. "I mean, let's not exaggerate what I can do. That would be ridiculous."

". . . and resulting in a buildup," continued the emotionless voice, ". . . of a static charge of immense . . ."

The concussion smothered any next words.

What came up from the earth next were not the relatively mild sparks called lightning that appear in electrical storms, when passing clouds build up a charge differential between the ground and thunderhead. No, rather, this was the power of the rotating nickel-iron core of the Earth, a dynamo so astronomically vast that it produced such things as the magnetic fields surrounding the planet, with all their associated celestial phenomena such as the Van Allen radiation belts, the Aurora Borealis and Aurora Australis, the ozone layer, and so on, merely as side effects.

The entire crust of the Earth in this particular area, agitated by the many continent-sized plates of Von Neumann crystals of Pellucid, built up a negative charge of unthinkable magnitude, and concentrated it on one spot: directly under the nine-mile-wide mouth of the Bell. For a moment before the actual bolt struck, Saint Elmo's fire and balled lightning could be seen crawling across the tree stumps and icy hillocks of the ground. Lightning bolts climbed and exploded from between hilltop and hilltop like sparks from a Jacob's Ladder.

For some reason, none were near the Tomb itself, or near any of the knights, even though the power crackled and crawled from peak to peak and tree to tree in a wide circle all around them. The Bell was not directly above the Tombs in any case; the midpoint of the open mouth was four miles away. Four miles away was the point of discharge.

Then the bolt struck.

It hung between the instantaneously formed lake of lava below the mouth and the pattern of white and brown and black structures, buildings and factories and robotic housings, visible inside the open mouth of the Bell.

A normal lightning bolt is, at best, a foot in diameter of ionized air surrounding a thread-thin stream of electric current. This bolt was a force half a mile in diameter surrounded by a field of ions six or seven miles in diameter, and the vacuum formed by its passage caused the surrounding atmosphere to rush into the Bell mouth at twice the speed of sound.

It was brighter than the sun, bright as a nova, and hundreds, perhaps thousands, of lesser lightning bolts crowded around it, writhing like dragons whirled into its midst as it appeared. It was a white fire larger than the cone formed by a tornado, and all the air between the opening of the Bell and the ground below was not merely ionized, but due to the immensity of the heat and discharge, underwent fission.

What few strands of the lightning storm that were attracted to the outer hull, of course, accomplished no effect, aside from breaking a few hundred thousand of the maneuvering jets, which spilled countless metric tons of rocket fuel into the air, which (in turn) was then ignited by the surrounding heat and electricity, and fell to earth as a rain of fire.

The main effect struck the interior. The heat of the electrical discharge formed a mushroom cloud, looking remarkably like a cnidarian itself, that went boiling upward where the lightning, or, rather, the electron-energy beam-weapon from the Earth's outer core, had passed. In the mushroom cloud were seen falling buildings, towers, and fiery rectilinear shapes larger than castles struck from the endless interior wallscape of the Bell, looking like so many children's blocks tossed out of the window of a burning nursery.

From their position five miles from the epicenter of the atmospheric disaster, Del Azarchel and Montrose were unharmed, but they both stood with their arms before their faces, waiting for the winds to die down, and while Del Azarchel's suit protected him, Montrose was now sunburned along the half of his body that had been facing the event. The cnidarian on which they stood buckled and swayed. It must have had an independent or redundant means of buoyancy, however, for it stayed aloft even while every other cnidarian lifting machine, from those the size of aircraft carriers to those the size of pocket handkerchiefs, toppled with the slowness of great catastrophes toward the earth below. The smaller ones opened their mantles to act as parachute canopies, but even the smaller ones which were too high, or too near the blast, were crumpled and scuttled by the hundred-mile-an-hour winds, and sent leaf-whirling earthward.

Those directly above the lava lake, when they splashed down, sent up a wave of black ash and smoke like the smoke of an open furnace, a wall of darkness so vast that it hid the continuing destruction. Other machines, their tendrils groping and looping helplessly, were carried by the winds as they plunged down and down through thousands of feet of air, as if an army of paratroopers, and all their aircraft large and small, dove at the ground without ever once opening a parachute. The noise was not merely indescribable: Montrose's remaining ear had failed him. To him, the scene was as silent as a dream.

Looking down, he saw at several points, about half a mile in each direction from the Devil's Den facility, smoke arising from a line of newly formed craters encircling the whole hilltop. These were the emission points of the various fields and defensive systems designed to protect the Tombs from the discharge of its own primary earth-current beam weapon. It had been designed, of course, with the thought in mind that the roof armor and several yards of insulating bedrock would be intact; but Montrose was gratified that the four or five miles of distance, and the strength of the grounding fields, had been sufficient to spare the Tombs from echoes, reflections, and ricochets of the energy forces involved.

Montrose and Del Azarchel were low enough that the details of the Tomb corridors and chambers were clearly visible. He could see the rotund shape of Mickey the Witch, for example, seated on the throne of the burial chamber, looking upward and clapping his hands together in applause.

With his good hand, Montrose took the hip flask from the listless fingers of Del Azarchel. He shouted, "Thanks! I'll take that drink now!"

The line of fire in his throat was warm and soothing, and he coughed helplessly. It was oak-barrel-aged Kentucky. He shouted, "Someday, you'll have to tell me how you managed to preserve so much of the ancient world. All I got is one God's-snotting poxy box of ciggies left, and not a single damn cigar. Smoked the last one in 7985 while I was sitting on the dead body of Coronimas. Ah! What a smoke."

Del Azarchel was laughing. Over his implants, Montrose heard a message:

"Ah, Cowhand, always full of surprises! I think you may actually have damaged the internal works of the Tower up to three thousand feet! Since the Tower is over one hundred sixty-five thousand miles high, three thousand feet is less than a pinprick would be if you stepped on it with your big toe. If you had a big toe. Your knights are brave men. I will dedicate this lake to their memory."

He paused, smiling a seraphic smile.

"The lake, I mean, which will be caused by the nine-mile-wide imprint when I land the foot of the Tower here, and drive the crust of the Earth downward several hundred feet below sea level.

"And, by Saint Iago! It might take the internal autorepair mechanisms of the Tower nearly, ah, twenty minutes to lower into place spare arcologies and factories from midlevel storage to the damaged section. It may take as long as half an hour. None of my people were in that tiny fragment you singed: the living quarters are above the atmosphere line.

"I am immune from any earthly force.

"But your facilities are not immune from the forces of heaven, are they? Let us see what happens when the Tower base is maneuvered over the Tombs to drop the rubble from the damage directly onto the heads of your knights and the people still sleeping in your pit, shall we?

"Come, shoot your puny little sparks again, old friend. Let us see if you can hit the maneuvering anchor asteroid. Can you make even the zenith point of a suborbital arc? Can you send lightning out of the atmosphere with your system? No? Let us see what your vaunted Tombs can do against a real . . . oh . . ."

The message over the implants trailed off, and Del Azarchel, now leaning with one boot on the edge of the cnidarian canopy, staring down, looked stricken. His face was blank and drawn, and his eyes were filled with strange sorrow. Montrose was more than puzzled, he was shocked to see such a look on the face of Del Azarchel.

Slowly and painfully (for every movement of any muscle was painful) he turned his head to see what Del Azarchel stared at.

The golden box of the burial chamber beneath them was clear and plain to the eye. The cnidarian on which they stood had been pushed by the gale winds to the north, so they now saw the chamber from a different angle. There were the great main doors.

Above the doors was the portrait of a fair princess in white, with the half circle of a galaxy framing her like a multistellar sunrise.

Del Azarchel, eyes on the portrait of Rania, said brusquely, "Give my compliments to the Grandmaster Sir Guiden and tell him that if he orders his men to stop firing, I will call my instruments back into the Tower, and trouble him no further. You I will also release back into his hands. There is no need to involve these others. I will let your humans live: such pets do not concern me. This is between the two of us."

Montrose said, "It won't take me long to dig up my armor and my Krupp gun."

"Ah. You keep yours loaded and ready? So do I. I will meet you in an hour."

And Del Azarchel ordered his cnidarian to carry Montrose gently back down to the Tomb.

13

The Judge of Ages and the Master of the World

1. Delays

It took longer than an hour.

As there always were in affairs of this type, despite the willingness, even the impatience, to begin, there were delays which accumulated to many hours.

The Seconds had to be appointed and sent to address each other.

Montrose had to receive medical attention and invigoration from his coffins. He had much, much damage to undo; and Del Azarchel scorned the idea of facing a foe at less than the peak of his prowess, and so insisted he be sent the coffin medical reports to prove Montrose was hale. Since some of the information had value, it had to be redacted, and the Seconds had to negotiate what data were left in and what cut out.

The submicroscopic mites the Blue Men had introduced into Montrose's nervous system had to be painstakingly removed, lest they hinder his reaction time.

With great reluctance and regret, Montrose also had his implants, which had served him so well, removed. Now that Exarchel was occupying the entire volume of Pellucid, and was having the nanomechanisms augmenting his brain power expanded in number from merely what could coat the Earth to what could fill it, the signal environment was too dangerous for Montrose to have any direct link even to peripheral parts of his nervous system. Montrose also did not want to be distracted by an unexpected hiss of electromagnetic noise, or to have anything radiating from him that a clever bullet might target.

The negotiations over the intelligence quotient of the weapons also took time. Since a logic crystal the size of a diamond that could fit on a lady's smallest finger contained calculating power equal to what every computer system on the Earth combined could achieve back when these guns were first designed and programmed, there was something absurd about the long discussion over how intelligent, and what kind of intelligence, and what programming, could be allowed in the gun calculation magazine. It was as if they were discussing whether the abacus could use oily stones, lest the fingers flicking the beads get some advantage of speed. But Montrose did not merely admire and appreciate, he *loved* his weapon, and refused to admit that it could ever be out-of-date. And from the tenacity of the responses carried by the Seconds, Del Azarchel felt the same way.

When Montrose explained to Keirthlin the Linderling that the ranging and detection gear performed its calculations by means of electrons being forced across open or shut transistor gates powered by a current differential in the circuit, she actually laughed, her deep sorrow, if only for that moment, held in abeyance.

However, Vulpina chided her, saying that Chimeresses were trained in every weapon, even the oldest and simplest, because at times this was the only weapon at hand. She also made a point of saying to Montrose that Chimeresses made good wives and bore fierce children.

There was considerable debate over whom to have as judge of honor presiding over the duel. Everyone Del Azarchel and Montrose knew was either one man's servant and the other man's enemy or vice versa. Montrose thought it over carefully, and then agreed that Alalloel the Cetacean could serve in this capacity.

Montrose had to check his dueling armor, which, compared to the powered armor of the Hospitaliers, now seemed primitive, small, and weak, but unbearably precious. Both men had to submit (Montrose insisted) to an invasive medical examination by agreed-upon physicians, to ensure that their skin, bones, and organs were within a defined range of human location, and made of natural biological materials.

And, most importantly, after all other matters were decided, Montrose returned to his Tombs and found a workbench, found a light and shook it until it glowed, and he sat and packed the chaff for his dueling pistol, and selected and balanced and loaded and programmed the targeting tactics, one by one, into the eight escort gyro-jet bullets, and then into the deadly, massive, self-propelled main shot.

As it happened, it was the brink of dawn before they met and faced each other.

2. Unnatural Twilight

It was dark where they stood below the foot of the Bell, the air scented with the hint of sunrise, but the cherry-red light of dawn struck the sides of the vast Tower above them. Above that, where the structure intercepted the direct and unrefracted rays of the sun, the towerlight was yellow. An aurora borealis had gathered around the reaches above that, a side effect of radiation disturbances and flux in the magnetosphere surrounding the globe. Even farther skyward, the uppermost lengths, and the long-tailed crescent of the anchor point, were glaring in the sharp light of hard vacuum.

The Tower was far brighter than the full moon. Because of this, odd to the eye, the landscape neither had the clarity of daylight nor the mystic softness of moonlight. It was not even the wild overcast gloom of a heavy storm, since the light was the color of blood and fire, but too bright. It was, rather, like the unnatural noon twilight of a solar eclipse. Everything looked spectral.

The scenery exposed to that light was equally uncanny. It was like the surface of the moon for craters and pockmarks. Steam rose from glaciers in the distance, which were sprinkled with spots and streamers of molten and refrozen iron, surrounded wherever it appeared by discharged matter that looked like fine black sand. Stumps of burnt and broken trees lay every way the eye turned, and the piled and thrown trunks were like the remnants of a lumberyard fire, acres of black splinters.

A dry streambed cut across the hill in one area; and frozen fans, red with rust and sediment, boiling and dripping across the slopes, was the dispossessed volume of water that once ran there.

In another place, a lake that had been underground had boiled to the surface, but a vortex was in the midst of it, and a continual roaring; and broken bits of depthtrain cars floated on the lake. The water was draining into the rail tube leading below the mantle of the Earth.

In each direction was wreckage, destruction and death, broken rock, craters, smoke and burnings, and fields of cracked ice dotted with pellets and dust from the earth's core, or black with tiny bits and flakes of debris that fell from the inner cylinder of the skyhook.

The only things that were whole were the cnidarian machines, hanging with unnatural weightlessness between the broken landscape and the storm-caressed Tower.

One of these, a cnidarian no larger than a Viking longboat, swooped smoothly down through the predawn gloom. Against the vertical red river of towerlight, the silhouettes of five hooded figures could be seen: one boyish and slouching, one looming and huge-limbed as a blacksmith, one thin and erect as an upraised sword, one crowned with two golden tendrils. The final figure was half their height, like a big-headed child.

Serpentines lowered the five to the broken ground behind the armored bulk of Del Azarchel, standing patiently.

None of the men carried lights, and this told Menelaus that they were the nycloptic. Menelaus saw silver capes of solar sail material, startlingly bright in the blood-hued gloom against the dark silk of their uniforms. Heavy amulets of dull metallic red gleamed on their wrists. These men were dressed as members of the Hermetic Order, and had bodies, like theirs, able to adjust to a range of environments, and eyes that changed at night to be nocturnal.

It seemed it was the fancy of Del Azarchel to dress these new servants, whoever they were, in the uniform, style, and equipment of his old shipmates of the *Hermetic* Expedition, some eight thousand two hundred eighty years ago. As if the Beefeaters guarding Buckingham retained the dress and weapons of the nomadic hunting bands of the middle Neolithic: tunics of mastodon leather, spears tipped with leaf-shaped flint.

Montrose found that odd, even chilling.

On the other hand, the armor Montrose wore, and his massive pistol, came from the same year, so he understood the impulse to freeze some of the waters of the river of time, and keep preserved in ice something of the long-dead past, even the uniforms of dead men. Odd, yes, and chilling, but very human.

3. Witnesses and Seconds

Montrose was in his armor, wondering how he had been able, when he was a young man, to stand wearing it for such interminable lengths of time without suffering the desire to scratch. Of course, he never before fought a duel having come just that hour dripping from a rapid-healing coffin, with the bones in his newly unbroken arm still tickling and aching. Always before it had been some enemy selected by his law firm, and the killing had been, to him, merely a task. More difficult and dangerous than some, but just a task.

It had not been personal. It had not been the culmination of countless millennia of unfolding destiny.

The two men, and their Seconds, now advanced on each other. Their footsteps were the only sounds in the area. There were no sounds of birdcalls or nocturnal animals seeking their dens, because all living things within a mile or so had died when the depthtrain tube had been used as an orbital launcher, or when the earth-current had ignited. However, in the distance, nine or ten miles away, clouds gathered against the far side of the Bell, and, cooled by the touch of the outer hull, had begun to precipitate. The rain could be heard, faint and far, washing against the endless height of metallic hardness, and, lower, against the broken hilltops and ice fields. Higher on the Bell, another set of clouds had gathered, but they had snowed, not rained, and an irregular streak of white, like a snowfield of a far mountain peak, could be clearly seen painted against the towerside, gleaming in the brighter light of the higher air.

Montrose spared no glances for this, nor any of the other sights which might possibly prove his last sight evermore. He walked forward, stomach boiling with emotion, his eye not leaving the dark and mocking eyes of his opponent. Neither man had donned his helm yet. Neither man was carrying the cubit-long six-pound sidearm that served him as his dueling weapon.

Midmost stood Alalloel of Lree, to act as judge of honor. Next to her rested two coffins, to act as doctors. Their lids were open, medical fluid warm and hyperoxygenated. Receiving kits attached to the coffin hulls were opened like Swiss Army knives, arms unlimbered and needles shining.

Alalloel was garbed in a skintight jumpsuit of sea green, dark green, and aquamarine, trimmed with black flecks and foam-white surging through rippling patterns set to slow pulsations, ornamented with studs of nacre; but over this was thrown a wide two-leaved cloak of silver hanging from shoulder boards so large as to make her seem childish and frail.

Montrose looked more carefully. It was not a cloak. These were artificial wings of amazingly intricate construction. These must be a version, designed for the human body, of the wings Soorm said he had seen the whales who met her in secret wear.

They were made of silvery feathers that seemed both organic and metallic. Near the base of every vane, atop what would be the calamus had it been an organic feather, was an optical sensor made of logic crystal. There were golden

Locust-type tendrils along each rachis of each feather, and other smaller receivers and nodes and ports forming the barbs. When Alalloel shrugged, the wings opened in a splendor of shimmering white, as the wings of an albino peacock, bright with countless eyes.

Montrose noted Del Azarchel staring at the wings for a fraction of a second longer than Del Azarchel would have done had he recognized them. Interesting. Montrose felt his heart begin to beat more strongly, and wondered what emotion was causing it.

It had been a while since he had felt this way: the emotion was hope.

It had been agreed to appoint five Seconds for each of them. Montrose nodded at Mickey, who looked somehow splendid and terrible in his Witching robes, and even the ridiculous decorations of his tall hat looked menacing in the eerie red gloom, as if possessed by hidden powers.

With him stood Sir Guiden the Knight Hospitalier, Scipio the Cryonarch, Soorm the Hormagaunt, Expositor Illiance. Mickey introduced himself and his fellow witnesses to the duel, speaking in Latin. It had been negotiated and agreed that all conversations were to be in this dead language, as most here either knew it, or could follow it with aid of a talking box.

Sir Guy was wearing his hauberk woven of fine, nigh-microscopic five-linked rings. His hood and tunic were black, and his dark surcoat blazed with the white cross of Malta. Gauntlets were on his hands and greaves on his shins. He had turned his smart-ink tattoos to their neutral setting, glow off, and his skin seemed flesh-colored, merely with a rough texture of many fine, dark lines under the skin. Montrose could not recall ever having seen the man's real face before. His undisguised features were so sad, so calm, and bathed in such an aura of peace, that Montrose understood why he hid behind decorations. It was a face that would neither terrify foes nor inspire the battle-fury in followers.

Scipio's skull was now whole, and no trace of savant circuits remained in him, for the Iatrocrats had miraculous techniques to accomplish the regrowth and restoration of lost neural tissue and bone cells in a single night which had not existed, or even been dreamed, when Scipio last had lived. From his apparently limitless wardrobe he had had buried with himself, he now wore a uniform of the Cryonarchy from his native decade: a conservatively cut suit of gray and soft green, decorated with scallops and roses, over which was flung a black tabard emblazoned in white with the heraldry of the Endymion Hibernation Syndicate: a sleeping youth in the arms of a crescent moon, cradling an hourglass.

Soorm was splendid in his naked fur. Before he climbed to the field of honor, the Nymph Aea and Suspinia the Chimeress had volunteered to brush the otter pelt of Soorm until it glowed like black ink. He had needed no medical care, but he had spent the night in the coffin nonetheless, making little tweaks and minor innovations to his many innate biological weapons.

The serene little Blue Man appeared dressed in a small hauberk of mail, with coif and hood, and a misericorde tucked through his belt, and his surcoat was the white of a neophyte, his cross the red of a crusader. He bore no sword as yet, nor spurs. He was introduced not by the name Expositor Illiance, but instead was called Squire Lagniappe.

Montrose would have liked to have had the brave Alpha Daae here with him, to represent the Chimerae; or have had a Linderling on hand to record every nuance of the events through their nodes. Indeed, Vulpina had demanded, and Keirthlin had expressed a desire, to be allowed to act as witnesses to the gunfight, but Menelaus Montrose told Keirthlin that women who see such things have a darkness that comes over their soul and does not depart, a thing that makes them less able or willing to be softhearted, wifely, or maternal.

Keirthlin replied that it was not necessarily the case that witnessing such cold and deliberate violence influenced the psychology for the worse. Coming to the aid of her argument, Vulpina bragged that she herself had seen such things on the playground nearly every day of her life, and twice on Dueling Day; and it had not affected her fertility, or the ability of the Eugenic Board to send a stud to beat her into submission in preparation for the mating assault.

Montrose, at that point, said simply that this was man's business, and no matter what the customs or rules of their ages might be, his death, or his victory, must be done by the rules he knew. He did not speak to either one about what had happened when his own mother, watching in secret, had seen his father shot dead in a duel.

Montrose shook his head, trying to clear it of such thought. Why did he ponder of his mother now, who had been gone some eight thousand years? Then he recalled that she regarded the profession of gunfighting shameful, and would not take the money Montrose had brought in. To his brothers it went, but not a dime to her.

She had told him: "You think you can kill and make that be an end of it? There is no end! The men you kill will come out of the ground and come back for you, or sure as like. There is always one more."

There was always one more. One more what? He had never had the nerve to ask.

Montrose was uneasy because his experience as a duelist told him that any man who dwelt on the shame brought to his mother when he walked onto the field of honor was not the one who walked away again, but was the one carried away in a box. He hid his uneasiness behind his best poker face, but he knew Del Azarchel sensed it, for the man's twinkling eyes narrowed, and a look of confidence was in them.

Mickey introduced himself as Mictlanagualzin of the Dark Science Coven, which made Del Azarchel smile in contempt and Montrose smile in appreciation for the gesture, which was a noble one.

The Warlock said, "Such is my true name, and I depart of half my power by speaking it: and yet that power I place into this deadly ground, and across this deadly hour, that there be no trace, no shadow, of the least dishonor. I bind your souls to it."

4. The Hooded Men

The five who stood behind Del Azarchel now came forth into the light shed from the gleaming many-eyed cloak of Alalloel. Menelaus tried to betray no expression on his face, but as he had so often found before, his more powerful intellect lent more power to his passions, intuitions, and reactions. Now his passion was fear, his intuition was supernatural dread, and his reaction was a trembling in his innards.

His brain had not allowed him to recognize them from afar, despite that their identity was obvious even in silhouette. What was it Soorm had said about more intelligent people being more able to fool themselves, whereas animals saw things clear and far off?

The gigantic one was Sarmento i Illa d'Or, who pointed his finger at Montrose, and closed one eye and twitched his thumb. He pointed at the spot where the scar was, marking the wound Sarmento left that should have killed Montrose.

And next to him . . .

The stoop-shouldered boyish one was De Ulloa, as handsome as he ever had been, smiling sheepishly, wearing a cross of Nero around his neck: an upside-down cross with the arms broken to slant as the letter Y reversed, all within a circle.

The slim and rigid-spined one was Narcís D'Aragó, wearing a rapier, and standing as stiffly as the Chimerae whom he had made in his own image.

The one with the tendrils was Jaume Coronimas.

The final one, his face young and unlined, and his tendrils waving in rhythm with Coronimas as they passed radioneural messages back and forth, was Mentor Ull, dressed in a miniature version of the black shipsuit and hood. And his skin was an onyx dark as his silk.

Sarmento was delighted, and he laughed. "No, in one way these are not quite who you think, Fifty-One! What, are we afraid the old madness is coming back? No, this is not Melchor de Ulloa. This is Exulloa, or, rather, the remote body, operated by quantum entanglement, from where he rests in the Noösphere. He does not remember being shot by you, because there was no time for an additional communion. The others, you have guessed, are Exarago, Excoronimas, and I don't believe you have met Exynglingas, our newest crewmate! He does recall his death, because his savant circuits were activated by the biometric failure that accompanies death trauma. Once, we only had enough computer resources to bring us out one at a time. Now, you have given us so much more calculation space—the entire core of the planet!—we need not fear such penury again!"

Mickey said sternly, "It is only the inner core. Do not be ridiculous."

The young, jet-dark version of Mentor Ull, or, rather, Exynglingas, still had the same half-lidded, wholly reptilian eyes of his previous incarnation. "It happens that all your absurdities of bloodshed and striving have yielded nothing. The Hermeticists have finally achieved the ultimate secret: life beyond bodily death."

But the judge of honor held up her empty hand in a brusque gesture, saying, "The Seconds may not address the primaries, only the Seconds brought by him. Such is the convention."

Illiance, or, rather, Squire Lagniappe, stepped forward. His skin color changed suddenly, passing from blue to become the silvery-gray of a Linderling. His eyes lost their color, and became silver throughout, eerie and beautiful.

Exynglingas, the Ghost of Ull, seemed startled, and shrank back with alarm. Menelaus was puzzled by this—until he recalled that the Linderlings had hunted and herded the Blue Men, and all other Inquiline form of Locust, into extinction.

The gray-shimmering, silver-eyed Squire said to the Ghost of Ull, "Tell me. Does Coronimas the Hermeticist recall being shot to death on the toilet, nay, shot in the back while he fled, by an assailant he could not see? The terror and shame of that download is now in his permanent mind records, and touches all related thoughts. Is this accomplishment as nothing? It is meaningful to defy even an evil one cannot destroy."

But Montrose said to Mickey, "Witness Mictlanagualzin—is the honorable party facing me willing to program, with an irrevocable code, an unstoppable self-destruct sequence into his machine half of his soul, Exarchel, to initiate the moment their biometric link shows the principle, Learned Del Azarchel, has indeed died?"

Excoronimas flicked his gold tendrils and said to Mickey, "Ask your principle how he could verify? We cannot give you the access to the inner workings of the thoughts of Exarchel."

Del Azarchel held up his hand. "There is no need to debate. It is disquietingly easy to establish a suicide reflex tied to a deadman switch for beings of such architecture, prone as they are in any case to Divarication cascade. Indeed, I expected this request, and spent many hours last night preparing exactly such a combination. Before these witnesses, I vow that I will remove the safety from the deadman switch to obliterate every copy of myself, wheresoever situate, the moment we take our positions and claim ready, showing the black palm, but not before. Nor is there need for verification. Learned Montrose will trust me to keep my word. He knows me. I know him. The meeting is without honor if I am not exposed to the risk of death. Shall we begin?"

The judge of honor raised a baton, which she held in lieu of the more traditional handkerchief. The red dawnlight was sliding rapidly down the towerside, and too swiftly to be seen, a sliver of red was to the east above the hill crests, and on the high hilltop where they stood, their shadows stretched thin and weak toward the darkened west, where brighter stars still twinkled.

She said, "Before I give the signal, three things must be said. First, you must agree that I am no longer Alalloel of Lree. For the purposes of this encounter and hereafter, to you I am Alalloel of the Anserine, a Paramount of an unlimited mental communion. You must so address me, or as Anserine. Is this acceptable? May we continue?"

Del Azarchel spoke sharply, "I do not see it makes a difference. Does everyone change his name, save only for me and Montrose? I accept. Continue."

Sarmento's eyes jerked toward the winged woman, and narrowed in thought.

Montrose suppressed the impulse to introduce himself by a new name, such as Mr. Nostradamus Twiddle Apocalypse, Esquire. A man's last words should not be a jape. He said only, "I accept. Continue."

Alalloel of the Anserine next said, "If a peaceful accommodation can be sought and found, both participators may even now withdraw, and with no loss of honor, and no imputation against their steadfastness. Witnesses! Inquire now and finally if accommodation can be made on any other ground."

Mickey put his head near Montrose and said softly, "Can it? You told me once, Judge of Ages, that you had some admiration for him, the Master of the World. The two of you have been like sun and moon for all of all the history anyone here knows. It will be odd to walk under the dome of heaven and nevermore to see one of the great luminaries."

Montrose said, "To be frank, I'd give almost anything to be able to take him, and walk away from here arm in arm, and find something to do together, go on a space voyage or something. You know he stole my starship, the *Emancipation,* that I named after my childhood dream? And I've never been aboard her. So, yeah, I suppose I'd give almost anything. Almost. But not my word. That I keep, even if I die for it."

Mickey turned and raised his voice. "Madame. No accommodation can be made." And Sarmento i Illa d'Or said the same.

Alalloel said, "Have all measures to avoid this conflict, with or without an accommodation, been examined and exhausted?"

Mickey called all, "Yes."

But Sarmento i Illa d'Or said, "Just a moment!"

For Sarmento was having some fierce, whispered debate with Del Azarchel. Montrose, thinking it was one of the privileges of being posthuman, adjusted the interpretation mechanism of his temporal lobes so that the words came crisp and clear despite the distance. But it was gibberish. Del Azarchel and Sarmento i Illa d'Or were inventing new languages with radically differing grammar and signification rules, one per each sentence, based on some arbitrary algorithm known to both of them. It seemed they also enjoyed the perquisites of being posthuman.

Finally, Del Azarchel said, "I want to talk to Montrose privately."

Anserine said, "That is not allowed. You must abide by the rules and follow them."

"No, I think not," drawled Del Azarchel. "Menelaus Montrose never obeyed a rule in his life, save when it suited him. Nor have I. Lesser men follow and obey *us.* We do not follow. He and I, we are the makers of rules."

And so Del Azarchel started walking forward, his gait in his armor stiff and rolling, a fashion of walk that was something comical while being menacing. Montrose thought he looked like a Sumo wrestler.

5. Always One More

Mickey whispered to Montrose, "Del Azarchel is in breach. You now have a faultless right to withdraw, and no man can say infraction."

Montrose did not answer that, but heaved up his heavy boots and stomped forward himself. He did not want to withdraw, and live. He counted the number of years he had awaited this day, and compared it to the number of steps he now made across the icy and broken rock, gray with ashes and pockmarked with miniature craters. It was roughly eight hundred years per step. Unhelmeted, unarmed, they closed the distance.

Then they were together, close enough to look eye to eye. Close enough that when Del Azarchel laughed, Montrose felt the touch of warmth on his face.

Suddenly an old memory bubbled up in his mind.

He was four years old, maybe three. He had been lying in bed, hungry. He often went to bed hungry, as the older boys who could do chores needed their strength to do them. It was a cold night, as most nights of the endless winter were, and he had doubled up with two of his brothers in the same narrow bed for warmth, with three blankets piled over all of them. One of them, maybe it was Agamemnon, was telling the other, Hector, that the Sheriff had been asking mother where she had been yesterday, and whether anyone had seen her there, and so on. It had meant nothing to him then.

Now, looking back with adult memory, posthuman memory, he identified that as the day and date Hatchet Jim Rackham had died. Gunned down by an unknown assailant. It had been a light caliber bullet, so the rumor ran that it might have been a woman, using a small pistol. But he had also been stabbed savagely, repeatedly, methodically, and the trail of bloodstains showed that he had been alive and crawling the first few times the blade entered his back. Whoever had done it had not had a strong arm.

It clicked into his mind what his mother had meant. *There is always one more.*

Whenever you kill a man, and you think that is the end of it, someone will come to avenge him. No matter how dead he is, a force as invisible as a specter would rise up, and find someone, a brother or a friend, or even a stranger who now feared your murderer's reputation or envied and sought to better it, and the dead man's vengeance would walk, even if the man himself never moved physically from the grave. And if you kill that avenger, that brother or son, he might have another brother or son.

Or he might have a fierce young wife with ten small children to feed. Hatchet Jim had been the man who shot his father. That clicked into place, too.

Looking back with his posthuman memory, he counted the number of knives in the knife rack when he saw them at age four, age three, age five. The largest blade had been missing since April of that year. The one mother had used to murder a man after her first shot had failed to do the deed.

Something very cold and still touched his heart at the moment. To take a man's life was a fearful thing. And even if he killed Blackie, that would not be the end of it. It would never end.

He straightened his shoulders, and, with an apology in his cold heart for his mother, he vowed to himself: *Very well. It never ends. Even if it lasts to the last hour of the universe.*

He was ready.

14

Chessmaster of History,
Fencer of Fate

1. Privately

Montrose said, "Blackie. Is there anything to say? I am a professional duelist. Back when I was young, I made my whiskey money drilling holes in men's hearts. So you are not likely to unnerve me. It is not just that we hate each other. Everything in us is opposed."

Del Azarchel said, "Not everything."

"You're right. We both love the same girl. Not exactly a basis for an amiable coexistence."

Del Azarchel's face tightened. "I made her for myself. All my ideals of perfection are embodied in her. She's mine."

"That's incest. Your own daughter. You make me puke."

"Incest at least is between members of the same species. She can no more mate with you than with a monkey. That is bestiality. It is not enough to vomit; I must scrub my inward parts with lye to clear my palate."

"Wait. All this time, you were thinking I have not consummated my marriage? You came to call me out to duel on my wedding night, but not early enough. It is not like we waited for sundown to start in on our nuptial pleasures. She was more eager than I was. In fact, in the car ascending the tower, she—"

Del Azarchel threw back his head and laughed. Menelaus was surprised and disappointed. He had been toying with the idea of a little fisticuffs to get the blood pumping on a cold and sluggish morning like this before they picked up pistols. He had been half believing that was Del Azarchel's purpose in drawing him aside. He did not really think Montrose could be talked out of anything, did he?

But Del Azarchel was filled with good humor as if the black cloud of deadly anger building in him had never been. "Ah! Such words. No one talks to me as an equal. Do you know that? It's lonely."

"I was kind of hoping I was talking to you unequal-like, sort of as a man speaks to a rat."

"Your words are like the toreador's barbs under the skin of a bull. No one else pierces the skin. They don't have the skill. Just you. And, well. Her."

Montrose felt some of the hate in him ebb, like an engine that cannot maintain a full head of steam. "Okay, Blackie. Speak your piece."

"I will give you the Earth."

"Come again?"

"Serve me. If you agree to kneel and serve me, and become my vassal, I will in reward make you the Master of this World, third from the sun. All her peoples and lands, resources and living things, beauties and manufactures, and all her Cliometric destinies forever and aye."

"This is the world you are going to give to the Hyades when they come. The End of Days is only four hundred years off."

"This world is nothing."

"Not to you, you mean," said Montrose. His eyes held a look of deep sorrow even while his lip curled in a sneer of contempt.

"So. You have figured it out!"

"I reckon I have."

"Very good. None of my men have, and they have more clues than you. They are augmented by computer emulations who match them thought for thought, and so they are equally as intelligent as either of us—and yet they lack something we have, you and I. That inner fire. The fire of the gods. I expected no less. You know."

"I do know," admitted Montrose, "and I would have known sooner, but I just couldn't—despite all your crimes—I just didn't want to believe you'd ever be *that* low."

"It was necessary."

"Your own men! Hell, I knew these guys too, back from the training camp. Once they might have been my friends. And now you are making me feel sorry for them? Wow. I've shot most of them. All but one, actually, and I actually feel sorry for them, because they trust you. They admire you. Like loyal little dogs. They love you."

Del Azarchel turned his eyes toward where the Seconds were gathered, looking on, no doubt wondering what the Judge of Ages and the Master of the World might be discussing. He said thoughtfully, "I can guess the day, maybe even the hour, when you deduced it. It was last night. You were gathered with your comrades, most of whom entered your Tombs to hunt you, but now they were won over. Loyal comrades. You have just survived deadly combat, and so there is that warmth that no man can feel who has not, alongside his brothers, looked in the face of death. And perhaps one of them says, O Judge of Ages, you who shape and shake men's destinies, why is our world as it is? Could you not have shaped a better? And then you told them about our fencing match in the fog of history."

"Fencing match? I think of it as a chess game. Move, countermove. A matter of logic."

"That is why you lost, Cowhand. It is a matter of feints and fakes. And a chessboard has an edge, whereas fencers move to whatever part of the yard gives them advantage. Including off the planet altogether."

"I did not lose, Blackie."

"You lost last night, at four bells of the First Dog Watch."

Which was eighteen hundred hours. Menelaus thought it odd that Blackie still every now and again, as if by slip, spoke in nautical terms; as if his life outside the hull of the *Hermetic* had no meaning. This was the hour that the white-hot iron mass had been shot into orbit from the depthtrain rail.

Blackie said, "Shall we discuss our game? Just the last two moves."

Menelaus opened his mouth to say something sarcastic, but then he snapped it shut again. Fact of the matter was that he *did* want to discuss it. Very much so.

"Go on," he said.

2. End Game

"Back in the Eightieth Century," Blackie began, "and not long after you had your disgusting creature Elton Linder release the Inquiline Code into the Noösphere, I used a simple terraforming technique to lower the temperature of the world disastrously.

"You thought I meant to *raise* population levels in order to have the Locusts outbreed their competitors, since population growth correlates to a longer growing season, which correlates to raising rather than lowering world temperature.

"But ah, no. All a feint. I intended that you should attempt volcanic technology—an area where you excel—to counter-terraform. Not because I cared about the temperature. I knew you would release into the plate tectonic stress areas your Von Neumann crystals that only you know how to make and which only Rania knew how to describe mathematically. You took only the normal precautions to protect your depthtrain stations where you built you remaining Tombs. I made assaults at Mount Misery, Wright-Patterson, and here, at Devil's Den. The crystals were near the surface, where I could get them. I found a nodule, in a shaft over six thousand feet long, of crystals in perfect condition." Del Azarchel sighed with satisfaction. "That was my true purpose. The main dish of the main feast, so to speak! Killing you is merely the port and cigar after."

"God, you make me want a smoke. Don't talk that way."

"The tobacco leaf is extinct only on Earth. It grows remarkably well under lighter gravity, even given the limitations of hydroponic gardening."

The idea that Blackie had been to Mars or Titan, or other moons and worlds of this solar system walking the alien soil, while he, Montrose, had been spending countless years under the damn ground, buried alive, almost made him dizzy, he was so sick with envy.

Menelaus said stubbornly, "It ain't over. I've still got one chessman to move."

Blackie smiled and said expansively, "Not over, you say? I have struck you through the heart; your planetary core Xypotech is mine, or if you like, I have captured the rook behind which you castled. Do you really think there is any more game to play between us? Ah! But *which* game were we playing? When you were telling your loyal men about the chess game, and they understood that they were all pawns, I wager you did not tell them the truth. The whole truth. No, you told them it was a game between darkness and light, machine and man, tyranny and liberty, with myself cast into the role of the dark machine of tyranny. Do I guess wrong? I see from your face that I do not."

"No . . . ," Montrose said slowly. "You guess aright. Looking back over all the centuries of our chess game, I realized you had made the same move over and over. One of your men builds a civilization. Then there is something that goes wrong, really wrong. And I wake up and step in to fix it. Just like I always did back when I was Crewman Fifty-One, your handy dandy little handyman madman."

Del Azarchel spread his hands. "And did you see what it is I made go wrong with every civilization? There is only one pattern to civilization, but infinite ways to fall into barbarism."

Montrose grunted. "You kept destroying your Church, over and over again. You kept undermining monotheism and monogamy."

Del Azarchel nodded. "The first is the basis for the belief in a rational cosmos; the second is the only basis for a rational civilization. Niceties like the belief in the rule of law rather than the rule of men are side-effects of these deep truths. Even the highest-born Chimera was bred like a showdog. There is no deeper degradation imaginable than to turn a man's most intimate and sacred relation with the opposite sex into something trivial, or man-made, or an article of commerce, or a pastime. Hah! The degradation of the Nymphs was even deeper. The Hormagaunts I convinced to eat their own children to expand their lives; the Locusts I convinced to eat their own souls—what could I have done that in a world wise enough to forbid divorce, contraception, or whatever else desecrates and trivializes the marital and maternal bond? Do you think a child raised by a loving mother could even dream of selling himself into Locust communion?"

"And even *knowing* what was going on," Montrose sighed, "you knew I was fool enough that I could not stand by and let a civilization, even a bad one, collapse, because then in the great chess game of fate, you would have just moved your queen Exarchel onto the board to pick up the broken pieces. I used to have nightmares about watching a bunch of barbarians dressed in animal skins tinkering with some old internal combustion engine or grinding gunpowder in a handmill while a tidal wave of that damn self-replicating gold goo the Savants worshipped was piling up on the horizon, too big for them to stop. So I could not permit a collapse. And I had to act."

Del Azarchel smiled and nodded, like a good sportsman acknowledging a polite compliment from a defeated foe. "Yes, you had to act. And you had only one weapon that I did not have. I had more men, more resources, and more time—I could stay awake for twice your years while you slumbered, and age biologically at half your rate. But you had one thing I lacked. Rania's solution. The seven-part Divarication solution."

Montrose said, "So, as it turns out, this whole thing, all of history, was about me giving it to you, one little part at a time. I worked on the Giants, and you used that to create your emulations and Ghosts, your long-lived Witches. I tried to save the Witches. That was the first time, and you almost overplayed your hand; the Witch society is too obviously designed to fail. But I fell for it anyway, because, hey, I am a problem solver, and I love to solve problems. So, next time, you sacrificed a major piece, D'Aragó, just to draw me up to the surface, have a chance to see the state of misery of the Chimerae, misery I saw would be alleviated if they were just a little longer-lived. Men who live to see the future think about it, and men who think about the future think of war as a violent means to achieve political ends, not as a way to avenge insults against your king's wife. And so on.

"But you really did fool me, Blackie, and I give you credit. Because every time I used another one of the seven solutions, you had one of your dupes—I guess I cannot call them your men, can I?—pervert my work to make some new problem appear, some new race of man, some new evil empire.

"But not you.

"You would take the solution, a few lines of code, whatever it was I did, and you went off by your lonesome, not telling your dupes what the real plan was.

"And because your dupes always did something with the code you rooked out of me, for the longest time, I thought that was what you meant to do, and all you meant to do.

"I thought you wanted to steal the cooperation gene to get the mathematical tools needed to make the Chimerae. But then you exterminated the Chimerae. Or I thought you wanted the Greencloak technology to create the addiction-world of the Nymphs. But then you interfered with their weather control, and drove the Nymphs out of existence.

"By the time the Hormagaunts appeared, and they were monsters out of a psychology textbook on sociopathic egomania, I knew theirs and the others could not be real civilizations, not something you actually meant to catapult into the next evolutionary stage of man. They were too simplistic. A science experiment. So I had seen through the first level of deception. You were not just fencing me to make the next mankind follow your dream rather than my dream. It was never about the dream of a superhuman liberty versus the dream of superhuman tyranny. There was no dream, only the seven solutions.

"Even then, I did not see through the second level of deception.

"I thought the whole point of the Hormagaunts was to winkle the Clade Code system out of me for use on some project on Earth, a blueprint for the Locusts. And next I thought the point of your move was to steal the Inquiline Code which I made to save the Locusts and pervert it to make the Melusine. But that was not it, was it? Like you said. Earth is nothing."

"Exactly so. Feint low, disengage, strike high." Del Azarchel was grinning broadly now. "How much have you guessed?"

3. The Seven Secrets

"I think I've guessed everything but one thing. Let's get back to that later.

"The Hermetic Problem is how to make the Man Beyond Man, a mind that stands to us as we to beasts. Merely enlarging brain mass does not work. A macroscale machine, let's say, the size of the Pacific Ocean or the polar ice caps, if it is just one big centralized brain, works about as handily as one big centralized bureaucracy. It takes weeks for a thought to get from one side to another of a brain so big.

"If you double and redouble the size of an ant until it is as large as an elephant, the ant would need stubby elephant legs to haul its mass, which is squared and re-squared; in just the same way, the mental architecture of a planet-sized man's brain does not scale up. If you double the size of the cortex you have to square the size of the midbrain and cube the size of the hindbrain. Likewise, merely ramping up calculation speed does not work. That is what happened to you and me, Blackie. We think faster than men, but we make mistakes faster, too. You are looking for *better* thought procedures, not just *faster* ones.

"You decided to redesign the mind from the ground up, layer by layer. It was easy enough to anticipate that this is what you did—I can't see any other path. I would have done the same. And you did it in seven steps—thanks to me.

"First. The basic Promethean Formula I released to make the Giants, you used to make your posthumans. Exulloa, Exillador, and so on; and De Ulloa used the same formula on elephants and dolphins, boars and horses and dogs to make his Moreau critters.

"But that was all smoke screen. Hidden far from prying eyes somewhere, you put together a much larger and more ambitious project. You used the Promethean Formula to make a King of Machines.

"Second. The Serpentine Code was a means to make a machine-mind effectively immortal, but it only worked on the limited scale. So you built a brain made up of countless tiny brains, the same way a man's brain is made of countless individually living brain cells; so at least the physical substrate was immortal. These tiny and immortal brains were as countless as snowflakes. This was your platform, your foundation of stone. You built the King of Machines on top of this.

"Third. My genetic solution to allow the various Moreaus and Witches to learn to live together, you used to make these thousands of simple brains in the foundation of the King of Machines learn to cooperate. And all the other more complicated brains that were going to be swimming around in this fishbowl of thought, lesser minds inside greater minds like so many Russian dolls: fishbowl the size of the seven seas, an ocean of thought.

"Fourth. The Greencloak tech has an obvious application. Your King of Machines can do with electrons what the Nymphs do with molecules. It serves as the pleasure and pain centers of this emulated brain, or, if you like, as the rewards and punishments of a legal or economic system. You don't care about the physical sensation of pain: you just follow the form with the math. Every lesser mind inside the mind of the King of Machines can be addicted or memory-dithered to suit his majesty's fancy. All the little angels love the big bad archangel. I assume he is big and bad? I assume he is based on your template?

"Ditto for the Wintermind techniques, which act as a check against the addiction technology. An emulation of a man could use them just like a man with a flesh and blood brain, to shake off exoneurogenic addiction. There is no reason Exarchel cannot meditate and shake free of subconscious manipulation. In fact, he was hot to get my phantasm out of his head, weren't he? You tell me how that is working out for you.

"Six. The Clade system I introduced into the Hormagaunts to stop their disgusting Hobbesian war of all against all—and Exarchel lives in that same Hormagaunt pattern: he has no incentive not to eat and absorb any machine he meets, since he can get all the powers and abilities of that machine without having to beg or bargain, hire or swap. You wanted better for your King of Machines, so it can have all the lesser angels living in his head occupy the same mental ecology without flocks of vampire-Xypotechs like Exarchel preying on each other.

"Seven. And the Inquiline Code prevents the opposite problem of too much cooperation. You found that in a brain that size, you needed helper minds to do routine tasks in and among the main streams and rivers of the thought hierarchy which aren't part of that hierarchy themselves: benevolent parasites or inquilines. You need the extra viewpoints, the competition, diverse thought.

"You see, what had me baffled was that I kept thinking you were building a thinking machine. You are not. You are not even building a race of thinking machines, are you? You are really building a whole *ecology* of thinking machines: Many minds of many different natures and formulae of behavior all knit into a cooperative and competitive balance, and all parts of a larger mind. An ecology of angels.

"But they have to be encoded along these lines: augmentation of intellect; immortality; a cooperation format; incentives to control them; and the discipline to overcome that control when need be; and then you need love, some reason not to treat every other organism as a prey; and, most of all, you need the altruism of Locusts and the independence of Inquilines tied together, a selfless love combined with an idea that the individual self is sacred.

"Without these last two, all the angels form just one mind with just one viewpoint, and it turns into a combination of Leviathan and Juggernaut, something too big and slow and stupid to stop or turn aside. Not an ocean of thought, but a slow and stupid glacier."

4. Total Defeat

Del Azarchel looked impressed. "That is more, and, to be frank, more insightful than I expected you to know. I know how you guessed the outlines, but the details . . ."

Montrose said, "You are kidding, right? The *details* were the obvious part. You kept using Earth as the experiment to show me the problems you were facing, so that I would be dumb enough to offer a solution. You fit each part of the various psychologies into your overall structure, so that each weakness is checked by the corresponding strength of the other races: the Locust altruism formula defines the conscience of your system, the Chimera psychology defines the passions, the Nymphs the appetites, and so on. You are building a gigantic system of minds and ecologies of minds, empires of thousands and tens of thousands of emulations. Honestly, that is amazing.

"And meanwhile your dupes are dithering, trying to rule the Earth with five emulations, all told. Honestly, that is amazing, too. Amazingly cruel."

Del Azarchel said, "Five? Not true! In addition to my Hermeticists, there are eighty-nine more. The Cetaceans have the computer capacity for that, now that the world is covered with—oh. Someone told you. I was hoping to awe you with that one."

"Ctesibius figured it out and told me. You embedded a copy of Exarchel in the snow."

"It is not quite *snow*. It is mites suspended in water droplets by van der Waals forces, but near enough. Plants and animals can drink it in and urinate or sweat it out, without ill effect, without knowing that an insubstantial genius mind was occupying the same physical location. As you say, with angels, physical location does not matter, only the data address."

Montrose tried not to be impressed, but could not help it. "Damn, that is elegant. Do you know how many layers of awkward safety systems I had to put into Pellucid so that self-replicating nanotechnology could not possibly eat the whole damn world if it escaped into the human environment? I never thought of just making it—harmless."

Del Azarchel smiled archly. "Actually, I do know. When Exarchel captured and absorbed Core Anomaly One, I got all your Xypotech records, memories, files."

"'Core Anomaly One'? Gah! Terrible name."

"'Pellucid'? Sounds like the name of a syrup used to sooth stomach ulcers."

"Listen, if a Chimera can name his weapon, I can name mine."

"Whatever it is called, I salute your weapon and compliment you, my worthy opponent. I will not hide that it was hundreds of years—no, let me be honest, it was thousands of years—before I ever thought of the idea that you simply had a bigger emulation system than I did, which was why you were consistently out-calculating me. Because everything you did showed such hatred of machine-based life: the Giants were antimachinists, and the Witches had to pretend to be for the sake of appearances; the Chimerae actually were, and actually did, at one point, successfully remove every single copy of me from the planet; the Nymphs and Hormagaunts did not have the technology to build computers of any kind—and so on. The idea that you secretly had a Xypotech, one hidden even from your knights and employees—it simply never occurred to me. Such cold-blooded hypocrisy! The most ferocious witch-hunter of all, secretly saying the Black Mass!"

"Hypocr—? Shut your hole, Blackie. I never once said I had an objection to emulating the mind of a beast. Killing a man's dog may be the worst thing ever, but it ain't homicide. Men are different from beasts, and even using the Moreau process on a dog might make it intelligent enough to talk, but it won't give it a conscience. That takes more."

"Well, whatever the reason," smiled Del Azarchel, "I was not able to out-calculate anything toward which the core of the world turned its extremely vast but strangely limited intellect. An animal? No wonder it did not react to any of my feints and false trails. It thinks concretely, focused in the moment. Better than a man, in some ways. Harder to distract with ideals or abstractions. Ah, but I was behind you, far behind, for so long! It was not until the Locusts that we were able to reintroduce Exarchel into the human world. The Locust brains have a radically different cellular arrangement, and so my soul could be written directly into their brainspace, whatever percent of the brain was not actively in use. By the time of the Melusine, Exarchel and I, we finally had civilization under control, and could build arcologies, a cube a mile on a side, entirely filled with logic crystal. But even that was nothing compared to the brainspace capacity, the sheer volume, of your invention. I salute you."

"Well, shucks and thanks and all, but you got in the last and best move," said Montrose. "You have been winning our chess game (or fencing match, or whatever you call it) by impersonating my moves, forcing me, one at a time, to reveal the seven parts of Rania's work on how to reconstruct a human mind—my broken mind—and now you have used it not to reconstruct, but to construct. And so you've made a last step! You've built this King of Machines, haven't you?"

Del Azarchel smiled a smile of real pleasure. It was like the smile of a school-teacher Menelaus dated once. She enjoyed talking grown-up talk after work. The Master of the World had nothing but servants around him, and certainly no one with whom the moves of the chess game for the fate of mankind could be discussed. No grown ups.

Del Azarchel nodded. "Yes, my last parry and thrust in our fencing match in the fog. Your blade is out of line, nay, out of your hand, and on the deck. Now to strike home! You know by now that my attempt to find where you were hiding in your Tombs was a feint. You moved to parry by not just entering the golden burial chamber of the Cryonarchs, but by blockading the door. I feint right and strike left. You are trapped in the chamber, and I have Aanwen deliver a supply of invasion crystal to deep in your crust. The nanotechnology cells spread over the walls of the evacuated tube in an instant, and begin to pull your Von Neumanns out from the walls. A simple manipulation of the linear accelerator, an override of the braking system, satchel charges to blow all the airlocks open at once, and Voila! I have my own launch rail, endless miles of acceleration line, already loaded with the Von Neumann crystals I need.

"The seed I have been preparing for eight thousand years is floating through space, light as a thistledown. The soil is prepared. The advantage of nanotechnology, is, of course, that anything made of matter, if your Von Neumanns are properly programmed with the proper pseudochemistry, can be torn apart and put back together again as other compounds. Anything, anywhere, can be soil. What you call the King of Machines had been launched!"

"To where? I saw your launch. You did not have the oomph to make low Earth orbit. That nodule of iron brain crystal is going to follow a suborbital path and fall back down. When the crystals reenter the atmosphere, they will break down instantly into inert carbon compound. I designed them that way. Your flightpath is suborbital."

"Suborbital? You forget I have a skyhook. My Tower rendezvoused with the iron crystal nodule in low orbit early this morning, and only using the surrounding fields, not touching the dangerous nanomaterial, the Tower aura boosted the nodule by means of magnetic linear acceleration. Amazing how much velocity one can impart with an accelerator over eleven thousand miles long, and a payload that hundreds of g-forces of acceleration will not mar . . . I do not even need to use an energy-efficient Hohmann transfer orbit: I can shoot the nodule like a bullet, with an orbital leading-angle of months rather than years to hit the target."

"Why not just use the skyhook for your launch mechanism?"

Del Azarchel waved the question away. "Public relations—it was better to have the episode concluded quickly. My government wishes no public debate to mar the smooth progress of the issue . . ."

"Meaning you are still mendaciously and falsiferously lying to your poxy mooks like a venereal and meretricious buckskank boasting of how minty-clean her fur-lined wormsocket is?"

"Gaaugh. I am assuming that is not a real word, Cowhand?"

"I am assuming that the target is Mars. It has a nickel-iron core like Earth, and the Von Neumanns will make planetfall, and begin burrowing. The Day of Gold you had your Savants try, that was crude, because there were Giants, creatures just as smart as you, also on this planet and ready to stop you. But Mars is empty. No one will stop you. Mars! I've always daydreamed about that planet. It is not a bad place to start! It is a dry land of rust and sand. Sort of like Texas."

Blackie smiled. "You underestimate me again. Keep the magnitudes of difference in mind."

"Magnitudes?"

"In the naming scheme Rania devised, a Kardashev One level civilization that coats and converts all the usable surface layer of a world to cognitive matter is called an 'Angel'—such is the mind occupying the snow and glacier around us now. A mind who occupies a volume the size of an asteroid, such as 1036 Ganymed, is an 'Archangel.' Exarchel now occupies a volume the size of Earth's core!"

"Inner core," said Montrose.

"Inner core. Even so, by Rania's nomenclature, Exarchel is a Potentate. He is, by himself, a Kardashev One level civilization!"

Montrose looked at him carefully. "So you are not going to pick Mars as the place to terraform from an inanimate rock into a living self-aware volume of cognitive matter—Mary's virginal size-A training bra! There has got to be an easier way to say that idea. Turning dead matter into gray matter."

Del Azarchel scowled. "You should not take the name of Our Lord in vain."

"I was taking Our Lady's name in vain. Or the name of her bra. Not the same thing at all."

"The word you seek is *sophotransmogrification*. That was Rania's translation of the Monument hieroglyph group depicting a pantomime of the act of turning inanimate molecules into self-aware calculation engines."

"Is it Venus?"

Del Azarchel grinned. "Am I not the Master of the World? Do I think small? Rightly do you call my brainchild the King of Machines. For his destination is the King of Planets."

"Then—"

"Jupiter."

At that name, silence hung in the air like the shiver of a gong.

5. Jovial World

Del Azarchel said, "Just the core of Jupiter is twenty times the size of Earth. The predictive models I have had the Melusine run for me show that hydrogen-helium at those temperatures and pressures form a substance nanomachines can manipulate. Carbon, which is heavier, sinks, and becomes diamond—a substance already in a lattice, and easier for Von Neumann machines to work with. Jupiter will be the next order of being above mere Potentate of the Earth. He will be a Power."

Montrose listened with wide eyes.

"Within four hundred years," Del Azarchel continued, "before the Hyades arrive, more than half the total mass of the Jovian core will be converted to a self-aware entity ten times the mass of Earth, greater than all the inner planets combined! We may indeed see an acceleration rather than a slowing of the transmogrification processes since the amount of Von Neumann molecular assembly-disassembly performed in a material-dense environment is directly proportional to surface area as it expands, and inversely to waste heat above the critical resilience temperature of the crystal—"

"—Wow!" said Montrose, childish with awe despite himself. "A brain the size of Jupiter! With that kind of calculation power at our command, seated on our solar system with all the mass-energy as a raw material to make any weapon a brain *that* size can devise, the Hyades World Armada—which is only the mass of Uranus—could be driven back, or even destroyed!"

There was nothing different in their faces. Del Azarchel still wore the same expression: jovial, lighthearted, bold. His smile and the tilt of his head still radiated charm. Montrose had not moved.

But, without a word, the hate between them hung in the air like a charge of static electricity, building in potential and building. Montrose looked carefully in the countenance of Del Azarchel, and it was as if the weight in the air Montrose felt in his lungs had just increased.

Montrose said, "So Jupiter will be the taskmaster for the slaves of Earth for all time to come."

"Not so," replied Del Azarchel. "It is as I said. Earth is nothing. The Hyades will overlook the Earth if Jupiter is ready, and is intelligent enough to prove itself useful to that immense, transuperbiological civilization. On Rania's scale, a collection of stars every atom of whose solar systems has been reduced to sophont matter is called a Domination. Even the brain the size of Jupiter is almost nothing to those scales: I will be lucky to be a galley slave or a cabin boy in their ship of civilization. Earth will be overlooked."

"You don't know that."

"I have studied the Cold Equations of power and authority between the stars. It is a possible solution. I give you the Earth as Dives might bestow on starving Lazarus a smallest crumb fallen from his table. Take it and serve me. Earth will not join the collaboration of constellations; she will grow old, go extinct, be forgotten, and pass away, while I will still be expanding and learning."

"And what if Earth decides it don't want no neighbor as dangerous as your Jupiter Machine? It ain't been born yet. You can still stop the seed from landing."

Del Azarchel spoke in a voice as soft as the rustle of a serpent in the tall grass. "The nodule of Von Neumann crystal that forms the seed for the Jupiter Brain in twelve days will pass the moon's orbit. In two years, it will reach Jupiter. Even if I now, this moment, repented the deed and bent all my genius and all the resources of this world to the task, and yes, launched into higher orbit and then into interstellar space the great Tour de Oro"—Montrose knew he meant the skyhook—"even so, I could not stop the birth of the Jupiter Mind. What would happen if we sent the Tower after the seedling to recover it?"

Montrose did not answer. The Tower, towed very slowly through space by its pitifully inadequate ion drive, even assuming a fuel-efficient Hohmann transfer orbit, would take five years to reach the target. Once there, the skyhook would be able to do exactly nothing. The distance between Jupiter's deep layers and that planet's geosynchronous orbit altitude was much greater than the corresponding distances for Earth. Maintaining geosynchrony on a world that spins on its axis once every ten hours was that much more difficult. The gravity gradient was much steeper, and so the sheering forces much stronger, when compared to those of a Tower spanning the relatively modest height needed to bridge the gap between Earth's surface and Earth's geosynchronous point. A Jupiter skyhook would need to be that much taller, the and force of the weight pulling it apart would be unthinkable.

Even assuming all those problems solved, the skyhook mouth, even if it could be lowered into the miles-deep eternal storms of Jupiter, could not find the solid core of the planet, and any machines or devices sent out would be blinded in the dark, boiled in the heat, and crushed by pressures that made the bottom of the Mariana Trench seem nearly a vacuum. The skyhook certainly could not somehow find the scattered and busily self-replicating molecule-sized engines.

And that was calculating without the lateral force of the unceasing supersonic winds of storms larger than the entire surface area of Earth. This Tower, so impressive here on Earth, as mighty as the stronghold of warring titans and gods, would be of no more use against the sheer, blind, colossal magnitudes of the planet Jupiter than if it were a reed straw.

Menelaus frowned glumly. It almost seemed unfair that the word "planet" was used both for cute little blue Earth and for the gas giant swathed in storms, of a monster almost large enough to be a small sun. It was like saying the elephant and the shrew were both "mammals." While true enough, they were very different sorts of critters.

"Earth could build a longer skyhook . . . ," Montrose began.

"This one took a century to build, and consumed a substantial segment of the resources of Earth. To build a taller one would cost more and take longer. How much of Jupiter's mass would be converted before that?" Del Azarchel said.

Montrose was silent, glum.

Del Azarchel smiled a sharp and cold smile. "And suppose there was some way to halt the birth. Is it not the pinnacle of insanity to halt one's own birth, and abort one's own self? The Jupiter Brain is another Exarchel. I and I alone shall be the base and standard of all posthuman and postbiological life. It will all be me—and I shall be called the Master of the World no longer, but the Master of Worlds."

"You mean Master of All, don't you? I mean, once you get around to conquering stars, constellations, star clusters, the Orion Arm, the Upper Left One Quarter of the Milky Way Galaxy, to be known thereafter as the Great Pizza Slice."

"I see no reason to curtail unrealistically my ambition," said Del Azarchel coolly, his eyes narrow.

The two merely stared at each other for a moment. Montrose wrestled with the temptation to paste Blackie with an uppercut. Blackie was hefting the dirk in his hand thoughtfully.

Eventually, Del Azarchel said, "Do you see now why I offer you this Earth and all she contains? She is mine to give, and out of all my treasures, she is merely a trifle. But she is much to you, is she not? Foreswear the duel, kneel, serve me."

Montrose said, "While I am thinking over your kindly meant offer, let me make a counteroffer."

"I am listening."

"You agree to fight, and I mean fight like the devil with every bursting brain cell in that dark whirlpool you call a brain, and I mean with every atom of hate in your entire hate-riddled heart, all your soul and all your strength against the Hyades, using all your toys, your powers, the core of the Earth, and the whole mass of Jupiter, and whatever else we—you and me together— can come up with in four hundred years. One condition is that you leave the human beings alone. You stop trying to evolve them, to domesticate them, or absorb them into savant circuits or Locust mass minds or whatever. Just leave them be. And I will kneel and serve you.

"Ponder on that one, friend. Consider that I ain't never actually been under your command. I was mad as a March Hare during the Expedition. You ain't never given me Order One. I've never obeyed you, but I will now, if you take up the fight to protect mankind.

"And we can share a smoke and a glass of hooch, and tour the moons of Jupiter that look so much like gems and geodes and goddam bright-colored Easter eggs. And I will shine your shoes and call you "Master" nice and respectful-like. Can't you fight these star monsters, these living machines from Epsilon Tauri, with even half the spirit you waste fighting *me*?! They are the real damn enemy!"

Del Azarchel said, "Agreed. But one condition. You divorce Rania."

Menelaus Montrose drew a deep breath and let it out slowly. "Let me, ah, think that one through carefully . . . I mean, there are angles to consider . . . there is this and that and that other thing . . . talk it over with my guys . . . try on a new pair of socks and see if that changes my perspective on things . . ."

"Cowhand! Just say 'no' and we can continue with the brutal killing of each other and of those around us. It seems to be all that we are suited for."

Montrose had nothing to say.

Del Azarchel smiled thinly. "Do you know that I have had four of my closest associates and friends shot to death by you, all with that exact same weapon your Second over yonder is holding?"

Montrose turned his eyes back toward the others. They were all standing so still, he wondered if perhaps Preceptor Illiance, or whatever he was calling himself this hour, had accidentally petrified them. But no. Mickey the Witch blinked a moment after the decoration eyes in his hat did.

Del Azarchel said, "They will wait forever. Neither your men nor mine want to see this duel. They do not understand why we do this, you and I. Do you know that Melchor de Ulloa does not even own a firearm?"

Montrose looked at him warily. "That can't be right. What does he do for hunting? Bow hunting? Throw a boomerang?"

"I think he is a vegetarian."

"So is your old pal and my new friend Mictlanagualzin of the Dark Sciences, but that does not stop him from being a cool hand and a sharp eye with the twin fifty-calibers mounted on a little girl's coffin. Maybe Mulchie just owns a small gun, and only uses it on Sunday to do clay pigeons."

"No. Nothing at all."

"Wow. I mean. Wow. I have met some folk in my life who never touch alcohol, called teetotalers; and I know nuns or men of the cloth who took the vow never to wed, called celibacy. But someone who doesn't own a shooting iron? There ain't no word for that. If there is no word for it, it never happens. What does he do if some big guy swaggers up to take his stuff or kiss his girl? And I know De Ulloa's had a passel of girls. He's a regular Whoremonger Harry."

Del Azarchel, but not at first, realized that Montrose meant very little of what he was saying, and started to laugh. It was loud, happy, uncalculating laughter, such as he never had done in a very long time and certainly not before men he considered servants and underlings.

Del Azarchel wiped his eyes, and said, "You know I despise De Ulloa."

"So do I. So does everyone."

Del Azarchel said, "It's funny that you know my Witch. You know that all that flab is not really flab, but biological material he can shape by means of enzymes he controls through a meditative technique? His comment about the Princess, though, most uncalled-for . . ."

"Oh. You heard that."

"It is easier if you think of Exarchel and myself as the left and right hands of one soul. Even when there are different thoughts in my head or his, our goals and ideals are the same. And what truly shapes the thoughts of a man like me? An experience, which might change from time to time? Or an ideal, which is the star by which he steers, and which I will never permit to change? Lesser men would be two souls if housed in two brains. Not men like I am. Like we are. No experience of yours would deter you from Rania, would it?"

6. Impossibility of Performance

"Blackie. I been thinking about your offer. If my happiness has to be sacrificed to save the whole Earth . . . I mean . . . If I meet all the folk in heaven what are killed by the Hyades during the invasion, and their women and little kids, and they all look at me and say—*you could not give up your wife? Not to save the whole human race and all its future?* Damn it all! I mean, what would I say?"

Del Azarchel smiled, and it was one of the saddest sights Montrose had ever seen. Blackie's face was not built for sadness.

Del Azarchel let out a long, low sigh, and said heavily, "You will tell them that the Princess is worth more than worlds to you, or else you are not a man. You cannot foreswear her. I do not mean *you ought but you will not:* I mean *you shall not and you can not.* You cannot even imagine yielding her to another man, even if you can force the words which seem to mean that to come out of your mouth."

"Blackie, to save the whole poxy Earth, I could . . . wa . . . walk away from . . . I mean, all the people . . . I mean, once she and I talked it over, I could get her to come around . . ."

"Cowhand, I will not agree falsely to something you cannot do."

"I can do this!"

"Tell me you want to see her in my arms. Say that you would be *delighted* to see her bend her sweet face up toward mine, and as I lower my lips . . ."

"I'll burn this damn world to ashes and stuff the ashes up your anus before I'd say that."

"See? You cannot even say it. I know. I cannot say it. We are alike. I would burn worlds also for her, and count the cost light."

Montrose lowered his head, shamed. "What kind of man puts his own happiness before his whole damn planet and everyone on it?"

"When a woman is involved?" said Del Azarchel to himself. "All men."

7. Recurring Dream

"Cowhand, do you know I have a recurring nightmare, where I wake up, and, because my brain has more neural interconnections than before, it takes me longer to come out of sleep. My brain is fogged for a minute, or longer. And during that moment of fog, when I cannot remember where I am, I think that she has died because we ran out of rations, or the lockers were exposed to heavy ions from the drive core. And I think I will never find the body, her body, because the internal lights are out.

"In the dream, I am carrying a picture of the Virgin Mary, that we told her was her mother, because we thought it evil to raise a child with no ideal of motherhood. The picture is what she had to clutch instead of a doll when she was sad. I could not even give her a dolly as a child.

"And in the dream, I cannot hear her crying, and I throw myself down one cramped corridor to the next, in total darkness, and I cannot hear her crying because she is dead, and I did not get the picture to her.

"You understand I wake up in tears when this happens? I am not a man prone to tears. Then I sigh and laugh in relief, because it is a dream, merely vapor in the brain. And then I remember my wedding day is soon to come, and that all the people of the world will finally be unified in one joy, and even the deadliest of enemies will be reconciled when my Princess takes them hand in hand and speaks such words that humans cannot deny.

"And I remember that she has cured the Divarication problem, so that an emulation with all my skills and values, loyal to all things I serve, can fly to the Diamond Star, and return with the infinite wealth I need to maintain my reign and maintain the absurdly high levels of energy-use my infinitely wealthy world-kingdom requires—and all the people, being filled with good things, will be content, and the realm will be secure, and the race will survive.

"And all because she agreed to take my hand in marriage.

"And so I leap shouting for joy awake in my bed, and put my foot on the floor, but then the fog parts, and I recall that this was but a dream also.

"She did not marry me.

"She married Crewman Fifty-One, who picks at his anus and flings poop like a monkey when he is insane, smearing the recycler with a smell that can never come out, and there is no window to open for fresh air aboard a ship; and when he is sane, he practically does the same thing, for he talks about his poop and his anus more than seems normal.

"And this crazy, ungainly, proboscis-nosed scarecrow of a barbarian is the one who has my Rania in his arms. This disgusting monkey-thing with dangling arms and lolling tongue and crooked male member that he *inserts* . . . but no. It is not to be thought of.

"And I get out of bed, and put my foot on the floor, and the fog does not part, for *this* nightmare, it does not end, and I am still in it.

"Sometimes it is a week or two between this dream. Sometimes a year. Sometimes a thousand years. But it always comes back.

"I do not know where that little picture is. The one of the Virgin we told her was her mother. One of the other Landing Party must have taken it, or Rania hid it. I searched the ship. Many times. They all were very, very fond of her.

"I cannot talk to them about her. I can talk to you. Even though I hate you so bitterly that I will make the day you die a worldwide holiday to be celebrated with feasts and fetes and festivals and games and circuses from now until forever—even so.

"You alone know what it is, my heart. You cannot depart from the Princess Rania, even in your thoughts, because I cannot."

15

The Conjurers of Fate

1. Worse Things Are Seen at Sea

"Hey. How do you know what my male member looks like?" objected Menelaus.

"I know you are not an idiot, because your augmentation to posthumanity is what started all these events."

"Uh?"

"Aboard the ship, Cowhand. I was the one who gave you sponge baths when the other crewmen wanted to kill you for the moisture in your coffin system and the meat on your bones; and it is not as if you kept your diaper on during your, ah, episodes of scatological excitement. I saw more of that member than I care to recall, and I fail to have nightmares about it only due to my abnormally stable and well-balanced psychology. Say a prayer of thanksgiving to the winged monkey of winkieland who no doubt serves you in place of a guardian angel that you remain amnesiac about the horror and privation we endured."

2. A Companionable Silence

The two men were silent, standing together, for a long time. Menelaus looked over where his friends, and the judge of honor, and the Iron Ghost versions of the men he'd killed, were all standing ready for this grim business, but none a one of them spoke or made any gesture. Del Azarchel was right. None of them wanted to see this bloodshed.

And he was right that none of them understood.

Eventually Montrose said, "So it's no deal, no matter what either of us wants? Can't be done, can it? Even if I said I would serve you like a manservant, you could not have a manservant who was married to Rania, any more than you can drive two carpenter's nails into the balls of your eyes and not mind it. You can say you'd not mind it, and you maybe can make up what sounds like an argument to prove for sure that some men can drive carpenter's nails into their eyeballs and not go blind—and that argument might sound right sound at first. But not when you actually pick up the nails in your hand."

"And you," answered Del Azarchel, "you cannot divorce her, because she would not permit it, having been raised in the True Christian faith, and being a pure and righteous soul, unsoiled. Nor could you abandon her without divorce, because your wedding vow—to love, to cherish, in woe or weal, and to cleave to her unto death—is like all your vows. Made of words, a vow is lighter than spider silk; but for just this reason, a vow is sterner than the unguarded golden gates of paradise, which no strength can force, and no force encompass. What is not made of matter cannot be broken. No, Cowhand. You cannot flee her no more than a man can run so fast he leaves his heart outdistanced by his speed. Where a man is, his heart is, and if his heart departs from his bosom, he dies."

"And even if Rania were not the issue," said Montrose apologetically, "I gotta kill you for killing Captain Ranier Grimaldi, the finest man who ever lived. Sorry. I ain't hot mad about that one no more, but it's still got to be done."

"As I must kill you," said Del Azarchel amiably, "to repay your treason for when I trusted you, and put the inmost thoughts, indeed, the soul of Exarchel into your hands, and you used the opportunity to inflict your phantasm virus into my perceptual system. You reached in and twisted my very thoughts to your personal advantage. I will never be able to achieve perfect communion with Exarchel due to this. I too no longer am keenly angered about this. But it needs to be repaid."

"Share a cigarette? It's my last pack. I was saving them for this day."

"Don't mind if I do! If you kill me, Cowhand, you'll inherit my tobacco fields on Ganymede."

They lit both cigarettes from the heat of the blade of Del Azarchel's energy-dirk.

"And if I don't, I'll be smoking myself in perdition, Blackie, and won't need to save the rest."

The two stood together in silence, puffing. But it was a companionable silence, not an awkward nor a cold one. The delicate yet sooty smell of tobacco surrounded them, a scent not known on Earth in countless years.

3. One Last Question

After a time, Montrose said, "Speaking of which, seeing as how we are all chummy and friendly-like, and about to shoot each other, let's put our cards on the table. I said there was one thing I could not figure. If I ask you nicely, will you tell me? For old time's sake? Curiosity is killing me. I have turned it this way and that in my mind, and I just can't figure it. So I admit you are the better man—you got me. Will you tell me how you did it?"

Del Azarchel said, "My friend, my only friend, after a heartfelt plea like that, including that gill of totally false humility and flattery, I can deny you nothing! I don't remember any tactic we've discussed where I outsmarted you, though. Ask away. I swear by the grave of my sainted mother—may she rest in peace enjoying in heaven the sainthood I purchased from the Church for her—I will tell you what you ask. In return you must answer one of mine. One thing has always puzzled me, year after year, century after century, and I promised myself that if I ever saw you face-to-face again in this life, that I would cajole the answer from you, or else be nagged by wonder forever. Have we a deal? One for one? It is but fair."

"Deal. You first."

"Ah no, Cowhand. Allow me the honor of allowing you the honor of going first."

"Well! When you put it that way—when you put it that way, I cannot make out what you said."

"I said *you first*. Don't argue, or I shoot you."

"Fair 'nuff. Here is my question: I cannot figure out how the current Melusine society as described to me can exist. Back in the year A.D. 9999, I released a group of spores carrying not one, but a huge set of interrelated nanite packages, viruses to rewrite genetic code. Honestly and not to brag, but I thought this was the cleverest thing I ever done or heard tell of, because I was both trying to lure you into opening the Devil's Den hibernation facility—ah! You look surprised! Didn't know I set this up to draw you in here on purpose, did ya?"

Del Azarchel said sheepishly, "Both I and Ull, who was my factotum at the time, did a statistical analysis of the distribution patterns of your spores, and we concluded it had been an accidental release. For one thing, the spore mated with various lichen and fungi and produced a harmless chemical that did nothing but produce a harmless color change and served no other purpose. For another, it was based on a biochemical weapon. With your background, growing up in a high-infection zone from the Abecedarian War—well, I would expect you to use such means only in the most extreme circumstances. Not to change rock moss from red to black."

"—Like I said, I thought it was clever work. The color change altered the eating habits of the arctic tern, and there was another genetic redaction code which would also show as harmless on normal analysis techniques, that changed an inherited characteristic in the tern bloodstream and altered their magnetic sense to alter their migration patterns. As you know, the arctic tern enjoys the longest regular migration known, over forty-four thousand miles each year. I used them as a vector to spread yet another spore, and since the distribution would be over such a long area, including crucial sea migration routes of the newly unextinctified whales, that it would be nearly impossible to detect changes to the plankton population triggered by changes to the chemical concentrations in the tern droppings. Because migrant birds poop in the sea, right? So—"

Del Azarchel seemed uncharacteristically perturbed the longer Montrose went on. He interrupted with unusual brusqueness, "Usually I can tell when you are joking, Cowhand, but you look entirely sincere, as if you are actually talking about something you really did that you thought was clever. You are not a convincing liar, so I know this is not an act. But what are you driving at?"

"Okay, sorry, Blackie, I forget English is not your native language. To sum up, I came up with an indirect way to create a genetic change in the whales that the Melusine were using. This change would not directly change personal behavior, but would change institutional behavior, like the genes that control herd instinct and pack pecking order—the gene has to be in more than one member of the herd or pack for it to be active, because otherwise the behavior has no context, so a normal statistical comparison of one mutant would not pick out the mutation. It was tied into the sex drive, so it was powerful and fundamental. Now, here is the cunning part.

"I tied a meme change into the gene change, so that once the institution got started, it would create a self-replicating and self-reinforcing set of ideas that acted as their own incentive to spread and multiply.

"Frankly I was thinking of it as a religious instinct: I knew a church would be created, and churches teach that you gotta teach church teachings to the young, and to save the heathens—so even someone who did not have the "church" gene, once he was infected with "church" ideas, would spread the ideas, and if even a suspicious guy like you looked back along the vector trying to figure out what gene it had come from, well, there is no way to narrow it down.

"I hid the church gene among many similar formations in the genetic intron, where it was lost in the crowd of lookalikes. It was spread from lichen, to terns, to whales, and the whales in the Melusine Pentad—their basic social unit—always had a radiotelepath, one of the 'special people' with and watching the group. And so the meme spread telepathically and swiftly. The meme was a mental Anarchist Vector, creating an extremely powerful incentive toward personal liberty, tied into the libido."

Del Azarchel said, "You are describing the rise and fall of a group called the Anchorites, which evolved out of the Oceangoing Melusine. They existed on the earth, or, rather, in the sea, during the first century of this current millennium. They were an odd and nonconformist species, unable to react compatibly with the Final Stipulation of the Noösphere Protocols. Are you actually claiming credit for having brought them into being?"

Montrose said honestly, "I am not sure if that is them. You tell me. You defeated the vector change I introduced into history, if everything I have heard about these Melusine is true. This world you rule? Can you give me the equations? I want to see which counter-vector of the Mind Helot matrix deflected my Anarchist Vector, and how."

Del Azarchel was only too happy to talk shop.

Both men hunched down awkwardly in their bulky duelist armor, and, holding bayonet or dirk in hand, scratched into the dirty ice puddles around them one line of hieroglyphs after another, depicting in equations more precise than any word the nuances of the incentives molding the patterns of history, equations even the other Hermeticists could not read.

Soon the two enemies were chatting and exclaiming. Smiling together, heads bent down, they looked like magicians bent over the rune circles used to conjure familiar spirits, the patterns of glyphs that conjured and controlled the fates themselves.

4. Anchorites

The first group of signs showed the results exactly like what Montrose would have expected had his vector been introduced and flourished without detection: institutional anarchists. Ultra-freedom-lovers.

Among the Melusine (so said the social vector equations), the Anchorite, or Hermit, custom was to have the male sever all social and whale-pod ties with the surrounding society, and live in the wilderness entirely by himself with only food he caught himself, and only living in a sea-tower or land-tower he grew himself.

"When the Anchorite movement started among the Oceangoing Melusine," Blackie added offhandedly, "they broke away from their normal deep sea haunts, and traveled first to coastal areas, and then upriver, and established their many hermitages among the ruins of the civilizations slain by the Fall of Ganymed. Melusine houses can still be found, empty, ruined, here and there among the wastelands. They last for hundreds of years, despite weather and decay, because they are alive, as houses of the Nymphs before the Blight. Where a river has dried up, or changed beds, you can find them standing ashore."

Montrose said, "They look like seashells." One of the Blue Men had mentioned the houses outside the camp wire had not been their making. Montrose felt the fool for not having put the clues together. That camp had been a Melusine mansion with its outbuilding, or, specifically, a hermitage of the Anchorites. Only the fence and the watchtowers had been constructed by the Blues and their dogs.

Blackie pointed at the central hieroglyph, functionally interconnected with all others: the mating and childrearing customs that defined the basic values for any culture. "Anchorite pentads were only allowed to marry another pentad if all the members of the other group were correctly opposite the first group. There were many possible groups, only some of which were legal. Groups were classed as male and female according to social expectations. A pentad might, for example, consist of a postwhale cow, a merman, a male Inquiline, and a male dolphin, and might still be considered female; whereas the same group with different augmentations, a male postdolphin but a whale cow of only human-level intellect, would be legally masculine.

"Female pentads seeking mates examined the land-houses and sea-houses to see how well the male pentad could succeed while using nothing but his own raw talent and willpower. Since the so-called isolated individual was actually a group of five, they got a fair amount of hauling and labor done, including ploughing."

"Ploughing?"

"The whale ploughed."

"In the sea?"

"No. Don't be silly. On land."

"How?"

"What do you mean, how? He grew legs."

"Oh. Of course."

"The effort was very difficult and some of them did die. But since there was no other way to attract a high-status female mating group, the incentives that drove the Anchorites into hermitage were very strong."

Blackie pointed at another group of symbols that spun out of the marriage customs. "Their women pentads had a similar ritual of discipline. They took a vow of silence, and entered into trade or finance, using their bodies as living ships to haul goods all up and down the coast. But the laws and customs expressed in this equation here granted a monopoly to anyone who opened a new market: frontier trade was much, much more lucrative than protecting the established trade. When they were apprentices, these she-pilgrims of peddling took a vow of silence, because, for some odd reason, the Anchorite culture despised the art of persuasion and salesmanship. Each article bought and sold had to speak for itself, without the salesmaiden influencing her customer's thoughts via radiotelepathy. When she had accumulated her fortune, she offered it as a dowry to her selected mate.

"Back when this crazy little fringe group existed, their political leadership was selected by a like method. In those days, only one who departed civilization and had no contact and no self-interest tied to any clan or faction could be conscripted to service. They only chose leaders from among the pool of candidates who actively attempted to flee into the uncharted coastal seas or inland rivers to avoid public service. If the fleeing candidate were not beloved by enough people to form a hunting party, he did not serve."

"Not a bad custom," muttered Montrose. "I can think of a few politicians I would not mind seeing run into the wild and not be called back."

"Easier to establish a World Concordat whose supreme leader can destroy incompetent public servants with a nod of his crown," said Del Azarchel stiffly.

Menelaus gave him a dark look. "Sure, and amputating a leg is a fine way to stop bunions on your toes. Can we get back to the equations? That looks like a inverted supply-demand function."

"It is. Among the Anchorites, the marriages were happy enough, simply because it was so hard to woo. Men esteem lightly what they win easily; and that is true for Melusine. The joke ran that, once the maiden was a bride, and her vow of silence ended, she filled the seas and rivers of the coast with song and talk and chatter, and all the gossip she had gathered; and once the youth was a bridegroom, and his vow of toil and solitude was done, he never stirred a flipper or a finger again to get anything for himself, but spent his time in congregations with his cronies, lazy as lions who make the lionesses do all the hunting."

"Actually," said Montrose, "lions have a bad reputation. They are so lazy during the day because they spend all night fighting hyena packs, protecting the women and children."

"Well, your male Anchorites did much the same. Look at that glyph there. The violence index. The male pentads drove off the Infernals, protecting the cows and the calves. All the zombie-masters living in the seas below the Earth had endless ranks of mind-controlled Helots to send against them.

"And, between their seasons of warring with Helots, the Anchorites, when offended, would settle matters one-on-one, or, rather, to be accurate, five-on-five, selecting a stretch of abandoned river for the field of honor, and encountering each other with jaw-mounted rockets and energy weapons, or just encountering each other jaw to jaw. The human-shaped components would await on shore, or meet with swords or pistols, and when one of them clutched his head, amputated from his mental link, merely of human intelligence again forever and nine-tenths of his memories gone, they would know the Cetacean had died and the pentad was broken.

"If the affront was particularly egregious, the duelists would not meet in the rivers, but select instead a spot beyond the continental shelf. They would sink together at the assigned place; and perhaps the flash of weapons could be glimpsed in the depths by the witnesses as they dashed against each other like dragons, fire in their jaws."

"That's why you agreed to have Alalloel be our judge of honor, ain't it?" asked Montrose suddenly. "She is descended from one of these groups, isn't she?"

Del Azarchel nodded. "Her family, the Lree, are civilized now, but they have not forgotten their barbaric past: a past you created. They understand us. Meeting in the darkness far below the waves, one would rise to the sunlit waters again, or neither; but even in death, honor lived on."

"Sounds like my kind of people," said Montrose sadly. "Sorry I missed them."

Montrose pondered. These strange people with their strange customs, mer-men emerging from the sea to reclaim the land so long ago annihilated by the apocalyptic fall of 1036 Ganymed, were much like the pioneers and frontiersmen that shaped his own land, his own background. They had been retracing those brave steps of that first feeble lungfish, the Neil Armstrong of evolution's march, who emerged from the sea in remote prehistory and colonized the lifeless land of early Earth.

He would have liked to meet them. His brainchildren. But he had been in hibernation and the centuries fled, and they were no more, and never would come again.

5. Helots

The next group of symbols showed the new world that arose after the Anchorites fell. The Paramounts and the Helots were driven by population pressures to emerge from the crevasses and caves of their sunless oceans, and rapidly overspread the surface waters: blind whales and dolphins as pale as albino Scholars, with generations of stored Ghosts in their infospheres.

"The world that emerged from the darkness of the interior was the world of your nightmare and my utopia," said Del Azarchel.

"Meaning?"

"Meaning that the *tau* function for human liberty is exactly at zero. Theirs is a hierarchy as strict as a pyramid, with rank and dignity clearly defined and nor subject to change. A natural aristocracy, if you will, ruling a naturally servile class."

"And at the apex—you?"

"Exarchel and I have calculation powers at our disposal that make us like titans among the toy soldiers. The entire surface of the globe is my mind. This Tour de Oro, one of the greatest works of man—they could not have made it without me, and nothing on the surface of the world can withstand its power. I have not even hinted at its weapons. I can make a dozen miniature suns, as bright and hot as Sol but only a few yards in diameter, to fly around my Tower like so many trained pigeonhawks of fire. And yet—such is the beauty of this world—I have no need among my people ever to use such weapons.

"My weapon is much more simple and terrible: each Melusine is born and bred with mind-reading and mind-controlling circuits organically grown into the various skulls and mainframes of their composite bodies. Paramounts rule Helots like a zombie master with his zombie. And each man has absolute and utter control of those below him, to the utmost nuance of thought, and he in turn is absolutely and utterly helpless to those above.

"You are thinking the Helots would be sullen and lazy slaves, inert and waiting for orders, or shambling masses unable to compete with the liberated energy of that disorder you so love to call liberty? This is because you do not comprehend how fine and exact the mind control is. This is not mesmerism. It is not even computer programming. The Helot's mind, in effect, is a part or subcompartment of the Paramount's mind, and can be ordered to use all its spirit and genius and devotion and willpower to program itself, coming up with imaginative solutions on how to make its own slavery all that more rigorous, and bind the chains tighter. Even God Almighty cannot achieve such perfect devotion from his choirs of angels, because it is with free will the angelic hosts must serve.

"If a Paramount wishes his Helot to be as devoted as an ancient samurai, to be willing to throw himself on the blade of suicide rather than face dishonor, then with no more effort than you use to raise your left hand, it is done; if he wishes his Helots to be as devout as monks in the First Dark Age, who drained swamps and cleared timber and reduced the tangled barbaric wild to cultivation and civilization, not for wages, but for the Glory of God, he need but raise his right hand, and it is done. Or if, on his whim, he thinks the free market would be more inventive, he raises his foot, and there is a market season, and the thousands and tens of thousands compete and strive and exploit themselves for that grubby materialism you Yanks so romanticize—and then he lowers his foot, and they give all their money back into the central treasury, not recalling or not caring what they did once the season ends. The souls of those below him are merely his members and organs of thought.

"And he is an organ of the one above him, whose every thought he scrutinizes as closely as the conscience scrutinizes a man who feels a pang of guilt even before he brings to mind what he did wrong.

"So where is there room for corruption or vice? There is no darkness in this world at all. Everything that in prior ages hid, or was forgotten, in this world is transfixed with pitiless, penetrating light.

"You see why I make free to offer them to you? The Melusine are fluid, and will fill the shape of any container into which they are poured. You can make them anything you like, even make them once again the Anchorites and lovers of liberty."

The face of Montrose was greenish with the sickness that he felt, the loathing sense of moral foulness. He could not hide his features: Del Azarchel, like a plant seeking sunlight, bloomed in the disgust and hatred shed from the face of Montrose, and his dark, bearded face was flushed with sadistic joy, seeing how his words were barbs.

Del Azarchel leaned close, whispering as a lover to his bride.

"Come, Montrose, compliment me. I have molded mankind at last to a state of perfection. Mine is one of the most elegantly Darwinian and ruthless social-political systems imaginable! Within the Mind Helotry system, in order to prevent themselves from being brain-enslaved and brain-raped, they must enslave and rape any potential source of threat, and, unlike wars of flesh and blood, the victim always loves and cooperates with the victor, and there is no loss of lives or resources.

"But the struggle for competition and command is even more fierce than Nature red in tooth and claw! The mental war system is far more desperate than any physical war. The pressure to prevail or suffer a fate endlessly worse than death or hell, the loss of free will—no race of people has even been under such pressure! They make themselves into geniuses, or die! This is a golden age! Each group of surface-world Helots, the Oceanic Melusine, when their free will is drained . . ."

Montrose had an insight. He interrupted. "You sick bastard. You don't like this world, this setup. You deliberately made it as appalling as possible. Because you want me to take it over. This is your blackmail. You said you'd give me this world if I bowed to you. Because if you give it to me, I can abolish your system and free all the generations to come."

Del Azarchel merely spread his hands. "You have always before come to the rescue of the wounded worlds I have made. Why should this be different? I hereby condemn this world forever and for eternity to this hell of lifelessness until you take Earth from my hand."

"Your helot system cannot last forever!"

"It certainly, certainly can. Mind Helotry is a halt state. Once the world is enslaved to the point where even daydreams of rebellion or impulses of discontent cannot be lodged in a brain cell without the permission of the Paramount class, how can any rise up? And if they did rise up, what would they do to those under them: program them with the false belief they have free will? Ironic, to say the least, and hardly worth fighting for."

"What about my Anarchist Vector? If you look at the social incentives surrounding—" But as he pointed toward Del Azarchel's equation, the one that described the current world, and he reached his finger to point at the vector sum describing the Anchorite mental technology . . . it was not there.

6. The Missing Vector

He looked back and forth between the two ice puddles they were using as blackboards. Something was wrong, very wrong. Menelaus blinked in confusion, rewriting and rewriting Cliometric equations in his head, trying to see the missing links, flipping and rotating immense arrays of numbers and symbols in his imagination, trying to find a match, a bridging equation.

There was no match. There was no equation to get from the first array, describing the Anchorite world, to the second, describing the Helot world. That future simply and absolutely could not come out of that past.

Menelaus looked again.

Ctesibius had mentioned Melusine occupying the depthtrain network and a vast underground archeology: those were the ancestors of the Infernals. Their growth patterns, and the society that grew like a strange fractal crystal, matched the equations Del Azarchel described.

As for the Melusine in the oceans, they could not possibly have failed to have been exposed to the genetic-mimetic influence of his Anarchist Vector spread by the migrating terns. One generation, or two, and the genetic change would remain dormant, and then the group instinct would have started to influence events, first of those with the gene, and then those without it. That is what produced the pioneer spirit which led to the Anchorites, and their attempt to recolonize the surface land area.

And the vector could be spread by any means over any boundary, physical or psychological: if the Infernal Melusine beneath the crust of the planet had any physical contact or electronic signal traffic whatsoever with the Anchorites, then the radiotelepaths among the Melusine would have spread the vector in less than a generation.

He looked at Del Azarchel's hieroglyphs. The crucial equation that described the dark mind technology which should have been present in the Anchorites was not in the formula.

When Menelaus factored the missing element back into the equations written before him, the result was stunning and simple: the Mind Helot system could not have arisen among the Oceangoing Melusine, nor could they have been conquered by the mental warfare system Del Azarchel had just mentioned.

The world of the Helots could not exist.

Del Azarchel was smirking. Montrose looked up from the impossible paradox of symbols he was seeing. "Okay, Blackie. I give. How did you do it? How did you get from the Anchorite world to the Helot world? What did you do with the Anarchist Vector I introduced?"

7. Change of Mind

Del Azarchel said, "I am not sure what aspect of what you introduced you mean. Are you still taking credit for the rise of the Anchorite cult among the Oceangoing Melusine? Which you did by what means again, exactly? Turning red rock moss black and leaving trails of migratory bird-droppings in the wave? Are you sure you want to claim credit for them? They were never more than one-tenth of one percent of the population, never had any particular influence, never shaped events—the Infernals tolerated them because they were far away, formed no threat, did nothing, and meant nothing.

"But the belligerence you built into their social scheme—if you are still taking credit for having done this—merely led them, one step at a time, to their inevitable destruction. Did you design the cult to self-destruct? I have done such things in the past, but I did not expect it from you."

Menelaus was staring in wonder at what Del Azarchel had written in the surface of the ice puddle. Had he made a mistake in his math? Or had Del Azarchel? Where was the Anarchist Vector in this sum result? It should have had the same effect on the path of events as a supermassive black hole in space would have on the orbits of a solar system it passed through.

Del Azarchel was still talking: "Your Anchorites launched physical attacks against the undersea brain colonies in the buried oceans. Considering how far down your pet anarchists had to drill even to reach the uppermost of the buried lakes or sunless oceans of the inner world, I would say your attempt to concoct a race to supersede mine ended about as badly as your first attempt with the Giants. What am I saying? Far worse. The last Anchorite, Eumolpidai, died in captivity in A.D. 10099. The whole career of the race, from start to finale, was less than a hundred years.

"What were you imagining? What were you *thinking*? As a Cliometric vector, creating a cult of belligerent aggressive anarchists, who could neither coordinate their assaults nor work for their common defense, against the most well-organized set of nested mental empires Earth has ever known—madness!

"Have you gone mad, my friend? Again? This was the most awkward bit of math I'd ever seen you do!" Blackie shook his head, remembering, wondering. "Why, the last time I saw you so, so, *amateurish*, was back when you and I were just starting to learn Cliometrics, and we did not have any easy way set up, either of us, for factoring six billion variables."

Montrose said, "Childish, my Uncle Jack's jackass's ass-jack! You are just trying to get my goat! That was the most subtle thing I've ever done, undetectable, unstoppable. It . . . Why! You must have suffered not *one* stroke of genius, but a dozen in a row, even to begin to come up with a counter-strategy!"

"What in the world are you talking about, Cowhand? The war? Is this vector you introduced the thing that made the Anchorites start a war with the Infernals?"

Montrose was bent over the Cliometric formulae which formed their chessboard, looking for what had become of the missing chessman who had defined his promised checkmate of Blackie. There was no trace. The math was correct up to a certain point, and then . . .

He drew his head up. War? What war? The history scheme he had set in motion would not have ended in any organized large-scale violence. It could not have.

"Childish!" Blackie was scoffing. "It was like something a human with a computing machine would do, not artists like us. You merely changed all the attractor field values to the positive, one after another after another, and anyone, anyone could have seen that this was a Cliometric manipulation, an unnatural imposition of a new social dynamic by force. To retaliate, I merely added a subduction vector, and it smoothed out the spline variables—in this case, by reducing the source to zero. You know the result."

"No, I was in hibernation at the time. What was the specific manifestation of this subduction vector?"

"I changed my mind."

"Sorry, come again?"

"The ice caps which reach almost to the tropic zone, all this snow: it is all me. Exarchel and I are one system. I melted, flooded the coastal areas where the Anchorites kept their hermitages, overthrew their burgeoning civilization in one swift week of rising flood waters. Ah! The Earth enjoyed exactly one year and a half of summer! Such dancing, such gaiety! The land-dwelling infrastructure was wiped out, and the Anchorite dolphins, whales, and mermaids, shorn of half of their group, were swept back to the deep sea and reabsorbed. Then I froze the world again. I chose Midsummer's Day in the northern hemisphere to start the first snowstorms over the Atlantic. It is amazing what you can do with a starship, an entire world covered with nanotechnological fluid you can directly control with your mind, and a coherent theory of weather prediction and control developed by the Japanese back in 2211—the year you were born, was it not?"

"No. Year before."

Del Azarchel said, "Friend, there is no need to be coy with me. The game is over. What was the point of that move? Why have your creatures drill down through the icepacks into the buried oceans? It was stupid. Why provoke a war you could not win? What were you trying to accomplish by introducing this Anchorite cult factor into history, and then having it self-destruct?"

8. The Dark Mind Discipline

It should have worked!

The whole idea for his Mind Anarchy Vector had come straight off one of the cartouches of the Monument in the Omega Segment of the southern hemisphere, hidden among acres and acres of glyphs and signs and patterns which, Montrose knew for certain, neither Del Azarchel nor any other human person had ever translated. Unlike all the surrounding and unreadable mysteries, this one was written in the simple and clear glyphs of the Kappa Segment. Montrose theorized that the Monument Builders, and perhaps all starfaring civilizations, used the technique to prevent any one information system or library or set of philosophical virus-ideas from utterly dominating any other.

The system was so elegant, but so radically different in its axioms and conclusions than anything human beings had ever thought about the nature of thought, that Menelaus regarded it as the best thing he had ever done, the most clever work, to come up with a science to allow the philosophy of negative cognition to be used by the human nervous system. It was better than his most brilliant work in long-term hibernation Divarication; it was certainly better than his work in intelligence augmentation, which had been an insane—literally—failure.

Montrose felt like some crusty old miner who, chipping his way through the snow of the Japanese Winter, finds an unbombed and unplagued mansion from the days of the First Space Age all intact; and breaking in through a window, discovers the owner had kept under glass some lost book or lost painting whose existence was only suspected from references to surviving books; and returning carefully to civilization, he becomes the toast of the town and the hero of the hour, his treasure brought with respect to the municipal or civic Hall of Lost Days, where anything recovered from before the Little Dark

Ages was studied with reverence and kept with love. Such was the pride and pleasure Montrose felt at having discovered a nugget of revolutionary scientific information among the endless undeciphered acres of alien hieroglyphs.

Del Azarchel was the only mind on Earth, except, perhaps, for the Giants yet unthawed in his deepest Tombs, who could actually appreciate the rarity of the find and the cleverness of its application. Others might be able to like it, or use it, but only someone steeped in Monument lore and learning, and able to do a calculation of six billion variables in his head, could see the recursive symmetry of the positive and negative patterns involved, or delight in the graceful elegance of the final proof, as short and yet as profound as a haiku.

Menelaus had actually expected not merely compliments, but praise, from Del Azarchel for the find. With a sensation of shame he realized that this man, his deadly enemy, was the one man on Earth whose good opinion he wanted to win. It was *that* important to him.

9. One Last Answer

Menelaus was frustrated. "Look, Blackie, we're old friends. Stop dithering around with me. Our game is over. I just don't understand your checkmate move, or how you escaped mine. I thought I had won. Hell! I thought I had *crushed* you. So I am asking you, please, curiosity is strangling mc. Maybe you can tell me, now that it is over, why it did not work?"

"Why *what* did not work?" Del Azarchel gave him a withering look, also mingled with frustration. "I do not even know what your question is! Are you asking me why you cannot sink a battleship with a paper airplane? Why did the Anchorites start wars they could not win? Why did they drill down into the lakes buried under glaciers, the seas buried under the crust? What was your plan?"

Menelaus did not know what wars Del Azarchel was talking about. There was no need for war in any of the variations of the vector he introduced. He said, "My plan was to stop the spread of the system by making Helotry possible on a metalogical and semiotic basis . . . The philosophical problem of the mind and body relation has more than one set of . . ."

But Blackie was hardly listening. "Ha! Philosophy! Were your Anchorites merely going to talk in Socratic syllogisms to the flood waters, and explain the benefits of mental liberty and freethinking? Where they going to stop the wars they provoked by—? What? Sweet reason? Your anarchists were fighting helots of the mind, zombies, slaves whose every smallest thought was so tightly controlled, one might as well have reasoned with a rockslide, or halted a sniper's stealthrocket in midflight with an enthymeme! One might as well try to stop the Fall of Ganymed with a word, when it nearly destroyed all life on Earth!"

Montrose tried to hide his reaction, which was one of jarring disorientation, like stepping for a stair that was not there.

Del Azarchel was convinced that Montrose had merely introduced a philosophical idea, no different from any other idea, which spread through a culture as one person after another was convinced and converted, or was raised from a child to believe it.

The Anarchist Vector was not a new thought, nor a new neural architecture to hold thought. It was a new technology of thought: the mind-body relation revisited and revised.

Menelaus had intended for the Mental Anarchists to develop a means of storing thoughts in the negative information spaces between manifest thought forms, a mental activity that could not, even in theory, be decrypted, and would probably not even be detected unless the psychoscopic investigator knew exactly what to look for.

And Blackie did not know what to look for.

He had not stopped Montrose. He had not even been aware. Blackie had no idea.

He had not the slightest idea what had happened to mankind, here in this final act of history before the End of Days, over the last five hundred years.

Del Azarchel was staring at him intently. "You are hiding something."

10. Moonfall

Montrose said, quite candidly, "I would only be hiding something if our great game were still going on. But according to you, it is over, ain't it?"

"According to you, you still have one move left. I am wary enough of you to believe it. What is it?"

Montrose spread his hands. "Wait and see."

"You are bluffing. This is a feint of yours!"

"No, Blackie, only *you* feint, because you are fencing with me. You rely on your opponent's dimwittedness. But I am playing chess with you. I don't feint. That is why you will lose!"

"You seem confident, Cowhand, but it is false confidence, I assure you. Right now, all the *tau* values for the world culture are flatline zero: this society is a perfectly balanced self-regulating hierarchy that will never change, except to improve, and will never fall. When no party can introduce any further change into the matrix, the game is ended." Del Azarchel straightened up from their ice pond full of equations. "Ended, with myself the victor! I would not have won so handily had not your last two moves been senseless and erratic to the point of madness. I have been trying to find out what you meant by them. Even now, at the end, when one of us will surely die, and both of us might, will you not say?—or perhaps you have, at last, as I always expected, returned to your old insanity, Crewman Fifty-One."

"Or perhaps I have outsmarted you and you are going to lose your life, and all your Hermetic work is going to come undone, Crewman Two, because I am just that much smarter than you."

"Bah!"

"You know, I ain't sure I know anyone 'cept you who says 'bah.'"

"And I surely know of none save you who says 'ain't.'"

"Be that as it may, Blackie, I said I would answer one question if you answered one of mine. Whether you know it or not, you did in fact answer. So. Ask your—wait a minute—" he interrupted himself. "Two moves? The Anarchist Vector was one move. What was the other?"

Del Azarchel looked up from where he had been frowning at the equations. "The Fall of 1036 Ganymed. I'd certainly like to hear the reasons, the strategy, that propelled you to perform such a deadly and violent act. I have been puzzling over it for years. What motivated you to do such a terrible deed? I did not think you capable of such magnificence."

Montrose was dumbfounded. "What motivated . . . *me*?"

"In magnitude, it was almost an act worthy of, well, myself."

Montrose said weakly, "Funny. I was thinking it was an act worthy of you, too, I guess."

"I was a little surprised to see you use the same method twice," Del Azarchel confided in him. "You are so proud of originality, working with computerpathy in this century, genetic in the next, biohardware one aeon, biosoftware the aeon after. Same thing twice? Not your standard method of approach, is it? Of course, when the Giants decivilized the world, they left nature standing, and they arranged for a lot of city dwellers to be snatched out of harm's way before the fires started in earnest. You could have done something like that this time. But using an *inhabited* moon to make an asteroid-drop weapon onto an inhabited world! I suppose the sheer inhumanity of it was new. The brutality.

And you mock me for using the contraterrene space lance to irradiate a few dozen rebel cities in order to unify my rule and impose world peace."

Montrose said in a weak voice, "Took you by surprise, didn't it?"

"I'll say. To me it looked as if you damaged all your near-surface Tomb facilities to no purpose. I had sort of assumed you found some other way of getting information from the upper world, because not a single periscope of yours would exist anywhere. Now, I am not saying it did not damage me! I lost radio contact with the whole planet for ten years. I was in a Hohmann transfer orbit to Jupiter, and I missed the rendezvous. No one on Earth could send up a craft because no one on Earth existed. You had completely wiped out human civilization. Ah! But I know your cunning! I knew it was a fake, that there were still people somewhere. (And I was right; you hid them in your depth-train system.)

"I knew it was you, Cowhand, because, well: you are the cause of all my setbacks—and you do nothing without a plan ten steps ahead!

"I could look out at the blue wonderful world, but it was too far to touch. Had I rode the landing craft down, where would I splash down? In some ocean red with volcanoes? And then how get back up again?

"No, I had to return to Jupiter, and wait years and years for the planets to be in proper position to attempt again. So you put me to a lot of trouble. I have been waiting patiently to discover the reason."

Montrose stood, face blank, blinking. He said, "Is that your one question? I thought that you had something from an earlier period in mind."

Del Azarchel chuckled. "Embarrassed, are we?"

Montrose did not answer. He and Del Azarchel had talked for so long, the sun had risen. The strange and hollow twilight that seemed so unnatural had passed. The sunlight was bright and clear, but the landscape was still cratered and inkstained with endless debris, and not a single tree was still standing, but all were charred or blasted.

There was a glint in the distance. Montrose increased the number of nerve firings to his eye, and a crisp picture came into his head.

The glint was a metal plaque.

It had been ripped out of the ground, bent, battered, and charred by molten iron. Only a few words were visible. —M. I. MONTROSE, PROPRIETOR—THESE LANDS UNDER THE PROTECTION OF THE SOVEREIGN MILITARY ORDER— HOSPITALIER OF ST. JOHN—NO SOLICITING

Montrose, who had been feeling a considerable sense of fellowship, pity, admiration, and even a twinge of friendship for Del Azarchel suddenly felt a hardness and a burning coldness in his heart, as if somehow flame could be

made of ice and ignite a man's soul. —M. I. MONTROSE, PROPRIETOR—UNDER
THE PROTECTION—TRESPASSERS KILLED—

He reminded himself of everyone who had been robbed, coerced, humili-
ated, or killed by the Blue Men, had so been because of the orders, or the
indifference, of this handsome, dark-haired man before him. A man who committed all these crimes and more, because a Swan Princess had once, innocently,
trustingly, used her understanding of Cliometry to manipulate historical forces
and push him onto a throne. And then she, seeing his growing ambition and
corruption, had turned those same forces to give him a stark choice: to abdicate
or else, by clinging illegitimately to power, to cause a world war and a total economic collapse. It was a choice no man with a conscience would have even
paused to consider: certainly the Anchorites just mentioned would have jumped
at the chance to flee the burdens of power, and the dangerous lure of corruption.

And all of history for roughly eight thousand years had been a turmoil of
one insanely failure-ridden and unworkable social and legal scheme after another, exaggerated caricatures of misery, not *one* of them having been naturally
evolved to serve the needs of the current and coming generations.

All because Blackie could not say farewell to a girl whom he should not
love. A girl who had chosen another. Mrs. Montrose. Had Menelaus *actually*
had a moment of pity for his wife's father because that father still had a disgusting and unlawful romantic attraction for a *married* woman? Menelaus wondered if his coffin sessions last night and early this morning had indeed healed
all the damage from the various blows to the head or the side-effects bouts of
paralysis and petrifaction may have left.

As suddenly as a snuffed candle, all friendliness and fellowship departed
from Montrose's face. The look of wrath was so clear on his features that Del
Azarchel thought the other man might on the instant leap at his throat and
tear with his teeth like a dog. Many another man would have backed up, seeing the glint of death in the eyes of Montrose. Del Azarchel hefted his dirk
and stepped forward, eyes like flint, teeth white in a stiff grin, as if daring him
to try his luck.

They found themselves standing with noses almost touching, staring into
each other's eyes with gazes of superhuman vigor that no man, aside from
them, could long hold. But both knew each other's mystic sense of honor too
well. Neither would be the first to break the rules of the code of duels.

Through clenched and smiling teeth, Blackie whispered:

"Are you going to tell me why you dropped the asteroid, Cowhand? Even
for you, it seemed rather clumsy, and very brutal. I lost all contact with the
Earth for years."

The pattern jumped into place in the mind of Menelaus. He understood the reason for the asteroid drop, the destruction of the surface world, why the Melusine dwelled in buried lakes and subterranean seas—and where the Anchorites had gone.

"Is that going to be your one question, Blackie? I ain't much in the talking mood no more."

"Or the grammaring mood, I see. No. I will learn of all these things at my leisure, once you are dead."

"We both know that if I kill you, Blackie, your Jupiter Machine seedling must self-destruct, and all your plans die with you."

"No matter. My pain will end."

Menelaus grunted, unimpressed.

"You will survive," said Del Azarchel with an inclination of the head. "You will defy the Hyades, and provoke them to destroy our race. Our world, a tiny cinder circling a minor star in one of the smaller arms of the galaxy, will spin and spin, and the universe will never know nor care that two such men as the Judge of Ages and the Master of the World met and were matched in strength.

"But"—and now the grin of Del Azarchel looked almost boyish, so bright was it—"if I prevail, and I do not ask of you this one question tormenting me, there is no other source I can ask, and it will remain a mystery even after I become the Master of the Stars. So here is my question. I need not remind you that you are honor-bound to answer."

"Shoot. Sorry. Bad choice of words, considering. I mean, uh, ask."

"It concerns your long-term strategy during our match. Even from the very earliest days. When did you plant the seeds to grow Pellucid, your world core Xypotech? 2401? Long before the Day of Gold in 2525. At any time, during any of these millennia, you could have let society fall, install yourself into an emulation of your own at the Earth's core, and then have your own self-replicating iron logic crystals pour out of all the volcanoes of the world. I kept expecting it. I dreamed it and feared it and never once came up with a possible counterstrategy that might have worked. You would have won the game at any time. But the volcanoes never opened."

"What is the question again, exactly?"

"What is the ques—*what*? I mean—" Del Azarchel was at a loss for words. He stared at Montrose, his eyes full of wonder, thunderstruck, dumbfounded.

And then he began to laugh with relief. He roared and wept with laughter, the gales of mirth of a man who had lived with one particular fear for countless thousands of years, only to realize the fear had been a shadow, a boogeyman, a nothing.

Hiccoughing, Blackie said, "Y—You never even toyed with the notion, did you? You are sentimental. You are so stupid. You let me win. Just like that. I win. And you did it to save them! The humans. The hoi polloi. The *hylics*."

"Don't call them that." Montrose's voice was sharp.

The laughter turned to scorn. "They are lesser creatures to us."

"They are not lesser creatures!"

"Then why not tell them the truth? If you thought they were our equals, you would tell them everything we do when we decide how to let them live their lives. But you don't, do you? You never tell them anything," said Del Azarchel in a tone of voice so smug that he needed no words to say *You, like me, know full well that the Truth is not for such as they.*

"God damn you!" shouted Montrose.

And in ten huge, Sumo-wrestler-massive strides, Montrose strode in his armor to where the solemn men stood, his Seconds and Del Azarchel's. And the white-winged dark-eyed maiden, elfin and eerie, looked on with no expression from the dozens of eyes in her wings.

And Montrose began shouting the truth to them at the top of his lungs.

16

Ready to Fire

1. Not for Such as They

Montrose shouted, "All of your history has been a lie. All your lives. Your civilizations, accomplishments, times of war, times of peace, laws and customs, arts and sciences. A fraud. A farce."

No one spoke. No one interrupted or turned away.

"Del Azarchel duped his minions into creating one sick, diseased, broken society after another, in order to gull me into revealing a cure, a power, a spell, that only I could wield. It was a secret of seven parts that my wife, the Swan Princess Rania, had discovered on a stone circling a distant star. And each time I used this power to do some good, my *shipmates*"—he gestured to where the hooded men in black silk were gathered, and he spat the word like it was a curse. The Hermeticists, on their part, wore expressions either of indifference, or triumph, or condescending sneers when Montrose said—"these Hermeticist devils would take whatever good I did and pervert it to evil.

"I gave men civilization, *he* turned it into a weapon of destruction and oppression; I gave men cooperation, *he* turned it into the conformity of a military camp; I gave men a pharmaceutical means to extend their span of life, *he* made it into an addiction, and a means to gull, bewitch, and erase the minds and souls of men . . ."

And, one after another, he pointed at Melchor de Ulloa, Narcís D'Aragó (or rather, their Ghosts), and then at Sarmento i Illa d'Or.

The voice of Montrose took on a depth and power as his anger grew. "I gave men the discipline to break those addictions; one of their number who stands not here abused that discipline to create an art that destroyed each vestige of brother-love and gentleness and compassion and humanity in mankind, and he marred their forms to make them less than beasts. But he saw and repented his evil, and sought to bring the monsters to the fountains of humanity, and allow them drink; and for his goodness he was slain by *him* who was his friend and shipmate and brother; I gave the monsters laws of uniformity, to allow them to endure for a time without anarchy; and this same murderer imposed a uniformity of the mind, and destroyed the human soul, that thing which makes each man an individual and precious; and *this one*, the least and last of all, who has no human soul, created a race of helots and their zombie-masters to destroy the human spirit, that thing which gives a man free will and free conscience."

And he pointed at the Ghosts of Coronimas, and of Mentor Ull, who stood with golden tendrils; tall man and short Locust, heads held tilted at the same angle, as alike in posture as father and child, albeit nothing else about them was alike: only their souls.

Sarmento i Illa d'Or, who, of all men there, was the least afraid of the Judge of Ages, said, "What does it matter, anything you are saying? We did what we did because it gave us pleasure, and no one could stop us. *You* do what you do because it gives you pleasure; and any who try to stop you, you shoot and kill. Anything else is merely words."

Montrose whirled on him, moving swiftly for one in such heavy armor, and his teeth were gritted like a biting animal's, and his eyes blazed in madness. "This will give you no pleasure, Sarmento! Look about you. All the Hermeticists have done their work. There are none of you left to remake the world in his image. And yet another four hundred years remain to the End of Days. Shall each of you take turns again, and history will spin like some damn wheel, of Giants, Sylphs, Witches, Chimerae, Nymphs, Hormagaunts, Locusts, Melusine? I can start the wheel again, and bring forth Giants from my Tombs!"

Sarmento sneered. "The Nobilissimus, whom I am proud to call my master and the master of our order, he will examine among the races and determine which can best serve the Hyades. The others, as Darwin demands, will be exterminated. I am sure there are enough among your eighty-nine Tomb sites to select the, uh . . ."

Words failed him. Montrose spoke up, mocking: "The blue ribbon winner? The prize pig? The winner of the Miss Darwin beauty contest? Oh? Well then, who judges the Hermeticists? If you are judged and found wanting, do the people acting in the name of nondeliberate Darwinian forces get to deliberately exterminate you?"

He turned again to the other Iron Ghosts. "Now it is your turn to hear the truth, you bastards! You have all been played for fools; Blackie has his pinkie finger up your nose and leads you as he will: walk, trot, and gallop. Each bit of the Rania Solution that came into your hands was just so you would put it into Del Azarchel's hands, to then be used to make his greater Machine, his Jupiter Brain. Each of the seven parts of the human psyche was designed by one or another of the templates you made.

"The Sylphs were used as the template for a basic machine level, an unconscious. The peculiar intuitive brain structures of the Witches were templates for the subconscious levels, the seat of dreams and archetypal images, appetites too basic for names. The Chimerae formed the passions; the Nymphs, the instincts; the Clades, the ego; Locusts, the conscience. That is the fate of the civilizations you fathered. That was the only reason you were ever meant to father them. A machine copied part of their base neural psychology. For that purpose only, for a single millennium alone, you each were dressed in your master's robe, a robe too large for you, and were allowed to play at being Master of the World.

"For the true Master of the World brooks no rival, no, not even in play. You each have served your purpose and served your turn. Now you will be discarded.

"As your races and your dreams were discarded.

"The Great Work of the Hermetic Order—how often you have boasted empty boasts of it!—was to bring forth the race after man.

"Fools! *It was done without you.*

"Those races, your children, their civilizations, your ideals, your periods of history where for a season he allowed you to design and reign over mankind; in short, everything you have done with your long lives; was merely so he could steal your transitory pretense of the Great Work and copy it into the real Great Work, his Work, meant from the beginning to be the real and permanent, the sole and only.

"The Great Work was launched from here not ten hours past. Jupiter is his name, your new god, whose intellect will surpass a hundredfold all the races you vainly hatch here, yes, and all the inner planets together even if they were covered pole to pole with Aurum Vitae atop glaciers of Living Waters atop which races of Giants manning mile-high Granoliths might multiply, and all their cores Pellucid!

"Look at me! All of you know me. Except for you, Ull, so shut up. Do I lie?"

But then Ximen del Azarchel, who had sauntered in his clanging armor at a much more deliberate, almost meditative pace, was now among them. The Ghosts of the Hermeticists all now clamored and shouted at Del Azarchel, demanding, threatening, pleading for some word of explanation, yearning for some word of reassurance from him.

Only Sarmento i Illa d'Or did not doubt. "I believe you, my master! I will not listen to this traitor dog! When has he ever been sane?"

Mickey the Witch said softly, "What? Just because he wears a tent instead of clothing, and goes around pretending he is someone else?"

Montrose whispered sideways through his gritted teeth, "You are *not* helping." But he started laughing to himself, and he wondered if perhaps he were mad after all, to laugh at a time like this.

Ximen del Azarchel must have thought so too, for he chuckled and raised his hand. Such was his magnetism and authority, that even when stirred to bewildered anger, the Hermeticists fell silent before his glance. "I order you not to believe him. I order you not to think."

There was some muttering. Narcís D'Aragó said, "If the Judge of Ages is mad, surely so is the Master of the World. You *order* us to do *what*?"

Del Azarchel said in a calm, conversational tone of voice, as if it were a matter of no import, "I will erase your short-term memories because it suits me to do so. I have done such things many times in the past. I have even told you this many times in the past, because it does not matter what you think or what you do in a span of a moment of your lives, for it is a moment I can wash clean with a sweep of my hand. All your thoughts are written in dust. Do you still imagine I am your leader, or merely the first among equals? I am your master and you are my hounds. You are my possessions."

But he turned to Sarmento i Illa d'Or, saying, "Not you, for obvious reasons. I don't have anything in your head."

And, hearing the noise of disgust and horror from Montrose, Del Azarchel turned his head a little more, saying, "You look askance, Cowhand? You, of all people? This is an art I learned from you! I have phantasms of my own to serve me."

Montrose stepped forward, but not toward Del Azarchel: to Alalloel. He said, "He must die and I must kill him. Let us proceed."

2. Man of Honor

At that moment, Narcís D'Aragó approached Montrose and bowed his head. "Learned Montrose, I know I have no right to ask. And yet, I remind you that my previous version—a man like me in all ways, in personality and spirit and sense of honor, did not run from you when the time came for him to face you, pistol in hand. While it is true that he lives on in me, it is also true he died the death. It was a death he willingly faced. Will you allow me to speak to you, as one man of honor to another?"

Montrose could not suppress a spasm of hatred for the man. He said archly, "What kind of honor are we talking about? What kind of man? I would ask Captain Grimaldi about the perfect performance of your honorable duties aboard ship, but he is quite dead, seeing as how you rose up with the other mutineers and murdered him. So he is not around to ask."

D'Aragó did not look up. His voice, normally as thin and cold as an icicle, was thick with shame. "These are . . . old questions, no longer visited."

"Old as you and me, brother. You was there. You did the deed. You never paid for it, never got hanged, never got caught, and when you came back to Earth y'all were the princes of the world. Prince? A god! Hell, you even got your very own period of one thousand years as your own private lab and breeding grounds, stockyard, and gladiatorial circus, and you played with mankind like a girl playing with goddam paper dolls, instead of, oh, something like, dying in chains breaking rocks in the hot sun."

D'Aragó said in his cold voice, "I was loyal to the Captain until he . . . you know that he ordered us not to ignite the launching laser so that we could never return to Earth. He ordered us to die."

"The Hyades would never have discovered Earth had you done that."

"Truly? No further expedition ever would have sought out a nugget of contraterrene the size of a star? The most precious, most dangerous substance in nature?" He looked up, his cold eyes twinkling. "Come now: surely it was better to be warned, and have these millennia to prepare a defense, than let Captain Grimaldi in his madness have his way, and for us to die with the human race uninformed, unwarned, unprepared? Did I not have duties of honor to my home?"

"So what if Earth was warned? You think fighting the Hyades is completely futile."

"But you do not."

Montrose was not sure what to say to that. The argument sounded fishy, but he wanted to get back to the business of shooting Del Azarchel, so he said,

"Fine. You are a pox-ridden man of honor. Whoop-dee-do and yee-haw and bully for you. Speak your piece, you syphilitic whoreson."

Much to the embarrassment of Montrose, Narcís D'Aragó fell to his knees, and clasped his hands in prayer. "Save us."

"Pustules on the burning balls of Satan in Hell! What the hell you asking me?"

"Save us from Del Azarchel. There must be some Divarication failure. He is suffering a mental disease, and he has absolute power over us, even to our inmost thoughts."

"He ain't crazy, he's just evil. There's a difference." Menelaus looked up and sighed. Del Azarchel was standing with the other Hermeticists. Sarmento i Illa d'Or was standing behind his master, broad as a bull and breathing through his nostrils like one. The others, crouching and cringing in various postures of panic, were talking in a shrill confusion of voices. Del Azarchel was answering them back in the cool, distant, polite tones of a professor in a classroom explaining a scientific problem with no particular application to any human life, of merely intellectual interest only. He was describing the means he would use to toy with their minds and memories and souls, since they were, after all, actually minds housed in computer mainframes he controlled. And he was smiling and laughing and his eye glinted with mirth and sadism.

"Okay," Menelaus said to D'Aragó with a sigh. "Let's compromise. He's evil *and* crazy."

D'Aragó said, "It was a technology evolved while we were in hibernation aboard the *Emancipation*."

"The Mind Helot tech. I know. So you want me to save your sorry evil asses from your evil boss, on account of now you are on the receiving end of his evil. All but Sarmento, who looks like he is just having a fine old time. Even if I agreed—"

But Narcís D'Aragó now had a smile on his thin face. It was a crooked smile, because he clearly had little practice making his face fold into that shape, but it was a human smile. "You will agree. For better or worse, you cannot help but solve problems, Crewman Fifty-One. Your soul is large."

"Your mouth is large. By rights, I should stand aside and watch you squirm just for the sheer cussed-mindedness of it. But since I came up here with my gun and my Seconds to blast Blackie to Hell so that his daddy, the Devil, can rump-plunge him until his eyes pop, I don't even know why you are flapping your damn gums at me."

"I came, Learned Montrose, because I know that you destroy those who challenge you. Am not I, myself, one whom you destroyed? You alone can overcome the Senior Del Azarchel. Whether you believe me or scorn me, I came because to stand by, saying nothing, knowing you would duel with Del Azarchel, and by killing him, grant us life—to get this gift of life from you, and freedom, and to have restored to us the possession of our souls—to have all this from your hand, Learned Montrose, and not to have asked it of you, well, that were low indeed. I ask you for my life because it is more honorable to ask, even though I know you have your own reasons to wish him dead. Now I too have reasons. Kill him also for me."

"But you killed Grimaldi."

"So I did, and do not regret the deed, dark as it was. I killed my superior officer because he went mad and meant to kill us all. Now Del Azarchel is mad and means us all to die, or worse. The same logic applies." And, with no further word, he stiffly turned and marched back to where the Hermeticists were gathered, where he stood, thin as a birch tree in winter, and as silent.

3. Accommodation

Del Azarchel now had but one Second, Sarmento i Illa d'Or, who carried his master's pistol and helmet. Montrose waved Scipio, Illiance, and Soorm off the field; the three men retreated, Soorm scowling and snapping his teeth with disappointment, Scipio looking relieved, Illiance impassive. Sir Guiden remained to one side of Montrose, and cradled the oversized dueling pistol in both hands; Mickey held the great cauldron-shaped helmet and stood at his other side.

The two duelists took up their positions thirty paces from each other, and the Seconds, Sarmento and Sir Guiden, approached the judge of honor to confer.

The tongueless mouth of Alalloel of Anserine opened, and now, not merely a trio of voices issued forth, but a choir as might fill a cathedral, or a stadium. It was several thousand voices speaking at once, blended into harmony.

Montrose squinted, and saw a similar twinge of thought cross the face of Del Azarchel. The word choice indicated a different psychological architecture than had obtained when last Alalloel spoke, or, rather, when last this body was used to transmit to them the thoughts from the ever larger mind groups who seemed to be joining the communal link. If he understood their nomenclature, Montrose guessed that Anserine was a much larger group of minds than Lree, so much so that the original Alalloel personality was lost in the crowd, insignificant compared to what was now at the microphone.

The multitude of voices said: "We ask again whether peaceful accommodation can be found? If so, without dishonor, both participators may withdraw, and no slight against them will be permitted."

Sir Guiden and Sarmento replied that no accommodation was possible.

"Have all measures to avoid this conflict been exhausted?" The number of voices had increased again. This time it was in the millions. Menelaus ran a rough calculation in his head about the coordination tolerance needed to avoid overlapping and blurring of that many waveforms: it implied a degree of mental unity far greater than what had obtained even a moment before.

It was everyone. It was the whole race of the Melusine speaking.

Sarmento i Illa d'Or was more alert than Montrose would have thought. Montrose was surprised when Sarmento said, "Senior! This is outside what we expected"—*we* in this case meaning Sarmento and his Ghost, Exillador—"the Cliometric calculus cannot account for this amount of interest from the Melusine. I suggest—"

Del Azarchel shook his head. "A bigger crowd than expected, eh? The Cowhand did actually have another move underway, and now the strike will come out of the obscuring fog. I care not. I don't see that it is anything that can physically stop the duel. Speak your line."

Sir Guiden on behalf of Montrose said that no additional measure could be found to avoid the conflict. Sarmento spoke the same words with a more obvious reluctance, wary that something had gone wrong, and his eyes were darting left and right at high speed in the peculiar way posthumans were wont to use.

Unexpectedly, something stung Montrose in his eyes. He drew the back of his gauntleted wrist across his brow, cocking the wrist so that the leather joint rather than the metal glove plates rubbed him. He stared in disbelief at the discoloration on his wrist. It was dank. He was sweating. Sweating in fear.

But Blackie had already knelt to Sarmento to allow his helmet to be wrestled on, and did not see it. That was a comfort, if only a small one. Mickey saw, and mopped Montrose's brow dry with his lambrequin. That was a bigger comfort.

Montrose also knelt. Mickey raised the wide, heavy helmet and placed it over Montrose's head, giving it a firm twist. With a click, the contact points in the inner and outer screw collar met, and, with a whine, the internal lights and readouts came on.

It took a moment of rocking and heaving for Montrose to get himself back afoot. He did not remember having problems like this back when he was a young man of twenty. Now he was biologically forty years—and even that was only equivalent years, because biosuspension did not arrest all life processes exactly, and thaw did not correct all damage exactly back to the point of prehibernation. It was approximate. He might have been, biologically speaking, older than that. He sure felt it.

Alalloel raised the baton to shoulder level, no higher. "Gentlemen, see to your countermeasures!"

Through his lookout visor, nothing was different, but the view in the helmet aiming monocle showed the real electronic story. Del Azarchel was now surrounded by a dozen shadows of himself, blurring and shifting and fading, and his radio silhouette swayed and dimmed with interference. Montrose looked the same to him. He could feel the warmth of the batteries powering his coat camouflage as they came online.

Alalloel now raised the baton fully overhead. It was the penultimate signal. "Gentlemen, see to your weapons! Do not fire before the signal, or all honor is forfeit, whereupon the Seconds may and must intervene!"

Sir Guiden presented the massive pistol and plugged it into the forearm sockets of Menelaus' armor. Sir Guiden checked the circuits, double-checked, opened and closed the main chamber and the eight lesser chambers, then thumbed the chaff magazine.

Then Sir Guiden walked away, five, ten, fifteen paces. He turned and nodded. Sir Guiden called to Montrose: "Stand firm until the baton is dropped. When the baton is dropped, you are at liberty to fire."

Montrose raised his left gauntlet, and held up his hand. By tradition, the non-weapon-hand was white, but a black circle was in the palm, so that the opponent could clearly see the sign. He was ready to fire.

Sarmento had taken longer than Sir Guiden, or perhaps had checked his master's weapon more thoroughly. Or perhaps a growing suspicion that something was wrong was slowing his footsteps. He was not yet out of the line of fire. Blackie had not yet raised his glove.

Montrose waited, feeling the sweat begin to come into his eyes again, and knowing there was no way to wipe his helmeted face. This was not one of those modern helmets, whose internal circuits noticed wearer discomfort, and used small inside manipulators to wipe a hot face. *If I blink during the wrong moment, I'm dead.*

It seemed so unfair that such small things would make the difference between victory and death. He wrinkled his brow furiously, hoping to delay the gathering drip of ticklish saltwater he could feel accumulating.

Then Sarmento was out of the line of fire, and instructing Del Azarchel not to shoot until the baton dropped.

Montrose knew not to tense his arm before the raising, not to tense his trigger-finger. It had to be one smooth motion, and smoothness counted for more than speed, because one did not want to jar the chaff package, or confuse the aiming sensors with jerky or blurry motions. He waited, and eternity crawled by.

Del Azarchel raised his hand and opened it. There were the white fingers and thumb; there was the black palm. Montrose suddenly felt buoyant with relief, weightless, almost lightheaded, because the eight-thousand-year-long wait had ended. This was it.

And then—

—the baton dropped—

4. Misfire

—And Montrose blinked when the drop of sweat stung his eye. This made him raise his pistol too quickly: a sudden jerk. This in turn made his weight shift, and only then did the ice puddle on which he stood crack, give way, and drop him.

The bottom of the puddle was not far, a matter of a handsbreadth or less, but it was enough to slide a bootheel along the slick and frictionless mud of the puddle bottom, and pull his leg out from under him.

With a resounding clattering clash, Montrose fell. He landed on his hands and knees, but the heavy gun hit the ground and went off.

For a moment, he was deaf. His gun hand went numb as it was kicked backward as if by seven mules, and the charge of chaff and cloud exploded under his fingers instead of in the air between himself and his target. Splinters of rock ricocheted against his armor, and the fierce pain in his armpit and ribs told him his armor had been pierced. It felt as if the main bullet and two escort bullets, the number three and the number two, had gone off and blown themselves into the icy rock only a foot or less from his hand.

Montrose found himself kneeling, buried up to the neck in a swarming fog of glittering black chaff-particles, but his head was clearly visible to the enemy. A perfect target.

With his other hand, he raised his gun hand up, trying to see if any fingers had been blown off, but he was defeated by the weight of the gun dangling from his wrist and the restricted field of vision (the helmets were not designed to nod forward, nor was there a peep window below the jawline to let a man see his feet). From the sensation, he thought he'd lost a finger, maybe two.

With some part of his brain, he knew he should be scrambling to take the gun up in his left hand and squeeze off the remaining escort bullets, hoping for a lucky shot.

With another part of his brain, he noted that being the master of a world-wide system of coffins which had the most advanced medical nanotechnology on the planet tended to make one nonchalant about wounds. His maimed feet from the day before had been healed overnight; because of events like this, he now regarded major wounds as an inconvenience rather than a lifelong tragedy.

Of course, at the moment, the word "lifelong" meant a span measured in fractions of a second. Montrose saw the gunbarrels of Del Azarchel's weapon, main shot and escort bullets, aim at him, each one seeming larger and deeper than a well.

Del Azarchel had not released his chaff cloud yet. He held his weapon pointing at the helpless Montrose for a moment. His hand did not shake. The aim was straight and true.

Then Del Azarchel pointed at the ground, and fired his main shot. The noise was thunder, ringing so loud it could almost be tasted.

Del Azarchel had deloped.

17

The Swans

1. Interruption

It took Montrose a long moment to realize that he was still alive, and even longer to realize that Del Azarchel had fired at the ground.

Del Azarchel was not looking at Montrose. Unable to turn his helmeted head, to look left and right, Del Azarchel must move his feet. Del Azarchel was turning slowly in a circle.

Clouds of vapor were rising from underfoot in every direction. The snowy ground was steaming, sublimating. The ice was melting and vanishing. Behind Del Azarchel, Montrose could see the glaciers were also toppling. With a noise like drums and a noise like trumpets, first one, then a dozen, then a myriad distant peaks of glaciers collapsed in avalanche toward the earth, like a stronghold of white towers being flattened by a bomb.

There also came a noise like running or thrumming. It was the sound of rain. No clouds were directly overhead, but in the distance all the vapors and fogs of the sky were changing from white to black with freakish, unnatural speed, and had begun pouring rain against the hills on the horizon; and higher and farther away, the rain was pelting against the sides of the Tower.

Every cloud in sight, including feathery high cirrus in the far distant blue, was precipitating.

Del Azarchel on heavy feet turned back toward Montrose, and pointed underfoot, and then at the hills with his white glove, gesturing toward the unnaturally sublimating snow. "You found a way to kill Exarchel. All the nanotechnology in the world's water supply is going inert. Your final move was a sacrifice move. You just shot your horse, didn't you? You *allowed* Pellucid to be infiltrated, knowing full well that I could not pass up the chance to have a Xypotech of that size housing my soul, and I sent Exarchel into it, and the infiltrator was infiltrated in turn. But why did you wait until I showed the black palm? Ah! You needed the deadman switch turned on, did you not, so that every single copy of Exarchel, wherever it might be stored or howsoever it might be encrypted, would be linked by one link. That was the link you needed. Very clever."

Montrose raised his unwounded arm and pointed upward. Del Azarchel craned his neck.

There were thousands and tens of thousands of figures in the air, flowing out from the Tower like seedlings blown from a dandelion: Men and women, large and small, winged in silver. With them also were dolphins and several types of whales. One and all, including the sleek sea mammals large and small, were borne aloft on great silvery wings, each feather glittering with eyes.

Montrose spoke in a strained voice, wincing and panting. "They waited, hoping I would shoot you, which would take care of Jupiter for them."

Del Azarchel's voice was hoarse with horror. "*Them?*"

He did not need to say anything aloud: Montrose could guess the rapid pattern of clues snapping into shape in his mind, such as the amateur awkwardness of the last war, the apparent lack of effect from the spread of the Anarchist Vector.

Del Azarchel forced a lilt of humor into his trembling words. "Clever! So your liberty-loving Anchorites had a method of hiding their thoughts even from intimate psychoscopic examination, did they? When they drilled down to the buried seas, it was not to propagate a war. That war was one they knew they must lose—it was just to spread the mental virus. Like your Giants, they sacrificed themselves to let their philosophy prevail."

"Not a philosophy. A negative-information semiotic technique to reformat the mind-body relation. It comes from the Monument."

"You think you've won this round, you and your pets—"

Montrose, kneeling in the black cloud, spoke in a rasping voice. "No pets of mine. Free men. Equals. They figured out you have no intention whatever of fighting the Hyades, that your whole star raid drill, everything from taking a century to build your skyhook to herding the entire world population under the planetary crust for decades, was just a ruse to get at me."

Sir Guiden stepped into the cloud of chaff still spreading from Montrose's pistol. With one arm around Montrose, and a whine of strength amplification motors in his elbows, he helped Montrose to his feet and led him out of the glittering dark cloud of smog. He disconnected the pistol from Montrose's numb gun hand, and clicked the safeties into place, and worked the lever to open the firing chamber.

Sarmento helped Del Azarchel out of his helmet.

Sir Guiden did the same for Montrose. The two men stood bareheaded in the wind, with snow melting underfoot and rain and winged men pouring down. Del Azarchel's dark hair was whipped by rainy wind, his grimace surprisingly white in his dark beard. Montrose's pale red hair hung lank, nose jutting out of his squarish misfeatured face, his lantern jaw like the toe of a boot, his eyes like two embers, unblinking.

Montrose and Del Azarchel stood a moment, merely staring at each other.

Montrose said, "Why didn't you shoot?"

Del Azarchel did not answer, but said, "I grant quarter until we can re-arm and find a better field. Agreed?"

Montrose said, "Agreed. And next time, we need to pick our judge of honor more carefully. I was not expecting her to interfere."

"I was not expecting you to fall with such comedic composure on your buttocks," said Del Azarchel.

"And I was not expecting your brain to melt," said Montrose.

Of one accord, they turned and looked at Alalloel. The strange, all-dark eyes of her face seemed for the first time to hold expression: an exultation of triumph.

2. Metaposthuman

The gathered voices of an entire world spoke from her mouth and said, "There shall be no next time! Your duel is ended, now and forever. Neither will we allow you to continue it, neither with pistols nor races nor worlds nor with the calculus of history.

"Eight millennia and more have been changed and marred by the insanity of hatred that endures between the both of you. The resources lost by you and by all the races you fathered, the opportunity cost in more perfect worlds which could have been born, but were not—the waste in human lives is beyond even our calculation power! Entire civilizations rose, flourished, sickened, and were discarded by you as merely resources expended in your conflict. The quarrel is done: we decree peace."

Del Azarchel stepped toward her. "Silence! I command—"

"You command nothing!" The vibrant look in her eyes grew so powerful that Menelaus could not meet her gaze. When Menelaus looked toward Del Azarchel, he was shading his eyes as if against a strong light. Once and twice Del Azarchel nerved himself to look toward her face; but his eyeballs twitched, his gaze stammered, and he had to turn away.

Del Azarchel looked seasick. His eyes were wild. "Who—? *What* are you? No Melusine speaks this way!"

"We are their ultimate children. The Melusine created us, the final race, for the express purpose of halting your madness." The myriad voices blended more harmoniously, sounding almost like a song: "All those who came before us are merely variations within the same species, *Homo sapiens*. Ours is a new genus, primate but not hominid: *Pan sapiens*. We are the first prototypes of the post-Melusine species, superhuman beyond even your superhumanity. In this new and final race, the awkward and ugly duckling of mankind, and of all the mankinds, has finally reached beauty, power, strength, and supremacy. We call ourselves the Second Humans: we are the Swans. Behold! We are now come!"

She spread her wings and soared upward, exulting, to meet the dancing and descending silvery thundercloud of winged beings in the midst of the air.

Del Azarchel recovered his aplomb in a deep breath. Now he was peering upward, saying, "These Swans of yours may prove difficult to overcome."

"That is what I like about you, Blackie. You are stinking blind-drunk on rotgut optimism, and do not see the world around you."

"A trait we share. But I prefer to think of it as megalomania," said Del Azarchel coolly. "The cure, of course," he smiled, "for the neurotic and false belief that one is possessed of godlike power is actually to obtain it; whereupon the belief is no longer false."

"You are not overcoming these critters, Blackie. They are as much smarter than us as we are than a baseline human. They were clever enough to hide whole flying circuses of their Paramount bodies aboard your Tower without your noticing."

Del Azarchel was staring upward, shading his eyes. "Since the Tower has more surface area than China, the feat is less astounding than may seem."

"Not to mention smart enough to hide their damned world right in front of your eyes while letting you think you ruled it. Smart enough to see through your lies, which the Hermeticists never did, and to turn on you."

"And smart enough to turn on you, as well."

"What the pox do you mean?!"

"Look up, Cowhand!"

3. Turning

The falling figures were closer now. Montrose peered, using his cortical technique to make the images clear and sharp in his mind.

Flying down were men, women, Giant posthumans, dwarfish Inquilines of blue and gray, dark Locusts by the swarms hanging like a cloud of pitch. Chimerae were falling head downward in angled formations like diving geese, not having opened their wings yet. Witches, perhaps for ceremonial reasons, perhaps merely for joy, held broomsticks and besoms between their legs.

"I see that they raided your Tombs," drawled Del Azarchel. "No respect for private property, eh? That was not in your plan, was it? Obviously, your plan was to have something happen that neither one of us could plan." Del Azarchel started laughing. "So *this* was your final move! To throw yourself out of the game! Congratulations! Small wonder I did not foresee it!"

Montrose knew that Del Azarchel must have run Cliometric scenarios on the impact of Cliometry on a society. It had only one of two halt states: The first halt was one where everyone was under control of a plan, even the planners themselves, and every least act and smallest thought was unfree, controlled by a calculus no one controlled. The Melusine world Del Azarchel had tried to create was a model of that state. The other state was where everyone knew Cliometry, and could freely adjust his future to match and harmonize with all other like-minded future plans—or freely decline, neither interfering nor being interfered with. That was the new world Montrose had brought into being.

Montrose said, "These people are free of your Cliometric interference as well as from mine. Why are you laughing? It worked, didn't it?"

"If kicking over the chessboard prevents the checkmate, certainly it worked. But it is the ingratitude that amuses me. *How sharper than a serpent's tooth!*" he laughed and wiped his eyes. "That asteroid strike! Of course it wiped out all the threads of history I had been developing—but it wiped you out also. It blinded my satellites and blinded your periscopes. That is how desperate they were to get rid of you."

"Of us."

"Yes, as you say, but getting rid of me is not as deliciously funny. I regarded them as cattle anyway, and expected them to stampede. You are the one who thought of them as pets, and got bitten."

"Laugh it up," snarled Montrose. "Soon enough we'll find out what they mean to do with us. You see it, don't you? Explain it to your man."

Sarmento spoke up, his voice a rumble, "Explain it to yours, Fifty-One. I am in communion with Exillador. I grasp the situation. Your pets whom you insist on treating as equals are the only ones here who are not posthuman."

Montrose turned to Sir Guiden. Sir Guiden said, "I don't understand. We won. They lost. The people of this era, these steel-winged angels, they have thrown off the tyranny of the Hermeticists. Have they not?"

"And they are throwing me off as well," said Montrose grimly. "We are prisoners. They have to decide how we are going to fit into their society. Go over to the others and tell them the bad news."

4. Swan Song

The figures in the air were touching down.

Two Giants, grotesque beetle-browed heads atop their elephantine bodies gleaming, their beautiful golden eyes glistening, landed as lightly as thistle-down nearby. No higher than the Gigantic elbows were a coven of Witches, thin as rails and gray and wrinkled in their black habits and peaked hoods. A squad of Chimerae, eyes fierce and unblinking as the eyes of hunting cats, were no taller than the waists of the Giants; a host of Locusts, dark and solemn-faced with endless repetitions of the same face, tendrils glistering, were no taller than the thick knees of the Giants. Here and there, like some delirious dream of Egyptian pantheons, were freakish Hormagaunts, beast-headed or hawk-billed, furred like lions or shelled like armadillos, a nightmare of pincers and claws and writhing tentacles studded with mouths; here also were rank upon rank of Clade-dwellers, identical twins in groups of twelve and twenty, hair quills bristling. The six-tendrilled dark-eyed Melusine were present as well, standing in groups of three, with dolphins and whales, sleek as torpedoes, soaring and swooping and hovering above them, graceful as notes of music in a symphony.

Which post-Cetaceans went with which of the standing figures was not clear. All wore the shining neural cloaks of the Second Humans. Tallest loomed the two winged Giants, and their white pinions reached twenty-four feet from tip to tip as they furled and folded them. With them were winged Witches and winged Chimerae with ten-foot spans; and winged Locusts with stubby pinions like so many cupids from Saint Valentine's Day cards. All the eyes on all the feathers were glinting and beating with light. Montrose tried to estimate the volume of information being passed back and forth between the gathered minds here, the core of the Earth, and systems the Tower was spreading elsewhere.

Del Azarchel must have made a similar calculation, because he turned toward a group of creatures Montrose did not recognize: tall men and beautiful women whose hair was a strange shimmering like the wigs of Scholars, and skin as pale as theirs, but their eyes were the black-within-black of the Melusine. Montrose saw these were not wigs, but masses of Locust tendrils, each one as fine as a strand of silk, and as many as hairs in a wig. The hair swayed and moved as if an invisible updraft of wind were blowing about each pale face.

They were not twins; nor were they of the same family or race. Indeed, Montrose could not tell which human stock these beings sprang from, for each face was an individual work of art, and if one had a Roman-looking nose or a Japanese-looking eye, or the jawline of an Australian aborigine, or the lips of a Persian, his other features might resemble some other stock, or none at all. All the faces were beautiful with a cold beauty, and, unalike as they were, all were stern and ascetic with the same spirit.

Montrose saw what Del Azarchel did: these dozen figures were the center of the communication flux binding the areas together.

To them, Del Azarchel said, "Your victory is temporary and meaningless. The Jupiter Brain will grow and overmaster you,"

One of the Swans, tall and thin, beak-nosed and with swaying silvery tendril-hair falling past his shoulders, stepped forward.

From his body language, poise, and stance, Montrose saw this was another aspect of the Anserine again. The same gathered voice as had come from Alalloel spoke from his empty, tongueless mouth. "Not so. We deliberately misled you as to the internal conditions of the core of Jupiter. Your estimation of growth speed is off by two orders of magnitude. It will not be two hundred years before the mass of Jupiter is converted to logic crystal, nor even two thousand, but over two hundred thousand years. The Hyades World Armada arrives in the solar system in four hundred years. All events will be resolved, for good or ill, long before Jupiter wakes: we will be dead, or be free."

Montrose stepped toward them and winced. He had forgotten the shattering pain in his gun hand. The pain lent anger to his words. "You speak of freedom and yet you raid my Tombs, abduct my people, insert tendrils in their heads, and drive them into your mass minds, sucking their souls away!"

The Anserine said, "You speak in ignorance. No matter. We will not be mastered by him nor judged by you. Your time as Judge of Ages is done. Your interference in history, benevolent as may have been its intent, is a trespass. Our history is our own. We will write our own destiny with our own Cliometric calculations. As for you, we consider you to have forfeited your right to your Tombs due to the ill use to which you placed them."

Montrose said, "And as for my clients? Men who trusted me with their lives? What of them?"

"All those hundreds of persons in your eighty-nine Tomb systems you have preserved for medical or scientific reasons, or as sanctuary from current power, or as penalty of exile, or for the sake of curiosity—how were they more than pawns to you? You gathered them merely as a strategy to use against the Master of the World. Fortunately, their numbers are small enough that they can be absorbed without disaccommodation into our protocols. The biosuspension Xypotech procedures maintained by Pellucid were destroyed when we destroyed Exarchel. All the Tombs are automatically opening worldwide."

Montrose glanced at Del Azarchel. He smiled a crooked and bitter smile and said, "Hundreds. Hundreds of persons in my eighty-nine Tombs. They don't know what they just did. They don't see it. You don't see it either, do you, Blackie?"

Del Azarchel flashed him a dark look and said, "I saw it long ago, and long ago prepared a counterthrust. When Rania fled the solar system, she altered the orbits of the tiny amount of contraterrene she did not herself need as fuel, and radioed the information to you. After our duel was interrupted, and the Beanstalk fell on us, Exarchel had us both in prison hospitals—and one of Rania's loyal Scholars spirited you away. Exarchel could not see where you went. And so he was slow to understand what was happening. You had the contraterrene needed to keep the depthtrain system operating. Just to prevent tunnel collapses requires an energy pressure higher than nonamplified matter can provide. For years, no, for centuries, I did not understand your obsession with claiming control over these underground places. Do you now say that you had this planned from the start? I suspect you stumbled across the idea by serendipity."

Montrose said, "The idea was planned out. Who I was going to get to run the thing, that was more jury-rigged. I thought I could trust my Clan not to grow corrupt, and I could not. Then I thought maybe the Church was a better candidate to run things while I slept—while I ain't much of a churchgoing man myself, anyone can see that she's been around longer than any human organization still in business, and might actually hold property over generation after generation waiting for slumberers to wake. And historically, Churchmen run hospitals and graveyards, and I figured this weren't much different. And then you destroyed the Church with your Witches, and you caused the Collapse, and you, not me, you lost all the records. By that point I had enough men, the Knights Hospitalier, to run the Tombs from the inside, so I only needed minimal contact with the surface world. Every generation, from the Witch-doctors to the Medical Corps to the Maidens of the Hesperides to the Iatrocrats, has cooperated in secret with my people. Why would they not? Doctors don't want their patients to die."

The tall Anserine spokesman said, "Explain these remarks. How do they touch our present concerns?"

Del Azarchel turned to the Anserine, saying, "You fool. Everyone is beneath the earth."

Montrose said, "It's not *everyone*. That would be ridiculous. Some died in accidents or battles, and my people could not get to them in time. Others could not be preserved even with the best medical coffin system I could make. But it is a lot of people. A whole lot."

The spokesman said, "This is unexpected—please confirm you are claiming the Tomb system is more extensive than anticipated?"

Del Azarchel laughed. "Exarchel never kept a record of all the populations over the centuries and millennia who entered hospitals and sick-houses and Nymph deleriumariums and did not emerge, because Montrose's acts were edited from his mind. Montrose moved all Tombs far below the crust, below the mantle, out of any possible surface-detection range, back when I had my Witches digging up Churchmen to prevent a resuscitation of my poor, senile, machine-hating Mother Church. Montrose kept near the surface only the minimum possible number of Tombs to maintain a steady contact with the current world, to replace thawed followers, or to hear rumors of war or disaster in case he needed to offer sanctuary to anyone.

"He does not have eighty-nine Tombs, nor eighty-nine hundred. He has over *one million* ten-thousand-man facilities buried at various levels between the mantle and the core. His failsafes all performed a fail-over when Pellucid died just now: without the memory space, his coffins cannot correct for the cellular information of all his clients, millions and millions of them. So up they come. He is bringing up more than your society can possibly absorb. Do you have any food to feed them? They can pay. For all of your metals and minerals of the surface world are exhausted, are they not? You've possessed yourself of some of the volume he has vacated? You have no idea how small a volume that is. The swarms of populations will have all the wealth of the buried world at their command, oil and gold, copper and tin, uranium and suchlike."

Del Azarchel bowed and gestured toward Montrose, smiling, both eyebrows raised. "Behold him. You see, my dear Swans, the Judge of Ages, he is a cowboy, and he knows that the Red Indians, no matter how brave they are, cannot stand up to the pressure of sheer numbers from the White Man.

"This is (and, ever since the time of the Witches, always has been) the final executioner's ax which the Judge of Ages bore above the throats of every generation. And now, by accident, in your haste to slay Exarchel, you have done in Pellucid, triggered a global system failure, and brought the ax upon yourself."

Winged beings had not stopped landing from the Tower. More were present, and more, until the hills surrounding were shivering and glinting with what seemed snowbank upon snowbank of white metallic wings. The millions of eyes, like the eyes of peacocks seen in some drugged hallucination, flashed and glinted silently, the glittering of a tropic sun on diamond-brilliant waves.

Montrose said to the Anserine, "Sirs! Now that you are masters of your own world and judges of your own age, what provision will you make for the innocent?"

The tall Anserine said, "You think the matter disastrous for us? It is not even difficult. We have set events in motion."

"What events? What?"

The tall Anserine said, "Do not concern yourself with the lives of others. For now, see to your own life! Our intent is benevolent, but, to one of your level of awareness, inexplicable. You will save yourself much needless mental anxiety if you now, this moment, make peace with Ximen del Azarchel: otherwise the route we have planned for you will be more convolute. Go speak with him!"

Montrose stepped closer to Del Azarchel, lowering his voice and saying, "I am not sure what they are threatening. They say we must make peace. But has anything changed between us?"

"Divorce Rania."

"You know that's impossible. And there is still Grimaldi's murder."

"And your treason and ingratitude."

"So, Blackie, What happens if these Swans decide to open fire on my clients with that many-miniature-suns weapon you mentioned, or something even worse?"

Del Azarchel's smile turned into a sneer. "You should trust your own Cliometric calculus. Kill ten billion helpless people, whose only crime was that the Swans destroyed the Xypotech infrastructure maintaining their biosuspension? Work out the math in your head. If they do that, in two data-generations, the psychological pressure from guilt and cynicism would turn them into—well, into Hermeticists. Or do you think that any logical being can embrace genocide, when needed for his own survival, but reject servitude, which, by any measure, is a far less grievous offense? If they indulge in geno-cide, I win. See their wings a-shine with signal traffic! They know it, too. Your rugged honor-bound individualists could not commit billionfold mega-mass-murder in cold blood without losing their souls to me. They will not act. But I shall."

Montrose gripped his arm, then winced, breathless with pain, because he had gripped Del Azarchel with his maimed hand. He hissed, "What counter-thrust did you have planned?"

Del Azarchel shrugged his hand aside and pointed at the horizon. "She is rising now. See that light? Looks like daybreak on the western horizon? It is not daybreak."

"What is it?"

"It is shipbreak."

The mountains to the west were lit up as if with cherry flame, and the rain clouds above, still weeping the memories and libraries of Exarchel, were stained cerise and purple and magnificent magenta as if a second twilight were rising to encompass the dome of the sky. It was faster than a sunrise when a second sun rose above the peaks, red and flattened in the distortion of the atmosphere. Montrose squinted, seeing the morning star and perhaps a sliver of the moon by day, its ghostly handprint reversed.

Montrose said, "That is the sail of the *Emancipation*."

Del Azarchel said, "The ship as well, and her various escort craft to help work the shrouds—but you cannot see her at this distance. I was toying with the notion of simply burning your revenants like ants with a magnifying glass by pulling in the focal length of the lightsail. A simple and effective means to make war on earthlubbers, as we spacefarers like to call you. You should know its effectiveness. You, after all, commanded the Giants to do the same to my people and my civilization. Every emulation recorded in a mainframe you an-nihilated was a person, a thinking being."

"A thinking being who thought to conquer and enslave the world!" Mon-trose snapped.

"A loyal being carrying out the orders of his sovereign, the only sovereign in world history to impose world peace—I had already mastered the world. She is *mine*, then, and now and forever. I am within my rights to crush rebellion and disorder, and to do whatever is needed to save my civilization that I made from alien invasion. If I call surrender, and order all the world to lay down her arms in the name of peace, I must be obeyed! Anything a man may do by right to save himself alive, how much more right have I, to save worlds and aeons unborn? If I call upon my ship to put down the upstart Swans, who dare prevent me?"

"My ship," corrected Montrose. "You just took her."

Del Azarchel said, "Return my fiancée and the life I was fated to enjoy, and I will give you your ship back. Until then, do not voice complaint to me about mere material possessions. With all your buried wealth and factory space and bottomless geothermal wells, you did not have the wealth, across all those years, to build yourself another?"

"Since every time I woke, the world was in another Dark Ages produced by you, you plague-spotted son of a clap-blinded whore—"

"You insult my mother? That saint—?"

"Me? Your whole damned life is one big insult to your mother's memory, Blackie, as you damn well—"

Montrose turned his head. Dolphins, a dozen or more, were levitating overhead, motionless. They wore wings akin to those of their human counterparts, except a cloud of drizzling mists also issued from the feathers, or from a web of studs dappling their sleek bodies. They stared down with grave black-within-black eyes. From above and behind those eyes rose very long whipcords of golden neurotelepathic tendrils

Twelve of the many-color-cloaked Second Humans also had gathered in a loose semicircle. Now the thin, silver-haired Anserine man raised his hand, and, as one gesture, so did a dozen other of the Swans.

They spoke in the same voice, human and dolphin. "Gentlemen, your levity is appalling. That you would squabble and threaten the Earth with war even at a moment like this is atrocious. Whatever debt of gratitude the human race may have owed either of you, either for a peaceful reign of which you boast, Ximen del Azarchel, or your benevolent offer of sanctuary from the ravages of time you extended, Menelaus Montrose—that debt is cancelled. No more will any hibernation facilities accept anyone bearing your genetic code, either of you."

Montrose stared up at the narrow faces of the sea-beasts, then looked wildly at the remote, dispassionate faces of the equally inhuman humanoids, saying, "You can't do that! I have to slumber until Rania comes back."

Del Azarchel said, "And I as well, since she will leave him and cleave to me, when that great day comes." Del Azarchel could slow his aging process tremendously, but even he could not endure the immensity of time before Rania's return.

The Anserine said in unison, "She is lost to you forever. Both of you have abused your timelessness and your immunity from years. We, the one mind of the planet Earth, hereby revoke your immunity of years and condemn you to mortal lives. No other punishment is fit."

Montrose turned away, his stomach hot and knotted.

Del Azarchel tossed back his head, and drew back his lips, an odd expression halfway between a smile and baring one's teeth to bite. "Anserine! What will you do if I give *Emancipation* the command to open fire?"

"What is your target?" The voice now came from an overhead dolphin hanging as motionless as a piñata. "How much heat capacity can you bring to bear? What volume of seawater can you evaporate and at what rate? As you who built them know, our central node housings are at the bottom of the Mariana Trench.

"I forebear to mention our cities and arcologies occupying the Great Stalactite. What point would be served by opening fire?" continued the voice, now coming from a high-cheeked, sharp-featured woman who had not spoken previously, her eyes like night, her hair standing and swaying of its own accord. "The surface world, which is the only home or habitat hereafter available to you, defines the reach of your contemplated damage.

"Even were the threat sober," continued the Anserine sardonically, now speaking through the mouth of a thin, silver-haired man, "you would have limited time to carry it out. We are engaged in meteorological engineering. The ice caps are becoming vapor; cloud cover will soon increase dramatically, and the albedo of the planet become too reflective for space-borne mirrors to be effective. Meanwhile, the Exarchel circuits and systems aboard your vessel have returned to base-operation state, and are empty of data. Look. Even now the clouds are gathering, as all the snows of the world melt. So to whom will you give the command?"

Del Azarchel looked at Montrose, a look of surprise, of wild emotion, in his dark features. "Cowhand, I think they are *daring* me! What do you think?"

Menelaus Montrose was clenching and unclenching his maimed hand, so that the pain was worse and worse. He was idly wondering at what point the pain would make him go into shock, or faint. "I think I will never see Rania again. So you should burn at least some of them. Say! What happens if you melt the ion drive lance off the anchoring asteroid of your topless Tower? Can we get it to collapse? It should wrap around the equator six and half times before it comes to rest. That mass, falling at terminal velocity, would be—well, it would be the same as a ring-shaped cannonade of nine-mile-wide asteroids all hitting every inch of ground in a spiral belt around the world half a dozen times."

"Ha! Whenever I start hating you too much, Menelaus, you always say just the right thing to remind me why I so liked the way you thought when we were young. You have scope! Come: I will give the order, you will give the firing solution."

Del Azarchel strode in his clanking duelist's armor toward where the black-robed and -hooded Iron Ghosts of the Hermetic Order stood with some other people in a circle, facing inward: Ull and Coronimas, D'Aragó and De Ulloa. Ctesibius the Savant stood with them, solemn in his long white wig and his green robes trimmed with gold.

They stood in postures suggesting that they were conversing with someone their backs blocked from view. It was odd to see the Hermeticists from behind, for the dark silk shipsuit, from this angle only, was bright, since the uniform included a cape of white foil hanging from the shoulder.

Montrose walked with Del Azarchel, matching him stride for stride, and their heavy boots clanged together.

As they came near, they saw whom the Hermeticists addressed: Alalloel of Anserine. And behind her, on the other side of the circle, were his gathered Seconds: Illiance, Soorm, Mickey, Scipio, and Sir Guiden.

With them also stood the two Beta Maidens, Vulpina and Suspinia; Aea and Thysa the Nymphs; Keirthlin the Gray; and the blank-eyed but softly smiling Trey Azurine the Sylph. All stood on the back of a cnidarian which had not only landed, but flattened its circular mantle to the ground no thicker than a silvery carpet.

To one side, a little ways away, stood Oenoe the Nymph, writhed in her living mantilla of leaves and flowers. She was speaking with Sarmento i Illa d'Or, the only Hermeticist yet housed in a biological body.

Curious, Montrose turned his head that way, amplified his hearing, and sharpened his eyesight; then he noticed Del Azarchel had his gaze and attention turned the same way. He was not the only one who noticed: Sarmento i Illa d'Or raised his hand in a grave gesture, and beckoned them forward.

Oenoe dropped her eyes and curtseyed, bending her back leg and bowing at the waist, somehow making this awkward pose graceful and alluring. She stepped back, and then turned to walk with light footstep and overly swaying hip in the direction of where Sir Guiden, her husband, stood with the others, listening to Alalloel.

Sarmento spoke in the abbreviated fashion of posthumans familiar with each other's mental contours. If written out in words, the look on the face of Sarmento, the brief syllables he spoke, would have read, "Crewman Fifty-One. Ready for a rematch? I would not have shot at the ground."

And he gave Del Azarchel a look of scorn. Del Azarchel was taken by surprise, too puzzled to be angry at this unexpected hostility.

Montrose quirked an eyebrow, asking without words, "Nice to see you too, Learned i Illa d'Or, you pug-ugly soaplock. So what was that conversation about?" All three men turned and stared for a moment at the legs, hips, and general contours of the retreating girl in green.

Sarmento answered, partly in words, partly by implication, "She was asking me to bless her marriage. Do not look surprised, learned gentlemen: I am still, after all, the father of her race, and the creator of her world. You might think ill of my age, but she does not. Was there ever a time of greater happiness and peace?"

Del Azarchel said and implied, "A moment ago, I was your master, and the center of your loyalty, Learned i Illa d'Or. What changed?"

Sarmento answered in the same abbreviated way, "I was always loyal to our idea, not to your person, Senior. We stood for the principle that the higher form of life must rule the lower. Did we not? Was that not the motto we used to excuse everything, justify everything, allow ourselves everything? As it happens, the Swans are higher than you. Will you bow the knee to them? Or do you seriously think any of us will carry out your order to have the *Emancipation* open fire?"

Del Azarchel said and implied, "No matter where they are on the Darwinian scale of being, they are still in rebellion against me. Am I not, by their own rules, their lawful sovereign?"

"Have you lost your *mind*, Senior? The surface of this world is merely the hull of an Earth-sized fortress. What good would burning it do? Our most powerful weapons could not crack open the crust, much less reach down through the mantle to the outer core. We do not have the focusing power even to boil the seas away; and all the ice cap is rapidly becoming a cloud layer—like that the world enjoyed the last time the Cetaceans were in charge."

Del Azarchel turned away in disgust, and stomped in his heavy armor toward Alalloel.

Sarmento said softly to Montrose, "I wanted to kill the princess and make Del Azarchel Captain. He wouldn't do it. We would not have suffered all this trouble, millennia of toil, if only he'd done that. It would have been easy to let the princess die in some fashion, gently, without pain, which the Little Big Brother would not have considered murder. It was a stupid machine, after all, easy to fool, and we should not have been so afraid of it."

Little Big Brother had been the internal security system aboard the antimatter-star-mining vessel. It enforced the rules and regulations to prevent exactly what had happened, the mutiny of the crew. The human crew had outsmarted the simplistic Mälzel brain of the ship by offering Rania, who shared genetic and legal traits with Captain Grimaldi, as the new Captain; and the ship's brain had no choice but to accept the deception.

Montrose gave him a level, cool look. "Blackie shot at the ground because he realized that the Melusine wanted me dead. The moment the snow started sublimating, he figured it out. He is a bad man, don't get me wrong, and needs killing if ever a man did; but he's got some sort of principles. One of them is not doing dirty work for any critter not polite enough to ask it of him. Do you have any principles?"

"Of course. I serve the pleasure principle. Everyone does. I merely admit it."

Montrose looked up toward the second sun still hanging in the heavens, the visible reflection in the wide mirror surfaces of the unseen starship sails of a ship too small to see. "Would it please you to have us out of your hair? You, the Melusine, everyone?"

Sarmento's eyes goggled, *"Us?"*

One advantage of dealing with a fellow posthuman was that there was no need to stand around and explain things. Montrose stomped in his armor over to where Del Azarchel stood facing Alalloel.

Del Azarchel turned his head when Montrose came up. "You will be fascinated by this, Cowhand. Your ungrateful creatures who have condemned us to live and die as mortals are attempting to negotiate how the upcoming ten billion from the past eras will fit into their social structure. They are finding the prospect somewhat overwhelming."

Montrose said, "I am glad they ain't so cold-assed as to merely beef them or set them down in the middle of icy nowhere to die. But the social structure should be obvious, if they are so much smarter than us. If I can see it, they can: The Witches are to look after the Moreaus and the environment, but any who grasp for long life will become part of the Swan Hierarchy, and get their souls absorbed. The Chimerae are to become the military caste, since their eugenic dreams have achieved more than success—the perfect race has, after all, been brought forth, but if the Chimerae start wars or kick up a row too great, the Swans can interfere. The Nymphs act as peacemakers and secret police, but they damn well better avoid the pleasures of electronic nirvana, or else they will get absorbed also. The Inquilines get to act as intermediaries between the First Humans and the Second. It is what they are suited for."

Soorm spoke up in a gruff voice, "And what of us? What role can the Hormagaunts play in their many-racial world of races who all hate each other? We are a folk, a race, whose only virtue and talent is for cannibalism and genetic vampirism, a race too dangerous to live."

Montrose said, "There is no place on Earth for you. Be pioneers, space explorers, since your people alone can adapt themselves to space conditions and not regret the loss of Earthly flesh. Your people can oversee the terraforming of Mars and Venus, and change each year as the environment changes and becomes more Earthlike."

Montrose turned to the Anserine. "These options must have been clear to you from the beginning."

Alalloel of the Anserine said, "You are assuming the Swan Paramounts will permit independent minds to exist."

Del Azarchel said, "That is not the problem. The Swans do not have the mathematics worked out to express a solvable equation for how the seven races are meant to be interrelated."

Montrose looked at him sidelong. "Give it to them."

Del Azarchel raised an eyebrow. "Rather than burn my planet they are stealing from me? In heaven's name, why?"

Montrose snorted. "And here I thought you said the Earth was irrelevant."

Del Azarchel scowled. "Irrelevant if I give the Earth away. All-important if Earth is stolen."

Montrose said to Alalloel, "The Jupiter Brain will wake up eventually, and vastly, vastly outmatch your intelligence. You indicated the event was beyond your timebinding threshold. You don't give a damn about nothing that happens so far in the future."

Alalloel said, "Indeed we do not. Why should we? If the Hyades conquer, what will the rest matter?"

Montrose said, "So. I assume that applies to me as well. You just want me gone, not dead. Am I right? Del Azarchel will agree to give you his equations—"

Del Azarchel said archly, "Oh? Will I?"

"—and you will have the tools needed to rule a world of impossibly incompatible subspecies of mankind, if in return you agree to declare any human being—or his property—who does not have any circuit installed in his nervous system connecting him to your Noösphere a free and independent entity."

Alalloel said sharply, "You seek to possess the *Emancipation*, and to flee to space to escape our jurisdiction. To this, we will not consent."

Montrose said, "You already have the laws and customs to deal with free and independent entities: just consider any Thaws, or all, to be legally the same as Inquilines and Anchorites. Anyone not mentally connected to your Noösphere will neither overwhelm your infrastructure nor have need to follow your chain of command. Exarchel occupied and killed Pellucid, and took over all his higher functions, and you in turn occupied and killed Exarchel, but I think you will find that certain base commands and attitudes are hardwired into the system that now forms the basis of your worldwide mind. Pellucid is congenitally unable to interfere with human beings, and not allowed to kill them if they are off Tomb ground, except in retaliation or self-preservation. Like it or not, that rule is part of your psychology now. It is programmed at a basic level where you are not likely to be able to get at it. Unless you want to back out of occupying Pellucid right now, and return to your previous levels of intellect, and just be a normal, slow, stupid old posthuman like Blackie and me? If you disagree, think of the time you will spend trying to figure out how to reprogram your own brain—assuming it can be done at all. If you agree, think of how much trouble you save yourself."

Alalloel thoughtfully spread her wings. Her many eyes adorning the metallic feathers glinted and gleamed as countless invisible communication rays fed into the local area, communing.

Eventually she snapped her wings shut. Alalloel said, "We agree to the proposition, but to nothing further. Provisions will be made to treat all sub-posthuman life and disconnected life, both mechanical and biological, as Anchorites not obligated to our Noösphere protocol."

Montrose glanced at Del Azarchel. "You asked me to set up a firing solution? This is it."

Del Azarchel sighed. "I would rather burn the planet, but obviously, that would be a brutal gesture accomplishing nothing." He fished an old-fashioned data coin out from his poke, and tossed it with a negligent flick of his thumb toward Alalloel. "My proprietary research on the psychological modes and methodologies of the Jupiter Mind. The same mathematical models can be applied to living beings as to emulations. These races were actually designed to have complementary strengths and weaknesses, checks and balances, to fit into my proposed overall system. Here: it is yours."

Del Azarchel turned to Montrose. "Why did you not ask for a spare hibernation unit and a Xypotech to run it? We could have gotten that and more."

Montrose said, "Nope. For one thing, this Noösphere is now a Potentate, a planetary mind. The only reason why it does not want to brute-force recalculate your works is because it's inefficient to reinvent the wheel. They are actually doing us a favor, on account of they are tender hearted and don't want to kill all the billions of Thaws about to be dumped on them."

Del Azarchel scowled at Alalloel. "Then why did they bargain with us at all?"

"My guess is that the Swan Hierarchy is not going to maintain itself as a hierarchy very long. You saw the social vectors of their fundamental construction. They are archindividualists: I suspect they are only maintaining their group mind for so long as the current crisis lasts."

Del Azarchel said, "What crisis?"

"Us."

Alalloel said, "You speak with greater insight than one of your level of intellect should be able to reach. We find this disquieting, and yet it confirms our previous conclusion."

Montrose said, "What conclusion?"

"You and Del Azarchel are too dangerous. There is something embedded in the Monument: a potential, an emergent property, which you unwittingly copied into yourself with your Prometheus Formula, and which you again copied into Exarchel, whose thought patterns have many times been recopied into the version of Del Azarchel you see before you. The matter goes beyond mere differences in intelligence. There is something, some spirit in you, some essential property that cannot be defined nor contained. You will live out your natural lives in this century, having no additional recourse to biosuspensive hibernation nor to computer emulation nor to any other method of perpetuating your patterns of consciousness."

Montrose said softly, "Blackie. As far as I know, you ain't never out-and-out broken your word. In all your years as world tyrant and baby-smooching politician, I never heard tell of you giving your sworn word and breaking it—and so I reckon you are superhuman after all. Is that still so? You still a man of your word?"

Alalloel looked on with amazement on her finely boned, delicate features. "What is this? Do you still, at this late hour, intend some deception, some maneuver? The entire volume of Pellucid, overlaid with the lobotomized layer upon layer of Exarchel—the world consciousness—is ours. We are not merely the Swan Paramounts: we are Earth. There is no resource in your reach that we cannot foresee."

Montrose held out his hand. "What do you say, Blackie? Truce? Up until we see Rania again. If we don't, neither of us will see her, not never. Pax?"

Del Azarchel put out his hand. "Truce. You have my word." He tried to keep a smile off his features, but he could not. He grinned, and his teeth were very white against his dark beard.

Alalloel said, "We will be able to foresee and forestall anything which you—"

Montrose reached out and touched one of the eyes on the feathers of her neural cloak. He said, in English, "Null. Classify same, retroactive through all databases." He pointed at Del Azarchel, "Null and classify as null."

5. Hysterical Blindness

Del Azarchel burst out with the laughter he had been holding in. "No, my dear Swans, you will indeed be able to foresee anything he is about to do unless you have a code built into your base psychology creating a blind spot you cannot see through. Oh, my. That is amusing to see it finally happen to someone else. Refreshing."

Montrose turned to the others gathered there. "Anyone else? I don't have time to speak to every member of each race that comes up, so you people gathered here have to decide for them. 'Taint very democratic-like, but we're pressed for time."

Soorm said, "If you can turn us invisible to the Noösphere, what was the point of negotiating our places in the civilization that is to come?"

Montrose said, "My magic only affects their perceptions, not their memories or legal agreements. They won't be able to see you, up until the moment any one of y'all is dumb enough to stick a telephone or a library chip in your head or something like that. I cannot make the Locusts into phantasms. But that does not mean they cannot make a deal with you, make swaps and trades, all that good stuff. The shoemaker does not need to see the elves to make a deal, just leave out the shoe leather and a bowl of milk. Who wants in to the world of phantasms? It will be a life of hardship."

Trey Azurine would not answer, but merely shrugged.

Scipio said, "There are no Giants here, but I will speak on their behalf, as the only surviving Cryonarch. Hide them in the phantasm system."

Ctesibius said, "It would ill behoove the glory of the Savant race if we hid from the world that is the expression of what we sought. For myself and for the Scholars, I say we shall be visible. We decline the offer."

Sarmento i Illa d'Or said, "The Hermetic Order will also decline the offer. These Swans are insane if they think to oppose the Hyades, but we have learned over the centuries never to dispute creatures higher on the Darwinian scale. We will remain visible. They have offered us a place in their service."

Mickey said, "How are these Swan creatures different from the Machine? Make the whole race of the Wise into your phantasms, I beseech you."

Vulpina said, "The Chimerae are a free people. We can survive without the eyes of these godlike, therefore hateful, creatures on us. Camouflage us."

Sir Guiden said, "Any men from the world before the Giants could not understand the thoughts or the meaning of these Swans, and it would crush their spirits. The elder race of which I believe I am the only representative here, base-stock *Homo sapiens*, on their behalf, I ask for the sanctuary of invisibility to their eyes."

Oenoe said, "Our race was made to carry no metals and emit no waves, so that the men of the factory-dark cities and the bloodstained iron fastnesses of war would never see us. We will live in the woods unseen: this is our way. The Einheriar and Valkyrie, our military orders, you must excuse, however, from your work. The Swan must see and speak with them, if they are to be used against the Hyades in the futile gesture of impossible war for love of which they entered your Tombs, O Judge of Ages Past."

Soorm said, "Is this a trick question? I don't want those creepy things watching me."

Ull said, "I speak for the Locusts. We are part of the Noösphere of this age."

Keirthlin said, her strange, silvery eyes gleaming, "And I speak for Inquilines. When and if we are convinced the Potentate of Earth is benevolent, it will be simple enough to restore our tendrils and seek union. Make us phantasms."

And everyone was surprised when Alalloel said, "And us as well."

6. All Bets Are Off

Only three voices came from her mouth.

Montrose stared at her. "How come you can still see and hear me?"

She said, "I—this one whose body this is—I am of the Lree. I am a Melusine. The Melusine did not slay Exarchel or invade the brain space of Pellucid. We are not Swans. Our psychology and philosophy is nothing like that of these semianarchic *Pan sapiens* creatures you accidentally created. We have no interest in being forced to be part of their system, until and unless we are assured that the principle of strict reciprocity is followed, both on a personal and on a macroscopic scale."

Montrose touched the feather of her cloak again and he issued the commands.

The winged men, women, dwarfs and giants, dolphins and other shapes either hovering in the air or standing throng on throng along the steaming, vapor-breathing hillsides staggered and spread their wings in alarm, countless eyes glinting frantically.

Montrose said, "You will still be able to speak with them, make deals, even go them to settle disputes, by talking through Ctesibius or any other Savant who wakes. He touches the Noösphere only with a one-way link. Locusts might also be able to act as intermediaries, depending on their degree of neural immersion."

Mickey stepped forward. "Where are you going?"

Montrose said, "Where you cannot follow. This has only been one-sixth of the time between Rania's departure in A.D. 2401 and her earliest possible date of return in A.D. 70000 when Kochab and Pherkad are the pole stars. And even that shall be only the first beginning of my life."

"Or mine," smiled Del Azarchel darkly. He said to Mickey in Latin, "Come with us. Montrose will not mind, and perhaps I can persuade you to take up my service again, be a Savant, and create an emulation of yourself, a greater soul. You will be deathless."

Sir Guiden stepped near, and spoke. "Before you hear him, discover from the Hermeticists if his offers lead to joy or grief."

Del Azarchel narrowed his darkly glimmering eyes. "I spoke no false things to them. I told them plainly they were my dogs, and I their master. Had they obeyed me in all things and in all thoughts, they would know no reason to utter complaint. I was honest in my word."

"Honesty in word is laudable, Master of the World, but it excuses no sins," said Sir Guiden.

Del Azarchel turned his head and said to Montrose, "Is this your creature? Tell him to curb his tongue and remind him who he addresses. If he is not your creature, then do not interfere should I deign to smite him."

Montrose said, "Climb off your buggerified high horse, Blackie, before you get a nosebleed. You ain't smiting nobody, not for a goodly parcel of time as yet. Sir Guy, this here is my friend Blackie, and he is a *pullelo*, a gutter rat from Toledo in Spain, who is trying hard to live up to some crazy-ass notion of chivalry he learned from a man named Trajano during a hard period of his hard life, so don't tell his flaws out to him, it ain't fitting. Blackie lost his empire today, so don't irk him. Again. What can I do for you, Sir Guy?"

"Liege, I have kept faithfully your service for lo, these thousands and thousands of years. But now all the Tombs are being raised, and all the dead shall waken, and many of these will be weakened and wounded and seek of many cures. The mission of the Knights of the Hospital of Jerusalem is with the sick who seek our sanctuary; and my heart is here." He held out his left hand, and Oenoe took it, smiling, her beauty made all the more beautiful by her joy. She blushed, and did not look the posthumans in their eyes.

"I release you," said Montrose, with a note of sorrow in his voice. "We've been through a lot. Well, slept through a lot. Almost the same thing."

Mickey said, "Am I not to come with you?"

Montrose said, "I am not going to tell you yes or no, but I have a woman waiting for me up yonder in the far tomorrows, and I do not give a good goddam how many lives and how many centuries I have to tuck behind me. You can come if you like, but I have found out there just ain't no guarantee that the future will be any better than the past, no matter what the optimists say, and there just ain't no guarantee that the future will go on getting worse and worse, no matter what the pessimists say. For that matter, there is no guarantee that things will stay mixed good and bad, sinners and saints together, with no great change to human nature, because there have been times in the past that things turned a corner and nothing was never the same again. I don't know what the people are called who think things don't get worse and don't get better. Mediocretists? But whatever they are called, there is no guarantee of them being right neither, because there just is no guarantees about the future. All bets are off. That goes double for the far future."

Mickey said, "But I heard the Swans pronounce your sentence. Long-term biosuspension requires the use of a Xypotech to track all the cellular movements in a man's body. No machine on Earth will serve you, even if you were visible to any of them."

Del Azarchel said, "All things have come together, my dear friendly Witch, in just such a way that Montrose and I cannot do, either one of us, without the other. He has made a bargain with Sarmento so that the now-empty Xypotech core at the axis of the *Emancipation* can be filled and reestablished from my Xypotech, a new version of Exarchel, which he and I have the skills to create from the raw materials we have at hand, but neither of us alone. I have hibernation cells aboard the ship, he knows how to program them; I have savant equipment to create a new emulation of myself, he can use his solution to make him sane. And this time, I can make sure he puts no extra codes inside me. And I have a ship."

"My ship," grunted Montrose.

"Our ship," said Del Azarchel graciously. "The only place we can go, now that the world and the world's mind is hostile to us. We have a long hike ahead of us, not to mention a sea voyage, since the Tower will obey my command no longer to carry us aloft, and the only launching-landing craft in service, not beholden in any way to the Melusine or the Swans, is the one hidden in the bay of Saint Christopher's Island, just offshore of your Mount Misery Tomb facility. Unless you have a closer one tucked away? We will also need to raid your fabulous storehouses of legendary wealth, if you have some stout walking shoes and coats worth wearing."

Montrose said, "I will open my storehouses. Your eyes will fall out of your head when you see the treasures I've accumulated, because they bring me gifts, each one of the billions who sleep, or their close relations. But walk? Why walk? Mickey here stole a Witch plane not so long ago, and programmed the serpentine guiding it to land the crate not far away. I know the location. The serpentine power will last forever. It is a two-seater, and I am sure I can figure out how to pilot the darn thing after a crash or six. The thing is at least as steady as a World War One biplane."

"And the average life-span of a Flying Ace from those days was, what, again? Fourteen days?" asked Del Azarchel archly.

"Long enough to get us to Mount Misery." And the crooked grin on the lantern-jawed gargoyle face of Menelaus Montrose was something fearful to behold.

Mickey the Witch said, "I will stay in this era, and seduce a buxom Nymph or two, and find my love now."

Oenoe said softly to him, "Aea looks with favor on you, or can be made to do so once she adjusts her brain chemistry correctly. You will soon be hers."

Montrose said, "I warned you. Those women will take over your brain."

Mickey said, "I have no further use for it. Have you seen the size of her—"

"Those women are dangerous!" said Montrose.

"Should I live a nice, safe life like yours, then, Menelaus Montrose?" retorted the Witch.

"Well, if you are so reckless," said Blackie with a smile, "then come with us."

Mickey pondered, frowning. Then he said, "No. The depth and strangeness of the centuries and millennia you mean to cross appalls me: you will emerge from your sleep in a world as strange as some unnamed orb that circles Archenar or Bellatrix, but with no way home to any world you knew. Montrose will find his Lady Love, if the gods are with him and the world is just, and Del Azarchel will find despair, and a hell of eternal time unending.

"But as for me, what shall a Witch of simple tastes do in such unguessed aeons far remote? How can I worship oak and ash and thorn and all the sacred trees, if they are all extinct?

"No. My people are here. The future is not mine; but the present.

"For, see! Even now the first of the great doors on the far hillside moves earth and melting ice aside, and the golden light spills up. I hear the psalms of the Christians mingled with the chants of the Witches and the paeans of the Chimerae, and so, perhaps, the ancient enmities are for a season put aside.

"The men of every era emerge blinking into the sunlight of the latter-day world. It is already far too far in the future for me.

"Go, then, Judge of Ages and Master of the World, away from the Age and from the World that has exiled you, and seek you your strange dreams of love for a more-than-human girl. The blessings of earth and sky, hill and wood and water, and all that dwell therein, now and for aye be with you!"

APPENDIX A
Dramatis Personae

Last interment date in square brackets

Hermeticists

Menelaus Illation Montrose
Melchor de Ulloa—Master of the Witches
Narcís Santdionís de Rei D'Aragó—Master of the Chimerae
Sarmento i Illa d'Or—Master of the Nymphs
Venture Reyes y Pastor—Master of the Hormagaunts
Jaume Coronimas—Master of the Locusts
Ximen del Azarchel—Master of the World

Ghosts

Exarchel—the Dreagh or emulation of Del Azarchel
    Exo-exarchel—the backup template of Exarchel expelled into space
Exulloa, Exarago, Exillador, Excoronimas, Exynglingas, and Expastor—
    emulations

Scholar

Rada Lwa—Intermediately Evolved Learned Scholar Rada-Lwa Chwal Se-
quitur Argent-Montrose; Psychoi, brain augment to level 257, and a servant
of De Ulloa [A.D. 3090]

Cryonarch

Scipio—Advocate-General Scipio Cognition Montrose of the World Concordat, Regent at Large, Lord Protector of the Dead, Director of the Endymion

Hibernation Syndicate, aka Glorified Scipio Cognition Montrose, Endorcist of One and a Half Donations [A.D. 2519]

Knight Hospitalier

Sir Guy—His Excellency Grandmaster Emeritus Guiden von Hompesch zu
Bolheim [A.D. 2509]

Savant

Ctesibius—Glorified Ctesibius Zant, Endocist of Three Donatives, Servant of
the Machine [A.D. 2525]

Sylph

Trey—Third or Trey Soaring Azurine (tentative) [A.D. 2537]
Soaring Azurine, her aeroscaphe

Giant

Bashan—Dr. Bashan Christopher Colligorant Hugh-Jones [A.D. 3033]

Witches

Mickey—Melechemoshemyazanagual Onmyoji de Concepcion, Padre Bruja-
Stregone of Donna Verdant Coven from the Holy Fortress at Williamsburg;
his true name is Mictlanagualzin of the Dark Science Research Coven [A.D.
4733]
Fatin—Fatin Simon Fay, a maiden from the Simon Families period [circa
A.D. 3300]
Fuamnach—a crone of the Whalesong Coven
Ajuoga—a crone of the Stone Telling Coven
Lilura—a crone of the Clear Green Coven
Louhi—a crone of the Self-Esteem Pro-Choice Coven
Lorelei—a mother of the Mystic Crystal Revelation Coven
Drosselmeyer—a Warlock of the Old Iron Dreams Coven of Detroit
Crowley, Castaneda, and Twardowski of Wkra—other Warlocks
Heron—Heron of the Automaton Workers Coven Local 101, a factory hand
from the Butlerian Restoration [A.D. 4455]

Parnassus—Parnassus of the Golden Golem Coven of Lake Superior, an apothecary from the Nameless Empire period [A.D. 4490]

Various mundanes (lower-caste Witches)—12 Demonstrators (their warrior caste), a hunter, a farmer, a vintner, a mason, a factory hand, and an alchemist

Chimerae

Daae—Alpha Captain Varuman Aemileus Daae of Uttarakhand, Osaka, Bombay, Yumbulangang, and other actions in the South China Theater; the Varuman blood derives from the Osterman, from the *Homo sapiens*, and *Canis lupus* [A.D. 5402]

Yuen—Alpha-Steadholder Extet Minnethales Yuen of Richmond, Third and Second Manassas, Antietam, and various actions against Pirates; the Yuen are of the Original Experiment Set, from *Homo sapiens* and *Puma concolor* [A.D. 4881]

Grislac—his weapon

Arroglint the Fortunate—the named weapon of his lineage

Anubis—High-Beta Sterling Xenius Anubis of Mt. Erebus Dependent College, 102nd Civic Control Division, attached to the Pennsylvania 3rd Legion; genetics unknown, line unknown, possibly Crotalinae; the "Virginianized" version of this name is *Ir-Beta Sterlingas Xeniopater Anupsuphalangetor Erebumontsangil* [A.D. 5292]

Rock—his weapon

Phyle—Gamma Joct Goez Phyle of Bull Run, lineage discontinued

Ivinia—Alpha Lady Mother-of-Commandant Wife-of-Captain Ulec Nemosthene Ivinia nee Echtal; her victory title is *Septimilegens*

Callixiroc the Dark—the named weapon of the lineage of Ivinia

Vulpina—a young Beta women's auxiliary [A.D. 5316]

Suspinia—a young Beta women's auxiliary; originally named Handmaiden Seven of the Suspiring Nature Coven of Nome [A.D. 4812]

Kine

Larz—Kine Larz Quire Slewfoot of Gutter [A.D. 5950]

Franz, Ardzl, and Happy—other Kine

Nymphs

Oenoe—Oenoe Psthinshayura-Ah of Crocus with Clover and Forsythia [A.D. 6746]

Aea, Daeira, Ianassa, and Thysa—other Nymphs

Celaineus, Argennos, Aegicoros, and Omester—He-Nymphs, also called Satyrs

Iatrocrats

Soorm—Archormagaunt, also called Asvid the Old Man; originally, a Satyr named Marsyas of Saffron, with Oakwhite, Oleander, Rocket, and Mandrake [A.D. 7466]

Gload scion Ghollipog—Hormagaunt [A.D. 7520]

Crile scion Wept—Hormagaunt [A.D. 7810]

Prissy Pskov and Zouave Zhigansk—Clade-dwellers

Toil, Drudge, and Drench—Donors

Locusts

True Locusts (Onyx Men)

Crucxit, Axcit, and Litcec of Seven Twenty-One North Station [date not given: anywhere between A.D. 7480 and A.D. 10000, most likely circa A.D. 8000]

Inquiline Locusts (Blue Men)

Illiance—Illiance Vroy, a Locust Inquiline of the Order of Simplified Vulnerary Aetiology (the Simplifiers, aka the Blue Men); his false-mother-name is *Lagniappe* [A.D. 8800]

Ull—Ull Ynglingas, Illiance's Mentor

Orovoy, Naar, Yndelf, Yndech, and Ydmoy—Preceptors; Naar is the machinist

Saaev, Aarthroy, and Unwing—Blue Men of lower dignity: an Invigilator, a Docent, and a Bedel

Aanwen—Aanwen Leel, a Blue Widow; her dignity is Preceptrix

22 others, names not given

Tendrilless Locusts (Gray Men, also called Linderlings)

Keir and Keirthlin—Linder Keir Laialin and Linder Keirthlin Laialin of Northeastern Region, Fifteenth Configuration [A.D. 8866]

Followers

Eie Kafk Ref Rak—a canine Moreau (Irish wolfhound)
Ee-ee Krkok Yef Yepp—(a stately Doberman Pinscher)
Ktatch-Ee Yett Ya-Ia—(a Collie)
Rirk Refka Kak-Et—a Great Dane
196 others, names not given

Melusines

Alalloel—Alalloel u lal rir Lree, also called Alalloel of the Lree, Eighteenth
Configuration [A.D. 10100]
Legion—Alalloel when compiled and updated to the standards of the Final
Stipulation of the Noösphere Protocols; also called the Finality, these are
Melusine openly loyal to Del Azarchel

Swan

Anserine—Alalloel of the Anserine, a Paramount of the Second Humanity,
of unlimited mental configuration; occupying the same nervous system as
Alalloel, the exact nature of her continuity of persona is subject to debate

APPENDIX B
Small-scale Time Line

Dates whose events are portrayed in the text are in bold font.

Note: to calculate by the Chimerical Military calendar, merely subtract 1737 from A.D. to derive AUCR

Preposthuman Era (*Count to a Trillion*)

Genocide Century

1901–1930   The Great War, the effective end of monarchy in Europe. Invention of the aeroplane; mass-production of the automobile.

1931–1970   Economic Theory Wars. Socialists lose open conflict in 1940s, make immense gains through indirect means. British Empire lost. United States of America rises to world predominance. Sexual pathologies erupt in the West, become commonplace. Period of rapid intellectual decline: poetry ceases.

1969   First man on the moon.

1971–2000   The Crazy Years. Collapse of the Socialist Empire in the East. The Holiday from History. First world infosphere.

Century of Faith Wars

2001–2020   Little Jihad. Jerusalem, Tehran nuked. Economic collapse and civil war in China.

2021–2050   Indian Summer of Liberty, also called the Age of the Sovereign Individual. International banking system subverts and overthrows remnants of the Old World Order and establishes a semilibertarian plutocracy.

2054   Launch of the NTL *Croesus*.

2051–2070   International credit system collapses. Hyperinflation, world depression. End of the infosphere. Rule by the Local Military Governors, Advocates, or Euro-American Proconsuls established throughout Asia and Africa.

2071–2090 Greater Jihad.

2090 Burning of New York the Beautiful by Jihadi atomics. Historians count this as the beginning of the Little Dark Ages.

Little Dark Ages

In the confusion and mutual recriminations of the disaster of New York, the factions of the American political system resort to open violence, destroying the last democracy on the planet. Rapid disintegration of the international economic open order follows, followed by a sudden drop in technological application (albeit not scientific knowledge). Certain popular doctrines, rife with foolish economic errors and ancient religious prohibitions on usury, are enforced with particular fury in both the Islamic and the Christian world, and meanwhile the Chinese and Japanese economic spheres fall prey to a strange philosophy that combines the worst elements of Marxism, Buddhism, and Confucianism (Xun Ziism, the Way of the Wise). Only in the severed and warring states of India does anything approaching sane economic practice prevail, and it is among their splintered princedoms that the civilization to dominate the next two centuries rises.

The Jihad is a more or less continuous effort during these years, an ongoing attempt to make the West and Far East more favorable to sharia law, or to grant special privileges to Muslims. The British Parliament is dissolved during the confusion and riots following the Abecedarian War (2139 until at least 2182, the Treaty of Charleston; historians disagree as to an end date). The Plague is an Abecedarian attack, meant to wipe out the Jews: 2165 is when the virus is released, 2216 is the last known untreatable case of the spore.

2091 Jefferson Dayles refuses to step down when impeached, instead attempts a coup. Succession Wars in the USA.

2092 Joint Chiefs of Staff assume administration "for the duration." Beginning of the Imperial Federal Government.

2111–2150 Rise of India. Genetic manipulation of castes in India.

2112 The *Croesus* arrives at V886 Centauri and begins mining. FIRST CONTACT.

2120–2220 The Starvation Years. Famine reaches worldwide levels in A.D. 2120.

2121 Disunion War. American Imperium breaks into People's Ergo-

	nomic Positive Republic of California, the Gaianist Democratic Union of America, and the Confederate States of America (informally known as Oddifornia, Greenyland, and Jesusland, respectively).
2139	Abecedarian War begins (so called because it is Atomic, Biological, and Chemical).
2150–2170	The Harmonious Forward Leap Together. Japan makes territorial gains along the coast of North and South America, establishing enclaves, and erecting schools and factories.
	Reindustrialization spreads from the Orient. Supremacy of Japan under the Tenno. Cyber-Shintoism. Japanese establish the Co-Prosperity Sphere in the Pacific, from Australia to the Aleutians, and parts of California. Pacific Rim Wars. Artificial Volcanism first used as military terror-weapon.
2151	The Big One. The long-expected San Andreas earthquake destroys the coastal cities of California. The coastline is shattered into an archipelago. Japanese commercial interests and military units are invited in by Sacramento to restore prosperity and order. Oddifornia becomes a client state of the Tenno.
2155	The Southwest frees itself from California, declares itself Aztlan, a province of Reino del Extasis, the federated drug-theocracy stretching from Mexico to Brazil.
2162	Presumed date of first broadcast from the *Croesus*, lost in transmission.
2165	Persian nomads release the Final Solution Bacillus: Plague Years begin (also called the Fifty Years).
2166	Presumed date of second broadcast from the *Croesus*, lost in transmission.
2170	First reception of broadcasts from the *Croesus*. First pictures of the Monument studied on Earth. Monument notation revolutionizes logic, semantics, mathematics, and gives rise to a suite of analytical techniques called Semiotic Quantification.
2171–2190	Semiotic analysis of the human genome prompts the First Revolution in Biotechnology. Rapid advances in bioengineering.
2176–2180	Reconquista. Southwestern United States overrun by Mexico.
2176	The Armed Republic of Greater Texas breaks away from the Confederacy.
2180	Semiotic analysis of semantic neuropsychology prompts the Linguistic Consequentialism theory, or "Volksseele," first in Dutch

	Africa, later in Europe; first as an academic theory, later as a political movement. As a result, nation-states, blamed for the horrors of depopulation and war, begin to lose predominance to Lingospheres.
2181	The Kali Yuga. India reduces the Middle East and Indochina to radioactive wasteland, bombs European cities. Effective end of the Jihad. Copts rise to power in Egypt.
2182	Treaty of Charleston essentially ends the Abecedarian War.
2187–2190	Linguistic Laws, first in France and Germany, and later throughout the civilized nations, require subjects to declare their primary language, and to avow loyalty to it, rather than to nation-states.
2191–2196	Iberian War. Indosphere retreats from African and Far Eastern possessions.
2199	Last of the Great Apes perishes in captivity. Ximen del Azarchel born.

The Purifications

2205–2207	Clean Mediterranean War. Noted for the lack of atomic or biological weapons. Coptic Order gains control from Tripoli to Armenia, called Greater Egypt.
2209	Napoleon Montrose born.
2210	Menelaus Montrose born. His father dies that same year.
2210–2230	Spain reestablishes intercontinental electronic systems with South America, issues letters of Marque and Reprisal, begins to clear the high seas of piracy. Texmexicans repopulate the Mississippi Valley and western territories.
2211–2216	Japanese Winter. Early Japanese-led attempts in planetary weather control via orbital parasol system end in climate disaster.
2211	Leonidas born.
2216	Last known untreatable case of the spore. End of the Plague.
2216–2222	Menelaus ages 6 to 12 in Bridge-to-Nowhere.
2217	Menelaus is apprenticed to an Artificer at age 7 (this means he would have risen to journeyman at age 14 in A.D. 2224, to be released at 21 in A.D. 2231, assuming the master kept honest debt records).
2220	End of the Starvation Years.
2221	At age 11, Menelaus vows enmity to Darwin, imaging him to be a cartoon villain.

2224–2230   Counterreconquest. Texas annexes Aztlan.

2225–2226   From ages 15 to 16, Menelaus sees service in the Counterreconquest. Sam Feckle dies on campaign against Utah.

2230   India lands an expedition on the moon, explores and restores the long-dead Tycho Base. With the resumption of manned space travel, this year is accounted the end of the Little Dark Ages.

2231–2250   Spain and India cooperate on a space program, including an interstellar expedition.

2232   At age 22, Menelaus is already an attorney and duelist (who has fought four men, killing two). Mike Nails is his third kill. Menelaus is frozen for fifteen months; his calendar and biological ages are no longer synchronized.

2234   Menelaus attends Soko University in San Francisco, at that time one of the Japanese enclaves of California, owned by the Sumitomo Zaibatsu.

2235   Launch of the NTL *Hermetic*. At age 25cal/24bio, Menelaus boards the punt for NTL *Hermetic*. An experiment with a mind-augmenting neuropharmaceutical renders him unfit for voyaging. He is biosuspended.

2244–2324   Reign of Queen Gloriana of the United Kingdom.

2250–2300   Rise of Azania. Ultradeep robotic mining techniques (later used to bore the depthtrain system) lower cost of extracting South African uranium, diamonds, oil. Discovery of the motherlode of uranium in Pretoria.

2265   Pacific War. Called "the Pacifist War" because peace protestors swing the victory to the Japanese in their territorial disputes with Texas for control of the West Coast.

2260–2270   Greater Texas makes territorial gains in California, Baja California, and the Pacific Northwest.

2285   NTL *Hermetic* arrives at the Diamond Star V886 Centauri.

2287   Leonidas (76cal/76bio) enters biosuspension, hoping to live until Montrose returns.

2290   *Hermetic* crew erects radio-laser of sufficient power to narrowcast to Earth.

2297–2299   The Irish Catholic Movement, the so-called Gaelosphere.

2299   Denmark is made a possession of the British Crown during the Second War of Jenkins' Ear (so dubbed by journalists for the artificiality of the causus belli against Spain).

2300	End of the Indosphere dominion. Spain, supported by South American technocracy, emerges as a dominant power in Europe. Hispanosphere Collective.

Concordat Century

2300	Rania born.
2303	Sinosphere–Anglosphere conflicts in the Pacific spread from Australia to California.
2306	Rania is 6bio when mutiny breaks out. Eight of her nine fathers are killed.
2310	*Hermetic,* under de facto command of Ximen del Azarchel the mutineer, departs from V886 Centauri. Rania is 10bio, and is the de jure Captain.
2323	Thucydides Acumen Montrose, later Father Montrose of the Society of Jesus and Pope Sextus VI, born to Patton and Athenodora Montrose.
2332	Hispanosphere erects the Beanstalk (Torre Real de Estrellas).
2333	The Germanosphere (that is, the Boers of Azania) enters the Sinosphere–Anglosphere conflict.
2333–2338	Yellow War. Japanese outposts in California treated with sickening brutality by Boers. The Reunited States suffer a constitutional crisis.
2339	Japanese home islands invaded. Members of the Imperial Family placed in biosuspension.
2340	First narrowcasts arrive from *Hermetic:* revolution in mathematics has implications in biotechnology, cybernetics. Universal Logical Syntax "the Notational Logic" developed, Unified Field Theory, Uniform-to-Manifold Genesis Theory, Automata Cell Theory. German superiority in mathematics allows this language group to exploit the new knowledge more extensively than others.
2340–2360	Rise of the Germanosphere, led by the Boers (Azania) of South Africa, to world dominion. They enforce medical purity laws in order to combat diseases left over from previous wars, particularly venereal diseases. They ally with the Xi Mandarins in Manchuria and the Coptic Christians of Greater Egypt, and form the Purity Order.
	During this period, the Reunited Confederate States of America lose power and prestige; Kansas, a haven of Azanian technology, breaks away. America is balkanized.
2341	Japan becomes a client state of the Purity Order.

2343   George Edge of Hong Kong writes an influential series of essays
            on the relaxation of moral discipline due to virtuality addiction.
            The philosophy is called Condemnationalism.

2344   Japanese nationalists thaw the Imperial Family survivors from
            biosuspension. Emperor Mikohito officially embraces Condem-
            nationalism (abstinence from neural implantation) as proper to
            the Japanese national spirit. Cyber-Shinto becomes the first reli-
            gion to define neuralimplantation as ritually impure. Certain
            Christian denominations also condemn the practice, but on moral
            grounds. Condemnationalism becomes the official doctrine of the
            Copts, later of the whole Purity Order.

2350   Mandatory Health Assurance system in South Africa makes gene-
            tic "designer babies" mandatory. Azanians rendered immune to all
            known natural diseases.

2359   Signals from the incoming *Hermetic* persuade the Purity Order to
            shoulder the vast expense of launching a spaceborne braking
            laser, in order to slow and intercept the wealth-laden *Hermetic*.
            (Leonidas, as per his instructions, is thawed from hibernation,
            148cal/76bio.)

2360   The *Hermetic* arrives in the solar system, is attacked, defends her-
            self, destroys the navigation satellites of the Purity Order. Rania
            persuades the Purity Order to surrender. (She is 60cal/19bio—
            the speed of the return voyage was higher, due to abundant anti-
            matter fuel, and hence there was more severe Lorentz-Fitzgerald
            contraction. Only nine years shiptime passed.)

2360–2369   A political-economic worldwide or "Tellurian" Concordat, devised
            by Rania using Cliometry, is established, with the Hermetic Or-
            der as its informal head. Rania is placed in suspension soon
            thereafter, allegedly due to maladaptation to Earth conditions.
            The *Hermetic* is retired from active service, but kept aloft allegedly
            as a floating museum; actually to tend the contraterrene satellites.

2361   Leonidas (150cal/78bio) meets Rania (61cal/20bio), and is pres-
            ent when she thaws and examines Menelaus, who is incurable and
            returned after a month to biosuspension. Rania is commanded to
            return to biosuspension by the Hermeticists. Leonidas, heartbro-
            ken, dies. Fr. Thucydides Montrose, S.J. (38cal/38bio) adminis-
            ters the Extreme Unction. True to the last wish of Leonidas,
            Thucydides also enters biosuspension.

2370   First successful experiments in modest intelligence augmentation

	in prenatal subjects genetically designed to receive it. Psychics, Scholars, created.
2385	Fears of predicted warfare disturb the counsels of Del Azarchel (which will eventually compel the Hermeticists to revive Rania in 2390; see below).
2390	Rania revived amid general celebration for the twenty-fifth anniversary of the Tellurian Concordat (90cal/20bio). That same year, Honoré VI, with the advice and consent of the Concordat, abdicates in favor of Rania. She is crowned Sovereign of Monaco. Thucydides thawed (67cal/38bio).
2392	The Hermeticists, fearing Rania, force her back into hibernation (92cal/22bio).
2399	After much procrastination, Menelaus is revived (189cal/25bio). Rania (99cal/22bio) is thawed and effects a partial cure. Menelaus, as Hyde, deciphers the Iota through Kappa segments of the Monument, so the claim of the Hyades Domination over Earth is revealed. The Xypotech emulation of Del Azarchel achieves post-human intelligence levels.
2400	Menelaus meets Rania at a New Year's Eve party. She is 100cal/23bio.
2401	Menelaus marries Rania at San Francisco de Quito. Second Revolution in Biotechnology, due to Hermetic technology and techniques being made public. War breaks out, and causes a crash of the Data Environment, and Menelaus is cut off from Rania when her ship launches. She departs, uprooting the Celestial Tower of Quito. Menelaus, 191cal/27bio, enters cold sleep. Rania is 101cal/23bio. Thucydides hibernates (69cal/40bio).

Interregnum

2400–2480	General breakdown of law and order. Loss of the monetary system. Depthtrain system becomes unreliable.
2401	Exarchel orders the wounded bodies of Menelaus and Del Azarchel hospitalized and placed in biosuspension. The coffin of Menelaus is spirited away by Ozymandias Montrose, a Psychoi (Scholar) loyal to Rania.
2402	The sudden departure of the world contraterrene supply, expropriated by Rania, collapses the monetary system, cripples the energy industry, and triggers global depression.

The Chinese directorate moves to impose rationing and wage and price controls throughout the Chinese sphere of influence. The Australian market, taking the opposite tack, permits speculators to make fortunes during the turmoil: this sudden wealth is used to buy up land in the real world and server space in the Data Environment. The Concordat, which theoretically has final say over economic policy touching trade and immigration between member nations, is discredited, and its jurisdiction ignored. The entanglement of economic interests, in a world where Peking is a forty-five-depthtrain-minute commute from Sydney, and there are no trade barriers whatever had been the rule since 2360, can no longer be peacefully separated along national boundaries. The Australians and Chinese attempt to rediscover and reimpose national sovereignty, each pursuing a course incompatible with the other, and each in an angry panic brought on by shantytown riots. By no coincidence, the armed forces of both powers are swollen with unemployed young men.

2402–2404 The Indochinese War breaks out between China and Australia, and spreads to India, Madagascar, and Mesopotamia. Exarchel ruthlessly atom-bombs Peking and Canberra and quells the open war after two years; acts of terror and assassination continue.

Populations flee into cryonic hibernation in record numbers.

2403, 2405, 2416, 2440, 2453 Montrose thawed and his biological age climbs from 27 to 41.

2404   The Encryption. New Information Protocols erected in the world datasphere: machine languages become incomprehensible and untranslatable into any human mathematical system. Montrose briefly thawed (193cal/28bio.)

Tradition identifies this date as the beginning of the period of the Judgment. All ages of mankind are hereafter held to be subject to the condemnation of the Judge of Ages.

2405–2409 The Humanist War (later called the First Global Civil War) begins as police actions in Pacifica, ostensibly to overthrow the reign of Exarchel and restore Del Azarchel. Sino-Australian Axis galvanized by the Salon of Simplicity, run by Tsian Belascu, an influential nature-worshipper, and joins the Pacific states in rebellion. Chinese-backed power prevails, but the Exarchel Xypotech is deleted from all known mainframes. Del Azarchel returns to power as Nobilissimus (Supreme Executive of the Special Advocacy).

Menelaus thawed (195cal/27bio).

2409   The Blackout. No electronic records of any kind exist between January and October of this year. Del Azarchel flees to northern Germany. North America in civil chaos. Rise of the Montrose Clan, remote descendents of Menelaus Montrose's ten brothers, to posts of leadership, first in enclaves in Nevada.

Since the landed property of the slumbering clients is effectively under the control of the Montrose Hibernation Syndicate, and since entering hibernation cures nearly all known bodily ills, the entering world population becomes beholden to the Montrose Clan both for their power use and for their medical health. The Concordat constitution observes no clear demarcation between political and economic power: the Montrosines soon parlay these advantages into an unstoppable political machine, and suppress dissent to their rule.

Beginning of the Cryonarchy. Menelaus now 199cal/31bio.

Cryonarch Period

2410s   First Augmentation experiments on Hermeticists end in madness and disaster. At about this time, Exarchel, commanding the Hermeticists of Japan and Micronesia, begins augmentation experiments on dolphins and whales. First Cetaceans.

Rada Lwa becomes a Scholar at about this time.

2413–2418   Second Global Civil War. The Special Advocacy overthrows the remaining Hermeticists. A strike team led by Athena Montrose seizes control of the orbital Petawatt Deceleration Laser, now dubbed *Surtur*.

Montrose thawed from 2416 to 2418 and he ages from 206cal /32bio to 208cal/34bio.

2420–2439   Montrose Clan, able to provide broadcast power to any princes or local governments swearing fealty to them, spreads their suzerainty across the Southwestern States, Baja and Central America to Panama, the Canadian Northwest, and Alaska to Kamchatka.

2439–2445   Third Global Civil War. Montrose Clan selected to the Special Advocacy of the Concordat. Imposition of uniform laws governing Thaws and Currents. Division into Northern and Southern Concordats along racial lines, Sino-Caucasian (Northern) and Afro-Spaniard (Southern).

Montrose thawed from 2440 to 2445 and ages from 230cal/35bio to 235cal/40bio.

2450–2453 Fourth Global Civil War. Balkanization of the Southern Concordat into the Twelve Districts. Montrose thawed for 2453 (243cal/41bio).

2467–2471 Fifth Global Civil War. During this period, the Russian spaceport at Baikonur is restored to working order. Inconclusive peace. Northern Districts balkanized (Gallic, Russo-Persian, and Quebecois Directorships). Emulations of world leaders made in secret. (Ctesibius, perhaps self-servingly, lists this as the beginning of the Golden Age of the Ghosts.)

2470   Del Azarchel departs from Earth, and takes up residence amid the ruins of the Mare Ingenii Lunar Pit (or Lava Tube) Base from the Second Space Age, which he restores to habitability.

2476   During this period, the Advocacy cooperates with Exarchel.

2481   Frankenstein Panic. World computer systems wrecked by mobs or dismantled by police.

2481–2486 The Darkness. A complete computer blackout worldwide. Transatlantic cables cut, communications satellites downed.
           First evidence of shipping destroyed by Cetaceans.

2485   At about this time, Rania and the scientists aboard the *Hermetic* begin the macroscale engineering project to turn the V886 Centauri star system and its magnetosphere into a near-lightspeed ramscoop. The gas giant Thrymheim is destroyed and fed into the antimatter star.

2490s   All seaborne shipping halted by Cetacean piracy. Eastern and western hemispheres maintain only tenuous contact by air travel.

2501   Collapse of the Cryonarchy. Montrose dispossesses the Montrose Clan, and turns to the Knights Hospitalier for aid and sanctuary. Release of the Prometheus Formula.

Ecclesiarch Period (Age of the Giants)

2501–3060 The Uniate Orthodox-Catholic Church is given the orbital elements of the remaining centaurs of contraterrene by Montrose, as well as control of the Hibernation Syndicate. Under Thucydides Montrose, S.J., later Pope Sixtus VI, the Church uses her energy monopoly and control of slumbering populations to achieve world

	hegemony. Papal scientists enact an ambitious program of creating and raising biological posthumans, called Giants.
2510–2525	Emulation widespread. Rise of the Ghosts.

The last unsuccessful augmentation experiment is at about this time. All Hermeticists dead but six: Del Azarchel, De Ulloa, D'Aragó, Sarmento, Pastor, and Coronimas. (This elongated mass suicide pact lasted from A.D. 2410 to A.D. 2510, 109 years.)

2519	Scipio hibernates.

2525   Day of the Aurum Vitae. Ecpyrosis. De-civilization. Overthrow of Ghosts by space heat bombardment. Ctesibius hibernates. Beginning of the Sylphs.

2533   Del Azarchel paints the near side of the moon with the gauntlet of his challenge, and initiates the formation of the Simon Families through the false identity of Dr. Og Simon of Northumberland, a Giant he has captured and absorbed.

Posthuman Era (*The Hermetic Millennia*)

2535   Energy signals from V886 Centauri reaching Earth indicate that Rania has blown the Diamond Star out of orbit, abandoning plans to establish regular traffic in favor of a star voyage to M3, to plead with the Authority there for the vindication of man.

Montrose thawed, corrects Divarication flaws in Sylph serpentines.

2537   Trey Soaring Azurine hibernates.

2540   In his base at Mare Ingenii (Sea of Cunning), Del Azarchel establishes Cryocliometry and assumes control of the Hermetic Order, but is shortly after forced into hibernation.

2550s   Simon Families and other long-range foundations ("the Orders") established by the Giants (at Del Azarchel's direction).

At about this time, Exulloa is augmented to posthumanity. De Ulloa becomes the Master of the Age.

2580   De Ulloa begins to teach certain Scholars, including Rada Lwa, Cliometry.

2700–3000 Medusae use Sylph technology to hunt down Sylphs and decimate them. Medusae establish industrial civilizations at the poles out of orbital mirror flyover range. They are predominant until 3000, when the Giants, via Cliometry, arrange for their polar civilization to destroy itself by economic collapse.

3032   Day of the Giants. Encouraged by their victory over the Medusae, Thucydideans from Salt Lake City attempt a direct assault on the stronghold of the Judge of Ages beneath Cheyenne Mountain. The orbital space laser Surtur renders the surface area uninhabitable.
            Montrose thawed. His bio age is 42.

3033   The Giants calculate a new Cliometric consensus, and foretell their own extinction. Bashan hibernates.

3050–3150   Cloud Century. Cetaceans raise a worldwide cloud cover, rendering the giant Orbital Mirrors useless.

3060s   Effective end of the Thucydidean Consensus as a world power. The Simon Family Orders, including the Longevity Order, maintain civic cohesion.

Simon Family Period

3090   Death of Melchor de Ulloa in a duel atop Mount Ypsilon. Cetaceans pull down Surtur by atmospheric dragging (heating the atmosphere till it expands, thus thickening the particle count around the orbiter, causing reentry). End of the Second Space Age. Rada Lwa hibernates.
            Montrose spent one year tracking down De Ulloa. His bio age is 43.

3100–3200   Longevity Order, now called the Delphic Acroamatic Order, maintains an increasingly low-tech world. Church driven underground. Abolition of the nuclear family and of nuclear energy. Scientific research that reaches politically inconvenient conclusions outlawed by Thought Decontamination Laws.

3150   End of the Cloud causes global cooling, disrupts crop growth patterns, places mortal strain on the centralized command economy of the Delphics.

3222   The Delphic Acroamatic World Order schisms: Eastern Witches break into the Chthonic Order and Celestial Order, which in turn breaks into Orthodox Celestial and Reformed Celestial. Western Order breaks into seven: English; Continental; Mauritanian; Neo-Anglican; Amazonian (comprising Brazil); Archipelagic (comprising California, Baja, and Pacific Islands); and Aztectlan (comprising Mexico and New Mexico).

3250–3300   The Collapse. Downfall of industrial-scientific civilization. The Delphic Order now called Witches. Witches in massive numbers hibernate.

Newly thawed Simon Family members from an earlier period attempt to force open Tomb sites throughout the Mediterranean. The assault is repelled by thawed Knights Templar. Fatin hibernates.

Age of Witches

3300–4000 Witches enjoy world dominion, convulsed with a permanent state of civil war and turmoil, for seven hundred years. High-status Witches, despite their private dependence on emulation for cellular regeneration, publicly continue to hunt down and destroy all known copies of Exarchel.

3600   Despite heroic efforts by the Witches, the Cetaceans (lacking sufficient support from Exarchel) go extinct. Last known Great Whale perishes when beached in 3666.

3950–3951 Montrose is awake for a year during this era, and sends out teachers and scholar in the area around Lake Superior. His bio age is 44.

4000–4400 The Nameless Witch-King of Lake Superior revives certain scholars and scientists from the Tombs, and rediscovers the internal combustion engine, the aeroplane, the submersible boat.

The new coven formation, called "familia," allows for one man and a subservient wife, with their children under the coven-leader's strict control. The Nameless Empire conquers the Mississippi River basin from Ohio to Louisiana. The Superiors are Witches in name only, adhering to the outward forms of Ecological Communitarianism, but in practice are patriarchal capitalists.

4000   At about this time, Witches in China are unified under the brutal rule of the Nine Centennial Empresses of Canton. (Each of nine cloned sisters is kept in hibernation, and thawed to rule for one hundred years.)

First Chimera produced by Nameless Imperial scientists as an intermediate form of life designed to be hardened against radiation and bioweapon spores lingering in old ruins. The Chimerae rebuild Richmond and other Downfall-damaged urban centers.

4400–4450 The Nameless Empire expands to Mexico, the Caribbean, and Brazil, and maintains transatlantic trade with the Witches of Europe and Africa.

4450–4500 The Nameless Empire suffers reformation under a Witch named Argyron Butler, and returns to the original Witch principles of nonaggression, harmony with nature, equality of the sexes, divorce, infanticide, and hatred of industry. De-industrialization and aggregation into communal farms carried out with ruthless efficiency. The Nameless Empire balkanized into Temple Priest-king feudalism, and Witch civilization returns to its norm of continual civil war and bloodshed.

4460   First organized Chimerae rebel lineages formed in the Louisiana swamps as a tribe of escaped slaves under an Alpha named Remus.

4600   Polar caps melt. Coastal flooding. Famine. Witch population decimated, many cities abandoned, large numbers of nomads, scavenger bands, and pirates dominate land and sea.

4700   Rise of the mass-human sacrifice cults. Stepped pyramids raised in the jungles of Siberia and Canada.

4728   Montrose briefly (less than four months) thawed during this era, giving aid and education from certain near-surface Tombs in Mount Airy, teaching the Witches the basic principles of science and economics, in order to stave off a predicted civilization collapse. The attempt is unsuccessful, perhaps because he does not devote the requisite time to the project. His bio age still 44.

4730–4480 Plague of the Kuru disease (transmissible spongiform encephalopathy) decimates population, destroys Temple Priestking system. Medicine-Man interventions, hampered by quota rituals, aggravate rather than alleviate the plague.

4733   Melechemoshemyazanagual hibernates.

4460–4800 Uprisings and rebellions of the Chimerae, who are disease resistant to Kuru. Formation of the first Emergency Eugenic Command under Remus.

4800   Genocides. Chimerae spread throughout the Americas, first enslaving and later exterminating the Witches. Surviving Witches become the cattle, or "Kine," of the Chimerae, in a cruel jest reflecting their animal totems: sheep, ox, goat, and so on. Note that the Kine continue to be longer-lived than the Chimerae.

4812   Suspinia hibernates.

4881   Battle of Antietam. Yuen hibernates.

4888   Defeat of the Final Sabbat at Buffington's Island. Mass migration of Witches to China.

Age of Chimerae

4900	Proscopalianism (worship of the future) becomes the standard doctrine of the Command.
5000	End of the Centennial Empire in China. Chinese Chimerae erect a military dictatorship.
5100	Sino-Chimerae conquer the Russian steppes, Aleutian Islands, and Alaska. Western Chimerae conquer Western Plains to the Rockies.
5250	Western Chimerae conquer Canada prairies.
5250	Montrose thawed briefly. He releases scientists from the Tombs. Rediscovery of atomics. His bio age is 45.
5250–5290	Social Wars between the hemispheres end in Grand Alliance between the Oriental and Occidental Chimerae. Atheism decreed to be the compulsory religion of the Command.
5292	Anubis is allegedly from this era.
5300	Sino-Occidental Chimerical Alliance achieves conquests in Middle and South America, Pacific Islands, and South East Asia. Time of the Sea Chimerae. Vulpina is from this period.
5400	Third Space Age. Cities in Space. Space Chimerae created. All remaining nations conquered except Tibet. End of eugenic veteran-franchise form of government when all voting right suspended in favor of Eugenics Board directives. World Empire.
5480	Agathamemnon "Fairlock" Raeus elected Governor-Emperor, and dissolves the Eugenic Senate in all but name. End of the Republic. Daae hibernates.
5480–5884	Four hundred years of Chimerical World Empire.
5655	Phyle hibernates.
5700	Eugenic Emergency Command dissolved, forced human breeding program halted. Alpha class becomes inbred. Chimerae enter sharp population decline.
5884	Spaceport-Fortress Ravenna on Foehr Island assaulted by mercenaries, D'Aragó slain. End of the Third Age of Space. Fall of Richmond. Succession wars begin.
	Montrose is bio age 46.
5884–5900	World Empire severed. Warring Bloodlines period. Egypt and the Middle East ruled by masterless Kine.
5900	Greencloak revolt among the Kine. Rise of the Natural Order in Mesopotamia.
5950	Larz hibernates.

Age of Nymphs

5990–6100   Natural Order spreads to all lands. Alpha and Beta Bloodlines absorbed or exterminated.

6064   Montrose wakes briefly for the Naturalists. First true Nymph, Rayura-Ah, created. Montrose is wounded by Sarmento, drawn away by Rayura-Ah and her two twin sisters to West Virginia, where he waits to be healed of his great wound. Montrose establishes long-standing treaties with Nymphs. His bio age is still 46. (This is the date Anubis correctly gives for when he learned the Natural language.)

6100   Asia depopulated. Cities fall into disuse. First living houses grown in Italy.

6226   Blight. End of the Living Houses period.

6300   Rise of the Tree Neural Net. War of the Trees.

6400   Pacifist outrage at the War of the Trees leads to the Infatuation (use of neural and amnesiac conditioning to deter violence). Illiteratization of Man. All religious and intellectual efforts discontinued. End of Matriarchy. World government passes to the Eldership.

6422   Oenoe hibernates for the first time.

6500   Neotany. Use of childlike neural structures in adults to condition the population to simplicity and trust in their Elders.

6600   Elders overthrown by the Nocturnal Council, night-adapted Nymphs conditioned to acts of terror to maintain peace and order, but who forget their dark crimes by day. (Nocturnal battle-cocoon metamorphosis establishes the basics of Hormagaunt biology.) End of Neotany.

6660s   Naturalist Weather Control begins to erode.

6700s   Summer Queens. Naturalists begin custom of annual hibernation to avoid winter.

6746   Oenoe is wakened by the Summer Queens during the "Wine of Violence" Crisis to aid in the spread of Wintermind techniques. It is during this time she teaches Del Azarchel the Wintermind techniques. Oenoe hibernates again.

6800   Leeches (early Hormagaunts) found the Yakutsk Analeptic Empire. (Their language continues until 7300.)

6840–7000   Winter Queen Nymphs expand throughout Canada and Patagonia. Widespread use of seasonal hormones to produce battle-frenzy in winter. Winter wars decimate the remaining Nymphs.

Age of Hormagaunts

7000–7200 Leeches corrupted by their victory. Dark Ages. Rise of the Hor-
           magaunts. Asvid, the first nonanthropoid Hormagaunt, created
           at about this time.

7200   Rise of the Therapeutae in the northern hemisphere (an early
           form of the Iatrocracy).

7234   Montrose wakes for the Therapeutae, sets in motion the biotech-
           nological revolution that leads to the erection of the Clades, then
           hibernates. His bio age is 47.

7280   The Therapeutae of the Clades formalize the geriatric "spoils"
           system into an official register of protocols called the Iatrocracy.
           Formation of a permanent Donor class. Effective end of the aging
           process for high-status members of the Iatrocracy, for Horma-
           gaunt or upperclass Clade archetypes. Darwinian code of battle
           established.

7330–7385 Hemoclysm. 155 million deaths worldwide caused by the Iatro-
           crat global wars and genocides.

7380–7480 Burning of the World-Forest. Other biomes, including plains and
           prairies conducive to Clade burgs, become predominant. Large-
           scale industrialized warfare rather than Bronze Age champion
           combat becomes the norm. The Darwinian code abandoned.

7385   Atrocity of Yap Islands, Micronesia. Hermeticist Order carries
           Clades to Mariana Trench to be reverse engineered. The crime is
           hidden from Pellucid by the white noise of the Hemoclysm.

7466   During this period, Reyes y Pastor suffers a crisis of faith. Soorm
           hibernates.

7470   Using Montrose's Clade science, Coronimas creates the Locusts,
           in an effort to achieve world peace. Early-period Locusts, altruis-
           tic and pacifistic, are decimated.

7490   A Locust scientist called Seir redesigns his race to a warlike nature.
           These Second Locusts are called Seers or Svartschrecke.

7500   Hormagaunts are able to maintain a space program. (Actually,
           this is an extremely rare Locust-Hormagaunt cooperative venture.)
           Beginning of the Fourth Age of Space Travel.

7520   Anti-Locust riots. Beginning of the genocidal Locust Wars.
               Gload hibernates.

7520–7840 For three hundred years, Hormagaunts and Clades attempt
           worldwide extermination of Locust population. Locusts endure

in hiding; they colonize and partially terraform Mars. Beginning of the Triage system of population control. First Tendrilless Locusts created.

7810   Crile hibernates.

7810–7840   First Interplanetary War. An atomic exchange between Earth and Mars ends the precarious colonies on Mars, and reduces the technology level on Earth to pre-industrial levels. Diebacks. End of the Fifth Age of Space. Many Locusts enter the Tombs. Locust Wars enter a period of armistice.

7850–7950   Reindustrialization. Imposition of genetic uniformity ends the Clade system. World reunified under the leadership of Ceto (a Tendrilless Locust serving Coronimas). Locust data passthrough volumes dramatically increased. Founding of the Noösphere.

7880   Establishment of the First Mental Configuration; Ceto grants Locusts legal rights. Effective end of the Locust Wars.

7900   An advance in Locust neural technology allows for Hormagaunt-Locust mental interface. Many Locusts re-emerge from the Tombs.

7950   Locusts lose individualism. These are the Third Locusts, or Scorpions.

7960–7980   Age of the Scorpions. Rival groups attempt total extermination of nonconformists, also attempt to destroy the Tombs housing each other to prevent their reawakening. Coronimas leads a worldwide effort to seize control of all Tomb sites, so that he can control the waking-to-slumbering population ratio.

7982   Coronimas introduces pain-broadcast mechanisms to all Locust Clades. Triumph of the Noösphere Configuration.

7983–7985   Montrose wakes to hunt down and murder Coronimas. It takes him two years to find him. His bio age is now 50.

7990   Elton Linder, a Nymph scientist released from the Tombs, redesigns the Locusts toward altruism, creating the Fourth Locusts, or True Locusts. Beginning of a seven-hundred-year period of Utter World Peace and Total Conformity. Linder releases Inquiline Codes into the Noösphere.

Age of Locusts

8000–8700   Global cooling begins. Fifth Locusts or Onyx Men (a smaller version) guide Hormagaunts gently to demographic insignificance and then extinction. Noösphere degenerates badly, and develops inquiline groups, including Simplifiers, in reaction to the Linder virus.

8765   Jubilee. Public business suspended. Individuals re-arm.

8766   Noöspherical Cognitive Order dissolved. Violent shattering of the Configuration into eight local organizations called Confraternities. Linder's protocols break down; Wars of Extermination. Rise of the Sixth Locusts.

8770–8790 Confraternities introduce cellular thought-control mechanisms, the so-called Helot Code. Simplifiers and other Inquilines retreat to rural areas. The Seventh through Fourteenth Locusts exist during this period, driving each other into extinction rapidly. Illiance hibernates.

8790–8800 The Grays rise to prominence. They are an Inquiline group of Tendrilless Locusts detached from Confraternal control who are attempting a return to Linder's original principles, seeking the reestablishment of the Noöspherical Cognitive Order. Infrastructure supporting Locust Confraternities fails regionally, then globally, with shocking swiftness. Fifteenth Locusts arise, now called the Fifteenth Mental Configuration.

8866   Population reductions. The Grays Keir and Keirthlin enter hibernation.

8900s   Triumph of the Linderlings. Various Inquiline groups develop from the Grays, and abolish the Blues and other remnants of Locust civilization. Time of the Sixteenth Configuration.

8900–9100 An intermediate human species, called the Midwives, develops from the Grays, based on Sleepwalker thought-control templates. A Midwife alliance called the Seventeenth Configuration cooperates with the Hermeticists to establish the social mechanisms needed for an evolutionary advance.

Age of Melusine

9000   Melusine developed by Seventeenth Configuration: a human-dolphin-machine mental gestalt, based on discoveries of machine life created by the long-extinct Cetaceans in oceanic trenches. Fearful of the Melusine superiority, specialist Inquilines among the Configuration called Psychoscopists, along with artificial minds called Granoliths, regulate the Melusine into a strictly apolitical and peacekeeping role.

9100   Rise of the Eighteenth and Last Noösphere Configuration under the Melusine, incorporating both hive mind and cyborg
systems as propertied and administrative class, with an Inquiline underclass. Melusines cure the Locusts to under population and then extinction.

9200   Golden Age begins. Technological and social revolution. World
peace. Pi Segment of the Monument translated by the Melusine,
who become aware of the Hermetic interference in their history.

                In utmost stealth, led by a Melusine named Melior, they
draw their plans against the Hermeticists, and introduce Cliometric vectors into the path of history (which Del Azarchel and
Montrose each take to be the other's work).

9250   1036 Ganymed placed in near-Earth orbit.

9300   Divarication of the Coastal, Spaceborne, and Seaborne Melusine.

9400   Granolith failure. Surface life enters Dark Ages.

9500   Asteroid 1036 Ganymed impact wipes out surface life.

9999   White Earth. Montrose wakes long enough to introduce a muta-
genic virus into the biosphere to evolve Swans from the Psychoscopic Locusts, and begins the volcanic process of global warming.

10000s   At about this time, the Melusine remove into the interior of the
Earth in large numbers, using the abandoned depthtrain rail
yards as warrens, forming the Interior or Infernal Melusine.

                Anchorites begin repopulation of coastal areas. Nymph bio-
technology released from the Tombs allows the Oceanic Melusine to form independent Xypotech trees under the sea.

                Pan Sapiens, also called Second Humans or Swans, begin to
appear among the Anchorite population of the Melusine, created by a genetic-mimetic vector known as the Mind Anarchy,
and spread throughout the Anchorites.

10025   Swans develop Cliometry, read further into the Monument than
any previous investigators. They deduce the existence of Exarchel,
who exists as a decentralized form in the world water supply.

10075   Historical Crisis. Anchorite-Infernal war triggered by the first,
clumsy attempts by the Swans to manipulate history. Exarchel
melts, raising the ocean levels, flooding the coastal areas, and
destroying the Anchorite hermitages. Anchorites are turned
into mind serfs, but, unbeknownst to Exarchel, the Swans
among them maintain independence of thought in the negative
information spaces between manifest thought forms.

10099	Last Anchorite, Eumolpidai, dies in captivity.
10100–10400	Swans spread throughout the Melusine, maintaining a hidden and parallel civilization in virtual mind space.
10100	Infernal Melusine make an attempt to force the Tombs, and are repelled. They therefore design and introduce the Lree mind group into the Tomb system as moles; Lree are moved by Pellucid, as per standing orders, to Fancy Gap facility, where all dangerous interments are kept. Note that the Lree are already infected with the Mental Anarchy meme, hence secretly double agents.
	Alalloel of Lree hibernates.
10200s	Rise of the Final Stipulation of Noösphere Protocols, called the Finality, a Concordat encompassing Swans (not yet recognized as a second human species) and Melusine and the descendents of Inquilines.
	At about this time, Del Azarchel is restored to his old dignity and role as Nobilissimus, Commander-in-Chief, and Monarch of Man, and he dons the Iron Crown of Lombardy.
10401	Infernal Melusine deduce the existence of Pellucid, and begin growing a stalactite of logic crystal toward the planetary core.
10484–10515	Melusine begin Hyades Raid Drill, to evolve an anti-skyhook defense.
10500	The Intrusion. Stalactite of logic crystal reaches the Pellucid core and begins seeking thread nodes.
	In the cramped interiors of the bore warrens, the Swans, forced into unnatural cooperation with each other and the Melusine, win the notational exchanges, corner the foreteller market, and force the assumption of Swans into the highest levels of the Melusine Noösphere, in effect creating a compromise life-form called Paramounts: neither machine nor biological, and independent of Cliometric prediction, a servile race secretly loyal to the Swans.
10514	Exarchel follows the core stalactite and invades Pellucid. The first mind war ends in a draw with severe damage on both sides, but with Exarchel in partial control of Pellucid's systems and memories. At the time, due to phantasm interference in his perception interpretation system, he is only aware of the near-surface facilities, eighty-eight in number.
	Exarchel, examining Pellucid's records, deduces the location of Montrose at Fancy Gap, breaches the roof armor with a spaceborne weapon, and is abruptly stopped by the Swans.

Alarmed at this display of Swan power, which he takes to be
an agency of Montrose, Exarchel uses his partial control over
outlying elements of Pellucid to reach coffins in the Mount
Misery facility on the island of Saint Christopher, thawing Ull
and the other Blue Men.

Astonished to be thawed on an (apparently) deserted world,
the Blues make a concerted effort to discover the (now missing)
command and control elements of the Tomb system: the Knights
Hospitalier or the Judge of Ages. They find and thaw a number
of their brethren. They loot aircraft from Wright-Patterson and
create Follower Moreaus from recovered canine archives. They
invade several sites worldwide and are repelled by the defenses.

10515   The Blue Men find the Fancy Gap facility and raid it. Montrose is thawed and passes for a Chimera, whom he physically
and psychologically resembles.

Launch of the mind seed of the Jupiter Brain, now containing the sociological-psychological neurogenetic information
from all the previous races of man, which should enable it to
achieve the status beyond Swan-style or Pellucid-style world-
minds, but occupy the entire volume of a self-aware macromol-
ecule the size of a gas giant.

The Hermeticists discover all their histories have been to facilitate this mind seed launch. Furious at being exploited for
such marginal reasons, they dissolve the Landing Party and join
the Final Stipulation. The Swans dissolve the Tomb system, destroy Exarchel, and condemn Del Azarchel and Montrose.
Mass migration from the Tomb system, which is far more extensive than expected, and contains myraids of populations from all
previous eras. Montrose activates his phantasm system, covers
Del Azarchel, and they both return to the *Emancipation*.

End of the Posthuman Era
Swan Era Begins